"The Gothic vein pulses strong in Boyle's latest, where a cursed cast of characters, one-by-one, meet their untimely fates, and where all the trappings of Victorian horror are polished and made modern. ...Strongly recommended."

Ronald Malfi, *New York Times*-bestselling author of *Small Town Horror*

"The parched halls of Temple Fall feed off the reader like the best modern haunted houses out there, making this black-as-pitch book a worthy addition to your bookshelves."

Clay McLeod Chapman, author of *Wake Up and Open Your Eyes*

"A creeping, clutching tale of doom and darkness inexplicably bound with hope and heart, Temple Fall will draw you into its hallowed halls and hold you there forever."

Delilah S. Dawson, author of *Guillotine*

"A clever, mind-bending, frankly terrifying haunted house mystery ... serves up delicious scares and sinister, hallucinatory set pieces, but it's the emotional truth at the center of it that's going to haunt readers the longest."

Andrea Morstabilini, author of *A Blood as Bright as the Moon*

"Like any great haunted house, Temple Fall is mysterious and labyrinthine, offering fresh surprises and terrors at every turn. The perfect read for a stormy night in a strange place."

Shaun Hamill, author of *A Cosmology of Monsters*

"Dark, persistent and unnerving, *Temple Fall* is an entrancing ghost story that gets under the skin with creeping dread. ...I was absolutely bewitched!"

Heather Davey, author of *The Ghosts of Merry Hall*

Also by R. L. Boyle
and available from Titan Books

The Book of the Baku

Temple Fall

R. L. BOYLE

TITAN BOOKS

Temple Fall
Print edition ISBN: 9781835414170
E-book edition ISBN: 9781835414187

Published by Titan Books
A division of Titan Publishing Group Ltd
144 Southwark Street, London SE1 0UP
www.titanbooks.com

First edition: February 2026
10 9 8 7 6 5 4 3 2 1

A CIP catalogue record for this title is available from the British Library.

EU RP (for authorities only)
eucomply OÜ, Pärnu mnt. 139b-14, 11317 Tallinn, Estonia
hello@eucompliancepartner.com, +3375690241

Designed and typeset in Adobe Aldine by Richard Mason.

Printed and bound by CPI Group (UK) Ltd, Croydon CR0 4YY.

For Maria
My Mum

For Owen
My Husband

And for Barney, Milo and Eric
My Heroes

Part of our psyche is not in time and not in space. They are only an illusion, time and space, and so in a certain part of our psyche time does not exist at all.

CARL JUNG, 'THE SYMBOLIC LIFE' (1939),
THE COLLECTED WORKS OF C.G. JUNG, VOL.18

PROLOGUE

Keep moving! Don't look back! These words keep time with Flynn's frantic heartbeat, singing a jagged song in her blood. Sweat glues her top to her back as she runs down the hallway, one hand clamped around Chloe's, the other clutching the back of Tyrus's T-shirt. Keeping close to Mei and Jonesy a step ahead, terrified if she falls behind they will abandon her to this insane house.

She has to get out. Out of this nightmare. Candles whicker against the walls, making the shadows twitch. Gaps in the floorboards reveal shadowy rooms below, chunks of fallen plaster expose the roof space above.

Half-blind in the darkness, Flynn bites back a scream. Every step sends pain through the soles of her feet and prints carmine kisses on the bare floorboards. She feels as though the house is savouring the taste of every bloody footstep.

The staircase creaks and groans as they hurtle down it. The wood is rotten, balusters missing from the sides. One of the steps has snapped in half, toothpick splinters jutting out, ready to turn a misstep into a fall. She sees dried bloodstains on the dust-coated floorboards, and realises in horror the blood is probably hers – that she climbed these stairs earlier, oblivious to the cuts opening in the soles of her feet, blind to the danger.

At the bottom of the stairs, they stagger down another hallway, move through decaying rooms that blaze with candles, sobbing, reaching for each other, until finally, they are back in the lobby.

Flynn's thoughts tilt at the sight of the paintings on the walls. The surfaces of the canvases are lifting, the colour flaking away so that the images that had repulsed her when they entered the house are now impossible to make out. The wine-red carpet is worn to the weave and ruined by black mould. The ceiling has buckled from the weight of the chandelier.

They pelt towards the door.

Mei twists the key in the lock, pulls it open.

Sunlight spills into the lobby.

Shock drops Flynn to her knees.

The heavens should be a churning vault of darkness, storm-tossed and thunderous, but the sun rides the hyaline sky of a renaissance painting, and the wind Flynn had heard battering the house has dropped to a soft breeze. The gravel driveway is dry, not so much as a single puddle on the porch decking. The only indication that a storm has passed are the fire-blackened trunks of the lightning-scarred trees.

Flynn gazes over the moors. The blaze of purple heather has gone, and in its place are fields of bare peat the colour of stewed tea, and the trees, which had been thick with foliage when they arrived, are now barren. Nude branches claw towards the quiet blue sky, like the outstretched arms of a dark coven.

It is as though, in the few hours they spent inside Temple Fall, time has slipped, the days and months skidding on greased wheels without taking them with it.

Slowly, Flynn turns to the house.

The desiccated walls of Temple Fall crumble beneath wreaths of moss and vines. The roof has caved in and fallen shingles lie in shattered pieces on the brittle, yellow grass. Rot has eaten away at the wooden decking. There are holes in the stone mullions. All the windows are boarded up, including the one that Jackson fell through. A sign, toppled into the bushes, almost illegible behind a scramble of weeds and thorny bracken: *Caution, Unsafe Building, Keep Out!* Only the cast-iron knocker on the door, that serpentine ouroboros, looks untouched by the passage of time.

But Flynn is not looking at the house.

She stares at the spot on the porch where Jackson fell.

Ripped police tape is tethered to the railing. It flutters in the breeze, like the dead skin of a snake.

And Jackson's body has gone.

PART 1

NOW

Sat in the back of the minivan, Flynn watches the scenery blur past. The grey of the motorway blends almost seamlessly with the grey of the sky, but the gloomy colours do little to dampen her mood. She is with her best friends, on her way to celebrate her boyfriend Jackson's eighteenth birthday, and while the idea of camping outside a crumbling old mansion doesn't exactly fill her with excitement, she can't think of anywhere else she would rather be.

Chloe managed to persuade her older brother, Andy, to drop them off, though he is clearly far from happy to be taxiing his sister and her mates halfway across Yorkshire. His eyes, framed in the rear-view mirror, are set in a scowl, and he and Chloe, who is riding shotgun, have been sniping at each other since they set off.

Flynn leans into Jackson, breathes the faint gasoline tang of his dark room, the peppery smell of his aftershave. On his lap, he holds the vintage Kodak Brownie that she gifted him for his birthday. She'd bid for it on eBay, despite the fact she thought it looked like an overpriced, archaic piece of kit. But then she isn't the shutterbug that Jackson is, and the instant he had unwrapped it, his beaming face had assured her she'd made the right call.

On the other side of Jackson, Mei nods her head to the music playing through the van. In the middle seats, Jonesy and Tyrus debate which superheroes they would shag, marry or kill.

'Shag Wonder Woman,' Jonesy says, placing the crutch in his joint, and scattering cannabis along the paper.

Mei snorts. 'Wonder Woman? You really want that kind of pressure when you lose your virginity?'

'Who you calling a virgin?' Jonesy quips.

Mei smirks, cracks her gum.

'Where was I? Yeah, so I'd shag Wonder Woman, marry Big Barda and kill—'

'Big *who?*' Flynn says.

Jackson leans closer to Flynn, says, 'Big Barda's the daughter of Big Breeda. Groomed by Granny Goodness to lead the Female Fury Battalion. Functionally mortal, physically more powerful than her husband, master of hand-to-hand combat.'

Flynn cuts Jackson a wry look. 'Sounds like *you* want to marry Big Barda.'

'No way.' Jackson's smile curls, irresistible. 'There's only one woman for me!'

'Didn't Big Barda make a sex tape with Superman?' Tyrus asks.

'I'll have you know they'd both been mentally manipulated by Sleez,' Jonesy says, leaping to the defence of his imaginary bride. 'Big Barda would never have cheated on Mister Miracle.'

'Mister Miracle.' Flynn frowns. 'So... that'd be you?'

'No, that's her real husband.' Jonesy shakes his blonde mop of curls, exasperated. 'Haven't you guys read the Female Furies?'

'No,' Mei and Flynn respond together, then share an amused glance.

'And I'd kill... I'd kill either Reed Richards or Batman.'

'Then you'll have to kill Reed Richards,' Flynn says. She has no idea who Reed Richards is, but thanks to her little sister she has an encyclopaedic knowledge of Bruce Wayne. 'If you touched a single hair on Batman's head, Riley would end you. You know how obsessed she is.'

'Good point, I wouldn't want to piss off your little sister, she's fucking terrifying.' Jonesy lifts the joint to lick and seal it just as Andy's eyes snap to the rear-view mirror.

'You're not smoking that shit in my van.'

Chastened, Jonesy lowers the joint. 'Course not, man.'

'Jesus, would you lighten up?' Chloe mutters to her brother. 'Honestly, you're worse than Dad.'

They resume their squabbling, but Flynn tunes them out and stares out of the window.

Even though she has been curious about her biological family for as long as she can remember, it is only in recent months that she finally committed to researching her past. Her reluctance to explore her ancestry sprang partially from fear: her birth mother suffered from severe psychosis, a condition which blighted Flynn's childhood and left her stricken with a dread of inheriting the illness. Conscious that her family history could play a large part in the likelihood of this happening, for years she had worried about discovering a long line of mentally ill relatives in her past. Finally, she had persuaded herself that it was possible her mother was the anomaly in her family tree, and the chances of Flynn inheriting her illness were far more remote than she expected. By delving into her past, she might be able to eradicate this long-held fear.

But alongside this pragmatic motivation, there resided another: Flynn had longed to discover someone remarkable, a connection perhaps to a celebrated war hero, a royal descendant, or some pioneer who had revolutionised modern science. The form or nature of their merit mattered little to Flynn, only that it did exist, for such a discovery would surely play a part in erasing the shame of her childhood.

And so, when she should have been studying for her A Levels, instead she carefully worked through her family tree, tracing her lineage back generation by generation; when she should have been sleeping she stayed up late, mining the internet for birth records; when she was looking after her little sister, Riley, she watched ancestry programmes in which celebrities discovered the admirable deeds of their ancestors, and imagined how she would feel when she made her own discovery.

Without any information about her biological father, she'd only had her mother's family line to work with, but she had managed to trace her ancestors as far back as her great-great-great-grandfather, Budd Young, who was adopted as a baby in 1884. His mother was a woman called Lyda Gray, but aside from her name, there was little else Flynn could uncover about her. With the trail cold, she had contacted a genealogist for help, but even he had struggled to find out anything, aside from the fact she had lived for a spell in a house called Temple Fall.

Flynn had searched the internet for information on the house but hadn't found anything. It was Jackson who had suggested she check out the 'historical imagery' feature on Google Earth. Only then had an image of the house filled the screen: a black and white taken some time in the 1930s.

The aerial shot didn't reveal much, other than it was a sprawling mansion deep in the moors. But its mysterious aura and isolated location were enough to capture Jackson's imagination. His passion for photography peaked when the subject matter was old houses, or as he called it, 'decay photography'. He suggested it would be the perfect place to spend the night of his eighteenth birthday, a creepy camping trip outside Flynn's ancestral home.

'What the fuck, Clo!' Andy yells, his voice jolting Flynn from her thoughts. 'We're on the fucking motorway!'

Ignoring him, Chloe crawls over the passenger seat, a bottle of prosecco wedged under one arm, a tower of paper cups in her hand. She perches on Jonesy's lap and passes the cups round. Despite the fact they are spending the night camping in a muddy field, she is wearing a skimpy vest, wet-look leggings and a cable-knit cardigan. Her stiletto nails are painted the colour of tin foil and her cornsilk hair falls down her back in waves.

'I can't believe you talked us into this, Jax,' she grumbles. 'We could have done just about anything for your eighteenth, but you want to camp in a muddy field outside a derelict old house in the arse-crack of nowhere.'

'Yeah, bro,' Jonesy says. 'It's not too late to bang a U-ey. My mum's away with work, we could all stay at mine, order Taco Bell, smoke a Fat One.'

'That's just a regular night with you,' Jackson says. 'And when it's your eighteenth, if that's what you want, then that's what we'll do. But this is *my* birthday, so suck it up.'

'When did you turn into such a diva, bro?' Jonesy grumbles.

'It's gonna be great, trust me.'

'I hate camping,' Chloe says, sulky.

'Really?' Jackson mutters. 'You haven't said.'

'Yeah, really. I'd sooner spend the night at The Pitfalls, and that's saying something. Actually, I think I've still got a bottle of vodka stashed there somewhere...'

'God, I can't remember the last time we spent the night there,' Mei says. 'I wonder whether it's even still standing.'

The Pitfalls, a derelict four-storey building that used to function as a university hall of residence until subsidence forced its closure. Reparation work was abandoned years ago, and these days the structure looks as though it is held together by the scaffolding and walkways pinned to its walls.

Almost nine years have passed since Flynn and her friends turned a room on the second floor of the collapsing building into their secret bolthole. Undeterred by its dubious condition, with rugs, blankets and throws, they had transformed the space into a cosy nook. Mei smuggled a gas heater from her dad's garage to warm the space, Chloe draped fairy lights over the bare brick walls and brought beanbags from her bedroom, while Jonesy contributed a giant wicker basket, which they all kept supplied with crisps and snacks. Flynn filched a deckchair from her foster family's garage, Jackson knocked together a bookshelf to which they had all contributed a stash of books. Tyrus added a stack of comics he had finagled from his big brother's bedroom, along with a collection of board games that grew as they each added to it, until they covered the entire back wall of the room.

After numerous trips to the local skip, Jonesy had found a ratty old sofa that he claimed was perfect for the space, and Andy – only seventeen years old back then, fresh from passing his driving test and more amenable to his cute little sister – had agreed to help when Chloe asked him to use his minivan to transport it to their den.

The electrics had been cut off when the building was vacated, but it remained plumbed to the water supply, and flushable toilets and running taps meant Flynn and the others could spend hours there without having to go home.

After a heated debate about what to name their den, Tyrus had suggested 'Nostromo', taking inspiration from his favourite film, *Alien*. They toasted the name by sipping whisky Jonesy had swiped from his dad's drinks cabinet, even though they all agreed it tasted worse than hot sick. Tyrus was the only one who abstained, announcing there and then that he would never touch a drop of booze.

It was an impassioned vow, and with her mouth and throat on fire, Flynn had not called it into question. Besides, even then, they all knew the reason Tyrus had sworn off booze was because of his dad.

Tyrus never spoke about his dad's drinking, but it was hardly a secret on their estate. Flynn and the others regularly spent their evenings in the games room of The Dive while their parents drank themselves stupid in the bar, so they knew Elijah Adebeyo was a mean drunk. He was regularly barred from the local pubs for fighting, and Flynn had lost count of the times Tyrus had come to school sporting a black eye or a busted lip.

In all the years that have passed since then, whenever his friends were splitting a six pack in Nostromo, or smuggling drinks from The Dive, Tyrus stayed true to his word and never touched a drop.

'Hey, Flynn,' Tyrus says, popping the tab on a Coke and twisting in his seat to look at her. 'What did Mr C want you for today?'

Flynn shrugs, watching Chloe work the foil from the top of the prosecco bottle. 'He just gave me a lecture, said I should know by now what courses and unis I want to apply for.'

'Ah, don't worry about that,' Chloe says, easing her thumb beneath the cork and pointing it towards Andy. 'You've got ages to decide.'

'I'm sorry, Flynn, but he's got a point,' Mei says. 'You've gotta start narrowing down your options otherwise you won't have anything at all lined up. You don't want to be stuck working in The Dive for another year, do you?'

The cork shoots from Chloe's prosecco bottle with a jocular *pop*, smacking Andy in the back of the head.

He jerks round and the van swerves. 'Do you want to fucking walk?' he yells.

Chloe sniggers, pours fizz into the paper cups.

'Have you even looked through those prospectuses I sent you?' Mei presses.

Flynn groans, shakes her empty cup at Chloe.

'I just think you should—'

'Mei, please don't start. I've had my lecture for the day. I thought this was supposed to be a birthday party, not a fucking careers advice meeting.'

The words come out harsher than Flynn had intended, but Mei just holds up her hands and sinks back into her seat. Flynn feels bad for snapping, especially when she knows Mei is only looking out for her, but she doesn't want to think about university.

In less than nine months, she will finish college, and while she still has no idea what she wants to do with her life, her best friends have already filled in their university applications. Jonesy plans to do a gaming degree in Cornwall or Bolton; Tyrus is hoping to study Film and TV Production in Cardiff; Mei wants to study Sports Science and is hoping to get into either Manchester or Glasgow; Jackson wants to land a place at Edinburgh Napier University to study photography; while Chloe has her sights set on London, where she plans on studying Events Management.

Flynn envies her friends their motivation and purpose. Without their sense of direction, university feels like a waste of time, money and energy. While they excitedly talk about the future, Flynn shies from it and secretly longs for everything to stay the same. She can't help but feel as though they are somehow leaving her behind, relegating her to the past in their eagerness to move forwards. She dreads their departure, especially Jackson's. They have been dating for less than a year, but in that time, she has fallen for him, hard. She would never admit to it, but the idea of him leaving, meeting other girls, *living* with them, stirs in her a thick, dark resentment.

To hide her insecurity, Flynn feigns a nonchalance about university, dismissing their concern and ignoring their offers of help. Pretending that it doesn't matter to her, that she doesn't care.

'Hey, is that the place?' Andy points at something in the distance.

Flynn follows his gaze across the mist-shrouded moors. At first, she doesn't see anything, but then the fog slides apart, revealing the solitary spectre of Temple Fall.

Flynn climbs out of the minivan and stares up at the house as her friends drag their bags and the camping gear from the back.

Behind skeins of mist, Temple Fall is grim and grey and somehow miserly. Walls of age-blackened stone dressed in threadbare ivy climb towards the lowering sky, worn steps lead up to a wrap-around porch with a sloped roof braced by stone columns. A turret, crowned by a cupola, projects from the left side of the house. Countless tall, narrow windows stud the walls, like hard black eyes fixed upon the landscape.

As she stares at the house, Flynn is gripped by the sudden conviction she has been here before. She tries to shake it off, to dismiss the eerie familiarity as a result of her preoccupation with the house over the past few weeks. But that doesn't quite account for the way the small hairs at the nape of her neck stir, or the tension that tightens the base of her spine.

It's just a house, Flynn tells herself.

Mei drops her bags beside Flynn, flings an arm over her shoulder as they both consider the house. Her wrist is bandaged from a recent parkour sprain and the familiar menthol scent of joint spray lifts from her skin. Her sleek black hair is fastened into a topknot, exposing her shaved back and sides, the assortment of piercings in her ears.

'Didn't you say the place was unoccupied?'

'It's definitely empty,' Flynn says. After discovering the location of the house, she had searched the Land Registry to see who owns the property now. A man called Mitchell Lister was the listed deeds holder, but according to the records, his current address is a care home in Leeds.

Mei snaps her gum behind her teeth. 'I mean, it doesn't *look* like no one's lived here for over a hundred years.'

'All I can tell you is the guy who owns it doesn't live here,' Flynn says. 'And it doesn't really look like the kind of place he'd rent out.'

And yet, a hint of uncertainty has edged into Flynn's voice. Because Mei is right. Despite its years of inoccupancy, the house doesn't look abandoned. The walls are weather-worn but not crumbling, the windows are intact, the paintwork in good condition. A few of the slate roof tiles have slipped but are otherwise undamaged, and while the lawn is overgrown, the steps that lead up to the porch are clear of debris.

'Does it matter?' Jonesy says, lighting the joint Andy refused to let him smoke in the van. 'It's not like we're spending the night in there.'

'I just want to be sure we're not camping in someone's garden,' Mei says.

Jonesy shrugs, eyes slitted as he drags on the joint. 'Maybe the National Trust bought it and renovated it.'

Tyrus moves up beside them. 'The National Trust only buys places of national heritage, doesn't it?'

Andy leans out of the van window, peers at the sky. 'You better pitch your tent. Looks like it's about to chuck it down.'

Flynn follows his gaze to the thick bars of rain-dark clouds overhead. The forecast had been cool but dry, and so the clotted, grey skies are an unwelcome surprise. She turns to the mist-clogged foothills, her imagination conjuring an image of a figure materialising from the smoky haze, ghosting towards them.

'Hey, dickhead, have you got your insulin?' Andy says, looking at his sister who is crouched on the grass rifling through her rucksack. 'Coz I'm not driving back here if you've left it in the van.'

Chloe flips him the bird without looking up.

'You're a real lady, you know that?' Andy casts a final glance towards the house, a dubious expression on his face. He shrugs, starts the engine. 'It's your funeral.' He winds up his window and steps on the gas, honks his horn twice as his minivan hits the rutted track. Flynn watches his tail-lights disappear into the murky fog, fighting the sudden inexplicable urge to shout him back.

2014

Flynn studies the letters on her rack as she waits for Heather to take her turn. Sand slips through the egg timer. Static plays quietly on the radio, a curtain of rain that falls day and night inside the house. Heather insists it protects them, helps conceal them from Outsiders. Flynn has grown so used to the sound, she barely notices it anymore.

She picks up the black biro on the table, mindlessly colours in the white letter 'A' of the word SCRABBLE on the front of the tile bag.

Heather sets her tiles on the board.

She writes her score down. 34 points. 'Your turn,' she says, and flips the sand timer.

Flynn leans over her tiles, as though a closer proximity might make a word materialise.

She considers ditching her letters for new ones, but she has already done that twice and she can't afford to miss another go.

She picks up the blank tile, absently rubs her thumb over the smooth surface. Funny, the way she sometimes thinks of herself as a blank tile. Something featureless. Invisible. She knows it's silly, but the feeling can be so strong, she fears that when she looks in the mirror, her face won't be there, that she will see nothing but a pale space where her eyes and mouth and nose should be.

The light patter of children's footsteps skitter past the window in a burst of giggles, and a man shouts, 'Stop! Wait for me!' Heather goes all still with fear, but Flynn feels their laughter as a splash of sunshine inside her.

The letters on her tiles shiver, seem to realign all by themselves, a word forming like a gift. And it's a Doozy. She grins, lines five tiles on the board, using the F that Heather played when she spelled FINITE *(9 points).*

F R E I N D

On its own the word scores 10 points, but the D is sat on a triple word square, which means she just scored 30 points! She scribbles her score in her column.

'Very good.' Heather's voice is pinched. 'But you spelt it wrong.' She leans over, switches the E and the I around.

F R I E N D

'It still counts.' Flynn's hands tighten into fists.

Heather won't look at her, but she shakes her head and strikes a line through the score Flynn has just written down, replaces it with a 0.

'A misspelled word doesn't count.'

'That's not fair!'

'The rules are there for a reason. You can't change them to suit you.'

Flynn's anger feels like a clenched fist behind her forehead.

'You're a cheat!'

Heather's mouth goes all flat. Her eyes move to the ceiling and slide side to side. Flynn can tell she's about to have An Episode, but she is too angry to care.

'That's not true.' Heather starts to rock. 'Not true.'

'It's true, it is! You're a cheat!'

'Stop it!' Heather drops her head into her hands. 'Stop it, they'll hear you.'

Outside, the kids squeal happily as the man chases them down the street, contented wriggles of sound bouncing on the air. Anger burns inside Flynn. She doesn't know why, but she feels as though she has been robbed of more than points in a Scrabble game, something bigger that she can't understand.

'Cheatcheatcheatcheat—'

Heather clamps her cracked palm over Flynn's mouth. Her fear smell is all over her and Flynn suddenly feels bad. She knows Heather is scared, that she is only trying to protect them both from Outsiders.

She goes still and quiet. Heather releases her, wraps her arms round her ribs and rocks. Shame sweeps through Flynn. She drops her eyes to the word on the Scrabble board, all the anger rushing out of her. FRIEND. Why does she care so much? It is just a stupid word.

NOW

Mei stomps the grass, trying to find a level patch of land on which to pitch Jonesy's tent, an eight-man behemoth he has borrowed from his dad. Jonesy and Tyrus unpack the tent poles, lining them up on the ground in size order. Flynn stands with her back to the house, unsure how to help. Her arms are tightly folded, body braced against the wind that has picked up since Andy dropped them off.

Jackson moves up behind her, slides his arms round her waist. In his hands, he holds a black rose.

'Where did you find this?' Flynn takes it and turns towards him, brushing her fingers over the satin petals.

Jackson nods towards a thicket of black roses that grow over the crumbling wall at the front of the house. The flowers form a clustered darkness amidst the spray of colourful wildflowers that grow around them.

'I didn't think roses could grow like that,' Jackson says. 'Even when they're dyed, it's impossible to get them truly black.'

But this one *is* truly black, like the silken pocket of the deepest shadow. Flynn turns the stem so that the flower twirls, petals spinning in a dark pirouette.

'It's beautiful.'

He hooks his fingers into the waistband of her jeans, pulls her close.

'You're beautiful.'

She rolls her eyes, trying to disguise the feeling his nearness elicits. His hand rests on the small of her back, his breath against her ear makes her feel hot and shivery. A feeling, silky and dark as the rose's petals, slides through her as the space between them shrinks and his lips brush against hers.

A slow scrape of frost down the nape of her neck makes her tense and pull back. She feels suddenly as though she is being watched, the weight of eyes like a subtle pressure against her skin. She glances round, but the others are all busy with the tent. Her eyes snag on the snarl of black roses. The wind whisks the trees, stirs the tall grass, but the roses barely move, as though they possess their own gravity.

'Hey.' Jackson's dark eyes run over her. 'You okay?'

In answer, she wraps her arms around his waist, leans into him. Breathes in the chemical scent of the fixer from his darkroom, a faint gasoline tang that always clings to him. As though it is part of his DNA.

'Hey, Jax!' Chloe yells, skipping up the porch steps. 'Take my picture!'

He pulls away from Flynn, but his eyes stay on her face. 'You look cold.'

'Yeah, well.' She glances at the clotted thunderheads in the sky, a swirling mass of silver-edged darkness that climbs towards the atmosphere in a rising cumulus. 'I'm not really dressed for the weather.'

Jackson removes his beanie and a comma of dark hair falls across his eyes. He pulls the hat over Flynn's head, works it over her numb ears.

'Jack*son*!' Chloe drapes herself over the porch railing like a model from a centrefold. Her yellow hair tangles on the breeze.

'This film's expensive!' Jackson yells back.

'Don't be tight, just take my picture!'

Jackson sighs but pulls the camera round on its strap. Holding it at waist height, he peers down into the viewfinder and fiddles with the dials to bring Chloe into focus. The shutter blades slash with an audible *ker-chunk*, followed by a high-pitched whir, like a tiny scream.

Chloe skips down the steps towards them, but Jackson's eyes travel from the camera to the house. He stares at the upper turret window, a crease between his brows.

Watching him, Flynn's unease tightens inside her. 'What is it?'

Jackson turns to her, his gaze unfocused. He opens his mouth to say something, but then his eyes shift back to the turret window. Chloe slides between them and flings an arm over Jackson's shoulder.

'Can I see?'

Jackson blinks, and the troubled look fades from his face. 'You'll have to wait until I develop the film.'

'You're kidding! Jesus, that thing's shittier than your battered Nikon.'

'It's an antique,' Jackson says, considering the camera as he turns it over in his hands. 'I like the mechanics of it, you know? Gears and springs and levers, gives it more character, don't you think?'

'But you don't even know how the pictures will come out.'

Jackson shrugs. 'I like not knowing how a photo will turn out.'

'And you can't, like, edit or filter.'

Jackson shoots Chloe a wry grin. 'Beauty lies in the imperfections.'

Chloe barks a laugh and punches his arm. 'Bitch, please!'

Flynn watches the two of them, smiling at their easy camaraderie. Had she not known them both for so long, she might have been jealous, especially considering Jackson and Chloe briefly dated when they were fifteen.

Chloe had been a different person then, far from the confident hoyden she was now. Skinny as a rake, riddled with acne and with track-braces glued to her teeth, she had been plagued by insecurity over her appearance. But over the summer between finishing high school and starting college, she had completed a course of medication that cured her acne, her braces were removed, and her toothpick frame began to fill out in all the right places. Suddenly, she was drawing admiring glances everywhere she went, and the same boys who used to call her 'Bean Pole', 'Tin Grin' and 'Pizza Face' were following her round like lovesick puppies and professing their undying love.

Chloe embraced her new position in the college hierarchy, ditching her trainers in favour of heels and swapping her baggy shirts and jogging bottoms for clingy designer tops and miniskirts. She became obsessed with her appearance, watching YouTube make-up tutorials for hours to perfect the feline flicks she swiped across her upper lashes and learning all the tips and tricks to master the art of contouring and highlighting.

'Flynn!' Mei calls, struggling against the wind with the tent's ground cloth. 'Get your arse over here and gimme a hand!'

The wind snaps Flynn's ponytail as she grabs an armful of tent poles and carries them to Mei, then lays them over the tarpaulin to hold it down. The roiling clouds have formed a wall overhead, a bluish-black mass with a cauliflower-shaped top. The air feels oppressive, charged with a sizzling energy that flickers over her skin, and she wonders how the weather forecasters could have got it all so wrong.

Tyrus blows into his hands, then picks up the blue rucksack, rummages inside. 'We're gonna freeze out here tonight.'

'Not me,' Mei says, holding down the ground cloth and flashing Tyrus a grin. 'This coat is lovely and warm.'

Tyrus shoots her an annoyed glance. He lent Mei the green canvas jacket months ago, but she is yet to give it back.

'If I was gonna be a prick about it, I'd make you return it now.'

'But you're not a prick, you're a gent,' Mei says. 'And anyway, it looks so much better on me.'

'You're not keeping it.'

'It's mine now.'

'Mei!'

'Tyrus!' Mei teases, mimicking his annoyed tone.

'I'm never lending you anything ever again,' Tyrus grumbles.

'You can have it back when I'm dead,' Mei says. 'Can you hurry up with those pegs?'

'They're not in here.' Tyrus drops the bag. 'Jonesy, where are the pegs?'

'Blue rucksack,' Jonesy calls back.

'No, they're not!'

Mei mutters something under her breath, crawls off the groundsheet. She grabs the rucksack off Tyrus, dumps its contents onto the ground. Head torches fall, spare batteries, a couple of flashlights, cable ties, a roll of binbags, a sewing kit, masking tape.

'They're not here.'

'That's what I just said,' Tyrus shoots back.

Mei unzips the side pockets, rummages through the smaller compartments. Watching her, Flynn feels the small hairs down her neck quill. She turns to the house, struck again by the irrational sense that it is watching her. Temple Fall is quiet, still, but there is a suggestion of dark energy behind the blackened windows, some strange vitality.

It's just a house, she scolds herself, turning away. *Just a house.*

'We have to pack up!' Mei yells to be heard over the wind. 'Jonesy forgot the tent pegs.'

Flynn feels a rush of relief at Mei's words, is already thinking of Chloe's bottle of vodka in Nostromo. While it's true, they haven't been there for months, at least it's somewhere warm they can all hang out together. Her chilled joints are stiff, her wind-slapped cheeks burn.

'Maybe we can pitch without them,' Jonesy says, shoulders hitched against the buffeting wind. He has pulled the toggles on the hood of his waterproof tight, so all Flynn can see is a small triangle of his face. 'We could use rocks to hold the tent down, or—'

'In this weather?' Mei scowls.

As though to underscore her words, a fine haze of rain begins to spit from the sky. The heavens groan, and the drizzle quickly broadens into a deluge that batters the ground.

'Did you leave them in the van?' Jackson shouts.

Jonesy shrugs, kicks gloomily at the ground.

'This is *shit*!' Chloe yells at the sky, wet threads of hair snapping in the wind.

'Clo, you better call Andy.' Mei's eyes are slitted against the rain. 'Get him to pick us up.'

'Have you met my brother? He'll *love* that we're stranded out here in the pissing rain.'

'Just ring him!'

'*You* ring him!'

Flynn wraps her arms round her waist as her friends start bickering. Darkness ripples across the moors, lightning throbs within the clouds. The rumble of distant thunder like roots ripping deep beneath the earth.

The wind suddenly changes direction, a body slam of warm air that makes Flynn stagger. Jackson pulls her close, briskly rubs his hands up and down her arms. Rainwater clings to his lashes, drips from his hair. He leans towards her and despite the cold, his warm breath against the shell of her ear sends a shiver through her.

'We need to take cover,' he says, nodding to the house.

'Leave all that!' Tyrus shouts at Chloe, who is trying to wrestle the metal poles back into the bag. 'It isn't safe out here, we need to go, *now*!'

'Flynn, come on!' Jackson grabs her hand and pulls her along behind him.

The sky gives an animal growl, low and primal. The small hairs down Flynn's arms stiffen, static electricity dances across her skin. The smell of ozone punches the air and a metallic taste floods her mouth. The heavens crack, the sound so loud Flynn could almost believe the earth had been cleaved in two. Somewhere behind her, a tree crashes to the ground.

Flynn sprints towards the house, her trainers slipping and skidding on the sucking mud. She takes the porch steps two at a time, desperate for shelter yet unable to shake the suspicion there is none to find there.

Huddled together on the porch, they watch the storm thrash the trees. The wind howls through the eaves and sweeps rain beneath the porch. Flynn's soaked jeans stick to her skin, rainwater squelches inside her trainers. The growl of thunder is so loud, it seems to drive fissures through the earth and shake the world on its hinges.

Chloe stares at her phone. 'I haven't got any signal.'

Jackson unzips his raincoat, pulls out his mobile. 'Shit,' he mutters. 'What about you guys?'

'Mine's dead,' Mei says.

Flynn takes her rucksack from Jackson. Her fingers are numb with cold as she unzips it and pulls out her phone. Her stomach drops. 'No signal.'

'Ty?' Jackson looks at his friend.

'Nothing,' Tyrus says, pocketing his phone. 'Jonesy?'

Jonesy's gloomy expression is answer enough. 'Not since we drove through–'

Veins of lightning sear the sky, striking a tree close to where they had been planning to set up camp. Branches explode in a shower of wood, the thick tree trunk blackens and splits with a spume of sparks. Fire flares in the unsnapped branches, a pulse of flames against the darkness. The accompanying thunderclap is almost synched to the flash of lightning, and it drowns out Jonesy's shriek of alarm.

'Holy shit!' Tyrus stares at the burning tree. 'We need to take shelter.'

'I thought that's what we were doing!' Flynn says.

'Lightning can travel sideways.' Tyrus turns, eyes Temple Fall. 'We need to break into the house.'

'I'll do it.' Jonesy starts towards the door, but Flynn grabs his arm, yanks him back.

'We're not breaking in!'

'Yes, w-we are!' Chloe's words are clipped between her chattering teeth. Her cable-knit cardigan is drenched, her long blonde hair hangs in soaked tails down her back. 'P-please, Flynn, I'm so f-fucking c-cold!'

'We'll freeze to death if we stand out here on the porch all night!' Tyrus shouts over the roar of the storm.

Jonesy takes a hammer from his rucksack – the one he had brought to drive the tent pegs into the ground – and moves towards the door. The others crowd behind him, pressing forwards in their eagerness for shelter.

Flynn's eyes move over the bubbling rust on the railing, to the vast stone walls, the oak door, stained to a shade so dark it is almost black. The cast-iron knocker is shaped like a snake eating its own tail. Exposed to the elements for so many years, it should surely have rusted, but it is pristine.

Jonesy squints through the keyhole. 'There's a key in the lock. There must be someone inside.'

Mei pushes forwards, knocks the rapper against the strike plate.

'Just smash it in already, there's n-no one here!' Chloe's words are like snapped icicles between her clashing teeth. 'P-please, I'm f-f-freezing my t-tits off here!'

Jonesy hefts the hammer, and as he swings it at the pane of glass above the door handle, lightning flares, like the flash of a camera, sealing one moment of time to celluloid.

The sound of shattered glass hitting the floor is barely audible over the roar of the storm. Jonesy sweeps the hammer round the edges of the frame, knocking away the jagged pieces, then reaches inside, twists the key in the lock. He turns the handle, starts to open the door, but the wind tears it from his grasp and blasts it wide open.

Tyrus swings his torch over a cavernous, shadow-cluttered lobby. A bifurcated staircase, carpeted in the deep maroon of old blood, sweeps up to the balcony. A chandelier hangs from the middle of the ceiling.

Jonesy whistles softly, turns a slow circle. 'This place is sick!'

As Flynn crosses the threshold, she feels a sudden heat pulse through the scars in her feet, as though they have been splashed by the scalding water that burned her all those years ago. She gasps at the pain, but already the sensation is fading to a faint tingle.

Avoiding the jagged shards of glass, she closes the door behind her. The others dump their rucksacks, start rummaging for torches. Tyrus pulls two storm lanterns from his own bag and turns them on. Flynn pulls Jackson's beanie off and turns to survey the lobby.

Walnut-panelled walls with intricate carvings rise to a high vaulted ceiling, maroon and gold brocade curtains cover the high arched windows. A chaise longue, upholstered in the same material as the curtains, occupies a space by the wall. The house smells of dust and mouldering flowers, but another scent lingers on the stale air, an animalistic musk that catches at the back of Flynn's throat. Wind flutes through the small gaps in the windowpanes, the floorboards creak beneath her feet.

She shrugs her backpack off and pulls out her own torch, tracks the circle of light over the oil paintings that decorate the walls, hunting scenes that make her stomach clench with revulsion: grey and grisly intestines unspool on lush forest carpets; fangs sink into furred flesh; muzzles wrinkle over blood-drenched snouts.

'This place is incredible.' Jonesy peels off his waterproof and shakes a hand through his corona of blonde curls.

'It's hardly degraded at all.' Jackson moves his torchlight across the high ceiling, where intricately designed patterns have been hand-moulded into the cornices. Dusty cobwebs tinsel the chandelier, like clusters of dirty grey hair. He walks through the lobby, inspecting the various trinkets and ornaments, photographing the side table, the chandelier, the iron candle sconces that line the walls.

Jonesy pulls a beer from his bag, pops the tab. The sleek *tsk* echoes around the lobby. Chloe flings herself onto the chaise longue and Mei drops beside her, drapes her legs over her friend's lap. Watching Chloe, Flynn feels a kick of unease she can't put her finger on.

'So, Jax,' Jonesy says, clapping Jackson on the shoulder. 'How does it feel to officially be a man?'

'*Officially*, I'm not.' Jackson fiddles with the dials on his camera. 'I don't turn eighteen until three twenty tomorrow morning.'

'Eighteen, man.' Tyrus shakes his head. 'And it feels like only yesterday you thought girls got pregnant by kissing their boobs.'

'They don't?' Jackson glances at Flynn, and his smile shoots a pulse of heat through her.

'You can do all the grown-up shit now,' Jonesy says.

'I don't think there's much I can do now that we haven't done already.'

'Yeah, but now it'll be legal,' Tyrus says.

'Bro, where's the fun in legal?' Jonesy grins.

'You can gamble.' Mei pulls her topknot loose, shakes her wet hair out. It falls across her cheeks in a spill of black ink.

'I've been gambling with Who-Shot-John since I was thirteen,' Jackson says.

'You guys gamble your lives working in that shithole,' Chloe mutters.

The Dive isn't the sort of bar where the landlord asks his workers to provide ID, and Flynn, Jackson and Jonesy have been working there since they were fifteen years old.

'You can get a tattoo,' Tyrus says.

Jackson pulls the collar of his T-shirt down, revealing the stick-and-poke Scorpio zodiac symbol Flynn inked onto his shoulder. Jackson tattooed a similar Leo sign on the inside of Flynn's wrist, despite the fact Flynn isn't sure she even *is* a Leo. The date on her birth certificate, 1 August, was an approximation, made by doctors and specialists after she presented in hospital for the first time as an Unidentified Female Child.

'You can legally drink,' Chloe says, reaching for the bag on the floor at her feet to grab a bottle of prosecco.

'Bro, you can smoke weed!' Jonesy grins.

'That's illegal whatever age you are, moron,' Chloe mutters, sliding the sharp point of her nail beneath the bottle cover, twisting the wire hood off the top.

Tyrus aims the beam of his torch up the shadowy staircase. 'Who wants to take a look around this place?'

'I'm not moving from this chair all night,' Chloe says, struggling with the cork. 'This house is well creepy.'

'Agreed,' Mei says. 'I say we stay right here and get smashed.'

Chloe and Mei high-five.

'Hey, Jax!' Chloe drops her head back, holds up the bottle. 'Come over here and pop my cork, will ya?'

Her flirty tone makes Flynn prickle with irritation, but Jackson reaches to take the bottle. As he works his thumb beneath the cork, Chloe peels off her wet cardigan. In the lantern-light, her skin is luminous, her eyes large and glossy. A sheen of rainwater glistens on her pearly shoulders.

The cork shoots from the bottle on a creamy spume of froth and Jackson passes the bottle back to Chloe. She lifts it to her lips and guzzles the booze as though it is fresh water.

'Hey, take it easy!' Jackson grabs the bottle from her, accidentally spilling fizz on her top. Chloe giggles, flops back down on the chaise longue.

Jonesy and Tyrus are crabbed over the rucksacks by the door, whispering to each other. Flynn watches Jonesy carefully remove a large white box from one of the bags. He opens it, lifting out the birthday cake he made Jackson, and starts to place eighteen small, thin candles on top. Tyrus flashes a look over his shoulder, checking Jackson isn't watching, but he is lost in conversation with Chloe and doesn't notice. Jonesy strikes a match, holds the flame to the first candle.

Flynn's gaze lingers on Jackson and Chloe, a strange ache pushing beneath her ribs. They are so at ease together, so comfortable in each other's company, that if a stranger were here observing them all, they would probably assume Chloe, not Flynn, was dating Jackson.

As Flynn watches Chloe, she realises what it is that has been niggling at her: only a few minutes ago, stood outside Temple Fall, her friend's lips had been tinged blue with cold, her teeth clattering hard enough to crack enamel. But now, her lips are pink, her skin glows and her eyes sparkle, as though she has been reclining by a fire for hours.

It is only observing these changes that Flynn realises that she no longer feels cold, either. The chill that the hard wind had driven deep into her bones has already thawed, and her limbs are suffused with warmth. Temple Fall is unheated, yet her breath no longer smokes on the air in front of her face.

The faint crackle of static washes through the lobby, almost imperceptible beneath the louder sounds of the storm and her friends' voices. So subtle she can almost dismiss it as imagination. She frowns, straining to hear where it is coming from. Her eyes track to the staircase, the quilted darkness overhead.

'Are you okay?' Jackson touches her elbow, making her jump and spin round.

'Yeah, I just... I thought I heard...' She glances up the stairs and the darkness dilates, like a giant pupil expanding. She turns back to Jackson, forces a smile. 'I'm fine.'

'Jax, check this out,' Tyrus says, straightening as Jonesy picks up the cake. 'Jonesy made you a birthday cake!'

The cake in question consists of a black sponge camera set upon a white base. *Nikon* is iced across the top and the strap is made of black fondant, *Happy 18th Birthday, Jax!* written across it in white icing. Black sugar paste buttons and dials, intricate in their detail, lend the cake a look of such lifelike authenticity, Flynn almost believes she could lift it off its edible base and snap a photograph of the moment. Eighteen flames bend and twist on the air as Jonesy walks towards them, a bashful grin on his face.

'Wow, Jonesy!' Jackson grins. 'That looks epic. You shouldn't have.'

'No trouble, bro. Flynn was threatening to bake for you, so I took one for the team.'

'Oh, in that case—'

'Hey!' Flynn smacks Jackson's arm. Ever since they started food tech in Year 7, the others have teased her for her questionable culinary skills.

Jonesy sets the cake on the side table, the glow of pride in his cheeks. Jackson folds his arms, eyes it with a trace of scepticism. 'Is this cake gonna make me forget my name and think you're Jesus?'

'It's clean, nothing but the finest quality ingredients, bro, trust me. Although there's enough fondant in it to put Clo into a hyperglycaemic coma.'

One of the candles flickers and shrinks, then winks out, trailing a thready wisp of grey smoke.

'Shit, it keeps doing that.' Tyrus lights another match, holds it to the eighteenth candle. Flynn's unease twists, a sharp tightening in her chest as she watches the flame of the freshly lit candle shrink low, as though it is about to wink out again.

'Come on, guys, while they're all still lit,' Chloe says, then breaks into a rendition of 'Happy Birthday'. Everyone else joins in and Jackson flushes, his hand catching and squeezing Flynn's. She smiles, kisses his dusky cheek, but sadness closes round her, the realisation that they are all reaching an ending of sorts, and that no matter how much she digs her heels in, there is nothing she can do to prevent it.

2014

Heather sinks onto the mattress beside Flynn, passes her the sleep drink. A Mickey Finn, that's what she calls it. Flynn always thought that was a funny name for a drink. Heather once told Flynn that someone had slipped her a Mickey Finn a long time ago, and that was how Flynn came alive inside her. Flynn had wanted to know how that was possible, but something about the way Heather said it had stopped her asking questions.

Flynn pushes the drink away.

Heather places Mama Doll on the pillow. She made the doll for Flynn years ago, a little Heather replica for when the real one wasn't around. Stuffed her cloth body with cotton batting, stitched big grey buttons on for eyes. Made her a navy dress just like her own, and a velvet brown cap that matches her cropped hair. She'd even sewn a tiny mole in the same spot she has one, a loop of brown thread stitched to her cheek. Mama looks exactly like Heather. Every bit the same, and nothing like her at all.

'Drink it,' Heather says.

Flynn feels her lower lip tremble, the press of tears behind her eyes. Heather sets the mug down and pulls Flynn onto her lap. In preparation for going Outside, she has washed in bleach, and her skin smells all sharp and chemically. Flynn doesn't like the smell, but

Heather rarely hugs her like this, and she has to fight the urge to fling her arms around her neck and beg her not to leave.

'I'll be back before you wake up,' Heather says, patting Flynn's hair then gently pushing her back onto the mattress.

Flynn shakes her head because it isn't true, not anymore. It used to be that Heather would return to find her still asleep, and she would have to smack Flynn's legs and pinch her cheeks to wake her. Once, she had pulled out a hank of hair trying to rouse her. Heather had laughed her nervous, brittle laugh, and said Flynn was 'such a Sleepyhead'. But the past few times she has been left alone, Flynn woke long before Heather returned.

She always feels terrible after she has the drink. The sleep it brings is so black and heavy it feels like a little death and when she wakes, her stomach churns and her head hurts like it's been kicked. Her heart pounds so loudly, she is sure the Outsiders will hear it, even though the radio's silvery crackling is meant to protect her. She hates being left alone, fears that one day Heather won't return at all, that the Outsiders will come for her.

And so, to distract herself when she wakes up, she walks round the house, counting her footsteps. It feels right, like one of Heather's Rituals. A Tactic. Holding Mama in one hand, the other hand brushing the wall, she paces, telling herself by the time she reaches the front door, Heather will be back.

'I've added an extra pill,' Heather says. 'Trust me, you'll sleep.'

Flynn takes the drink, she has no choice. Her stomach squirms when she swallows, threatens to eject the bitter liquid. The tablet dust is gritty between her teeth.

Heather takes the empty mug and goes back into the kitchen. Flynn holds Mama to her chest and lies down. She hears Heather flicking switches on and off, tapping things and muttering to herself. Spellcasting.

She has been cleaning all morning, getting ready to go Outside. She washed the fridge out with bleach, defrosted the freezer, scoured the oven, cleaned the cutlery drawer, descaled the kettle, scrubbed the bathroom tiles, hoovered the sofas, sanitised the door handles. Flynn hadn't offered to help, not because she is lazy, but because she barely has the energy to stand. Hunger chews her insides, a toothy gnawing, making her feel crumpled and empty. Besides, Heather always insists on doing it herself.

Now, Flynn hears her turn the tap on and pump the soap dispenser three times. Heather likes to do lots of things in threes.

Flynn's muscles are starting to feel funny. Floppy and soft like Play-Doh. Tiredness crashes through her, a rising tide that lifts her off the mattress, bobs her along on an invisible ocean. She hears the splash of water hit the sink again, Heather pumping more soap from the dispenser. Her vision wavers, blurs, and she floats in the grey sea between waking and sleep.

Her heart suddenly quickens in the silence, a panicked rat-a-tat-tat *that makes her eyes snap wide. The house is quiet. She is alone. But fear flickers beneath her skin, panic jogs in her pulse.*

A flurry of hard knocks shake the door, and she realises this was the sound that roused her. But Heather never knocks, and Flynn knows better than to answer.

She sways to her feet, clutching Mama. The drugs in her blood make her thoughts run like treacle, her movements feel slow. Her body possesses all the strength of a ragdoll. She stares at the door, paralysed by fear.

Hide! *Heather's voice, bright as a flare in her mind.*

Flynn staggers into the kitchen, her knees threatening to give out with every step. She crawls into The Cupboard, closes the door behind her. She hates hiding in here. It smells bad, like popcorn and wet bricks and bleach, but right now she doesn't care about that, because she feels Mickey Finn spreading through her, sleep pulsing behind her eyes.

But she has to stay awake.

She has to be alert.

She can't let them take her... Can't let them... Can't...

Again, the knocking – harder this time. Insistent.

Darkness crowds her vision, warmth slides down her spine, across her temples. Her eyelids slope. She slaps her face, hard. Nips the skin on her elbows. But it is like fighting in quicksand, and she is sinking, sinking.

A hard kick against the door, the sound of splintering wood.

They are in the house!

Her terror widens as she realises she can't fight it any longer. Her body is collapsing, falling, her tear-damp lashes fluttering closed, even as her mind rails, furious with herself, her body, its weakness. She squeezes Mama tightly, folds herself around that small cloth body. Sleep is a warm glove slipping over treacherous skin and bone and muscle, but her thoughts flail, panicked, desperate to shake free, to escape. That word – Escape! *– beats like a drum within her, as insistent as her heartbeat, a command that won't be quieted.*

Gruff, muffled voices from the living room, something crashes to the floor. They are so close to her... so close... but Flynn's body sinks, succumbs to the darkness.

Escape! Escape! Escape!

She feels a tearing deep within her mind, and something inside her rises, born aloft on a violent expulsion.

She is simultaneously falling and flying.

The sensation is over before Flynn can register what has happened, but when she blinks her eyes open, she is no longer in The Cupboard.

She is crouching on the patch of grass at the back of the house.

She is Outside.

At first, she is too stunned to move, can't understand what has happened. The fear that twists through her feels dull, distant. As though her senses have been dialled right down.

The grass is waterlogged, but she doesn't feel its wetness beneath her bare feet. She is wearing her thin pyjamas, but she doesn't feel the cold. She doesn't feel anything. *She wonders if she is dead, presses a hand to her chest, feels her heart beating. Its slow, steady drum feels distant, removed, quiet like the constant bath of static that plays in the house. No, this isn't Dead, this is something else. Something In-Between. Like her mind and body have... Split.*

She stands up, moves round the side of the house. She feels oddly weightless, floaty. She listens to the commotion within the house, the banging of cupboards, slamming of drawers, and understands her sleeping body is still in The Cupboard, vulnerable to discovery. The thought should be a shock, but it passes through her with a dull tremor.

She steps onto the street, almost walks straight into an Outsider. She opens her mouth to cry out, backs away. But the Outsider looks straight through her, as though she isn't there, his eyes sweeping up and down the street.

Flynn looks down at herself, blinking. She is stood in a puddle, but her feet don't send any ripples through the water. The sun is sinking behind her, yet her body casts no shadow. She is here and not here. She feels the pull of her sleeping body, a little tug in her belly. She knows she should be scared, but fear doesn't touch her in this strange other-place.

She carries on walking, quicker now, wanting to see everything that has always been hidden from her, everything she has been hidden from. *She starts to run, something she has never been able to do before because her house is so small and her legs too thin and weak from hardly being used.*

She gathers speed until she is racing so fast her feet feel as though they might leave the ground, and it is as though the thought alone lifts her, floating into the air. She opens her arms to hug The Night, and her breath snaps in her throat and her stomach drops, and she is sure she is about to fall. But she doesn't.

Flynn flies over rooftops, like a shirt snatched by the wind from a clothesline, tossed and tousled skywards. She holds tight to the cord, that tug deep in her core, and even as she spins higher and higher, she doesn't let that band snap too tight.

NOW

Flynn peels her wet trainers and socks off her feet, pours vodka and Coke into a paper cup. Mei has lit the small black candles that are mounted on the walls, and their light, combined with the illumination from the storm lanterns, brightens the lobby.

Flynn's gaze keeps sliding to Jackson, who is stood with Chloe in a darkened corner. His previous reticence to waste film photographing her has morphed into an eagerness to capture as many shots of her as he can. Now, he has her posing with a black candle, playing with the light and shadows that move across her face.

Jackson rarely shoots portraits, and when he does, it is usually Flynn he photographs. And while she avoids taking selfies and inwardly cringes when she has to pose for shots, she feels different when it is Jackson on the other side of the lens. He sets her at ease, and always seems able to capture something in her face that she likes: the freckles on her cheek, a play of emotion across her face, her hair splayed on a pillow. She has never admitted it, but she has always found the steady way he considers her through the camera lens to be deeply erotic, his attention like a drug, his focused intensity addictive. Now, watching Jackson photograph Chloe, the jealousy that has plagued her since entering the house sharpens. She feels its heat behind her eyes, her pulse beats hot and fast.

'Hey.' Tyrus sits beside her. 'You were miles away.'

Flynn's gaze sweeps the lobby. 'I wish.'

'Come on, it's not that bad.'

'Hey, Jonesy!' Jackson calls. 'Check this out!'

He tosses something to Jonesy, who is sat on the chaise longue working his way through a tube of Pringles. Jonesy snatches it from the air.

'Wow, a tin,' Jonesy deadpans.

'Open it,' Jackson says.

Jonesy cracks the tin open and his eyes light up. 'Sweet!'

'What is that?' Flynn stands up, moves towards him.

The metal tin is the colour of mustard, the lettering across the top so scratched and faded it is illegible. But it isn't the tin that Jonesy is interested in. It's the long, brown cigarettes inside.

'You're not smoking those,' Flynn says.

'Why not?' Jonesy slides one of the cigarettes out.

'Because they're fucking ancient! They've probably been sitting there for over a hundred years.'

'Besides,' Mei says, moving closer, 'the Victorians put all sorts of poison in their cigs. Radium, opium, belladonna.'

'Bella*what?*' Jonesy sniffs the cigarette.

'Belladonna. It's a powerful hallucinogenic.'

Jonesy grins. 'Cool.'

'C'mon, Jonesy,' Mei says. 'Please don't smoke that shit.'

'Relax,' Jonesy says. 'It's probably full of cloves and cabbage leaves. Anyway, if they're as old as you say, then they'll have lost all their potency...' Jonesy falters, staring at Tyrus, who is stood beside Flynn. 'Bro, the fuck, man? You're *drinking*?'

Flynn turns to Tyrus, only now noticing the tin of Stella in his hands. Tyrus frowns at the can, as though perplexed to find it there.

'Just one can't do any harm,' he says, but his voice sounds uncertain, his expression foggy. 'It's a special occasion, not every day you turn eighteen, hey, Jax. Here's to you, bro.' He lifts the can, salutes the air. The muffled sound of thunder echoes through the house. He drains the tin and crumples it between his hands.

But Tyrus doesn't drink. Flynn stares at him, the thought like a broken cog in her mind, locking her thoughts. The air in the room seems to thicken. Her skin bristles, the roots of her hair stiffen.

She drains her drink, hoping to dull the queasy tension that crawls through her. She feels strange, her thoughts muzzy, hypnogogic. She passes a hand over her face and the moment before her fingers touch her skin, she is convinced there will be nothing there, that her palm will slide over a smooth plane of flesh. A featureless oval. The thought is so overwhelming, she almost cries out with relief when her fingertips trace her lips, her nose, the sockets of her eyes.

Like mother, like daughter.

The voice whispers from the back of her skull, as subtle as breath-warmed air, yet it blows like a gale inside her, blasting goosebumps across her arms.

She turns back to the others, but none of them are paying her any attention. Her gaze snags on Chloe, who is standing a little too close to Jackson, whispering something that makes him smile. She puts her hand on his arm and giggles. It is a low, intimate sound, and it sets Flynn's teeth on edge.

Whore.

The word pulses red inside her, like a blade slashing flesh. She flinches, appalled by the vehemence of the thought, yet something of its savagery thrills her, too.

Flynn picks up a storm lantern, moves deeper into the lobby. The swinging light makes the shadows caper and sway.

She passes through an archway which opens onto a large room with box-panelled walls and a coffered ceiling. A three-piece suite upholstered in purple velvet and edged with plum-coloured tassels. A denuded mahogany side table. Red and mustard paisley carpet. The curtains are open, and beyond the glass, the rain blurs the moors and the storm beats saturnine bruises into the night-dark sky.

She hears the low rumble of Jackson's voice, Chloe's muted reply. Flynn trails her fingertips across the surface of the side table and her jealousy inexplicably sharpens. She imagines Chloe peering at Jackson from beneath her lashes, leaning towards him, her perfect face turned up to his, her satin lips parted. Anger pulses up into Flynn's throat.

Whore.

She welcomes the voice now, takes pleasure in its savagery.

She doesn't want to turn back round, doesn't want to be in the same room as Jackson and Chloe. There is a door on the opposite side of the room. Flynn walks through it, finds herself in a long hallway. The door softly closes behind her, cutting off her friends' voices. The animal musk Flynn had detected earlier has faded, and the rooms smell of springtime after rain, crushed leaves and cut grass.

Her hand floats to the wall, trance-like, and she keeps walking as her thoughts unravel through time.

She had fallen for Jackson long before their first kiss at the college party last Christmas, and she can count on one hand the days they have spent apart since. Walks in the park, trips into town, stolen kisses at college, entire Sunday mornings sprawled on his bed listening to music or fooling around.

And yet, Flynn can't shake the conviction that one day, Jackson will move on from her. There is a wildness about him, a fey quality, an aura of tragic charisma and magnetism that burns so intensely, she fears it can't last.

Now, as she moves through the rooms of Temple Fall, Flynn's thoughts turn back to when Chloe and Jackson dated. She recalls their lingering kisses at The Pitfalls, how they would snuggle together on the ratty sofa. Always glued together, hip to hip, their legs tangled on beanbags, arms entwined, fingers interlaced. As though they had needed to touch all the time.

And yet hadn't Jackson admitted to Flynn, after he and Chloe broke up, that they had shared no real spark? That though he loved her, he was not *in* love with her?

Yeah, but that was before she turned into such a knockout. All the other lads at college are crazy about her, what makes Jackson immune?

Flynn's jealousy twists, an alien musculature flexing inside her. She feels as though she has mentally brushed against something that has attached itself to her thoughts, the way warm skin welds to ice.

She blinks at her unfamiliar surroundings, feels a kick of unease. *What am I doing?* She is standing in a narrow hallway with bare wooden floorboards and dark green wallpaper decorated with tiny emerald-coloured flowers. The light from her lantern falls no further than a few metres ahead of her, so that the only way to push back the darkness is to walk towards it. She feels strange. Off-kilter in a way she used to feel as a small child, waking with the bitter taste of Heather's drugged tea on her tongue.

Flynn realises she can taste the tea now. A furred sweetness lacquers the roof of her mouth, the sediment of crushed pills coats her teeth.

Her hand, which had been brushing the wall, drops to her side. She freezes. *I was counting my footsteps. Oh my god, I was counting my footsteps...*

Without even realising it, she had fallen back into that old childhood compulsion. She sways, leans against the wall to steady herself. Giddiness bubbles up in her chest, warm and effervescent. So much more pleasant than the bitter taste of her jealousy. *What does it matter if I was counting my steps? It's not such a big deal.*

She presses the heels of her hands against her temples. Her thoughts are like sludge, thickened by contamination. The urge to keep counting is almost overwhelming, a comfort she longs to reach for, but she has a sudden image of herself, counting each footstep as she endlessly walks round and round the house, forever lost.

She glances over her shoulder, wonders whether she should double back, but is not sure she can navigate her way through the labyrinthine corridors. It occurs to her that the rooms and hallways are far more numerous than the house can accommodate. As though the building is larger inside than out. Temple Fall is a maze, and she is the mouse lost inside it.

'Squeak squeak,' she says, and giggles.

Her voice sounds small and frightened, a tiny scratch of sound against the cavernous silence.

She opens the next door she comes to, steps into a formal dining room. A low-slung chandelier hangs over a vast table that is bracketed by high-backed chairs. A silver tea service on the table gleams as though it has recently been buffed to a high shine.

She can't understand how she came to be so lost. It feels as though the house is growing as she moves through it, the hallways stretching, rooms materialising, as though the air stirred by her passage is flushing life through its walls, causing it to grow and expand, like proliferating cells.

She crosses the room, passes through another door. The darkness in here is thicker, despite the high arched windows that line the far wall. Shadows pool and stir, like swirled eddies of water. The wooden floorboards are cold beneath her bare feet. The sense that there is something wrong with this room – *with this house, there's something wrong with this house!* – touches the edges of her thoughts, but it is a muted fear, dulled by some mysterious anaesthesia.

Again, she considers turning round, trying to navigate her way back the way she came, but the thought is interrupted by a distant strain of music.

Happy birthday to you!

Flynn stills, listening. The well-worn song sounds different, echoing and strange, the chorus of voices somehow leering, grinning. Flynn feels as though she is on a carousel, music flaring and fading as she spins. She realises Chloe must have turned her Bluetooth speaker on, and that all she needs to do to navigate her way back to the others is follow the music. Why then, do those faint, echoing notes scatter chills down her spine? Why the urge to cover her ears and run in the opposite direction?

Happy birthday to you!

The music sounds muffled, crackly, as though it is playing through an ancient gramophone, and the celebratory tone she is accustomed to hearing in the song is absent, replaced by an insidious, creeping malice. Off-key and drawn out, the voices scrape in her head, like an axe dragging across the ground.

Happy biiiiirthday, dear Jacksooooonnnnn!

The darkness twitches, contracts.

'Hello?' Flynn's voice is a dry rasp that barely carries to her own ears.

Lightning strobes the sky, a finger-snap of light that reveals high wood-panelled walls, an iron armchair beside an unlit fireplace. In the corner, a silver-dapple rocking horse, its mane and tail the colour of rotting cobwebs. And standing against the far wall, four metal-framed cots...

At the sight of those small beds, the strange numbness that

furs Flynn's thoughts is ripped away, like a scab from a wound, and fear spills through her, hot and red as blood. She hurries from the room, her heart a piston, her pulse thrashing her temples, fighting the urge to run, knowing that if she does, her terror will skid out of control and erase her.

The music swells in her ears, seems to echo from every corner of the house so that she doesn't know which way to turn. It fills her head, so loud she doesn't hear when someone says her name, does not sense the cold hand reach out of the darkness until it touches her shoulder.

2014

Flynn peels a corner of the newspaper from the window and sneaks a forbidden glance Outside. Heather is upstairs, oblivious to her transgression, but Flynn's heart drums wildly, thrilled and terrified by the prospect of being caught.

She knows it is dangerous, stealing looks like this, but she can't help herself. Something about Outside calls to her. Tonight, the moon looks huge, a perfect silver ball floating above a reef of clouds. Flynn feels as though she could reach out and pull it from the sky. Of course, to do that she'd have to open the window, and she thinks her heart would burst if she did that.

The street lamps splash yellow pools of light across the pavement. The lawn in front of the house is overgrown, a tiny jungle. She longs to run her hands across the tall blades of grass, to feel it tickle her knees. It is so overgrown, she could probably crawl through it on her belly and no one would ever see her.

Movement across the street snatches her attention. An Outsider, male, standing on the street corner. A rucksack is strapped to his shoulders, and his hair is long, knotted at the base of his skull in a ponytail. He is carrying a wad of leaflets. He lifts his face, stares straight at Flynn.

She freezes, fear zipping through her as he turns and starts to walk towards the house.

'Come away from the window!'

Flynn jerks round at the sound of Heather's voice, shrinks back as she moves towards her. Heather's breath catches between her teeth when she sees Flynn has peeled a section of newspaper from the window.

'What were you thinking?' Anger ticks like a bomb in her voice as she tapes the newspaper back to the glass. 'How many times do I have to tell—'

Knocking at the door turns her to stone.

'Hide!'

All the anger suddenly blanched from her voice, the word is a whisper, light as a feather falling down the dark well of her throat.

But Flynn is already moving to the kitchen, to The Cupboard. She shutters herself into the darkness, hears the slide of the bolt as Heather locks her inside. The sound of knocking is muffled. Her heart punches hard, breath hot in the small space.

She wonders whether he saw her, this Outsider, whether it is her fault he is knocking on their door. Heather will know. She always knows. She can read patterns that Flynn can't see, and will later be able to tell Flynn exactly what brought him to the house: Heather hadn't switched the hallway light on and off the right number of times (five) or she had lost count of her footsteps from the bathroom to the living room (eight) or from the living room to the kitchen (four) or she had tripped on a step on her way up the stairs, or she had forgotten to touch all the books on the shelves, or she had found a fly or a spider or a woodlouse in the house, or she hadn't tapped her hand against the doorframe as she walked through it, or she had found a chipped mug on the shelf, or she had knocked a glass over and it had cracked, or...

Cramp tightens Flynn's calf, but The Cupboard is too small to stretch it out. Heather will want to clean every inch of the house now that they've had a Knocker, and Flynn knows she will be locked in for hours yet. She remembers what had happened last time she crawled in here: the Outsiders. The Split. She knows it wasn't a dream, because when she'd woken up, Heather's tear-streaked face looming over her, the lock on the front door had been busted open, and the room's contents, ransacked.

She later found out the Outsiders had taken an envelope of cash from the kitchen cupboard, as well as the few items of jewellery Heather kept in her dresser. Upon discovering this, Flynn had wondered whether they had broken in only to rob them, but Heather told her that what they had really come for was her. Flynn. That if she hadn't hidden, they would have taken her away forever.

The Split. Flynn wonders if she can do it again.

She closes her eyes, listens to her breath as it slows. She tries to remember how it had felt the moment before it happened, the strange sensation of being scooped outside of herself, a white-knuckle propulsion within her mind. She reaches mentally for the edges of the Split, and quickly finds it, like a scar that has not quite healed, a seam that might be wrenched apart again.

She recalls how she had floundered in terror as the Outsiders tore through the house, her thoughts pushing outwards, straining beneath the cage of her skull, the bars of her bones, her jail of muscle and sinew. Held fast by her body, a straitjacket made of meat, pinning her. But with the voices of the Outsiders so close, the knowledge that they had finally come for her, it had suddenly been so easy. And like a drowning person shrugging off a heavy coat, she had slipped through the confines of her skin, floated free.

Holding the ragged seams of that first Split in her mind, she peels them open again.

Feels her consciousness begin to slide...

A pushing through her torso, those bulbs rooting spirit to host ripping... ripping... an untethering of the soul.

And she is falling, flying.

When she blinks her eyes open, she is Outside. Her bare feet are sunk in frost-stippled grass, yet she does not feel the cold. Her eyes slide to the swollen moon, the ink-black sky. She smiles, opens her arms to The Night, not quite able to believe she has really done it.

She starts to walk, her feet skimming the pavement. She stops to peer through the windows of houses she passes, but the Outsiders inside don't see the girl staring wide-eyed through the glass, don't feel the weight of her gaze as she observes them.

Heather once explained to Flynn how babies are born, and how afterwards, they are still connected to their mother by something called an Unbiblical Cord. That it was through the Unbiblical Cord that the baby breathes until a doctor or nurse cuts it and breaks the connection. When she explained this, Flynn had asked her who had cut her Unbiblical Cord, because she knew Heather wouldn't have let Outsiders do it, and Heather had said she had cut it herself with a pair of bleached kitchen scissors.

Flynn doesn't remember breathing through an Unbiblical Cord, but that is how she thinks of the tug in her belly now. A subtle pull right beneath her navel. And even though she can't see it, somehow she understands that the Unbiblical Cord is what keeps her alive, that it is her tether to the living world.

The cold breeze whispers across her skin, passes through her, seems to sing a silent song, laughing, teasing, begging her to come and play. Because they are the same now, bodyless, boundless, free.

Flynn allows herself to be swept up, into the arms of The Night. She sails over houses, chases wind-whipped clouds. But she holds fast to her Unbiblical Cord, careful not to let that connection snap too tight.

NOW

Flynn slaps the hand away with a cry, swings her body round, ready to pelt away from her attacker.

'Jesus, Flynn!' Jackson flings his hands up. 'It's me!'

Flynn sags, weak with relief. But then her eyes move past Jackson, to Chloe who is stood behind him. She has changed out of her wet clothes into flesh-coloured hot pants and a crop top that cleaves to her skin like a slick of oil. Amusement sparkles in her cut-glass eyes, her full lips are quirked in a smile. The needle of jealousy pierces Flynn again, a slip of poison in her blood. Her pulse quickens, her hands tremble. She passes a shaking hand over her face, sickened, overwhelmed, by the turbulence of her emotions.

'Hey, I'm sorry I made you jump,' Jackson says, misinterpreting her reaction. He pulls her into his arms. 'Why did you wander off? We've been all through the house looking for you.'

'I told you she wouldn't have gone far,' Chloe says, her eyes dismissively flicking over Flynn. 'Come on, it's freezing down here.'

Put some clothes on then, the voice in Flynn's head pipes up.

'We've found a room upstairs,' Jackson says, lacing his fingers through Flynn's. 'It's better than spending the night in the lobby.'

Flynn allows herself to be steered through the house, noting dazedly how easily Jackson and Chloe seem to navigate their way. In the space of a few turns, they are back in the lobby, and then they are climbing the sweeping staircase, moving down a long hallway. Jackson and Chloe's chatter washes over Flynn. She feels shaky, confused. The haunting music she had heard playing through the house echoes in her mind, sings beneath her skin.

'We're just in here.' Jackson opens a door, holds it open for Flynn and Chloe.

'Thanks,' Flynn mumbles.

She steps past him, into a small room with a low coved ceiling. The walls are curved and covered in dark green wallpaper. A fire burns in the hearth beneath a large bevelled mirror. Trembling candlelight makes the shadows twitch. Tyrus's storm lantern sits on a red oriental rug which covers bare floorboards. Damask curtains are pinned open by ornate brass fixings. An oak drinks cabinet and sideboard line one wall, and two sofas set across from each other brace a low table. An armchair is tucked into the corner of the room beside a freestanding candelabrum.

Tyrus is sat drinking from a can of Stella, and beside him, Mei has changed out of her rain-soaked clothes into white-and-green checked pyjamas. Jonesy sits on the floor in front of the table, rolling a joint. A log fire blazes in the hearth and the air is sticky with weed.

'Ah, the wanderer returns!' Mei says.

Chloe sags onto the empty sofa, and with her eyes on Jackson, pats the space beside her. Jackson sinks next to her, and says nothing when Chloe swings her bare legs over his knees.

Flynn swallows, drops her eyes. 'I got lost.' Anger squeezes her chest, so tight it is hard to breathe around. 'This house...' These two words, as dense and broken as collapsing masonry in her throat.

She moves to the drinks cabinet, stacked with bottles and

beer cans. She sets the storm lantern down, pours herself a large measure of vodka, adds a splash of lemonade. The sharp taste of the drink blunts the edges of her nerves, but it does nothing to cool the heat of jealousy moving through her blood.

Thunder cracks outside, the wind pummels the windows with a violence that rattles the panes.

Tyrus's head slopes towards his chest, his beer can starts to tip. Mei reaches to take it before it spills, but Tyrus's eyes snap wide and he sits up, lifts the drink to his lips.

'Clo, put some music on,' Jonesy says.

Chloe climbs off the sofa and roots through her rucksack, pulling random items out, flinging everything onto the floor.

'Shit,' she mutters.

Tyrus watches her with booze-dimmed eyes. 'What's up?'

'I think I forgot my speaker,' she says, plunging her hand deeper into the bag. 'Damn it.'

'What are you talking about?' Flynn stares at her. 'I just heard you playing it a few minutes ago.'

'Huh?' Chloe shoots her eyes at Flynn. 'You must be hearing things.'

'No.' Gooseflesh breaks down Flynn's arms at the recollection of that creepy rendition of 'Happy Birthday'. 'No, I heard it, I heard music.'

'Ah ha!' Chloe pulls her speaker from her bag, switches it on. 'Let's get this party started!'

She rifles through the music on her phone, selects a dance mix. Bass drums, hi-hats, synthesisers fill the room. Flynn stares at Chloe, blood crashing in her ears.

'Is this some kind of joke? Coz it isn't funny.'

'What are you on about?'

'The music you were playing when I was downstairs.'

'Have you completely lost it? I haven't been playing any music, I've literally just turned it on.'

'How do you explain it then?'

'Well, that's easy.' Chloe's eyes slip sideways to Jackson. 'You imagined it.'

'What are you saying, that I'm fucking crazy?'

Chloe looks up at Flynn through a curtain of glossy hair and lets the silence pool. Her lips curve into a snide smile. Flynn tenses, a sway of anger making the room tilt.

'Hey, no one's saying that.' Mei cuts Chloe a sharp look, then mutters, 'Jesus, Clo.'

Jackson moves up behind Flynn, brushes his fingertips down her arms. She wants to push him away, ask what the hell he and Chloe are playing at, but that ghostly music is still turning in her mind, chords that shiver with some unspoken threat. She turns to him, her body curving into his, seeking his warmth, his comforting solidity.

'This house is big, sounds travel,' Jackson says. 'Maybe it was one of our phones you heard. Jonesy playing one of his shitty games.'

He catches her hand and his eyes move over her face, stop on her mouth. The cold clutch of fear in her gut melts in a sudden pulse of heat that has nothing to do with the alcohol she has just swigged. She drops her gaze, flustered, as he slides his hands around her waist, pulls her closer. His touch sends electrical currents dancing across her skin.

'What's going on with you? You've been tense since we came into the house.'

Flynn shakes her head, but Jackson slides his palm along her jawline, lifts her face to his.

'You know you can tell me anything, right?'

His dark eyes are warm, open. The haunting notes in her mind fragment and fade. She wonders what Jackson would say if she told him she'd tasted Heather's drugged tea as she walked through the house, that the gritty sediment of crushed pills at the back of her throat had been as real to her as the dust that hangs on the air. Would he think she was losing her mind? Assume she'd suffered some sort of psychotic episode?

Like mother, like daughter.

The voice whispers from the back of Flynn's skull, secretive and sly.

Since stepping into Temple Fall, Flynn's faded childhood memories have sharpened in clarity, forgotten details and blurred recollections singing forth in vivid technicolour: the time she'd fallen into the scalding hot bath when she had been too small to climb out, the skin on her feet blistering, peeling, before Heather ran in and picked her up; the way she had smothered Flynn's screams with her hands, terrified the Outsiders would hear her cries; the pain of walking in the days and weeks that followed. She can suddenly recall the sourness of fear sweat on her mother's skin; the way her cracked hands were always moving, fluttering, like wild birds skewered to the ends of her wrists; the horror stories she used to tell her about the Outsiders and the terrible experiments they would carry out on Flynn if they were ever discovered, stories she re-enforced with newspaper clippings, television programmes and films. Fictions passed off as reality.

She rarely thinks of Heather anymore, has trained herself to press down the traumatic memories of her childhood, but they bubble up now. The way her mother's eyes would dart round the room, seeing bugs that were not there; how she turned every knock at the door, every ball bouncing into their back garden, every blaring siren into a conspiracy; how she would go for weeks without showering, her body exuding the stink of sweat and fear until she decided it was safe to wash; the bleach baths she used to make Flynn take, scrubbing at her most tender parts with an abrasive pumice, as though she was scouring all the way down to bone; the cracks in her raw skin afterwards, so pink and tender she felt as though the light itself would bruise her.

Is this how it starts? Am I losing my mind?

Oh god. Am I sick like my mother?

'Flynn?' Jackson's eyes, like gravity, pulling her. His expression, so full of concern, removes the sting from the ugly memories. Flynn can't bear for him to look at her any differently than how he does right now.

'It's nothing.' She leans into him. 'I just let myself get creeped out, that's all.'

Jackson lowers his face to hers, and the world shrinks to the feel of his hand gliding down her back, his other hand cupping the side of her face. His mouth on hers, slow and searching, slides a delicious warmth through her.

A cushion whacks into them and they pull apart.

'Get a room!' Jonesy catcalls.

Grinning, Jackson picks up the cushion and hurls it back at Jonesy. It thumps him on the head, then lands on his pile of hash, scattering it across the floor.

'Hey!' Jonesy throws his hands into the air.

'You feeling left out, man?' Jackson launches himself on Jonesy, planting noisy kisses on his face.

'Get off!' Jonesy curses, pushing him away.

Jackson stands and ruffles Jonesy's hair, mussing up his curls. Scowling, Jonesy scrubs at his cheek with his sleeve, then scoops up the spilt tobacco and cannabis. He grimaces at the small pile on the table that he has salvaged.

'You've ruined it!' He pokes at the stash. 'I can't smoke this, it's probably full of carpet mites and shit.'

'Stop whining,' Jackson says, opening the sideboard. 'You'll smoke anything.' His gaze runs over the shelves and he picks something up – a small green bag. The contents give an insectile rattle. 'Anyone want a game of Scrabble?'

He turns, tosses the bag onto the table.

A Scrabble purse. Flynn stares at it, her hair standing like quills down her arms. It is small, made of green velvet, with yellow pull ties at the top. Printed across the front – SCRABBLE – in blocky white text, it looks like any ordinary Scrabble bag.

Only the 'A' in the word SCRABBLE has been coloured in with black pen.

Chloe tips the Scrabble tiles onto the table. They clatter against the wood like clicking fingernails.

'How are we supposed to play without a Scrabble board?' she says.

Flynn picks up the empty velvet bag.

'Scrabble sucks.' Jonesy slides the letters around the table. 'I can think of a more interesting game.'

Flynn smooths her fingers over the green velvet. The inked 'A' is completely black. *It isn't the same purse. It can't be.*

Jonesy's eyes are swimmy with drink and weed. 'Let's do a seance.'

'No chance,' Mei says. 'Are you nuts?'

'Yep.' Jonesy sinks the dregs of his beer, belches. 'Who's in?'

'How are we supposed to do a seance with Scrabble tiles?' Chloe asks.

Tyrus, who has been dozing on the sofa, sits up, his heavy-lidded eyes sliding over the room. 'We're doing a seance?'

'We're not doing a seance, Jonesy,' Jackson says, dropping back onto the sofa. 'You shouldn't meddle with that shit sober, never mind when you're newt-pissed.'

'Ah, c'mon, nothing's gonna happen,' Jonesy says.

'Then why bother doing it?' Jackson shoots back.

Jonesy rolls his eyes. 'I mean nothing *bad* is gonna happen. It's just a bit of fun.'

Chloe slides onto the armrest of the sofa, tucks her bare feet beneath Jackson's thighs. He wraps one hand around her bare ankle. Flynn's breath catches. The casual affection of the gesture is somehow even more shocking than a passionate kiss.

'Jax is right,' Chloe says. 'You shouldn't mess with that stuff.'

Flynn stares at her boyfriend's hand braceleting Chloe's ankle and the edges of her vision shimmers. Jealousy flares, so intense she feels light-headed. A smile skims Chloe's lips and her cheeks are flushed with pleasure. *Whore*. The word pulses in Flynn's throat, so sudden and unexpected she has to grit her teeth together to keep it inside. She can almost feel it in her throat, alive and fluttering, like a bat beating leathery wings against the roof of her mouth.

Flynn tears her eyes from Chloe and kneels in front of the table.

'Let's do it,' she says, moving the lettered tiles into a wide circle.

Jonesy grins and claps his hands together. 'Alright! We need one of those things to put our fingers on.'

'A planchette.' Mei opens the drinks cabinet and takes out a green shot glass. 'This should work.'

'Nice one,' Jonesy says. 'Someone turn the lamps down.'

Mei moves round the room, blowing out the candles and turning the dials down on the storm lanterns. Jackson slides onto the floor in front of the table. Chloe slips down beside him. The fire crackles and spits as they all sit cross-legged on the rug around the low table. Mei sets the glass in the middle of the lettered tiles.

'I really don't think this is a good idea.' Jackson's voice sounds pained.

'No one's forcing you,' Flynn says, her eyes on the table.

'Okay, some ground rules.' Mei's eyes move over each of them. 'Rule number one: I do the talking and you all keep your mouths shut.'

Chloe mimes zipping her lips.

'Rule number two: no one takes their fingers off the glass until I say so.'

'Why?' Chloe asks. 'What will happen?'

Mei shrugs. 'Probably nothing, but it's a rule, so stick to it. Rule number three: if the shot glass starts to move in the shape of the infinity symbol, or if it looks like it's gonna spell ZoZo, then we have to say goodbye. Like, immediately.'

'Who the fuck's ZoZo?' Jonesy says.

'ZoZo is supposedly this demonic entity that stalks people through Ouija boards.'

'We're not doing a Ouija board though, are we?' Chloe frowns at the Scrabble tiles.

'What's the infinity symbol?' Flynn says.

'The infinity symbol is the figure eight. It's a demonic sign that implies eternity, or eternal anguish.'

'Eternal anguish,' Jonesy says. 'Not optimal.'

'It's also how a spirit frees itself.'

'Got it,' Flynn says. 'Anything else?'

'Yeah.' Mei meets Flynn's eye. 'Don't ask when you're going to die.'

'Why the hell would anyone ask *that*?' Flynn mutters.

'Okay, fingertips on the shot glass.'

They all lean over the tiles. Shadows leap into their faces, deepening the hollows of their eyes and planing away the softness of flesh.

'Is there anybody there?' Tyrus calls.

Jonesy giggles.

'Rule number one, Ty?' Mei glares at Tyrus.

He grins back, presses a finger to his lips. Jonesy wipes the smirk from his face and bellies closer to the table.

'First, we move the planchette in a circle to warm it up,' Mei says.

They circle the shot glass around the table a few times. A blast of wind rattles the panes in their windows, the rain hisses like static. The dark corners of the room seem to bulge, as though filling with a presence. Flynn is suddenly convinced that there is someone behind her, that if she reaches back, her fingertips will graze black crinoline skirts. The thought shoots a spray of ice down her spine.

Mei bows her head. A dark sheaf of hair falls across her face as she draws in a slow, deep breath and sighs it out.

'Close your eyes.'

Darkness pulses behind Flynn's eyelids. A pinprick of fear at the base of her skull.

'We call upon our spirit guides to protect us from malevolent entities and negative energies. Cloak each of us with the armour of righteousness and watch over us. We ask only spirits of light and goodness–'

Jonesy snorts on repressed laughter, which sets Tyrus and Chloe into another giggling fit.

'I'm sorry!' Jonesy says, swiping tears from his eyes. 'But what the fuck is the "armour of righteousness"?'

'Look, if you can't take this seriously–'

'I'm good, we're good,' Jonesy says, holding his hands up. 'I'm sorry. Serious now.'

'Serious,' Tyrus slurs.

Once everyone has placed their fingertips back on the shot glass, Mei waits a beat, checking the silence, then says, 'We wish only to communicate with spirits of light and we ask for protection for this house and the people in this house. Let there be nothing but light. Amen!'

'Amen,' Jonesy whispers, a grin in his voice.

Tyrus's sniggers taper to silence and the sounds of the house steal into the room. Flynn's nerves feel raw and tight. It is all too easy to imagine the door creaking open, footsteps climbing the stairs, an arm wreathed in black lace reaching from the darkness to lay a desiccated hand on her shoulder. *What the fuck are we doing? What possessed me to agree to this?*

Jackson sighs. 'How long do we have to sit here like this?'

'I need a drink,' Tyrus mumbles.

'I need to pee,' Chloe says.

'Guys,' Mei hisses, 'if you don't shut it, I swear to–'

Flynn gasps as the shot glass jerks across the table beneath her fingers. Her eyes spring open.

'Who did that?' she whispers.

'Jonesy, was that you?' Mei says.

'Why do you always blame me for everything?'

Mei chews her bottom lip, as though mulling over her next words. 'Is there anyone here with us?'

A chill rises through Flynn, the feeling that there is someone stood behind her solidifies into a conviction.

'Is there anyone here with–'

The shot glass slithers across the wood with a sound that drags nails down Flynn's spine. Her breath catches and she looks up at her friends. Their shadowed faces are rapt and fearful, but a grin twitches Jonesy's lips, his eyes sparkle with mirth.

Flynn shoves him. 'You jerk!'

'Hey, what did I say about taking your hands off the glass?' Mei says.

'That was you?' Chloe grabs the cushion she had been perched on and smashes it against the back of Jonesy's head.

Jonesy cackles, throws his hands up to protect himself from her assault. 'You should've seen your faces!'

'Moron,' Mei mutters, standing up. She starts to move round the room, turning the dials on the storm lanterns up, filling the room with light.

'Ah, don't be like that,' Jonesy says, watching Flynn as she picks up the Scrabble tiles, drops them into the velvet purse.

'Come back, come on, best behaviour now. I promise. Mei, for real. I'll be good, I can be good.'

Flynn pulls the ribbon ties closed, tosses the bag onto the table. She feels suddenly light with relief, glad to be done with it, and vaguely surprised that she had gone along with the idea in the first place.

~

Tyrus's chin drops, the beer in his hands tips.

'Woah!' Mei is sat at the low table playing Devil's Grip with her cards, but she lunges, grabs the can from Tyrus's slack fingers. He blinks blearily, grins, and then his eyes slope closed again.

'Jesus, he's shitcanned,' Flynn says. 'How much has he had to drink?'

'I don't know what got into him,' Jackson says. 'When we came in here, he started on the vodka, just drank it neat from the bottle.'

'And you let him?' Flynn stares at Jackson.

'I told him to ease up, but…' Jackson shrugs.

'He's a big boy,' Mei says, scooping up the cards, slicing them between her hands. 'If he wants to drink, we can't stop him.'

'Lighten up, Flynn,' Chloe says. 'He's only making up for lost time, aren't you, Ty?'

Tyrus snorts in his sleep. His mouth hangs open, and his breath rattles softly in his throat. The sight of him earlier holding a beer can had been jarring, wrong in a way that had made Flynn want to knock it from his hands. But seeing him like this is worse.

Jackson tugs Flynn by the hand to the armchair, pulls her onto his lap. Despite her annoyance, she sinks into him, her eyes slashing towards Chloe.

Jonesy takes a cigarette from the tin Jackson gave him earlier. He sniffs it. 'Hey, I think these are loaded.'

'For fuck's sake, will someone take those things off him,' Mei says.

Jonesy ignores her, holds a struck match to the joint, inhales. A hush falls over the room as the filter flares orange, as though he has pulled all sound into his lungs. The music playing through the speaker fades, the crackling fire grows muted, and the house holds itself still, poised and watchful. Even the storm seems to quieten.

The sensation lasts moments, and when Jonesy expels the smoke from his lungs, sounds surge around them again. Smoke drifts round his face, flat and leaden, forming a mushroom-shaped cloud.

Flynn stares at him, her breath trapped in her chest. The smoke breaks apart around his face, and behind its foul clouds, his eyes lose their jocular blue shine, hardening and shrinking into a socketed darkness that is lumined by a strange phosphorescence. His forehead broadens, his hairline slides forwards into a sharp widow's peak. Darkness licks across the blonde ring of his hair, his mouth flattens, his skin droops loosely.

A stranger's face holds its form for a pulse and then dissipates, unravelling like an image momentarily rendered in wind-whipped clouds.

Flynn feels dizzy, as unmoored as she had when the rooms had shuffled around her. She shutters her eyes, takes a steadying breath. *It's just the weed, just a hallucination. Every breath in this room is like a toke on a blunt.*

'What's it like?' Jackson asks.

'Strong,' Jonesy says, his voice thin and choked. He pinches something off his tongue, studies the tip of the joint. 'Earthy, a bit like a cigar.' He takes another pull on the joint, deeper this time, giggles as he taps ash into an empty beer can. 'Man, it's really fucking strong.'

'Here, gimme.' Chloe plucks the joint from Jonesy's fingers.

Flynn climbs off Jackson's lap, moves back to the table to pour herself another drink. Her pulse hammers her temples, the edges of her vision waver, basalt glisters sparking like pulverised stars. She reaches for the bottle of vodka, hesitates. Listening to the rain tick against the windowpane. She knows she should slow down, switch to lemonade, eat something. Her hand tightens on the bottle as she wills herself to set it back down. But she thinks of Jonesy's face changing behind the smoke, and fear drums a painful rhythm beneath her chest.

All she wants is to dull that feeling, to drink herself unconscious and not wake up until Andy picks them up in the morning. Vodka hits the glass before she even realises she has poured it, a comforting splash that instantly steadies her. *Just one more*, she tells herself, lifting the glass to her lips. *Just one more...*

2015

Flynn wakes in the dark, shuddering with cold. Her throat is hot and swollen, her breath fast and shallow. Every inch of her body aches and she never knew it could hurt so much to breathe.

Heather slept on the mattress beside her last night, her body curled around Flynn's like a question mark, silently asking if she was going to be okay, and the only time she left her side was to replenish the warm, salty drinks that she pressed to Flynn's lips, or to rinse the damp cloths that she draped over her scalding forehead.

Now, Flynn turns her head on the pillow, expecting to see Heather lying beside her. But she isn't there. In her place is Mama. One of her grey button eyes fell off the other day, and snapped thread dangles from the socket, like a severed optical nerve. The button is still stuffed in Flynn's pyjama pocket.

She feels weak, can barely lift her head from her pillow. She blinks, stares at the doll. Heather only gives her Mama when she goes Outside, but she never leaves without telling Flynn she is going. She listens for the sound of Heather moving around, but all she can hear over the static hum on the radio is the wheeze of her own breath.

'Paramedics! We're coming in!'

A man's voice, an Outsider, inside the house! Panic cracks a whip beneath Flynn's skin. She pushes herself up, and her head swims with the effort, spots of light flickering across her vision. She opens her mouth to call out for Heather, but it's like the air is full of smashed glass and every breath tears a wound in her throat.

'Hello? Is anyone here?' The second voice, a woman.

Footsteps on the stairs.

Flynn's heart cracks her ribs, blood whooshes in her ears. Heather's voice fills her head – Hide! *– and she swings her feet over the side of the bed, but it is as though her bones have turned to liquid, and when she tries to stand, she collapses onto the floor. Her throat feels as though it is being crushed by a giant boot. Can't pull enough air into her lungs.*

She crawls towards the wardrobe. Her vision blurs. Her fingers and feet are numb, her lips tingle.

'Jesus Christ!' The man's voice is muffled behind the closed door. 'Alicia, in here! Quick! Help me get her down!'

A scuffle, muttered voices. Flynn can't make sense of it. Her breath whistles in and out. Time stutters, wavers.

The bedroom door swings open.

A woman flicks the light switch on. Flynn flinches back, tries to cry out.

The woman steps into the room, her eyes widening with shock when they land on Flynn.

'Dan, come here!' she calls over her shoulder before turning back to Flynn. 'Sweetheart, we're here to help you.'

The Outsider's voice seems to come from far away, an echoing, disembodied sound. Her hands are lifted, palms up, like on TV where someone is scared of being shot. A man appears behind her, holding a red bag with yellow stripes on it. Flynn shakes her head, staring at the bag. Her heart thuds painfully, each hard kick driving the light from her eyes.

The woman crouches beside her, and the shock of being so close to an Outsider makes Flynn want to scream. She doesn't realise she is trying to fight her off until the man pins her hands by her sides.

'Alicia just needs to take a look at you, darling,' he says.

The smell of Outside on his skin, a forbidden tangle of scents Flynn can't even begin to pick apart.

Her eyes slide to the woman. Alicia.

Alicia is holding a needle.

Flynn bucks beneath the man's grip, detonating more explosions in her skull. Alicia grabs her hand, jams the needle into her arm. It sinks like a fang and Flynn screams for Heather, but her voice is a thin whistle that barely reaches her ears. The man slides a mask over Flynn's face, shunting air into her lungs.

Her panic stutters… and sinks.

NOW

Flynn is sprawled on the sofa, watching Mei thrash Jonesy at poker. Her gaze keeps sliding towards Chloe and Jackson, who are squirrelled away in the corner of the room. Chloe is perched on the edge of the table, a bottle of beer balanced between her naked thighs, and Jackson is standing so close to her, his leg brushes against hers.

Mei had offered to deal them into a game of cards, but they had declined, engaged in some intimate conversation that continued through multiple games of poker, Spit and Mafia. At one point, Flynn had tried to join them, but they had barely looked at her, and she had slunk away, her face burning with humiliation and anger.

Mei grins, turns her cards face up on the carpet, and Jonesy tosses his own hand down in disgust.

'You're cheating,' he says. 'No one wins this many times on the trot.'

'You always were a sore loser.' Mei smiles, pirouettes one of the cards on the tip of her middle finger like it's a basketball.

Sulking, Jonesy flicks the card and it drops to the floor. Mei laughs easily, scoops up the deck, shuffles them one-handed. 'Shall I deal you in again?'

'I'm out.' Jonesy heaves himself to his feet. 'I need to go for a slash, and you're coming with me.'

'What? You want help to go peepee?'

'I'm not walking round this creepy house on my own.'

'Take Jax or Ty,' Mei says, as Jonesy reaches down and hauls her to her feet.

Tyrus mumbles incoherently without opening his eyes, but Jackson and Chloe don't look up from their conversation at all.

'Chloe said she needed the loo earlier,' Flynn says. Jackson murmurs something in Chloe's ear, and she throws her head back, her throat bobbing with laughter. There is something obscenely provocative about the gesture, and it makes Flynn want to smash things. It doesn't help that Chloe is so skimpily dressed. Her tiny vest and hot pants cling like a layer of skin.

As though sensing Flynn's gaze, Jackson turns and looks at her. His lips curve into a smile and he starts towards her, the touch of his gaze like a spray of sunshine, flooding her with warmth. But then Chloe touches his forearm, says something low and secretive. His attention swings back to her and Flynn's heart falls.

'Fine, let's get this over with.' Mei picks up a hurricane lantern and moves to the door. 'Later, 'gators.'

'Love you, Spider-Mei,' Tyrus slurs without opening his eyes, using his old nickname for her.

'Stay together, yeah?' Flynn calls after them.

'Don't worry,' Jonesy says. 'If I take a dump, I'll leave the door open so Mei can watch me the whole time.'

Mei grimaces, punches his arm. They slip out of the room, their voices fading as the door closes behind them and they move down the corridor.

'Shit, it's dark out here... can I hold your hand?'

'You're kidding, right?'

'Mei, gimme your fucking hand!'

'Oh my god, fine. Ouch, ease your grip, buddy.'

'Sorry.'

Flynn glares at Chloe and Jackson, but they are too engrossed in each other to notice. She snatches up the tin of cigarettes Jonesy left beside the deck of cards, takes one out, then sinks onto the low window ledge. One side of her body pressed against the cold glass, gaze turned to the sky. Veins of light pulse within the dark clouds. The wind beats pillowed fists against the window, bleeds icy ribbons of air through the gaps in the panes.

Wary of leaning too heavily against the thin, aged glass, she shifts her weight. Taps the cigarette against her knee. She can't remember the last time she had a joint, had quit the habit years ago, but the feel of it between her fingers is enough to send her spinning back in time.

She slides it between her lips and reaches for Jonesy's lighter. Behind her, Chloe laughs, deep-throated and husky. Flynn's hand tightens on the lighter. She thumbs the flint wheel, stares at the flame, then touches it to the tip of the joint, inhales.

Pain flares in her throat and chest, a searing heat that briefly overpowers the corrosive burn of her jealousy. The taste of smoke fills her mouth, a subtle hint of cloves, the rich dark taste of earth... and something else just beneath it all. Vaguely metallic, as though she has just bitten her tongue and drawn blood.

She feels a tug inside her thoughts, a sudden nakedness. She rarely allows herself to think about her time in foster care, has learned to stifle those painful memories, but now, her thoughts flash back through the years, as though that one toke has opened a door in her mind that she usually keeps locked and bolted.

She had been nine years old, and living with her first foster family, Beverley and Carl Slaughter (The Slaughterhouse, as she had quickly come to think of it), when she tried her first joint.

The Slaughters already had a daughter of their own when Flynn moved in with them, Carrie, the same age as Flynn. They were also fostering a thirteen-year-old girl, Reese, who Flynn ended up rooming with. Carrie had taken an instant dislike to Flynn, but Reese, a potty-mouthed pothead with a foul temper and a deep disdain for her new foster family, had taken her beneath her wing.

It was Reese who had encouraged Flynn to try pot. Flynn can still remember how that first hit had made her feel, the terrible burn in her throat as she inhaled, the sick squirming in the pit of her belly, followed by a light-headed, happy-floaty feeling after.

It was during her time in The Slaughterhouse that Flynn met Carrie's friends, Mei, Tyrus and Chloe, who lived nearby. Unlike Carrie, who had to abide by a strict curfew, the Slaughters made it quite clear they preferred their foster children out of the house as much as possible. Rather than feel ostracised and rejected, Flynn relished this freedom, because it gave her time to hang out with Mei, Tyrus and Chloe without Carrie always being there.

Their friendships began in the small things. Tyrus would be kicking a football about on the street and pass the ball to Flynn, drawing her into playing; Mei would deal her into a game of cards on the pavement or show off her backflips and tricks; Chloe would exclaim over her thick, dark hair and beg permission to plait it.

Soon Tyrus was giving her backies on his bike round the estate, Mei was inviting her over for dinner and sleepovers, and when Chloe visited The Slaughterhouse, it was for Flynn, not Carrie, that she called. Chloe was fascinated by Flynn's past, curious about her reclusive mother, and what it was like to live in a children's home. She would paint Flynn's nails or make up her face while asking questions no one else dared ask with an unflinching directness that amused Flynn, and made her open up in a way that she had never done with any of her therapists and doctors.

They helped her heal: Chloe with her make-up bag, Tyrus with a football, Mei with a pack of cards. Little mechanics of the heart, with small kindnesses they patched her back together.

After the summer, Beverley and Carl Slaughter moved Flynn from her old school to Elliott Dean, which was closer to where they lived, and it was there that Flynn's small group of friends grew to accommodate Jonesy and Jackson.

Jackson Darrow was a sullen, introspective boy in her form group, but Flynn had noticed him straight away. With his pale complexion, serious eyes and unkempt mop of dark hair, he possessed a quiet magnetism, and it was his face Flynn always sought in the classroom. His presence tugged at her, like the moon tugging the tide, his presence like mute music playing beneath her skin.

If Jackson was the moon, his best friend, Teddy Jones – or Jonesy as he insisted upon being called – was the sun. With his infectious laugh and wild spume of white-blonde ringlets, which he was not afraid to accessorise with headbands or fasten into pigtails, he'd possessed an exuberance and *joie de vivre* that drew people to him.

Flynn began to spend more time in her friends' homes than The Slaughterhouse, which had never really felt like home to her, anyway. And as her friendships deepened, she came to realise the Outside was not as frightening as she had once thought. She stopped bunking off school with Reese, her grades improved, her confidence grew.

And then Jackson discovered The Pitfalls, and they built Nostromo within the shell of the abandoned building, a secret space that became the only true 'home' Flynn had ever known. It was where they congregated after school, the place they met at weekends; where they did their homework, played board games and watched films on Tyrus's iPad. Andy even helped Mei anchor some battle ropes to the wall outside and installed a pull-up bar over the doorframe in Nostromo, so she could use the building site as her own personal training ground. While the others sat filling their faces with junk food, Mei would be flipping over walls and staircase banisters, vaulting railings, bunny hopping obstacles.

For almost six months, Flynn knew a level of happiness she had never before known existed. But it was a spell of time that was to prove all too brief. Because while Flynn was spending time with her new friends, Carrie's previous resentment of her foster sister was deepening into something more malicious. Furious at her exclusion from the group, she started to leave the key in the lock when Flynn stayed out with the others, so that even when it was tipping down, Flynn couldn't come inside. She stole her schoolbooks, graffitied on her homework and started rumours about her at school, spreading details of her past that she could only have picked up from her parents.

But these petty cruelties only widened the growing distance between Carrie and her old friends, who took Flynn's side and condemned Carrie's behaviour.

Even now, eight years after it happened, Flynn still flinches from the memory of what followed: returning to The Slaughterhouse after spending all day at The Pitfalls, finding Bev Slaughter waiting for her in the living room. The sour, hateful look on her face. Flynn's belongings packed and standing by the door.

The recriminations began before Flynn could even understand the crime for which she was being accused, and it was only later, when she was back in Crickwell Children's Home, that she pieced together what had happened.

Carrie had snuck into the bedroom Flynn shared with

Reese, stolen some weed from the older girl's stash and planted it in her own bedroom, where she knew her mum would find it. When confronted by her mother, Carrie had accused Reese of giving it to her, and said both Reese and Flynn had forced her to smoke it.

Whatever allowance Bev and Carl received to care for Reese and Flynn was evidently not enough to risk the safety of their precious daughter, and any attempts to explain what had really happened fell on deaf ears. The foster kids were sent packing and Flynn never saw Reese again.

Outside, the wind glissades into a high-pitched scream that pulls Flynn's wandering thoughts from the past. A glance towards Chloe and Jackson makes her breath catch painfully. Jackson is stood between Chloe's parted legs, their faces kissing close as he looks at something on her phone.

Flynn tears her eyes from them, feeling suddenly hot and sick. She takes another long pull on the joint. Lets the smoke roll across her tongue. Her thoughts spill backwards through the years, but instead of turning away from those painful recollections as she usually does, she follows them through the fog of her past, tracing the shape and contours of time-dimmed memories.

Her swift eviction from The Slaughterhouse had been a devastating blow, not because she was upset at leaving her foster family behind, but because she'd had to say goodbye to her new best friends. Though Crickwell Children's Home was only on the other side of town from Hocking Estate, at the age of nine and without parents to shepherd her back and forth, it may as well have been in another country.

Flynn started acting up, bunking off school again and hanging round town, sometimes with other older kids from the home, sometimes with people she came to recognise from the streets. She drank and smoked and shoplifted – at first, small things, like sweets, bubble-gum, chocolate bars, then later bottles of booze, pain medication, cigarettes.

It scares Flynn to think what might have happened to her had it not been for Jenna. From the moment they met, Flynn understood her new foster mother was different to the Slaughters. It was in the way she spoke to her, the way she listened. Strict, but always fair in her discipline, she never condescended to Flynn the way many of the doctors and therapists did, nor did she hustle her from the house with instructions to stay out. Unlike the Slaughters, Jenna seemed to take genuine pleasure in Flynn's company. She helped her with homework, spoke to her teachers about her grades, ensured she attended appointments with her therapist.

Flynn was no longer barred from helping herself to food in the kitchen, or made to eat the leftovers of cooked meals alone in her room. Jenna cooked dinners with a passion and flair that was infectious, and at mealtimes, they sat together to eat, trading pieces of their day.

It was over one such meal that Flynn confessed how much she missed her friends. The next day, Jenna approached the head teacher of Elliott Dean and put Flynn on the waiting list. Not six weeks later, she was back in the classroom with Mei and the others.

Jenna drove Flynn across town when she arranged to meet up with her old friends and picked her up at a negotiated curfew. She took her to the cinema, the park, the ice rink; they explored Otley, Ilkley, York. There was always somewhere to go, something to see, and every new discovery pushed the edges of Flynn's world a little wider.

The day Jenna sat her down and asked her how she felt about adoption, Flynn had felt like she had swallowed the sun.

The warmth of the memory suddenly sharpens to a very real flame-hot burn in her chest. She coughs, wincing. Her mouth tastes of ashtrays, her throat aches. She is astonished to see she has smoked the joint down to the roach. Jackson and Chloe are still deep in conversation, but now Flynn feels pleasantly buzzed and the sight of them together does not hurt the way it had before.

She ashes the joint out on the windowsill, and without thinking, reaches for the tin. She takes out another cigarette, lights it, and sucks the poison deep into her lungs.

Jackson lowers himself onto the ledge across from Flynn, the left side of his body pressed against the glass, his legs splayed in front of him so that their feet touch.

'So... you're smoking again?' His eyes drop to the joint in her hand.

'I'm surprised you noticed,' Flynn says, a snip in her voice that makes her inwardly cringe. She glances at Chloe, who is lying on the sofa, her flaxen hair splayed around her as she takes selfies on her phone.

A perplexed look flickers across Jackson's face, but then he opens his arms, a crooked grin on his lips. Flynn hesitates, watching him, but her thoughts feel blurred, her previous anger dulled to a mild, nebulous irritation. She scoots towards him, turning so her back curves against his chest. He lowers his chin onto the dip in her shoulder and plucks the joint from her fingers. He takes a drag, exhales a thick stream of smoke.

'God, that's disgusting.' He passes it back. 'How can you smoke that shit?'

Flynn shrugs, stubs the joint out. Her head is swimming, her lungs are heavy. Jackson wraps her hair around one hand, then gently brushes his lips over the curve of her neck. She closes her eyes, surrenders to the dark and liquid longing that spills through her.

'What do you say we take a walk?' Jackson's stubble-dusted chin scratches her shoulder.

'Oh yeah?' Flynn drops her head back, closes her eyes. Reaches for the anger she had felt earlier, feels only the heat of lust. 'And why would we do something like that?'

His lips trail her collarbone, and she feels his grin against her skin, low and teasing. 'You know why.'

His hand covers hers, squeezes. Her heart quickens, a flutter that makes her breath catch.

Tyrus snorts loudly, then jerks up on the sofa, looks round blearily.

'Hey, Sleeping Beauty,' Chloe says.

'Clo?' He frowns, his face slack with booze. 'I love you, Clo.'

Chloe giggles. 'Love you, too, T-Rex.'

He squints round the room, his head wobbling as though it is too heavy to hold aloft. 'I love all of you.' *Iluffalluffyou.*

'Holy shit,' Flynn mutters. 'He's so wasted.'

'Thirsty...' Tyrus croaks, sitting up.

Chloe rolls off the sofa, the bottom of her hot pants riding the high curve of her buttocks. Without adjusting them, she knee-walks towards the table, grabs a bottle of unopened gin.

'For fuck's sake, he doesn't need more booze!' Flynn sits up, a cold space opening between her and Jackson.

Chloe ignores Flynn and Tyrus takes the drink, chugs the neat spirit. He starts to lower the bottle, but Chloe places her fingers beneath it, tips it back so that he keeps drinking.

'Down it, down it!' she chants.

Flynn surges to her feet, the sudden motion making the walls rock around her. She crosses the room, snatches the bottle from Tyrus. His eyes are glazed and an uncanny light frills the edges of his pupils, a silky sort of gleaming similar to the glow Flynn had seen in Jonesy's eyes earlier. She tells herself it is a trick of the light or an effect of the smoke-choked room, causing her to see things.

I'm not seeing things. We should leave this house, now. Before it's too late.

Outside, the heavens groan, the wind smashes fists against the windows. The storm sounds as though it is gathering in power, not receding. And she knows they can't leave, not yet.

'I'll get you some water,' Flynn mutters.

'Jeez, Flynn,' Chloe slurs. 'He's just trying to have a good time. For once can you not be such a vibe killer?'

'What is wrong with you tonight?' Flynn glares at Chloe. 'Look at the state of him!'

'He's fine! He's having *fun*! Maybe you should try it. It's your boyfriend's fucking eighteenth birthday.' Chloe flops back onto the sofa and shuffles through the playlist on her phone, mutters, 'Honestly, this feels more like a wake than a party.'

She cranks up the volume on the Bluetooth speaker before Flynn can reply. Flynn turns from her, her hands shaking as she pours lemonade into a paper cup and passes it to Tyrus, but he lowers the drink onto his lap without taking a sip.

Flynn turns to Chloe, ready to tell her to turn the music back down, but her friend is on her feet and shimmying towards her. She is grinning widely, and the Bluetooth speaker is balanced on her shoulder like an old-fashioned Boombox. All combativeness seems to have fled her, as though carried away on the song's opening bars. She grabs Flynn's hands, tugs her into the middle of the room.

The music is so loud, Flynn feels the bass vibrate the floorboards beneath her bare feet; so loud she wouldn't have been surprised to see cracks haze the fragile single-paned glass. It drowns out the house's chilling symphony – the wind shrieking through the small spaces around the windows and gusting through distant rooms, the pop of contracting joints, the sigh of expanding wood, the creak of timber – and in the music of bass and snare drums and hi-hats, she feels the tension slide from her shoulders.

Chloe spins her round and Flynn laughs, her anger dissipating in the face of her friend's delight. She feels the heat of Jackson's eyes on her, slips him a glance. He has stood up, is leaning against the wall, a hungry, almost vulpine cast to his face. In the shadows, the dusting of stubble on his face looks thicker, darker, and Flynn aches to run her fingers through his unkempt hair, to brush her lips over the line of his jaw. His face is lit with feverish desire and Flynn feels an answering pulse of lust and longing.

The song finishes, transitions smoothly to a slow ballad. Flynn twirls away from Chloe, drops onto the sofa beside Tyrus. He looks at her, but his eyes shift and slide, as though he can't get a fix on her face.

'Wanna dance?' He grins at her sloppily.

'You're pissed.'

'Pissed.' He grins, but there is something broken and confused in his expression, and his smile does not touch his eyes.

'Don't beat yourself up about it.' Flynn nudges his shoulder. 'We've all been there.'

Not Ty, though. Never Ty. Flynn pushes the thought away, tells herself she is overreacting. *Vibe killer.*

Chloe is still dancing, her ear tipped to the Bluetooth on her shoulder, her movements fused to the music's slowed tempo. Her long hair brushes the dip in her narrow waist. Her eyes are closed and her free arm weaves like a pale snake over her head. Her face looks ivory-carved, lips parted, the pink tip of her tongue glistening between her perfect white teeth. She seems to glow in the room's dim light, her sweat-jewelled skin pearlescent.

As Flynn watches, she could swear that Chloe's scent is becoming heavier on the air, her fruity perfume thickening, salted with the faint tang of sweat and something else layered beneath it all, an aroma that reminds Flynn of the house's musky scent. She rocks her hips back and forth, and her lissom body quivers with a percussive energy, radiating eroticism. Her nipples have hardened beneath her vest, the subtle cleft between her thighs looks suddenly prominent, the material cleaving to her skin. As though the music arouses her.

Flynn shoots an uncomfortable glance towards Jackson and the look on his face hits her like a punch to the gut. His expression is hot and yearning and lust has blown his eyes into black craters. Pain cleaves Flynn's chest, her cheeks flame with humiliation, the realisation that Jackson has not been watching her dance at all; he is watching Chloe.

Chloe opens her eyes, her gaze finding Jackson's, as though in that instant, she senses him watching her. Skin slippery with sweat, a silky invitation. She drags her teeth over her lower lip. Time stutters, stops, and Flynn is in freefall. It is as though Jackson and Chloe are alone in the room, sharing something secret and urgent and electric.

Flynn stands up, grabs Chloe's phone, stops the music.

Chloe whirls round, rocking unsteadily, the grace and fluidity of moments ago suddenly abandoning her.

'Hey, put the music back on!'

Flynn is trembling, blood pounding in her ears. The sounds of the house wash back into the room, and Jonesy's and Mei's voices float down the hall, growing in volume as they return. Flynn tosses Chloe's phone onto the sofa, turns away from her friend. She pours more vodka into a paper cup, adds a splash of lemonade. She wants to obliterate her anger, eradicate herself. The door opens and Jonesy and Mei walk back in.

'We found the bog,' Jonesy says.

'A chamber pot is not a bog,' Mei mutters, dropping onto the sofa.

Flynn downs the drink, pours another.

'You guys pissed in a pot?' Jackson's voice is full of wry amusement.

'There isn't a flushable toilet in this place,' Mei says. 'We brought another one of those chamber pots back with us, left it in the hallway. Bloody heavy.'

'I'm not pissing in a pot in the hall!' Chloe says, snatching a lantern. 'Jax, will you come with me? I don't want to walk around in the dark on my own.' Her half-lidded eyes find Jackson, coy, inviting.

Flynn sees the slip in Jackson's expression, the pull of hungry desire, and it locks her heart in her chest. Chloe reaches for his arm, tugs him towards the door. Her hand slides into his back pocket, and he does not remove it, does not resist, does not even look at Flynn, as they push the door open and walk out of the room together.

2015

Flynn's consciousness slips and skids, the ambulance's wail slices the night. Colours, noises, smells, it is all too much, an assault on the senses. She wants to cover her ears, but she can't because the woman – Alicia – strapped her hands down after she kept trying to pull the mask from her face.

The bed rattles as the tyres bounce over the road. The needle squirts drugs into Flynn's vein and a mask pushes air into her mouth. Dan is driving, but Alicia is sat on a chair beside her. She keeps telling Flynn that everything will be okay, but she is an Outsider and can't be trusted.

The pain in Flynn's throat and chest is lessening, but her thoughts feel funny. Gluey and slow. Soon, the Outsiders will start their experiments. Flynn has seen it on TV, the way they hurt people who are different. Pushing needles into their eyeballs, squirting diseases into their skin, smashing hammers into their knees and elbows, locking them in white rooms and playing angry music through the speakers. Taking them to pieces with plyers and pincers and scissors and scalpels.

She is shackled and weak. Powerless. She has to escape, to Split. She knows how, has done it many times now, torn her spirit from its host and floated free, but she can't think beyond the pain, can't focus her mind. Her body holds her, a prison of flesh she can't escape.

She slides back into unconsciousness, awakens on a bed in a white room. Surrounded by Outsiders wearing blue overalls, their eyes slits between face masks and skullcaps. Two huge round lights hang over the bed, and there are screens on one side that blip with lines and numbers.

Flynn tries to sit up but her body is a sunk ship. One of the Outsiders tells her she is going to be okay, that she is safe. His words are meaningless. She knows they are going to kill her. Nightmare images flash through her mind, a thousand deaths delivered in a thousand ways, a waking fever dream of grisly torture.

She shakes her head, tries to fight off the hands that hold her down, to twist her body from their touch, but they are so much stronger, and each snatched breath is smaller than the last as her lungs scream for air. Her vision dims. She scrabbles for the light, but feels herself falling back into darkness. She has seconds, moments, one last chance...

Like a hand snatching for the ledge of a cliff before a fatal plummet, her thoughts converge and lash out. Her consciousness heaves against the confinement of skin, the tethers of muscle, a bloodless labour of the mind.

She feels the tearing inside her, that violent detachment she can never quite get used to.

The sensation of falling, flying, soaring.

She is filled with light, unencumbered.

She opens her eyes.

She is crouched on the floor of the white room. The terror that coursed through her blood is quiet now, like the colours have been washed out of her feelings. She doesn't feel sick anymore, her breathing is even and steady, her throat doesn't hurt.

The Outsiders are still gathered round the bed, but they don't turn to her. She moves towards them. Her unconscious body swells the sheet on the bed. Flynn can never quite get used to seeing herself this way. It always looks wrong, somehow, like a sock without a foot or a pillow without its stuffing. Very pale and very still. A plastic cap covers her hair and a band encircles her arm.

Name: Unknown Female Child
DOB: Unknown (aged 6/7)
Hospital No: YSR4739573
NHS no.: 364 509 6457

The Outsiders pull blue sheets over her body, covering her arms and chest.

One of them fastens a metal pole into her mouth, wedging it open. Like she is screaming her biggest scream. Flynn backs away, her gaze on the tray of instruments. She doesn't want to be here, doesn't want to see this.

She fades through the wall, into a long corridor with white-painted walls and a shiny floor. Outsiders pass by without noticing her, as though she has as much weight and texture as a stray thought. Some of the Outsiders carry dark smudges on their shoulders, and Flynn keeps her distance from these. She has seen such entities before in the Split, felt the chill that pours from them, and she always avoids them. They make Flynn think of leeches, sucking something vital from their hosts, because the Outsiders burdened by their weight hold themselves differently to everyone else. Their bodies are hunched, their shoulders buckled, and their expressions are worn and jaded.

She reaches a set of double doors beneath a sign that reads: EXIT. *The doors are propped open. Cold air tumbles inside, but it feels like a ghost-breeze against Flynn's skin, whispery-silver. It slides* through *her like she isn't there at all.*

She walks through the open doors. Hesitates. Thinks of her body, lying exposed on the hard bed, pinned by the glare of harsh lights, vulnerable to Outsiders. But her fear is far away in the Split, as distant as the cold stars shining down on her, and The Night is a warm cradle that gathers her up, and bears her softly, silently, aloft.

NOW

Mei, Jonesy and Tyrus are huddled together on the sofa, watching a film on Tyrus's iPad, while Flynn sits alone in front of the fire in her sleeping bag. She turns the green shot glass over in her hands, watching the flames flicker in its reflection.

She can't shake the way Jackson had watched Chloe dancing, her lubricious movements turning his eyes to dark wells. She tries not to think what they are doing now, but unwelcome images taunt her: Jackson, his hands sliding down the curve of Chloe's back, trailing his lips down her slender throat; Chloe pressing her body against Jackson, her thighs wrapped around his waist, her fingers tangled in his scruffy hair.

They're probably fucking right now.

The sly voice speaks from the darkest corner of her mind, but it does not feel as though it belongs to her. She shakes her head. *No, Chloe was just flirting. She wouldn't do anything. She wouldn't betray me like that. And Jackson, he'd never cheat on me. He just wouldn't. I* know *him!*

The door swings open and Chloe walks in, Jackson following a few paces behind. Flynn tenses, watching them. Something is wrong. Chloe had practically swaggered out of the room earlier, a kick in her hips and a looseness to her movements that sizzled with sex. Now, she walks stiffly, her arms crossed over her chest, chin lowered. She looks shrunken, diminished. As though trying to fold herself away. Or hold herself together.

Jackson's gaze is inward-turned, his face drawn, tense. The indigo bruises that squat beneath his eyes are more pronounced. He wordlessly pours himself a whisky while Chloe wraps herself in a blanket and curls up on the empty sofa.

Flynn glares at her, her heart beating up in her throat. She can usually read Chloe's tics and tells like punctuation in a book: the small vein that pops between her brows signalling her anger, the subtle hitch in her voice that betrays a lie, the small red mark that appears in the groove between her nose and mouth when she is stressed. But now, Flynn feels as though she is looking at the face of a stranger.

And then it hits her, the truth like a kick to the gut, and she can't understand how she missed it. The evidence of Chloe's indiscretion is scrawled all over her face. It is in her kiss-bruised lips and mussed-up hair, in the stubble rash on her chin and the hickey that is already blooming on her slender neck. It is in the rip that slackens one of her vest straps.

Tears prism Flynn's eyes. She feels as though her heart is buckling, shrinking like a piece of crumpled origami.

'Jax, man!' Jonesy says, without looking up from the film playing on the iPad. 'It's nearly your birthday! Three twenty, right?'

'Huh?' Jackson turns round, dazed. His dark eyes slide to Flynn, and he starts towards her, but she tightens her grip on the shot glass, turns away from him.

'Flynn—'

'Leave me alone!'

'Please, can we—'

She whirls round, the shot glass inexplicably burning in her hand, a smouldering ember she longs to smash into his beautiful, treacherous face. Instead, she slams it down on the table, then grabs the Scrabble purse, shakes the tiles out. Her hands tremble as she spaces the letters in a wide circle.

'Let's try this again.' Her voice shakes, betraying her tears.

She had not planned the words, had no idea what she was going to say until she opened her mouth and they tumbled out, but anger and jealousy blend into a toxic stew, a fuel for recklessness and impulsivity. She knows she is acting out of character, that something is not right, but this recognition is crushed beneath the storm of her rage.

'Flynn, please, can we just talk?'

Flynn flashes a look at Chloe, hunched on the sofa. Her eyes are hollow, her knees tucked beneath her chin. *What has he done to her? Did he* hurt *her?* Concern is eclipsed by the memory of Chloe dancing earlier, her body shimmering, pellucid, luminous; the playful way she had slid her eyes to Jackson, as though she'd known exactly what effect she'd had on him.

Whatever he did, she was asking for it.

The words sear Flynn's thoughts, so blistering in their viciousness that they sweep a chill down her spine. It feels as though someone else is speaking from inside her own thoughts, riding on the coat-tails of her rage.

Flynn drops to the floor in front of the table. 'What do you say, Clo?' Her voice drips with saccharine spite. 'Let's see if we can get a special message from beyond for our birthday boy.'

They sit around the table, a hushed, sombre-faced group, not quite meeting each other's eyes, as though the tension between Flynn and Jackson has soaked into the atmosphere. In place of joking and laughter, a skin-crackling tension, the sense something between them all has changed. Only Tyrus, swaying where he sits with a vacant grin on his face, remains unaffected by the soured mood.

A log drops in the hearth, red sparks dance up the flue.

'Spirits, we open the circle for you to enter,' Mei says.

No banter this time, no cleansing incantations, no smothered sniggers. Outside, the wind is a base roar that smashes the trees and shreds itself against the walls of the house; it whistles through the gaps in the window frames and skirls through the eaves.

Deep in Flynn's subconscious, a voice urges her to stop, but it is blurred by alcohol and weed, and too quiet to hold her attention. Besides, she doesn't *want* to stop; she needs a distraction from the terrible ache of betrayal inside her. She focuses on her breath, drawing the weed-laced air deep into her lungs, expelling it slowly.

'Is there anyone there?'

Shadows twitch in the flickering candlelight. Flynn has a sudden intimation of impending catastrophe, can almost taste the seconds on the tip of her tongue, a bitterness of fear that she still has time to spit out.

A creak from down the hall, like a footstep on the wooden staircase.

Jonesy's eyes widen. 'Did you hear—'

'Shhhh,' Mei scolds.

They sit and listen as the house breathes, awakening around them.

'I didn't hear anything,' Tyrus blurts, his eyes sliding in and out of focus.

'Ty, shut up!' Mei snaps.

Tyrus closes his eyes. A grin is plastered to his lips, but Flynn sees a tear roll down his cheek. That *wrong*ness flares inside her again, the whispered warning of earlier rising in pitch.

Tyrus tips his head back, calls, 'Izzanybodythere?'

His voice clatters into the silence. Mei glares at him, but he doesn't notice. A charge is gathering on the air; it prickles against Flynn's skin like static. Her fingertips, delicately touching the shot glass, begin to tingle.

'Come out and play, we don't bite!' Tyrus giggles, but the sound carries no humour, only a strained terror.

'This is a bad idea,' Jackson mutters, watching Tyrus.

'It's Jackson's eighteenth!' Tyrus slurs. 'Say happy birthday!'

Mei hisses, 'Ty, if you don't stop—'

The wind suddenly drops and the temperature in the room plummets. The fire in the hearth leaps high, the wicks of candles in the tiered stand flicker to life. A hush falls, deeper than any that preceded it, a silence that spills around them in ripples, distorting the hiss and spit of the fire, the wail of the wind, the rattle of the windows in their frames.

'Don't move,' Mei whispers.

A coldness washes through Flynn's body. Her breath swirls on the air, each exhalation tinged with an eerie phosphorescence. The shadows spill forwards, stretching towards the table. She imagines a woman's face sliding from the gloom, dead fish-eyes sunk in darkness, lips split around her scream, skin ghastly white.

The shot glass quivers.

'What the fuck...' Jonesy gasps.

'Don't,' Mei whispers, 'move.' Her face is ashen, her eyes fixed on the shot glass. 'What is your name?'

The glass shivers against the wood, like a stuck needle on old vinyl. The room is cold, but Flynn's hand feels as though it is plunged into a freezer. Her skin is studded in gooseflesh and the small hairs down her arms press against her shirt. Every tainted exhalation paints foul clouds on the air.

'Mei...' Flynn breathes.

Mei lifts her voice. 'What is your name?'

Icy breath stirs the small hairs down Flynn's neck. She gasps, twists to look behind her, but there is no one there.

'Did you die here?'

'Mei, I don't like it,' Chloe sobs.

'Keep your hands on the glass!' Mei snaps.

Flynn's hand trembles, but she realises it is taking no effort to hold it over the glass; it is as though her fingers are magnetised to it. Her heart slips as the shot glass slides across the table. It stops at the Y, slides across to E, down to S.

'Oh Jesus... Oh shit...' Jonesy gasps.

Mei's throat bobs as she swallows. 'Why haven't you moved on?'

The planchette feels like a live cable beneath Flynn's fingers as it moves around the table, pausing at individual tiles before it slides back to the centre.

TRAPPED

'I don't want to do this anymore,' Chloe says. 'I don't want to do this.'

'Ask its name.' Tyrus's voice weaves drunkenly. 'You should ask its name.'

Chloe suddenly whips round, as though someone has dropped an ice cube down her back. 'Something touched me!' Tears clot her voice. 'Oh my god, something *touched* me!'

'Clo, it's alright. If the spirit's lost, maybe we can help.' Mei stares at the shot glass, perhaps hoping to see reflected in its surface the face of whoever they are communing with. 'What is your name?'

The glass doesn't move.

'Mei, that's enough,' Jackson says.

'What was it you said,' Tyrus slurs, 'about dying?'

Mei spears Tyrus with her glare. 'Ty, would you just shut the fuck up?'

'Oh, yeah,' he says, sitting straighter, that strange bilious tinge swirling in his eyes. He leans forwards, until his lips are nearly touching the shot glass. 'How old will we be when we die?'

A fine crack slides through the glass, a jagged hairline fracture. The air, already cold, drops to a glacial chill so intense, each inhalation tightens Flynn's throat. A rank stench pollutes the room. Flynn turns towards the sound of a soft splintering, sees feathers of frost crackle across the windows.

Mei stares around the room with fear-fattened pupils.

Slowly, the shot glass slides across the wood, sketches a long, straight line down the centre of the table. Like a finger tracing a shape on the air, it leaves no mark behind, but in her mind's eye, Flynn feels it drag down her spine, like a one-tone note of terror. The glass stops for a beat, then slides diagonally upwards, draws a curve beside the line, like a giant 'S'.

'Mei, make it stop!' Chloe cries.

The shot glass picks up speed, sweeping through the 'S', framing the number '8'.

'I can't move my hand!' Tyrus yells.

Over and over, the glass slices the number '8' into the wooden surface of the table, until it is moving so fast, Flynn's shoulder burns in its socket. She tries to pull her hand from the planchette but that previous subtle tug is now a vice-like grip.

'Jesus *fuck*!' Jonesy shrieks.

Flynn strains to free herself, but it is as though her hand is welded to the shot glass. She sees her own fear leap like flame into her friends' eyes as they too try and wrench their hands from the glass, their outstretched arms like the spokes of a giant wheel that won't stop spinning.

'Spirit, leave in peace!' Mei yells. 'We thank you, spirit, leave in peace! *We thank you, spirit, leave in peace!*'

The shot glass flies across the room and smashes against the wall in a hail of jagged green rain. Flynn and the others fall backwards as warmth floods back into the room, the fire in the hearth drops low.

Tyrus scrabbles away from the others, vomit spraying from his lips onto the carpet; Chloe is sobbing, her pupils blown wide with fear; Mei staggers to her feet, her breath tearing in and out; Jonesy's fists are clamped in his curls; Jackson stares at his hand, as though that fierce, ghostly grip has left an imprint there.

Flynn inches towards the table on legs that feel ready to buckle beneath her. In the room's dim light, she can't at first see what is scarred there, but when she runs a hand over its surface, she feels the indentation in the wood, markings from the chipped shot glass.

Two numbers.

18.

Flynn feels exhausted, like an athlete who has run a race, but with none of the accompanying exhilaration. She and the others have decamped to a room down the hallway from the turret room, snatching only a few belongings that were close to hand before they fled.

There are no candles to light in the room they now occupy, no fire to press back the darkness. Furnishings comprise little more than a heavy oak wardrobe and an iron bedframe, and the only illumination comes from their two hurricane lamps, one at the centre of their circle, the other by the door.

Jackson has tried again to talk to Flynn, but she shrugged him off, and now studiously ignores him. She notices him glance at Chloe a few times, but the lustful glaze in his eyes has been replaced by a vaguely confused, questioning look.

Flynn muses on how different they are now to the rowdy group they had been a few hours ago, drinking and toasting Jackson's birthday in the lobby downstairs. For the past twenty minutes, they have sat hunched over the light in this spartan room, barely speaking, and only then in hushed whispers, fearful that whatever entity had communicated with them might hear them and return. Pale-faced, shaken, they stare fixedly at the storm lantern in the centre of the room, its glow a small comfort against the terrifying images playing over in their minds.

Without Chloe's music blaring or the constant stream of chatter, Flynn is acutely aware of the sounds that echo through the house. Each creak and sigh of ageing timbers makes her heart kick and her body tense. The wind is an orchestra, finding its voice in the throat of the chimney, gusting through empty, cavernous rooms, fluting through the leaky windows. Sometimes it rises like a cry and acquires a distorted human quality. At one point, Flynn even thinks she hears Andy calling them and, convinced he has returned early to pick them up, she dashes to the window, expecting to see his minivan outside. But the driveway is empty, and his voice tapers and dies on the fading cry of the treacherous wind. At other times, she hears distant strains of music, soft echoes of the 'Happy Birthday' song she had heard earlier.

The first time she heard that haunting melody, she had frozen, her head tipped to the side, and asked the others if they could hear it, too. Their blank looks had chilled her almost as much as the song, and after that, she hadn't mentioned it again, even as the music echoed faintly through the house, the words fading in and out, a frequency she could not quite attune to.

'I need a drink,' Tyrus mumbles.

'Seriously?' Mei gives him an incredulous look. 'You literally just chucked your guts up, now you want more booze.'

'Yeah, well, what can I say?' Tyrus says as Jonesy rummages through his rucksack and brandishes a bottle of Jack Daniel's. 'I'm shook.'

Tyrus takes a swig, then passes it round. Flynn still feels

heady and buzzed from the joints and the booze, but takes a nip anyway. She presses the back of her hand to her lips as heat sears her throat and chest.

'What time is it?' Tyrus asks.

Jackson checks his watch. 'Gone three.'

Mei takes the bottle from Flynn, turns it over in her hands. 'What do you think that was back there?'

'I don't know,' Jonesy says, 'but I don't think it was one of your "spirits of light and goodness".'

'It felt so... angry.' Flynn shudders, remembering the way the atmosphere had so quickly and tangibly altered.

'Yeah, well, I'm not surprised it was pissed,' Jonesy says. 'Mei and Ty just kept asking questions about dying. Not exactly a cheery topic.'

'I suppose you'd have preferred me to ask where it kept the rest of its stash,' Mei snaps.

Jonesy opens his mouth to say something, then hesitates, as though the idea hadn't occurred to him but that it was a good one.

'We should try and get some sleep,' Jackson says. 'It's gonna be a long night.'

'No way I'll be able to sleep,' Mei says. 'Not after that.' She takes a sip of whisky, grimaces, then holds it out to Chloe, who is sat a little further back from the others.

'Clo?' Mei sets the bottle down, watching Chloe.

Her eyes are glazed, tear-tracks of mascara cut black rivulets down her cheeks. Her face has acquired a deathly pallor and sweat stands out on her skin.

'Shit, she's hypo,' Flynn says, a hardness to her voice that she barely recognises.

Chloe blinks up at her, as though her voice has somehow filtered through the haze of her sugar-depleted brain.

'Where's your glucose?' Flynn says.

A scribble of confusion appears between Chloe's brows as her gaze slides over the room. Panic flares in her eyes, her hands float to her mouth, fingers trembling.

Excessive sweating, tremors, confusion – Flynn recognises all the symptoms of hypoglycaemia, and knows if Chloe doesn't consume some sugar soon, she will lose consciousness. Then, without medical help, she will slip into a coma.

'Has anyone got any food?' Flynn turns to the others, but they are already turning their pockets out, shaking their heads.

'Fuck. She must've left her glucose back in the room. Right—*fuck*!' Flynn stands up. 'Okay, I'll go and get it if someone comes with me. I don't want to go back out there on my own.'

Jackson bounces to his feet and Flynn glares at him, but now he is the one avoiding her gaze as he moves to the door.

'Maybe we should all go,' Jonesy says.

'No, you stay with Clo,' Jackson says. 'We won't be long.'

Flynn grabs one of the hurricane lamps. Pushing down her fear, she steps into the hallway, Jackson shadowing her as they head back towards the turret room. The lamplight slides over green damask wallpaper, bare wooden floorboards and unlit wall-mounted candles, but the deeper reaches of the hallway remain cloaked in darkness.

'Flynn, please... Won't you talk to me?'

'Not now, Jax.' Her voice, sibilant and cold, sounds almost as though it belongs to someone else.

'Don't do this. Don't shut me out. Won't you even let me explain—'

She whirls round so sharply Jackson takes a shocked step back.

'I don't want to hear it.'

Jackson drops his eyes. His tousled hair shadows his face and Flynn has to fight the urge to brush it back, to reach out and trace her fingertips along his jaw. She turns away from him, silently cautioning herself against her own tender feelings.

They reach the turret door, but Flynn hesitates. She recalls the violent speed of the shot glass moving across the table, the terrible cold that flooded the room, the manacle grip that had seized her hand. Sweat gums her palms and her heartbeat skids into a tachycardic rhythm.

Jackson moves in front of her. He turns the handle, steps inside.

Flynn swallows, follows behind him. Her gaze moves over the room. In their absence, the fire has almost burned itself out and shadows hang like drapes in the corners. The table is a lodestone, dragging her gaze. In the darkness and at this distance, she can't make out any markings on its surface, but she sees them in her mind, the number '1' nothing but a faint whisper against the wood, the '8' beside it, gouged deep as a cerebral scar.

She tears her eyes from the table, reminds herself what they are there to do. Chloe's rucksack is on the sofa. Flynn sets the lantern down, moves to the bag. She unzips the side pockets where she knows Chloe normally keeps her glucose tablets, but finds only a lip balm, a pocket mirror, tampons, a lighter, hand sanitiser, chewing gum. She opens the main compartment, tips everything onto the sofa.

'Shit. It's not here.' She casts round for something else Chloe can eat, but every sweet wrapper and crisp packet is empty.

Rather than diminishing, that sense of unease she had felt upon entering the room is growing, pressure building at the base of her skull, lifting the small hairs along the nape of her neck.

'Flynn, please listen to me. You have to let me explain.'

'Explain what?' Flynn walks round the room, picking up blankets and coats, searching for the multipack of Haribo Jonesy brought, or Mei's giant tube of Smarties, a packet of biscuits – anything that Chloe can eat to elevate her sugar levels. 'You cheated on me, now you want to talk me through it? I'd rather not know all the details.'

'No, that's not...' He falters, his expression lost. 'You don't understand–'

'Chloe's hand was on your arse and you were practically making out with her right in front of me. What exactly don't I understand?'

Jackson passes his hands over his eyes. 'This fucking *house*.'

Flynn whirls round. 'The *house* didn't cheat on me, Jax. *You* did.'

'No.' He turns his eyes away from her, confusion buckling his brow. 'I didn't–'

'We don't have time for this,' Flynn mutters, turning from him before he can see the tears spilling down her cheeks. She pulls the throws off the sofas, checks beneath the cushions, but all she finds are more empty wrappers. Panic flutters at the thought of what will happen if they don't get some sugar into Chloe soon.

She deserves it.

Flynn stills, chilled by the sound of that creaking, insectile voice in her head, and revulsed by the savage happiness the prospect of Chloe's suffering brings her. She backhands her tears away, tells herself that she is just angry, that she doesn't really wish her friend any harm. But the thought lingers, skulking in her subconscious, like a snake beneath a rock.

Her gaze catches on something on the windowsill and she moves towards it, relief rushing through her when she realises it's a packet of glucose tablets. Outside, thunder cracks, the muscled clouds roll and heave, slinging fulgent javelins onto the black and sodden moorlands.

'Flynn, you're saying I walked out of this room with Chloe,' Jackson says, moving towards her, 'but I swear I walked out of here with *you*.'

'You can't be serious.' She picks up the glucose. The packet is almost empty, only five or six glucose tablets left.

The tassels on the curtain ties stir, a faint agitation on the air.

'I'm dead serious.' Jackson's pleading eyes are fused to her face, but she can't bring herself to look at him. 'Listen, I know how that sounds, believe me. But it was always you, Flynn, it was always only ever you.'

Truth drips from his voice and Flynn feels something give inside her, a chink of light piercing the dark cave of her chest. Besides, she knows Jackson is guilty of many things – anger, jealousy, moodiness, recklessness – but he isn't a cheat.

She starts to turn to him, her hand moving to his face, the tight band around her heart relaxing. Seeing the change in her, Jackson's dark eyes soften with relief. But then, Flynn's gaze catches on two thin scratches along his jaw. Her vision washes scarlet as she imagines Chloe's stiletto nails snagging him in the heat of passion. She recalls her friend's kiss-bruised lips, the love bite spreading across her white throat, the rip in her vest strap. So dishevelled she looked as though she had been *mauled*. Jealousy spills through Flynn as she realises Jackson has never lost himself in pleasured excitement so deeply that he left bruises on her skin, has never hungered for her so intensely that he ripped her clothes in the heat of desire.

Does he expect me to believe that he hallucinated Chloe in place of me? Does he really think I'd buy that?

Sensing her withdrawal, Jackson reaches for her, his dark eyes pleading.

'Don't touch me.' She takes a step back, starts towards the door.

'Flynn.' Her name in his mouth is a knife twisting in her side. Serrated, raw. Agonised. It stops her in her tracks, the pain of it. She turns to him. He hasn't moved, only stands framed by the window, rumpled and broken. 'You *know* me. I'd never do anything to hurt you.'

'It's too late for that. We're finished, Jax.'

The words gust from her lips, leaving her cold and empty inside. Something behind Jackson's eyes collapses, and Flynn feels suddenly like the little girl she had once been, sick with fever, every breath crushed beneath an invisible boot-heel.

She tears her eyes from his face.

'Flynn, no.' A crack in his voice. 'You don't mean it. Flynn, come on, don't do this.'

'*You* did this, Jax.'

'I love you.'

She hesitates, her hand on the door handle. He still hasn't moved, only stands there, watching her, and again she feels herself soften. She wants him to fold her into his arms, wants to brush away the tear that is rolling down his cheek and taste his whiskied breath as she kisses him. Instead, she turns, opens the door.

'Flynn, please. I've never–'

His voice breaks with a gasp of shock. The temperature in the room drops, Flynn's breath snaps in her throat. Fear lurches through her as, slowly, she turns round.

Jackson is still staring in her direction, but his face is rigid, panic swimming in the dark pools of his eyes.

'Jax?' Flynn takes a step towards him.

The cold that had enveloped her hand when she held it over the shot glass earlier now slides over her whole body as a rancid stench fills the room.

'Jax!'

A shape steps from the gloom behind Jackson, parting the shadows. A woman. Her skin possesses a sick, chartreuse tinge, darkness swirls in the dark pits of her eyes. She slides her hands over Jackson's shoulders. Blistering terror sears Flynn, the taste of fear a flood of battery acid in her mouth. An answering smile eels across the woman's lips.

Jackson's body trembles, his breath frosts the air. Flynn senses him straining towards her, but he is held in check by the woman at his back. Pinned by the dark gravity of her presence. Flynn tries to take a step forwards, to shout out, but the air feels suddenly solid, rooting her to the spot.

Frost feathers Jackson's eyebrows and gathers on his dark lashes. A scrim of ice sheets his eyes. The tear gliding down his cheek freezes to his skin, glistens like a tiny pearl.

The woman leans closer, her eyes on Flynn as she whispers something in Jackson's ear. If he understands her words, he has no time to register them, because her grip on his arms tightens, her grime-gummed nails digging into his skin. She wrenches him violently backwards and the aged glass behind him breaks beneath his weight as both he and the woman plummet through it.

A scream blasts through Flynn's body, horror searing her skin in an explosion of unborn sound. She is stood at the window, her feet planted on the floor, yet she is falling, falling, braced for a landing that does not come. Over and over, she hears the sound of Jackson's body thudding against the ground.

Hands grab her, pull her away from the window. A chasm opens beneath her, a darkness so complete, so profound, she can see no way out of it, no blade of light. Voices buzz around her, shrill with confusion and hysteria.

What happened? What's wrong with her?

Where's Jax? Oh god, where's Jax?

Oh no, oh nonono! We need to help him! Jax!

Clo, stop it! Come back... Don't look... Oh god... Oh god...

No, please, Jax, please no...

Oh, Jesus. Don't look!

Jax!

Flynn feels someone grab and shake her. They are shouting at her, but their features blur and waver, like a face viewed from deep underwater.

'Flynn! *Flynn!*' It's Tyrus, but his voice is waterlogged and so far away. 'We need to go. *Now!* We need to help him.'

'Jesus, look at him, Ty!' Jonesy's voice. 'He's dead, Ty, isn't he? Oh my god, he's dead!'

What's happening? Why does Jonesy sound so strange? A shifting framework of images, captured in negative and brief as lightning flashes, sear Flynn's thoughts: Jackson, lying on the ground, his left leg horribly bent at the hip, his knee canted unnaturally; his right arm snapped at the elbow, the left tucked beneath him; his tangle of dark hair, fluttering around his too-still face; head twisted, one eye glazed and sightless, fixed on some distant horizon; brain matter spilling across the ground and a pool of spreading blood, wet and gleaming silver in the moonlight.

Jackson... Jackson... His name floods Flynn, spills through her like hot rain. *JaxJaxJax...*

Her eyes track to the window. Cold cuts into her bones, turning her tremors into violent convulsions. *Jackson... Jackson... JaxJaxJax...*

Someone grabs her shoulder, wrenches her around.

'What happened?' Chloe's eyes are wild, her fingernails dig into Flynn's shoulders. '*What the fuck did you do?*' Spittle flies from her mouth, her eyes roll. A crust of something on her lips. Sherbet? Jonesy must have given it to her. He loves sherbet.

'We found your glucose.' Flynn's lips feel numb and her voice sounds so far away.

'You pushed him! You pushed him, didn't you? *Didn't you!*'

Flynn tries to shake her head, to deny it, but she can't move, can't speak. *Had* she pushed him? She'd been so angry... Her thoughts feel soupy, like half-formed things that might take any shape in her mind. All she can think of are the cruel words she spoke to Jackson, the splintered look on his face, the devastation in his eyes.

Guilt must flash across her features because Chloe's jaw tightens. Her hand lashes out, cracking Flynn across the cheek, a hard open palm that whips her head to the side. Tears stab Flynn's eyes, but she feels numb, as though she has mainlined novocaine. She tells herself she is dreaming as the scene around her devolves into mayhem and hysteria. Tyrus is dragging Chloe away from Flynn, Mei is crying, Jonesy is hunched on the floor, his hands plunged into his halo of blonde curls. None of it is real. *None of this is happening!*

Flynn takes a step away from the others, but the moment she does, sharp glisters of pain shoot through the undersides of her feet. She gasps, staggers, catches herself on the edge of the sofa. She lifts one foot, sees dozens of lacerations there. Dried blood has congealed between her toes.

I cut myself. The thought is distant, but the pain in her feet sharpens, pushes back the fog in her head. *No, I would remember cutting myself...*

Flynn feels as though she is re-entering the room in tiny increments, her shock-blasted senses re-forming. The first thing she notices is the smell. Earlier, she had thought the house smelt green, faintly mildewy. But the room doesn't smell green – it smells *red*. Ferric and gamy, the ripe foulness of bowels and blood, the mammalian stink of fear.

Her eyes track to the mirror above the fireplace.

Her vision sways.

She blinks, sees herself and her friends in the reflection – but the room in the glass is *different*. Wallpaper hangs in sagging strips, revealing water-stains and bulging plaster riven with deep fissures. The window casements are corroded, grey with encrusted grime. The tiles around the fireplace are crumbling, black soot cakes the wall above the hearth. The room's vivid colours have faded, the woodwork is blistered and rotten.

Flynn slowly turns from the mirror and stares around the room.

It is just as foul and diseased as its reflection.

The curtains are grimy and the fabric of the sofa almost completely rotten away. Mould beads the plasterwork and saturates the oriental rug, billows of black obliterating the intricate patterns she had seen in it earlier. The floor is covered in rubble and debris, fallen chunks of plaster from the ceiling. Splinters of wood jut from the floorboards. She must have been walking barefoot across this jagged carpet all evening, slicing her feet without even registering the pain.

She lifts her hands. They are grimy with dirt. Her hair is thick with dust, clumpy with filth. As though she has spent hours sitting in the rotting corpse of a building. *This isn't real... This can't be real...*

'What's happening?' Chloe backs into a corner, her eyes skittering over the walls. '*What's happening?*'

Flynn sees her own horror reflected in the faces of her friends as they stare around the room with bulging eyes.

'We need to get out of here,' Mei says.

Tyrus grabs Flynn's hand, pulls her after him. Chloe backs into the hallway, her chest heaving with each ragged breath, but when she turns round, she screams.

'Who did that?' Her terror-choked sobs echo down the hallway. '*WHO LIT THE FUCKING CANDLES?*'

Flynn's eyes move down the candlelit hall. The same one she and Jackson had navigated a few minutes ago with only their storm lantern to guide them through the pitch-black. Now, countless flames illuminate the full length of the corridor, burning tallow fills the space with a foul stink.

Tyrus swallows. 'Just keep moving.'

Keep moving! Don't look back! These words keep time with Flynn's frantic heartbeat, singing a jagged song in her blood. Sweat glues her top to her back as she runs down the hallway, one hand clamped around Chloe's, the other clutching the back of Tyrus's T-shirt. Keeping close to Mei and Jonesy a step ahead, terrified if she falls behind they will abandon her to this insane house.

She has to get out. Out of this nightmare. Candles whicker against the walls, making the shadows twitch. Gaps in the floorboards reveal shadowy rooms below, chunks of fallen plaster expose the roof space above.

Half-blind in the darkness, Flynn bites back a scream. Every step sends pain through the soles of her feet and prints carmine kisses on the bare floorboards. She feels as though the house is savouring the taste of every bloody footstep.

The staircase creaks and groans as they hurtle down it. The wood is rotten, balusters missing from the sides. One of the steps has snapped in half, toothpick splinters jutting out, ready to turn a misstep into a fall. She sees dried bloodstains on the dust-coated floorboards, and realises in horror the blood is probably hers – that she climbed these stairs earlier, oblivious to the cuts opening in the soles of her feet, blind to the danger.

At the bottom of the stairs, they stagger down another hallway, move through decaying rooms that blaze with candles, sobbing, reaching for each other, until finally, they are back in the lobby.

Flynn's thoughts tilt at the sight of the paintings on the walls. The surfaces of the canvases are lifting, the colour flaking away so that the images that had repulsed her when they entered the house are now impossible to make out. The wine-red carpet is worn to the weave and ruined by black mould. The ceiling has buckled from the weight of the chandelier.

They pelt towards the door.

Mei twists the key in the lock, pulls it open.

Sunlight spills into the lobby.

Shock drops Flynn to her knees.

The heavens should be a churning vault of darkness, storm-tossed and thunderous, but the sun rides the hyaline sky of a renaissance painting, and the wind Flynn had heard battering the house has dropped to a soft breeze. The gravel driveway is dry, not so much as a single puddle on the porch decking. The only indication that a storm has passed are the fire-blackened trunks of the lightning-scarred trees.

Flynn gazes over the moors. The blaze of purple heather has gone, and in its place are fields of bare peat the colour of stewed tea, and the trees, which had been thick with foliage when they arrived, are now barren. Nude branches claw towards the quiet blue sky, like the outstretched arms of a dark coven.

It is as though, in the few hours they spent inside Temple Fall, time has... slipped, the days and months skidding on greased wheels without taking them with it.

Slowly, Flynn turns to the house.

The desiccated walls of Temple Fall crumble beneath wreaths of moss and vines. The roof has caved in and fallen shingles lie in shattered pieces on the brittle, yellow grass. Rot has eaten away at the wooden decking. There are holes in the stone mullions. All the windows are boarded up, including the one that Jackson fell through. A sign, toppled into the bushes, almost illegible behind a scramble of weeds and thorny bracken: *Caution, Unsafe Building, Keep Out!* Only the cast-iron knocker on the door, that serpentine ouroboros, looks untouched by the passage of time.

But Flynn is not looking at the house.

She stares at the spot on the porch where Jackson fell.

Ripped police tape is tethered to the railing. It flutters in the breeze, like the dead skin of a snake.

And Jackson's body has gone.

PART 2

Time and the bell have buried the day,
The black cloud carries the sun away.

T. S. ELIOT, *BURNT NORTON*,
THE FIRST POEM OF *FOUR QUARTETS*

NOW

'Two... Three... Four...'

I count each footstep, the numbers like a silken ribbon between my fingers, guiding me through the darkness. Doors appear and disappear in shifting curtains of mist. The house is alive, a vast neural network, forming new synapses while others die.

I float down the hallway, my voice the only sound in the hushed silence. Sometimes, I catch my reflection in the window. My face is as pale and featureless as a pane of glass. No eyes to see, no mouth to speak, no ears to hear, even though all my senses remain intact. I don't question it. The house makes everything possible, and I am part of it now, as much as it is part of me.

'Eight... Nine...'

The numbers crash over me in waves, concealing memories I don't want to face. I trail my hand across the textured wallpaper, savour its luscious feel beneath my fingertips. The carpet whispers beneath my feet. Candles flicker against the walls, hot little tongues licking the darkness. I can almost hear them, burning whispers scorching the air, chanting with me.

'Fourteen... Fifteen...'

I reach a dead-end, place both palms against the wall. It is warm, slightly damp, like sweat-perfused skin. I press my cheek against it, a child leaning into her mother's soft belly. I feel happy, held by the walls, folded from the world like a secret. I'm home.

'Seventeen... Eighteen...'

Fear slides down my spine.

'Eighteen...'

The smell of swamp rot fills my nose, the wall turns boggy. I pull away, repelled by the clammy feel of it. The waves that beat over my memories creep back, a receding tide, and something rises on that dark shore.

'Eighteen...'

My throat is tight and dry, my voice a choked rasp. Because I know now that I am not alone. I feel it in the tightening of my hair follicles, in the cold pinch between my shoulder blades.

'Eighteen...'

Terror has jammed the gears of my mind and all I can say is this, over and over, as though no other numbers come after. Not for me. I'm sobbing now, watching the tide slide away and memory take form. A swirl of black sand kicks up from the floor, solidifies into a figure. Thin shoulders uncurl from the massed darkness, a shrouded head lifts, ebony skirts riffle on the breeze.

A voice spills across the ocean, shaped by the diseased and rotten mouth behind the mouldering shroud, and it echoes my own. I press my hands over my face, feel my features move somewhere below the surface, a strange, liquid undulation.

'Eighteen... Eighteen... Eighteen... Eighteen...' Panic whisks a frantic beat into my voice as I speak faster and faster.

A cold breeze stirs my hair.

Slowly, I turn, stare at the candlelit hallway. I had thought the figure existed only in my mind, but I was wrong. It's there, standing at the end of the hallway. Its veiled gaze drills into me. I can't move, can barely breathe.

An arm snakes out of the darkness, shedding black rose petals into the air like flakes of dead skin. The wrist peeking from the cuff is startlingly white against its wreath of dark lace. It pinches the flame of a wall-mounted candle, snuffing it. The rustle of skirts as the figure moves closer to me and the hand slides out again. Finger and thumb nip another flame. The darkness widens.

My back against the wall, I'm trapped, but then I reach out, feel an opening where there hadn't been one before. I slide down the hallway, sobbing, and the space opens, a solid wall melting away to reveal another corridor.

A scream of pure hate and rage blasts from the figure and I sense it hurtling towards me. Flames wink out as it passes in a whirl of flapping black skirts and a snapping veil. Thrashing like a trapped crow hurtling towards the light. A face slips from the gloom, a siren scream pours from the open rip of its mouth. Two glowing white eyes blazing in the darkness.

I spin away but hands snatch me, and pull me into the waiting darkness.

Flynn cries out as someone pulls her from the path of the car she had been about to step in front of. Tyres spray rainwater over her, the driver leans on the horn.

She blinks, turns round. The sky is dark, the streets slick with rain. She does not recognise where she is or understand how she came to be here. Only a handful of people are out, and none of them are close enough to have grabbed her. A single black petal corkscrews to the ground. More float on the puddle beneath her feet, like shreds of night-time shaved from the sky, and the air is painted with the delicate aroma of roses. Subtle, fleeting, a heady inhalation of a sweet bouquet.

She realises she is clutching a shopping bag in one hand, and her rucksack is strapped to her shoulders. Chills stagger down her spine and she starts to tremble so violently, she fears she will collapse in the street.

It happened again.

Wary of being recognised by people who have followed the Temple Fall case in the papers or on the news, she backs into the shadowy recess of a shop's awning, leans against the window. She looks in the shopping bag, hoping to glean some clue to unravel her mysterious appearance in the middle of the street. A bag of onions, carrots, garlic, two packets of pasta. A memory sparks: her mum had asked her to pick up some ingredients for dinner. Flynn remembers filling the shopping basket, paying for the food at the checkout, walking out into the mizzling rain, and then... nothing.

She takes her mobile from her pocket. She has five missed calls from her mum, two from Chloe. Her stomach twists. She has barely seen any of her old friends since that night in Temple Fall, and she has not spoken to Chloe at all.

The time on the phone display reads *18:53*. Flynn recalls calling her mum from the shop to ask what type of pasta she wanted. She checks her call history, sees that they spoke at 17:58.

I left the shop almost an hour ago.

A fresh wave of horror ripples through her at the realisation she has probably been walking the streets for all that time. She is soaked to the skin, her calves ache dully and her face is numb with cold.

They are happening more and more often, these absences. She hasn't told anyone about them, not even her mum, who would only try again to persuade her to talk to a therapist. Flynn is sick of talking. Besides, a therapist would only pass off her blank fugues as sleepwalking episodes. But Flynn knows that is not what they are. Even if she was exhausted to the point of collapse, she wouldn't fall asleep while walking home laden with shopping or, as happened last week, while standing at the school gates waiting to collect Riley. No, this is something else.

These blackouts descend sporadically and without warning,

smothering consciousness and transporting Flynn back to Temple Fall where she walks the empty corridors like a wraith. It is as though the house is scooping the spirit from its host, which is left to wander, mindless and mislocated, in the physical world. Even now, miles from Temple Fall, she can taste its foul miasma at the back of her throat, feel its dust against her skin, like a slimy skein of filth.

She taps her home address into Google Maps, sees she is only about two miles away. She fires off a quick text to her mum apologising for taking so long and telling her she will be home soon. Then, she starts walking.

As her shock fades, grief slides in to accommodate the space it leaves behind. Barely a moment passes without Jackson in her thoughts. The feel of his hand in hers, the tilt of his head when he framed a photograph, the kink in his smile. Flynn misses him on a cellular level, craves him with every atom in her body. The knowledge she will never see him again is sometimes more than she can bear. She has no appetite for food, and when she does manage to eat, everything tastes bland. She feels hollow, as though there is nothing left inside her, only a cold and aching darkness.

Flynn dwells in ghost days, a living spectre haunting the past. Even now, as she walks home, she pictures Jackson walking beside her, the Cupid's bow of his mouth, his Nikon F2 camera hanging round his neck, a scoop of dark hair falling across his tired, russet-ringed eyes. Sometimes she catches the smell of his peppery aftershave, the faint chemical scent of his darkroom, and she turns, her heart lifting, half-expecting to see him standing behind her. But of course, he is never there.

Flynn's all-encompassing grief leaves no space for her to stay angry with him, but she can't think of Chloe without feeling an accompanying surge of hatred. Her friend's betrayal hurts no less now than it had the night they spent in Temple Fall,

Flynn's bitterness perfectly preserved, as though it has been bottled in brine.

Now, as she walks down the moon-silvered street, Flynn replays the day she and her friends fled Temple Fall. The memory is so visceral, she almost feels the ghost sun of that day burn her eyes, shock singing beneath her skin, the pulse of remembered pain in the scarred soles of her feet.

They had been a ragtag group then, clinging to each other in bewildered terror, but even as Temple Fall receded behind them, Flynn had not been able to shake the feeling that she was somehow still inside the house. Or that part of the house was inside her. The mineral smell of water and the earthier scents of dirt and grass tangled on the air, but Flynn could still detect the foul tang of rot, the meaty stench of burning candles.

Only Tyrus and Chloe had any charge remaining on their mobiles, and they kept glancing at their screens, waiting for reception so they could call for help, until Tyrus stopped dead in his tracks. The way his eyes slid from his phone to the surrounding moors, confusion morphing into a stunned incomprehension, had tipped the ground beneath Flynn's feet, and she had snatched the phone from his slack fingers.

The display should have read *Saturday 7 September*. Jackson's birthday. Instead, it read *Thursday 16 January*.

She tried to dismiss it as an error, a glitch in the mechanism, but a quick check of Chloe's phone confirmed the date.

They had walked into Temple Fall hours ago, and yet somehow, over four months had passed.

It was impossible, yet it was the only thing that made any sense: the change in weather, the transition from the early hours of the morning to midday, the boarded-up windows, the scraps of blue and white police tape on the porch, the dramatically altered scenery. Jackson's missing body.

Flynn's phone buzzes in her pocket, pulling her back to the

present. She takes it out, expecting it to be her mum. Chloe's name flashes across the screen.

Flynn's hand tightens round the phone. The sudden urge to pitch the mobile grips her, and she starts to pull her arm back to hurl it as far away as she can, but then realises, with a jolt of alarm, what she is about to do. The extremity of her reaction chills her. It is as though someone is steering her thoughts, inflaming her anger, inciting her hatred.

She swipes to answer.

The instant she does, something in the back of her mind hisses. The breeze feels suddenly oily, repellent. Watchful. And Flynn knows that she had been right to feel as though the house had been stalking her. She has picked something up inside its walls, like a parasitic fungus, a blight in her thoughts that contaminates everything.

Her hand trembles as she holds the phone to her ear.

'Flynn?' Chloe's voice sounds raw and scratched. 'Hello?'

'I'm here.'

'Oh, Flynn...' Chloe snatches back a sob. 'I've been trying to get through to you. I didn't think you were going to answer. Have you... Have you heard?'

'Heard what?'

A beat of silence. 'About Mei.'

Flynn stills, breath held.

'There's been an accident.'

Flynn closes her eyes. Chloe is talking but her voice sounds suddenly far away, inaudible over the memory of the wind gusting through the smashed turret window, the wet thump of Jackson's body smacking against the ground, and Flynn's scream painting the air scarlet. Only one word Chloe says – *fell* – slips beyond the roar of noise that fills her head, slices at her over and over, like a jagged shard of glass: *fell... fell... fell...*

'Is she okay?' Flynn forces the question past her lips, and silence drops behind her words.

Please tell me she's okay, tell me she's broken bones, she's cracked her ribs, tell me she's got a skull fracture, she's in intensive care, tell me it's serious but tell me she's alive, please tell me she's—

'No, Flynn.' Chloe's voice, thick with tears. 'She's dead. Mei's dead.'

Flynn sits on the window ledge in her bedroom, her tear-swollen eyes fixed blankly on her phone screen. It had taken her over an hour to walk home, a journey which she can now barely recall, her senses so blunted by shock that it was almost as though she had slipped into another fugue.

The moment she had opened the front door, her mum rushed to meet her, her pale face streaked with tears, eyes shimmering with grief. It was obvious she had heard the news, but Flynn had not wanted to talk about it and had hurried upstairs with barely a word, closing her bedroom door behind her.

Now, she scrolls to Mei's number. The photo of her friend in her contacts is one Flynn took at The Pitfalls last year. She had lain on the ground between two brick walls as Mei backflipped from one to the other. Flynn's shot frames Mei upside down against the high blue sky, her toes delicately scraping eggshell clouds. Bandages cover her hands, sweat darkens her sleeveless T-shirt. With her topknot, shaved back and sides, and perfect grace, she looks like an anarchic ballerina, let loose from the stage and given invisible wings.

Mei isn't dead, she can't be. Chloe made a mistake. Flynn's finger hovers over the screen. *I'll call her and she'll answer and everything will be okay. And if she doesn't answer, it'll be because she's doing press-ups in her bedroom, or hanging out at the skatepark, or playing cards in The Dive. She's always shit at answering her phone. It doesn't mean anything.*

Flynn tosses the phone onto her bed, drops her face into her hands. Behind her shuttered lids, memories of Mei surface like bubbles rising from the depths of her consciousness: she sees her blazing across The Pitfalls, vaulting rails, leaping over vast domes of sand and rubble as though there are springs in her knees. Muscles taut and lean, she contorts her body in flips and rolls, bar kicks and Kong vaults, scrabbles up walls, her strong hands finding the shallowest grooves and ledges.

Flynn remembers the myriad ways she could shuffle a deck of cards and make them walk between her hands; the time she'd tried to teach Flynn how to do dive rolls and wall runs at The Pitfalls; giving her backies round the estate when Carrie Slaughter refused to let Flynn borrow her bike; laughing manically as Flynn spun her round on Carl Slaughter's swivel chair before she projectile vomited all over his desk; the card she had made Flynn to celebrate the finalisation of her adoption; sitting beside her on the top of the scaffolding at The Pitfalls, their feet dangling over the sharp drop and Mei nervously confiding that she had a crush on Poppy Nielson, her dark eyes filling with tears when Flynn shrugged and said she'd known it ever since the two of them sat together in Year 9 chemistry.

There's been an accident.

Mei's past injuries flash through Flynn's mind, too many to catalogue. Scuffs, sprains, rolled ankles, bloodied limbs, snapped tendons, broken bones, all consequences she was willing to face, and did, every time she attempted a wall spin or dash vault, a shin slide or tic tac.

She fell all the time. But she always got back up.

Fractions of what Chloe had said play over in Flynn's mind. *A rooftop run... Must have slipped... A fourteen-storey fall... Died on impact... An accident... A terrible, terrible accident...*

She drops onto her bed, eyes on the ceiling. As though it is a screen replaying the day she and her friends stumbled out of Temple Fall, she sees them all staggering down the porch steps, the cold of an imposter winter filling her lungs. Chloe listing beside her, blinking at the landscape, as though its alteration wasn't real to her, merely a symptom of her hypo, an illusion. Flynn had forgotten, in her shock, that she was still clutching the glucose tablets, and had passed them to Chloe, who shovelled them into her mouth with trembling fingers.

It wasn't enough though, and after an hour of walking, her sugars plunged again. Flynn knew she wasn't alone in her worry that her friend might pass out before they made it to civilisation, but eventually that longed-for bar of signal had bounced up on Tyrus's phone and they had called an ambulance to collect them.

Later, they found out that Andy had discovered Jackson's body the day he returned in his minivan to pick them up. He had searched the house for them, and though he found evidence they had been there – abandoned shoes and socks, coats, empty beer cans and prosecco bottles, crisp packets and stubbed-out joints – Temple Fall was empty.

Chloe's hard-as-nails brother had been devastated by his sister's disappearance, and so traumatised by finding Jackson's body that he had been seeing a therapist ever since.

An investigation was immediately launched, their faces circulated on news channels and in national newspapers, pasted to lamp-posts and posted on social media. The urgency surrounding the search was heightened by the fact they were all under eighteen years old, and that Chloe was a type 1 diabetic.

The public were captivated by the mystery of what had happened to them, baffled by the fact that there was no evidence to suggest they had left Temple Fall after Andy dropped them off: no footprints leaving the front door, no tyre marks in the wet grass, aside from those left by Andy's van. Police had tried to track their mobiles but had been unable to do so. Their phones had been picked up passing a mast less than ten miles from Temple Fall, before they had all disconnected from the network. It was as though they had been sucked into a black hole.

Over the following weeks, police and volunteers systematically searched the area around Temple Fall, and a cadaver dog, Bullet, was deployed with his handler. Gormire Lake, which was a few miles from the house, was dragged, but no bodies were found. The families of the missing teenagers made public requests for help finding them, and filmed tearful appeals, begging them to come home.

An inquest into Jackson's death was opened, an autopsy carried out. Forensic pathologists examined the velocity, height and angle of his fall and concluded he had died on impact after he jumped from the window. His death was ruled a suicide and his funeral took place on the morning of 27 September. Almost three weeks after he died. His family were there to mourn him, but his friends were not.

The more time that passed without news, the more the mystery surrounding their disappearance grew, and in the absence of a rational explanation, superstitions and conspiracy theories began to circulate.

Despite the fact Gormire Lake had already been dragged, some people insisted the teenagers must have gone swimming in the tarn-like water and drowned. Much was made of the storm, the fact that some trees around the house had been felled by lightning and the surrounding moorland was flooded with rainwater, while the nearby village of Brinley Cliffe saw nothing more than a light drizzle. According to one wild theory, this localised storm was caused by a portal opening and sweeping the teenagers into another dimension. Someone else came forward, claiming he had seen a silver disc-shaped object the night Jackson died, hovering in the sky close to Temple Fall.

As if all that wasn't bad enough, the media picked up the story of Flynn's unconventional childhood: Heather's psychosis; the fact she had delivered Flynn alone at home and failed to register her birth; how she had committed suicide following her 999 call reporting Flynn's illness; Flynn's subsequent spell in hospital, Crickwell Children's Home and foster care. Even the Slaughters crawled out of the woodwork, claiming Flynn had been a 'challenging' and 'troubled' child, who tended to 'gravitate towards other miscreants because of her past'.

Now, she hears her mum's footsteps on the stairs, a hesitant knock on her door. Jenna enters the room, wordlessly sits on the edge of the bed. Flynn notes, numbly, how much the past few months have aged her mum. She has lost weight, and the wrinkles that frame the corners of her eyes and mouth have deepened. She no longer tries to cover the spray of grey hairs at her temples, just as she no longer bothers with make-up. Threads of red capillaries worm through the whites of her eyes, and sadness is pressed into her features, like an indelible mould.

Riley has changed, too. Only four years old when she first moved in with Jenna and Flynn, the trauma of living in an abusive household had left its mark. She would wet the bed almost every night and resist sleep for fear of the nightmares that woke her, shaking and sobbing and begging not to be sent away, sent back. Wary of adults, suspicious of other children, she spent much of her time alone, talking and playing with her imaginary friend, a little girl she called Murphy Brown.

Eventually, Riley began to form friendships at school, and Murphy Brown faded away, relegated to the scrapyard of infant imaginings. The night terrors and bed wetting stopped, and she emerged from her shell, a boisterous, quirky, courageous little girl.

But since Flynn's disappearance, Riley has regressed to the scared child she had once been, acquiring again those old habits, as though they were a heavy load she had only briefly set down. She has even reverted to addressing Jenna by her Christian name, and while Flynn's mum never comments on it, pretends everything is fine, Flynn sees the small flinch behind her eyes every time Riley fails to call her 'Mum'.

Now, Jenna places her hand over Flynn's.

'I'm so sorry.' Her voice cracks with emotion. 'Sylvia called me when you were out.'

Sylvia. Mei's mum. Flynn closes her eyes, but tears slide between her shuttered lids.

'She asked me if you'd seen much of Mei since... If you'd spent time with her since...' She falls silent, looks away. Her eyes harden. *Since Temple Fall.* It is as though she can't even bring herself to say the name of the house, as though the thought of it alone brings with it waves of pain and resentment.

Flynn inhales a sharp pang of regret and shakes her head. More tears spill down her cheeks.

'Oh, sweetheart.' Her mother wraps an arm around her shoulder, pulls her close.

'How can this be happening, Mum?'

'Flynn, how can I answer that?' Exasperation bleeds into her mum's tone, the helpless frustration of someone who feels unjustly kept from a secret. 'How can I make any sense out of it when you won't tell me what happened inside that house?'

Anger sweeps through Flynn and she pulls back. She knows she can't blame her mum for being sceptical; Flynn's explanation for her disappearance must have seemed like a slap in the face for its implausibility. After all, anyone can lose track of time, but no one loses months of their lives in the space of one night. It sounds like a wild story concocted by a group of teenagers trying to cover something up, a lie that makes a mockery of the terror and anguish their parents lived through in their absence.

Every minute of Flynn's disappearance had been unbearable for her mum. Desperate with worry, she had frantically called the local hospitals to see if Flynn or the others had presented there, and when that heralded no results, she had expanded her enquiries to every hospital in the country. She had contacted jails and hostels, praying she would find her daughter there, then finally the coroners, praying that she wouldn't. She had trawled the streets with Flynn's photograph, showed it to hundreds, thousands of people, and when Temple Fall was no longer deemed a crime scene, Jenna had driven there herself, determined to find some hint or clue that the police might have missed.

But the days turned into weeks and months, the heartbeat of time staggered onwards and still there was no sign of Flynn or her friends. Jenna and Riley spent a sombre Christmas together, terrified every time the phone rang that it would be someone calling with bad news. New Year came and went without acknowledgement, the depth of their worry precluding celebration. Four months, one week, six days. How slowly that time must have passed for them.

And then, just when the furore around the Hocking Teens Disappearance was beginning to die down and other stories nudged their own to the back pages of the newspapers, Flynn, Tyrus, Chloe, Mei and Jonesy returned, wearing the same clothes they wore the night they disappeared, like revenants who had met their end on the same night as Jackson, but with a story that sounded more like a shared delusion than a true account of what really happened.

Flynn knows it would be easier to placate her mum with a fake story to account for those missing months, but she refuses to lie about what happened. Doing so would somehow be a betrayal to Jackson. Her only alternative is to shoulder the burden of her mum's disappointment and accept the suspicious glances and hurt recriminations.

'I did tell you what happened.' Flynn backhands tears from her cheeks.

'So you're sticking with that story?'

'I'm sticking to the truth.'

Her mum sighs, looks away.

'Flynn, I've tried not to push it, I really have, but I can't ignore what's happening.'

'Mum, I'm sorry, I can't do this right now.'

'You can tell me anything – *anything* Flynn.' She pushes her hands through her hair, and Flynn doesn't think she has ever looked so care-worn, so sad. 'I thought you knew that. Whatever you did, wherever you went, it doesn't matter. I won't be angry, but I need you to tell me.'

'I don't know what you want me to say.' Flynn's voice is flat, tired of this seemingly endless battle of wills. 'I haven't lied to you.'

'I suppose you're going to tell me it's just a coincidence,' her mum says bitterly.

'*What's* a coincidence?'

'That Mei died on her eighteenth birthday, too.'

Flynn's head snaps up, but her mum is staring into the corner of the room, oblivious to the sudden pallor of her daughter's face. She is still talking, but Flynn is no longer listening.

Since leaving Temple Fall, grief has blurred the passage of time, and she feels as though her feet are skimming the surface of days, weeks, months, unable to touch the ground. She mentally tries to find her bearings. She remembers Riley making a Valentine's Day card for a boy in her class a few days ago. She had given it to him yesterday... yesterday, the day Mei had died.

February 14th.

Mei's birthday.

'No.'

In her mind, the thin screech of a chipped shot glass scrapes against wood and the air is suddenly redolent of dust and weed and mould. Tyrus's slurred question echoes from the vault of memory: *How old will we be when we die?* Gelid fear tightens Flynn's chest as she recalls the glass spinning and spinning around the table before flying across the room and crashing against the wall in a spray of splintered shards.

I suppose you're going to tell me it's just a coincidence.

What's a coincidence?

That Mei died on her eighteenth birthday, too.

Flynn pictures the faint '1' traced into the surface of the table, the deeply gouged '8' beside it. Mei had called it an infinity symbol. Her words echo in Flynn's mind now.

It's also how a spirit frees itself.

2021

Flynn knows she has been in the Split too long. The tug in her belly is becoming more insistent, a dragging sensation deep inside her, an ache that is beyond physical. But she doesn't want to go back, not yet. She is having so much fun, sweeping through the clouds, racing unseen on the fading breath of The Night.

She has travelled a long way, maybe further than ever before. Covered mist-blanketed hills and rugged coastlines, crashing waterfalls and brilliant white cliffs. Below her now, deep gorges tower over a twisting river, a ribbon of black beneath the star-spattered sky.

She sweeps low, dips her fingers into the river, but she does not feel its cold wetness against her skin, and the surface of the glassy water does not ripple or distort at her touch.

The tip of the sun shimmers as it rises behind the high peaks, a molten crack that bleeds threads of colour into the clouds. A flock of birds soar through the air, black wings scissoring the peach-coloured sky. Laughing, Flynn chases them, but they keep formation, as though made of one mind, oblivious to their invisible companion. Flynn is one of them, a bird, flying free. She reaches out to touch one, to feel that shiver of energy, the percussive rhythm of life that flows through everything.

Then she feels it.

A hard pull at the base of her Unbiblical Cord, like the string on a balloon being sharply jerked. The sensation is all-encompassing, and for a moment, it erases all thought, the shocking wrongness of it. She rears back, seared by an agony beyond anything she has ever felt before. A rending in her soul, a deep, slow tearing.

Fear is usually a remote feeling in the Split, but it is as though that rent in her cord allows her emotions to spill through, and terror grips her, the realisation she is lost, unmoored. She has never cried in the Split before, but she is crying now, her breath catching in panicked, desperate sobs. She tries to focus on her sleeping body, wills herself back to it. But... nothing. Her Unbiblical Cord feels slack, a rope loosed from its anchor, and she is the ship, drifting untethered into the fathomless black of the sea.

Wake up!

It is normally so easy, so quick, the thought alone reeling her back to herself in the blink of an eye. But she remains where she is, floating above the cold river, a bird abandoned by its flock. Alone.

She bites back her sobs, tries again to reach for her connection, and she feels the agony of the wound, an injury caused by the strain of distance and time in the Split. She is sure if she tugs on it too hard, the frayed link will snap completely, and then she will never wake up. She curses herself for staying too long, for allowing this to happen.

Over the rush of blood in her ears and her own ragged breath, she hears someone crying. She stills, listening, trying to place the sound, which seems at once distant and right beside her. It floats up from the body of water beneath her, echoes faintly from every rock face.

Riley.

The sound clarifies, and as it does, Flynn hears her mum's voice.

Flynn. Flynn, wake up! Come on, now, Flynn. Flynn! Come on come on come on, *Flynn!*

Flynn closes her eyes, focuses on her voice.

Flynn, please, sweetheart, come on now, wake up! Please, baby, please, wake up!

She keeps her eyes closed, pushes herself towards her mum's voice and Riley's cries. But it is like working against an overwhelming G-force, as though her incorporeal body suddenly weighs as much as the mountains at her back. She drags herself through the darkness, clinging to her mum's voice, and the effort is almost more than she can bear: a slow, soul-burning agony, more effortful than climbing a rope hand over hand.

But she keeps going, keeps moving, like a deep-sea diver following but barely touching the line that leads them to the surface of the water. The pain in her cord sings out, invisible threads fraying, the damage worsening every time she reaches out to trace the feel of it, the faint tug at her navel.

The voice calling her back grows sharper, clearer, losing that distant, silvery quality, and Flynn clatters back into her body with a convulsive gasp. She lurches up in bed, her eyes wide.

Riley is stood in the corner of the bedroom, sobbing into her cupped hands, while her mum is sat on her bed, speaking into her mobile.

'Oh my god, oh god, she's awake!' She drops the phone and starts to cry, pulls Flynn into her arms. Rocking her as though she is a baby, asking over and over if she is okay, pulling her away to peer into her eyes.

Flynn blinks, a weariness settling deep in her bones. Dawn light pours through the windows. She has been asleep all night, but exhaustion sinks through her. She sags against the bed, and the speeding bump of her heart begins to slow.

She knows that if the cord had snapped, she would have died on the bed in her mum's arms. Such a close call, she is lucky to be alive. And yet it is tears of sadness, not relief, that blur her vision. Because she felt the rent in her Unbiblical Cord, the irreversible damage she has inflicted on that sacred connection. And she knows that if she ever Splits again, the chances are it will break completely.

NOW

Moonlight bathes the thin curtains, casting a blue-hued glow across Flynn's bedroom. She lies in bed, wide awake, her thoughts whirling. The sleeping tablets should have taken effect by now, but she has built up a tolerance over the past few weeks, and they don't seem to do anything for her anymore.

The timing of Mei's death has confirmed what, until now, Flynn has tried to pass off as paranoia: Temple Fall is *inside* her. Forced to acknowledge its presence, she can almost feel it, a sickness around the edges of her thoughts, an infection that can't be cut away. Like a house seeping radon, it has leeched part of itself into her, some malignancy not of the body, but of the mind. It is the thing that flares and flexes every time she thinks of her friends.

But that isn't the worst of it.

Something from the house is coming for them, bringing its dark gift on the day they each turn eighteen.

Jonesy's birthday is in less than two weeks, Chloe's in little over a month, while Tyrus doesn't turn eighteen until June. Flynn has a little longer, her birthday falling on 1 August – but how accurate is the date the doctors assigned as her birthday? In reality, her true birthday could be next week, tomorrow. It could be today...

She could turn eighteen at any moment.

Flynn remembers the shadowy figure that materialised behind Jackson moments before he fell through the window. She had managed to convince herself that she had imagined it, that the booze, the weed, the atmosphere in the house, had caused her to hallucinate the woman's appearance. But she had been fooling herself, because now she is sure that she was the entity who cursed them that night in the turret room.

Flynn pulls her laptop from beneath her bed, switches it on, and types *Temple Fall* into the search bar.

Most of the links that come up are for articles written during the time she and the others were missing. Salacious headlines, tasteless clickbait. *VAST HUNT ON MOORS FOR VANISHED TEENS; JACKSON DARROWS'S FATHER HELD FOR QUESTIONING; MOTHER'S TEARS FOR SON WHO TOOK HIS OWN LIFE; MISSING TEENS SEEN IN VEGAS; £25,000 REWARD TO FIND HOCKING TEENS; FLYING SAUCER OVER MOORS NIGHT OF TEENS' DISAPPEARANCE; STILL NO CLUES IN MYSTERY OF HOCKING TEENS DISAPPEARANCE.*

Flynn scrolls further, past a Wikipedia page for Temple Newsam Manor and Castle, an old estate that is now a Grade I listed building. Temple Fall Rentals, Temple Fall Dentist Practice and a Wikipedia link to a Joseph Stewart Temple Fall, a Canadian military officer in World War I.

Frustrated, she changes the search to *Temple Fall Haunted* but that only throws up dozens more links to Temple Newsam and the Blue Lady who supposedly haunts the estate. It is the same problem she ran up against when she first heard from the genealogist that her ancestor, Lyda Gray, had lived in the house.

She is about to give up the search when her gaze catches on a website titled Skeleton Key. Beneath the link, the article's opening lines begin:

Search any list for the most haunted properties in England, and you'll find no mention of Temple Fall. Its dark history has been covered up, the house itself left...

Flynn's pulse quickens. She clicks on the link and a photograph of Temple Fall fills the screen. The sight of it scuttles goosebumps down her arms and neck, an insectile heave that flows beneath her skin.

Behind the house, flamingo-pink clouds frill a lavender sky. The sloped moors are quilted in heather, a lush patchwork of purple swirled through swathes of green grasslands. The scenery is so pretty it almost looks surreal, and yet its beauty acts as a sharp counterpoint to the house, which appears even more imposing and inhospitable by comparison.

The building gloats over its surroundings, ruinous and darkly majestic. Trees crowd close to its walls, a verdant cloak that seeks to conceal it from view. The house's aged stone walls, choked in vines and darkened by moss and lichen, should make it blend with the surrounding nature, yet it remains somehow apart. As though the earth itself has heaved it forth, a misbegotten and malignant pregnancy it sought to reject.

Above the external shot of the house, two rows of thumbnails show its interior. The sight of those derelict rooms makes Flynn's stomach clench with remembered terror. The article below is dated 12 May 2005.

The Chequered History of Temple Fall

Search any list for the most haunted properties in England, and you'll find no mention of Temple Fall. Its dark history has been covered up, the house itself left to rot, and yet Temple Fall is one of the most dangerous houses in England.

It was the summer break from university, 1998, and I'd picked up a job working in the Old Crown Tavern in Brinley Cliffe. That's where I was when I overheard some of the regulars talking about Temple Fall. I can't remember what they said now, only the grim, furtive way they spoke the name of the house. It was strange, out of keeping with their usual manner. I asked them about it, but they wouldn't be drawn on the subject, and when I pushed, they told me to mind my own business and let it go.

I could tell that something about the place unnerved them though, and I was baffled. These were gruff, plain-speaking, salt-of-the-earth old men with weathered faces and work-scarred hands, not the sort of rattle-brained new-age airheads I'd have expected to believe in ghost stories or superstitions. I suppose it was curiosity over what could have spooked them so much that motivated me to research the house.

Temple Fall was a black hole on the internet. I couldn't find anything out about it at all, but I got the address from the public archives, and the name of the current owner, a Mitchell Lister. I decided to visit, thinking maybe I'd take some photos, then get the shots doctored, really give people something to talk about.

The morning I drove to the house, the sky was clear and blue, scrubbed clean by recent spring rain. Everything gleaming and bright, daffodils and gorse blossoms and fresh green shoots scattered and swaying in the breeze. I drove with the windows down and breathed it all in. I was young and healthy and life was good. I think that drive was my last truly happy memory.

As soon as I saw the house, my mood sank. I know it sounds melodramatic now, but my reaction felt physical, like the gut-drop you get when you receive bad news or relive a traumatic memory. That sensation of falling, even when your feet are planted firmly on the ground.

It's pointless to wish now that I'd listened to my instincts, turned round and driven home, but it's the truth. There are a handful of decisions in life which seem innocuous enough at the time, but that looking back, you realise were pivotal moments, a crossroads of sorts. This was one of those moments.

That realisation didn't hit me until I stepped foot inside the house, and by then it was too late. I didn't see or hear anything, but every hair on my body lifted, like the house was this huge electrostatic generator. Something singing beneath the skin. Or screaming.

The place was a ruin. I snapped a few quick photos in the lobby, but I didn't dare explore the house any further than that. I was pretty freaked out. I'd only been in there a few minutes, but every second took a sledgehammer to my nerves. And that staircase... It was one of those grand, bifurcating ones, and I remember looking at it, the middle rolled out like a tongue and the yawning darkness above, and I was struck by the idea that the house was hungry.

I pelted back to my car, practically stood on the accelerator as I drove away, tyres spewing mud. I couldn't stop shaking, and my eyes kept flicking to the rear-view mirror. I don't know what I expected to see, only that I felt as though something had followed me out of that house, that it was with me in the car.

That night, I barely slept. Every time I closed my eyes, I was back inside Temple Fall. I drifted off at some point, but when I woke, it was to an agonising pain at the back of my neck.

At first, I put it down to the fact I'd spent hours tossing and turning, but over the next few days, the pain spread. My knees felt as though someone was driving hot pokers into the cartilage, my wrists and ankles throbbed. Every joint in my body felt overblown and hot and the pain was so intense I could barely move without sobbing.

A blood test was conclusive: rheumatoid arthritis. A case more severe than almost any that the specialists had seen. The new term started at university, but I could barely get out of bed. I started to miss my lectures and eventually, fell so far behind that I had to drop out.

People argued that the onset of my symptoms coming just hours after my visit to Temple Fall was nothing more than a coincidence. That there is a history of the condition in my family, nothing too shocking about my diagnosis. That while the house is undeniably creepy, it isn't sentient, and certainly isn't actively evil. That if anything infected me, it was the fear and paranoia of other people. That it's just a house. They would point out all the other people who have passed through its front door and escaped unscathed.

In answer to that, I would say the house has periods of dormancy. Like a living organism, it possesses its own circadian rhythm, latent spells where it sleeps unaware of those who wander through its rooms and halls. But when it rouses, it feeds.

Sometimes, I catch myself thinking about the house, not with any sense of fear, but a strange sort of nostalgia. As though it's a past home full of fond memories. When I come round, I can smell its rooms on my skin, can almost hear its corpsing laughter in my head. It's enough to drive anyone insane.

Flynn's eyes track back to the name of the owner of Temple Fall. Mitchell Lister. She types his name into the search engine, which throws up another piece, titled: *Leeds Man Released without Charge for Murder and Attempted Arson*. Flynn clicks on it.

Mitchell Lister, a high school teacher from Otley, Leeds, who was being held on suspicion of the murder of his wife and son and arson, has been cleared of all charges. Mr Lister, who has no criminal record, was arrested at his home in the aftermath of the fire that claimed the lives of his wife and son.

Police found three empty petrol cans in his car, but later evidence exonerated him of the crime. His car was captured speeding over fifty miles away from the fire at the time it took hold, and CCTV images from inside a gas station some forty miles from his home, taken only ten minutes before the fire started, show him buying the cans of petrol that were later discovered by the police.

When questioned about the purpose of the petrol cans, Mr Lister claimed he had bought them with the intention of burning down Temple Fall, a property he had inherited from his deceased mother, Eliza Lister. But in a bizarre twist, while Mr Lister was attempting arson at Temple Fall, a fire started in his own home, claiming the life of his wife Amanda Lister (31) and their son Benjamin Lister (19 months).

Investigators found no evidence of arson in the charred ruins of Mr Lister's home, nor any evidence of accelerant.

Flynn types: *Eliza Lister, property developer* into the search bar, clicks a link to a newspaper article, headlined: *PROMINENT PROPERTY DEVELOPER TAKES OWN LIFE.*

Eliza Lister (54), a well-known property developer, has been found dead in her apartment after an apparent suicide. Ms Lister was involved in property all over West Yorkshire and is said to have completed over fifteen property deals in the UK worth approximately four million pounds.

Ms Lister had no previous history of mental illness and was not being treated for depression. Her suicide is said to come as a complete shock to her family. Her son, Mitchell Lister, said she had been eager to commence work on her most recent acquisition, a country estate on the edge of Brinley Cliffe.

The circumstances of Ms Lister's death are said to not be suspicious.

Flynn chews her lip, frowning. Eliza Lister, a successful property developer, dead by her own hand. Her son, Mitchell Lister, a high school teacher with no criminal record, arrested on suspicion of murdering his own wife and son.

A creak on the landing makes Flynn's eyes snap to the door. A floorboard pops softly. She sits up, blood beating in her temples. It is almost one in the morning. Riley should be fast asleep and Flynn heard her mum go to bed hours ago.

There is a rustle of movement outside her door, then silence closes around the sound. A shadow falls across the strip of light beneath Flynn's door, a thick bar of darkness.

Flynn's heart thuds against the chopping block of her sternum, her vision jumps. She wonders if this is it, the end. She stills, listening, but all she hears is the hard thump of her pulse.

'Who's there?' Her voice is thready with fear, her breath, fast and shallow.

The door swings slowly open, the creak of the hinges like a drawn-out death rattle, a sound that floods cold terror through Flynn and shrinks the skin down the back of her neck.

Riley stands in the doorway.

Flynn sags against the headboard as her little sister shuffles into her room. She is dressed in her Maleficent costume, the black and purple dress and the skullcap with the long black horns and widow's peak, but instead of dark feathered wings, she has a Ghostbusters proton pack bolted to her back. Her skirts rustle as she moves towards Flynn's wardrobe, the wand of her proton pack held in front of her as though ready to blast a hiding ghoul.

'Ry, what are you doing? It's the middle of the night.'

'I thought I heard a noise. A *ghost* noise.'

'Ghosts aren't real.' Flynn thinks of the woman standing behind Jackson the moment before she pulled him through the window and represses a shiver. 'And if they were, I'm pretty sure they wouldn't make any noise.'

'This one did. I heard it.'

'Ry, come on, it's late–'

Riley shoots Flynn a querulous look and presses a finger to her lips. She turns back to the wardrobe, places one hand on the door handle, then flings it open, grasping her wand in both hands and aiming it at Flynn's clothes. Her little shoulders relax as she turns back to Flynn.

'This room's clear.'

'What a relief,' Flynn mutters, slapping her laptop closed and sliding it beneath her bed. 'Interesting costume. I didn't know Maleficent was a Ghostbuster.'

'Maleficent doesn't need to be a Ghostbuster, she's *Maleficent*. She can crumple a proton pack with her *mind*.'

'Seriously, you should be asleep.'

'Can I sleep in here?' Riley says. 'I've adapted my utility belt so I can keep you safe!'

Flynn's gaze drops to the Batman belt Riley has fastened around her Maleficent dress. Something metallic glints in the one of the pouches. 'Jesus, is that a carving knife?'

Riley glances down, as though she has forgotten what she has stuffed down her belt.

'Fucking hell,' Flynn says. 'You've got Mum's cheese knife, too.'

Riley's eyes widen. 'You said "*fuck*".' She mimes the swear.

'Put those knives down before you cut yourself.'

Riley scowls, but pads across the room, pulls the cheese knife and the carving knife from her belt and places them on Flynn's desk.

'Come on, weirdo, what else are you packing?'

Riley sighs, reaches behind her, pulls the meat prongs from the back of her belt, and slaps them beside the knives.

'You're a psychopath,' Flynn mutters. 'Now go to bed.'

Riley looks stricken. 'But I'm unarmed!'

Flynn punches her pillow, then collapses onto it. 'It's safer for you that way, trust me.'

'I'm sleeping in here.' Riley folds her arms and glares at Flynn.

'No, no way. Go on, get.'

'Oh, please, Flynn,' Riley begs, then in a small voice. 'I'm scared.'

Flynn rolls over, shuts her eyes. ''Night, Ry.'

'Please please please please please pleeeeeeeeeeeease...'

'Riley!'

Riley falls silent, but Flynn doesn't hear her shuffle out of the room. She can practically feel her little sister's huge anime eyes fixed on her, silently begging.

Flynn groans into her pillow. 'Fine, but you're going to have to lose the fancy dress.'

'Can I keep my batarang?' Riley asks, pulling the small bat-shaped projectile from a pocket in her skirt.

'You know, normal kids take teddy bears to bed.'

Riley giggles, then starts to peel off layers of fancy dress, revealing Mickey Mouse pyjamas beneath. She removes the cap with the Maleficent horns attached, making her hair stick up in wild clumps.

'Hit the switch, weirdo.'

'Okay!' A happy skip in her voice now. Riley turns off the light and dashes back across the room, as though terrified something will reach out of the darkness and grab her. She scrambles into bed, clutching her batarang to her chest. Flynn pulls the duvet over her little sister's shoulders. Her hair smells like strawberry shampoo, her warm skin like Crayola and candy necklaces. Flynn listens to Riley's breathing deepen, feels her body relax beside her. She watches the shadows turn on the walls, listens to the swish of cars passing outside, and the knot of tension behind her eyes begins to unravel.

'Don't go away again, Flynnie,' Riley murmurs, her voice blurred by the sleep which is already smudging the edges of her consciousness. 'Don't leave me.'

Flynn turns to look at her. In the shadows, Riley's face crackles with a febrile tension, a small frown pinches her brow. Guilt spears Flynn. She knows that she is the reason her kid sister is struggling at school, why she no longer sleeps at night.

'I won't,' Flynn says, ignoring the voice at the back of her skull that whispers that she will and that there is nothing she can do to stop it. Her gaze hardens in the darkness. 'I promise.'

~

It is the morning of Mei's funeral. Flynn sits in the back of a taxi, her reflection in the mirror as bleak as any mourner, but she is not going to the woodland burial site where her friend is being laid to rest.

Flynn's mum had tried numerous times to persuade Flynn to join her at the ceremony, making it quite clear she considered her refusal petty and selfish. She thinks Flynn is clinging to grudges, which is incomprehensible to her after what happened to Mei. But alongside her mum's evident disappointment, Flynn recognises a brittle hurt and confused bewilderment over what she perceives as her daughter's continued refusal to open up and confide what had really happened in Temple Fall. She knows Flynn is keeping secrets, and the knowledge is eating away at her.

Flynn leans her head against the window as they roll past unfamiliar streets. She presses back the guilt over not attending the funeral, tells herself that she doesn't have the luxury of time to grieve for Mei; Jonesy's birthday is only eleven days away.

But while this is true, other reasons for avoiding the funeral scratch below the surface of her subconscious.

Part of it is denial, the simple fact that she just isn't ready to see Mei being lowered into the ground. Her death doesn't feel real, just as Jackson's still doesn't feel real. Over the past few weeks, Flynn has retreated so far from reality, she can almost trick herself into believing they are both still alive, waiting patiently for her to set her anger aside and call them, and that when that time comes, they will answer.

Another part of it though, is reluctance to see Chloe, Tyrus and Jonesy. Every time her thoughts turn to them, she remembers the shadow of scepticism she'd seen in their faces when she told them about the figure that had materialised behind Jackson, the silent recrimination in their eyes, the suspicious glances. Even now, the memory of it stokes the anger skulking at the back of her mind, a violent pulse in her thoughts.

When she thinks of her old friends, she again sees the wretched fury on Chloe's face – *What the fuck did you do?* – feels her fingernails digging into her arms as she shook her – *You pushed him, didn't you?* – the burning sting of her hand across her cheek.

Resentment gnaws at Flynn, a constant gripe in the pit of her stomach. In flashes of clear-sightedness, she realises these darker thoughts are not entirely her own, that the house is somehow inflating her paranoia, spreading its poison inside her. Manipulating her. That it *wants* to turn her against her friends. But however hard she tries, she can't rationalise away the raw emotion these thoughts evoke, can't reason the anger away.

Her brief return to college had failed to help her reacclimatise to normal life. Because of her troubled past, the attention focused on her by her peers was far greater than that which Mei, Chloe, Jonesy or Tyrus had endured. Lingering gazes and sly whispers mutated into malicious rumours and small cruelties. Students scribbled insults on her locker door and in her textbooks – *psycho*, *freak*, *weirdo* – and even her teachers seemed to look at her with an air of distrustful wariness.

Worse than the bullying was the conviction that Chloe was responsible for the rumours. Since starting back at college, she had been hanging round with Nola and Macy, two of the biggest gossips at Elliott Dean, girls that only a few months ago Chloe would have gone out of her way to avoid. Flynn would often turn to catch the three of them huddled together, watching her, only for their eyes to drop away, their expressions shifty, sly.

Possessed with neither the motivation nor the desire to knuckle down and catch up on all the work she had missed over the course of her disappearance, less than two weeks after restarting college, Flynn dropped out. The grief she refused to fully acknowledge flattened into a deadening depression, and her old anxieties flared, fear of the Outside making her turn increasingly inwards so that she spent long hours locked in her bedroom.

The taxi stops at a set of traffic lights. A young girl on a skateboard sails across the pavement, her hair snapping behind her in the breeze. She reaches the underpass of a bridge, flips the board into her hands and barely breaking stride, jogs down the steps. Her laid-back grace and casual athleticism remind Flynn of Mei. A fine crack hazes the surface of Flynn's denial. *She'll be in the ground by now.*

The lights change, the taxi driver drives on. He turns into a car park and pulls up outside Greenfields. The psychiatric hospital is a large red-brick building surrounded by landscaped gardens. Neat squares of lawn are spaced like green picnic blankets between meandering pathways. Benches occupy shady spots beneath the trees.

Flynn climbs out of the taxi, zips her coat up against the chill. Nerves churn in her stomach as she approaches the entrance. She wonders how severe Mitchell Lister's mental decline has been since the death of his wife and son. Will she meet with a catatonic old man, incapable of answering any questions about Temple Fall? Or will Mitchell Lister have the presence of mind to recognise the lie that has gained her admittance to visit him? Perhaps he will be angry, refuse to talk to her at all, or fly into a rage, become abusive, violent...

Flynn takes a deep breath, reminds herself why she is here: Jonesy's birthday is a matter of days away. If anything bad happens to him when there was something she could have done to prevent it, she will never forgive herself. Whatever information she can glean from Mitchell Lister will help her decide what to do next.

The walls of the reception area are decorated in colourful pastels that match the modular furniture; sheet vinyl flooring shines beneath squared recessed lights. A curved reception desk occupies one side of the room, a small Costa Coffee stall nestles in the other.

Flynn's heart thumps as she approaches the woman sat behind the desk.

'Hi, my name's Flynn Lister, I'm Mitchell Lister's great niece.' She feels her cheeks flame with the lie. 'I called yesterday to see if I could visit him.'

Flynn had not anticipated any real problems getting in to see Mitchell; from what she could gather, Greenfields seemed to operate more as a rehabilitation home than a secure psychiatric hospital. Still, there was no way to be certain, and she figured the small white lie might bolster her visitation request.

The receptionist gets her to sign in and points her towards the waiting area. A few minutes later, a nurse is leading her down the corridor towards the 'recreational room'. He is dressed casually, in jeans and a T-shirt, a name tag – *ALFIE* – clipped to his breast pocket.

'So, you're Mitchell's niece?' Alfie says.

'Yeah, that's right. I mean... *great*-niece,' Flynn answers without meeting his eyes.

'Ah, that's nice. He'll be happy to see you, it'll make his day to get a visitor.' Alfie stops at a door and swipes a key card over a sensor. The pad flashes green and he pushes the door open. 'He hasn't had one for a long time.'

'Oh.' Guilt squirms inside Flynn as she follows Alfie through a lobby. 'I'm sorry to hear that.'

'Well, you've a small family, haven't you?' Alfie darts Flynn a look that makes her wonder if he knows she has lied her way into the building. 'So anyway, this'll be good for him. It makes a big difference to patients when people from outside come to visit, gives them a lift, ya know?' He holds his key card over another sensor and pushes a door open. 'We're just in here.'

Flynn follows him into a large recreational room. A TV, bracketed by three sofas, plays a film to a small group of patients. Freestanding bookshelves, thick with books, occupy the opposite side of the room, and a middle-aged man quietly browses the reading material. Tables are set up with various activities and board games. A girl who can't be more than a couple of years older than Flynn sits at a desk, colouring in a picture. On the opposite side of the room, there is an opening in the wall, a member of staff sitting on the other side, like a ticket-teller in a booth. Flynn watches her pass someone a steaming mug from a small kitchen to which, presumably, patients are not permitted access.

Flynn had anticipated an atmosphere of sickness and mayhem, imagined patients sitting blank-faced and drooling onto their starched gowns, or wailing and shouting until they had to be restrained. But there is not a white gown in sight, and for the most part, everyone appears cognisant and self-controlled. The atmosphere is calm, almost serene.

Alfie leads Flynn to an old man who is sitting in front of the window. He is painfully thin, his arms like pipe cleaners sticking out of his baggy shirt. His skin is almost translucent, his white hair so fine, it barely covers his liver-spotted scalp. In profile, Flynn can see the lattice of blue veins spidering across his temple.

'Mitchell, your niece is here to see you.' Alfie places his hand on the old man's shoulder, but Mitchell continues to stare out of the window. 'Sorry, *great*-niece.' Alfie smiles at Flynn. 'I'll leave you both to catch up.'

Flynn shifts her feet, feeling like an imposter and a fraud. She wonders whether she has made a mistake. The accident that killed Mitchell Lister's family happened in 1984 when, according to the newspapers, Mitchell was twenty-nine years old, which means he can't be any older than seventy now, yet the man before her looks well past his hundredth birthday.

Flynn glances over her shoulder at Alfie, fighting the urge to call him back and make an excuse to leave. Because this frail and desiccated man can't be Mitchell Lister.

'Temple Fall.'

Flynn's head snaps back to the old man. His voice is raw and ruined, a faint rasp of sound. And yet, as quietly as he speaks, those two words open a trapdoor beneath Flynn.

'How did you—'

Mitchell turns to Flynn. His eyes are an age-rinsed blue, clotted with cataracts and sunk in darkness. His cheeks are collapsed hollows. A life of pain is carved into the deeply riven lines of his face. His lips quiver, as though with repressed emotion, but then they twist into a strange, sly smile. The shadows beneath his eyes deepen and Flynn tenses as she feels something slither to the surface of her consciousness in response, like a snake sliding its head above the water.

'How did I know?' Mitchell finishes her question. His voice scrapes like wet gravel, and Flynn wonders if he has throat cancer or polyps. 'It's inside you. I can *smell* it. It works its way inside so it can eat its way out again. That's how it *feeds*.'

Flynn sinks into the seat beside him.

'What do you mean?'

'It feeds,' Mitchell says, speaking so quietly that Flynn has to lean towards him to catch his words, 'and it doesn't stop. It doesn't quit. And now it's feeding on you, isn't it? You're on the hook, yes you are, I can see it. Your soul, hooked up like a bag of saline as you drip... drip... drip-feed yourself to the house.'

Flynn's skin crawls at the thought, but she does not question the veracity of his words; she can feel the house moving inside her, a dark uncurling at the back of her mind.

'Mr Lister, a few months ago, I went to Temple Fall with my friends and now... now two of those friends are dead.'

Saying it out loud doesn't make it any more real to Flynn. The words taste like the lies she told to gain admittance to visit Mitchell. The old man's eyes move back to the window. Feathers of snow have started to drift from the sky, embroidering the trees and benches in a chilly lacework.

'There's nothing I can say that will help you.'

'Please. I just want to hear what happened to you in that house.'

Mitchell closes his eyes. Pain trembles behind his closeted features.

'I tried to save them,' he says, 'but there was nothing I could do.'

He opens his eyes again, and the emotion in his gaze is raw and fresh, as though the horror he has lived through happened only yesterday.

'I'm so sorry,' Flynn says, a clutch of pity in her chest.

Mitchell stares out of the window, at the slow tumbling snowflakes, memories turning in his faded gaze.

'It started as soon as she bought the house...'

Mitchell starts to talk, slowly at first, as though testing the waters of the past, wary of what might rise from those murky depths. Sometimes he stops, presses a clenched fist to his lips, pained by some agonising memory, or pauses to take a trembling sip from the glass of water beside him. Other times, he seems to forget what he is saying altogether, his face growing still as his memories snag like wool on a hook, lost in his own recollections until Flynn prompts him to continue.

MITCHELL

1984

As I moved through Temple Fall, I couldn't help but think I'd made a terrible mistake. I'd only visited once before that day, but once was enough to convince me that Mum had been right: the house was diseased.

I'd felt it in the way the small hairs down the back of my neck frizzed when I stepped inside, in the chill that slipped over my skin. The building felt sickly. Infective. Standing in the lobby, old aches and pains that had not troubled me for years flared, and as I moved through the rooms, I felt off-kilter, as though I'd just knocked back a few hard shots of gin. It was then, during that first visit to Temple Fall, that I considered the possibility that the house had been the catalyst for Mum's mental decline.

But that day, standing in the lobby with the sun's sullen heat seeping through the glass and the breeze trickling through the open door at my back, I felt none of that oppressive menace.

It's just a house.

I'd repeated these words to myself many times since my first visit there three months before, but that was the first time I believed them. I felt suddenly foolish about calling the priest over. It seemed so... melodramatic.

My mum, Eliza Lister, had been a successful property

developer before her death shortly after her acquisition of Temple Fall at auction. The house was a wreckage, with sagging floors, crumbling walls and a collapsed roof, but none of that had mattered to Mum, because she'd planned to tear the building down and build eight small cottages where the old house stood. The nearby village of Brinley Cliffe had become a tourist hotspot in recent years, and the rural setting was ideal for luxury holiday rentals.

Prior to purchasing the house, Mum had submitted plans to the planning department, requesting permission to carry out the work. They had been approved without a hitch, but after she'd signed the contract, bat droppings were discovered in the loft space. Mum had been forced to delay building work until an ecologist's survey could be completed, which would advise on plans to protect the bats during the demolition, but before that could happen, they had to wait for the bats to roost there again.

The wait had abraded Mum's nerves like nothing ever had before. She became obsessed with the house, constantly calling the ecologist for updates, enquiring about the hold up and questioning the report's necessity. Her behaviour had baffled me; Mum was an experienced professional, accustomed to building delays. Besides, Temple Fall was far from the only project to which she could have turned her attention.

The delay stretched on for months, and as Mum waited for news, she became increasingly reclusive. When I visited, she was jumpy, nervous and eager to usher me out of the door. She had always taken pride in her appearance – nails manicured, clothes tailored, her diminutive figure propped up on towering heels even when visiting building sites, as though they were as essential as her hard hat and high-vis jacket – but in the weeks and months following her purchase of Temple Fall, she became increasingly slovenly, drifting round her apartment in her night clothes all day, oftentimes failing to get out of bed at all.

She stopped eating and her weight plummeted. Even my son, Benjie, who she had always doted on, failed to hold her attention. The only thing that seemed to occupy her thoughts was Temple Fall.

After a couple of days of her failing to answer her calls, I drove to her apartment. When she didn't answer the doorbell, I let myself in with my own key. I found her lying on her bed in a pool of vomit, empty pill packets scattered across the bedside table and a bottle of gin on the bedstand. She had been dead for days.

Later, working through her effects, I found a receipt for the hire of a bulldozer. Sick of waiting, it seemed she'd been planning to bulldoze Temple Fall herself. I was devastated, and yet the image of my Lilliputian mother operating a bulldozer shocked from me an amused chuckle, which turned into full-bellied laughter before it tipped into something else, and I realised I was bawling on the floor like a baby.

As her only child, I inherited all Mum's properties. Most were rentals that brought in a steady income, and so rather than sell them and incur hefty capital gains taxes, I allocated their management to a letting agent. Temple Fall was the exception that I decided to sell. That was, until I visited the property a few days after Mum's funeral and realised there was something very wrong with the house.

But as I stood in the lobby, waiting for Father Heskin to arrive, I began to suspect I had allowed paranoia and stress to get the better of me. Temple Fall wasn't evil. It was bricks and mortar, glass and stone. Nothing more.

I turned to leave, already thinking of what excuse to give the priest when he arrived, when my gaze fell on a wooden rocking horse. It was standing in the shadowy space between the two staircases, a beautiful silver-dapple mounted on a bow, with a glowing white mane and black-painted hooves. Bronze stirrups and polished buckles, a red saddle of leather and velvet. Glass eyes of burnished amber seemed to smile out at me, impish and playful.

I slid the palm of my hand down its smooth flanks and wondered how I missed it the first time I was there. The wood felt warm, almost *alive*. Benjie wasn't two years old yet, too small for something as grand as this, but in a few years...

I pulled the rocking horse from the darkness, dragged it to the door. My muscles strained, sweat popped up on my brow as I carried it down the porch steps to my car. I realised I was grinning, though I couldn't understand why. I didn't notice the clumps of cobwebby hair falling from the horse's mane, the paintwork flaking from patches of black mould, the wood crumbling beneath my touch. I didn't even realise when I cut my hand on a rusted screw, lifting the rocking horse into my car boot.

I slammed the boot closed just as headlights splashed the dirt road and a car pulled up outside Temple Fall. A tall, slim man with horn-rimmed glasses, dark hair and a priest's clerical collar climbed out.

I walked towards him. 'Father Heskin?'

'You must be Mr Lister.'

'Mitch, please.'

We shook hands, and Father Heskin frowned at a smudge of blood on his palm.

'I think you've cut yourself.' He nodded at my hand with a faint wince. 'Do you need a bandage?'

I blinked, startled to see blood dripping down my palm. '*Shit!* I mean, I'm so sorry, I didn't realise.' I cringed, mortified. 'I was just clearing things up in the house, I must've caught it on something. Here, let me get you something to clean it off.'

'It's nothing, really.' The priest pulled a handkerchief from his pocket, wiped the smudge of blood away. 'Is it deep?'

I glanced at the cut, baffled by how I managed to draw that much blood without noticing. 'It's fine, I think it's stopped bleeding.'

I considered the priest. I had expected someone much older, an imposing grey-haired man with a supercilious air and a booming voice that would carry from the pulpit. But Father Heskin looked to be in his mid-forties, and his voice was low, gentle. Behind his glasses, soft grey eyes were framed by a fine spray of wrinkles that deepened when he smiled. Stubble dusted his chin, giving him a pleasant, rumpled look and a demeanour that was instantly endearing.

'It's an impressive house.' Father Heskin's eyes moved over the high walls.

'You're very diplomatic, Father,' I said. 'It's a collapsing ruin, and it hasn't been lived in for over a hundred years. The locals are very superstitious about the place, and I suspect that's partly why it sat empty for so long.'

'It's not unusual for traumatic events to leave an imprint on a place,' the priest said, his gaze lingering on the darkened windows.

I frowned. 'Traumatic events?'

He turned to me with a look of faint surprise. 'Forgive me, it's probably just as you say – local superstition.'

'About that...' I felt heat climb my cheeks. 'I think I owe you an apology. You see, my mother – she was very unwell towards the end, and she became convinced there was something wrong with the house. She was delusional, obsessed with tearing it down. I suppose I blamed the house for her death, but to be quite honest, I was in a dark place and not myself at all when I came here for the first time. It was so soon after her funeral...'

I spread my hands, embarrassed, hoping the priest could read between the lines.

'You think you've overreacted,' Father Heskin said. 'That

you allowed your mother's delusions to cloud your thinking.'

'Exactly,' I said, grateful for his understanding. 'I feel so silly about it all now, especially after dragging you all the way out here.'

Father Heskin turned and regarded Temple Fall, his expression thoughtful. 'Your mother,' he said. 'What was she like?'

'Well...' Disconcerted by the change in topic, I nevertheless considered the question. 'She was a single mother, a businesswoman. Tough as nails, but then she had to be, I suppose, the property industry as it is, dominated by men. She was pragmatic, hardworking – very hardworking. It must've been tough for her, bringing me up on her own after my dad left us, but she was always good to me.' I heard pride edge into my voice and was surprised and embarrassed to find my eyes were misting with tears.

'And you,' Father Heskin said, still watching the house, 'would you say you're a credulous man?'

I smiled, understanding now. 'I know what you're getting at, and no, I wouldn't say I'm a credulous man. I learned scepticism very early on, I'm afraid. It's hard to believe in magic when you're a kid brought up by a hard-headed single mother working to support herself. Too many Santa mishaps and amnesiac tooth fairies.' I shot the priest an apologetic smile. 'I'm sorry, Father, but I can't say I even share my mum's belief in God. Blind faith seems so... irrational to me.'

Father Heskin nodded. 'Quite unscientific, I agree.'

'Yes.' I offered an awkward smile. 'Quite.'

'And yet you walked into this house, and you felt something was wrong. Felt it keenly enough to change your mind about selling it. I remember when we spoke on the phone, you sounded quite shaken. As I recall, you said the house was *evil*.'

I followed the priest's gaze to Temple Fall. A chill squirmed through me, like a maggot breaking through smooth, blemish-free fruit.

'Did I say that? Well... I don't know what came over me, but it's just a house.'

My voice sounded weak, lacking the conviction I had felt before the priest showed up.

'Perhaps you're right,' Father Heskin said, turning his clear grey eyes to me. 'But I'm here now and it won't do any harm to look around. At the very least, I can perform a house blessing.'

If Father Heskin felt the same menacing atmosphere that I had felt the first time I entered the house, he didn't show it. He walked from room to room, explaining that he would begin the blessing upstairs and systematically work his way back down to the lobby, so he could leave a final blessing at the front door.

He chatted amiably as he picked his way across piles of rubble, his manner relaxed, friendly, but I found myself only half-listening to what he was saying. I felt increasingly uneasy, though I couldn't quite pinpoint the cause of my escalating tension. A musky scent clung to the air, vaguely feral, as though we were stood in the domain of wild animals. I recalled the bat droppings discovered in the loft space and wondered whether the colony had spread through the entire house.

Father Heskin chose one of the bedrooms on the top floor to begin the blessing. An iron bedframe stood against the back wall, a heavy oak wardrobe occupied the corner. Exposed wooden beams in the ceiling were festooned in cobwebs, the windows were coated in dirt and dust that smothered the crepuscular light.

He slipped his purple stole over his shoulders, and removed his bible from the bag, as well as what looked like a saltshaker, which I assumed must contain holy water. The priest began to pray, his voice as hushed as a parishioner speaking in the middle of a sermon.

With a solemn, 'Amen,' he crossed himself then walked towards me. 'In the name of the Father, the Son and the Holy Spirit,' he said, marking the sign of the cross on the air in front of me.

'The Lord is our shepherd and leads us to streams of living water. Let this water call to mind our baptism into Christ, who by his death and resurrection has redeemed us.'

As I watched the priest move round the room, the air seemed to thicken. Tension curled in the pit of my stomach. I told myself that I was imagining it, but I couldn't shake the feeling that the house was agitated. I realised I was ascribing human emotion to an inanimate building, but my unease persisted, alongside a growing conviction that Temple Fall was seeking to repel us.

Father Heskin walked round the room, shaking holy water over the walls and praying softly. My heart beat up in my throat, heat prickled over my skin, and I felt a sudden urge to turn and run out of the house. I wanted to believe I was imagining the gathering charge on the air, that strange tension I couldn't quite put my finger on, but I was suddenly convinced that our presence had stirred something inside the house to anger.

'We pray for those who died here, that they may move on in peace.'

The priest's voice was low, soothing, but when he turned round, I saw his face had grown pale and his brow was stippled with sweat. The house blessing felt as though it was turning into something else, the prayers changing, acquiring an urgent intensity that had not existed at the start. As though the priest and the house were in some sort of private communion.

Father Heskin hesitated, wiped the back of his hand across his brow. Then, instead of spraying holy water from the saltshaker, he tipped some directly into his hand and used it to mark the sign of the cross onto the wall.

'In the name of Jesus Christ,' he murmured, moving to the window, which he started to mark with another cross. 'Our God and Lord, strengthened by the intercession–'

He froze, his thumb pressed against the window. His eyes were glassy, fixed on something outside that I couldn't see. Water slipped down the glass like a tear down a grimy cheek. Rashes of gooseflesh broke across my skin.

'Father?'

He blinked, sucked in a convulsive gasp of air, then slashed a horizontal line through the vertical one. He moved back into the hallway, drew the shape of the cross on the air.

'We drive you from us, whoever you may be, unclean spirits, all satanic powers, all infernal invaders, all wicked legions, assemblies and sects.'

'Father, maybe we should stop,' I said. 'This doesn't feel right.'

Ignoring me, the priest opened the door to the next room. He used the holy water to mark crosses onto the walls, then on the bedframe.

'In the name and by the power of our Lord Jesus C-Christ, may you be snatched away and driven from the church of G-G-G–'

Father Heskin closed his eyes, and a tremble passed through his body. The fine dew of perspiration on his brow was now a lather of sweat that covered his face.

'Snatched away and driven from the church of G... G... *God*!' He almost shouted the word, then swayed, as though he had been dealt a dizzying head blow. 'And from the souls made to the image and likeness of God and redeemed by the p-p-precious blood of the d-divine lamb.'

He shot a darting, frightened look round the room.

'Father, are you okay?'

But one glance at the priest was enough to see he was far

from okay. Palsied tremors rippled through his body and his skin had taken on a bloodless pallor. He leaned one hand against the wall, his hair falling over his eyes.

'Father, I really think we should stop now. Please, sit down for a minute.'

'We mustn't stop now... Mustn't stop...' The priest swallowed, his throat clicking audibly.

I pictured all the glistening wet crosses scored into the fabric of the room, like tiny wounds on a huge beast, and I was struck by the sudden urge to knock the shaker from Father Heskin's hands and swipe my sleeve over all the damp marks.

'The most high God commands you,' the priest said, speaking louder now, 'and he with whom in your great insolence you still claim to be equal.'

His voice was hard-edged, commanding. Somewhere in the last few minutes, this had turned from a house blessing into something else entirely.

'G-G-God the Father commands you and G-G-G...'

I winced, covered my nose in the crook of my elbow as a foul stench swilled on the air. Father Heskin shook more holy water onto his hand, but this time, instead of marking a cross on the wall, he smeared it beneath his nose, the way a coroner would smear Friar's Balsam beneath their nostrils before an autopsy.

'G-God the son c-c-commands you and G-God the—'

An expression of anguish filled his face and he shook his head violently from side to side. His voice, eloquent and clear when he had spoken to me outside Temple Fall, was now slurred, as though he had chased half a bottle of whisky.

'Be silent!' he hissed, then shook more holy water into one cupped palm, dragged it over one ear then the other. It dribbled down his neck, soaked into his collar. '*Be silent!*'

'Father?'

'Submit yourselves therefore to God,' the priest muttered to himself. 'Resist the devil and he will flee from you.'

His back straightened and his eyes moved over the room. He lifted his voice. 'God the holy ghost commands you—'

His eyes locked on something in the corner of the room and he stilled.

I took a step towards him. 'I must insist that we stop—'

'The s-sacred sign of the cross commands you, as does the p-power of the mystery of the Christian faith.'

Something rippled behind the priest's features, a brief look of malice that plunged shadows into his face and doused his eyes in darkness. He giggled, a strange, high-pitched sound that sprayed goosebumps across my skin. But the giggles quickly turned to sobs. He shook holy water into his cupped hand and dragged his wet palm over both his eyes.

'The glorious Mother of G-God and the virgin M-Mary commands you.' He set his teeth, planted his feet, as though anchoring himself to the ground. 'The faith of the holy apostles P-Peter and Paul, and of the other apostles c-c-commands you.' He ground the words between his teeth, as though they pained him to speak. 'The blood of the martyrs and the pious intercession of all the saints c-command you!'

He lifted his right hand, started to make the sign of the cross on the air. 'Begone, Satan, inventor and master of all deceit, enemy of man's salva—'

His arm locked, as though the air had sealed around it like a block of ice. His body stiffened, his eyes flooded black with panic. The shaker of holy water dropped to the floor.

The foul smell in the room thickened, animalistic, metallic – *alive*. The fingers of the priest's outstretched hand splayed wide, some invisible force wrenching them apart. His thumb snapped with a dry *pop*. Father Heskin howled but his hand remained welded to the air, as though his wrist was pinned by an invisible nail, and it remained there as each of his fingers snapped, one after the other, the sound like dry kindling cracking underfoot. His eyes rolled in pain, his knees sagged.

The light from my torch dimmed, darkness swooped. Father Heskin dropped to the floor. I started towards him, but the priest curled into the shadows, cradling his hand to his chest and jabbering nonsensically.

I crouched beside him, tentatively placed a hand on his shoulder.

At the contact, the priest's head snapped up and I peddled back with an alarmed cry.

Father Heskin's sweat-greased skin was the colour of old cheese and saliva dribbled from his quivering lips. His pupils were black coins, wet and sliding, fear pulled his lips into a clenched grimace.

Still babbling, he pulled himself to his feet and lurched towards the door, but as soon as he passed into the hallway, the door banged closed behind him with a force that shook splinters from the frame. I cried out, grabbed the handle. The door wouldn't budge.

I felt a presence in the room, a swelling pressure in my skull. I swept my torch over the shadows. The darkness seemed to peel away too slowly from the bright light, as though it possessed a texture, a malevolent sentience. I rapped the side of my fist against the door, yelled at the priest to come back. The darkness swelled, tension stretching like a thin-lipped smile.

I grabbed the handle again, hysteria bubbling up inside me at the thought of being stuck in that room all night. This time it turned easily, and I pelted down the hall. My torchlight arced over the faded wallpaper as I ran, rubble crunching beneath my feet. I hurtled down the staircase, longing to feel fresh air on my skin, to slam the front door to this terrible house closed behind me.

I was halfway across the lobby when I heard Father Heskin's car engine roar to life. By the time I reached the porch steps, the priest's tail-lights were fading in the distance.

When I arrived home, both Amanda and Benjie were fast asleep. The events of the evening combined with the emotional trauma of the past few weeks had left me weary to the bone, but I knew I wouldn't sleep. The house clung to my thoughts like a stain I couldn't wash away.

I showered, turning the heat up as high as I could tolerate and scrubbing my skin until it was raw. I brushed my teeth to try and rinse away the foul taste of the house, wrapped myself in a dressing gown, and went downstairs.

The radiators ticked with heat, the house slumbered. My skin tingled from the scalding shower, but my bones felt steeped in a brittle chill. In the kitchen I chased a shot of whisky, and winced at the unpleasant taste as it mingled with the lingering toothpaste. I poured myself a second measure, which I sipped more slowly.

Taking both the bottle and glass into the sitting room, I lit the fire and sank into the armchair beside the flames. The logs popped and cracked, reminding me of the sound Father Heskin's fingers made as they snapped. I closed my eyes, but the priest's face swam up in my mind, his youthful features cragged with terror, spittle flying from his lips as he jabbered and rocked on the floor.

Finally, I drifted off into a restless sleep.

I was roused by a chill breeze playing across my skin. I sat up, disoriented, my thoughts muzzy with whisky and sleep. Darkness frilled the edges of the curtains. The fire was still burning, the radiator behind me was warm to the touch, but the room's heat had been sucked out, as though a window had been flung wide.

I moved to the hallway. The front door stood open.

'Mandy?'

The answering quiet implied I was the only one in the house awake, but the prickling down my arms and neck signalled that the opposite was true. Dread dropped in my stomach. I walked towards the front door, peered outside. The streets were quiet, the sky black. Lamplight splashed pools of light on the waterlogged road in rippling skeins of silver.

I closed the door, locked it.

Back in the living room, I picked up my whisky, but before I could drain the glass, I heard a thud behind me. I swung round, listening. Slowly, I set the glass down.

Silence... *thud*.

Silence... *thud*.

It's just a door banging in the frame. But there was no breeze, not now that I had closed the front door, and besides, this banging did not have the firmness of wood meeting wood. It was a dulled, dampened sound, the sound of something solid striking fabric.

Thud. Silence... *Thud*. Silence...

Coming from the staircase. As though someone was moving up them, dragging something that knocked against the riser with each step.

'Mandy?'

Fear turned my voice to a choked whisper. I couldn't move. Because I knew whatever was moving up the stairs, it wasn't my wife. The air was leavened with the stench of Temple Fall, the ripe aromas of mouldering rot and unaired rooms. And even though I had closed the front door, an inhuman cold crackled on the air.

The knocking stopped, turned to a slither across the carpet on the landing, moving towards Benjamin's bedroom.

Benjie!

I started forwards, as though my son's name was the gunshot and I the runner waiting with hair-trigger nerves on the starting line. The immobilising fear of self-preservation was replaced by the galvanising fear that something terrible might happen to my child, the urge to protect him overpowering the terror of what I was rushing towards.

The foul smell became almost unbearable as I neared his bedroom, a corruption of decay and sickness, greased by the scent of tallow candles. I was a few paces from the door when an unholy racket started up inside. I grasped the handle, threw the door open.

Every musical toy in Benjie's bedroom had been switched on or wound up. Notes filled the air like shards of glass, nursery rhymes collided, dancing lights skipped across the walls. The lullaby lightshow rotated, spraying glowing moons and stars across the walls; the pullcord puppy on the wall sang 'Frère Jacques' as its eyes rolled; the Happy Apple on the windowsill chimed and rocked; the musical mobile above Benjie's cot played a melody as it spun; the toy monkey clashed his cymbals.

It was as though a hyperactive child had rushed round the bedroom, winding up every toy, flipping every switch on. The tumult of sounds bludgeoned my senses, but that was not what made my breath stop and my legs buckle beneath me.

Benjie was stood up in his cot, bouncing his knees and babbling contentedly. One dimpled fist gripped the bars, the other reached between them, his plump fingers curling around the long silver hair of a rocking horse.

I had forgotten all about it in the aftermath of Father Heskin's hasty flight from Temple Fall, and only now remembered carrying it down the porch steps, wrestling it into the boot.

But I had not taken it out of the car when I arrived home.

It was barely recognisable from the gleaming antique that had so enchanted me earlier, but I knew it was the same one.

The wood was rotten, the paintwork flaking away. The horse's mane and tail, a glossy silver a few hours ago, were now filthy and snarled, the stirrups rusted. Its eyes, which had been polished amber, now possessed an unnatural gleam, and they rolled in its skull, skittish and wild, as though it was in paroxysms of pain.

These details rippled through my consciousness, lesser shocks to the horror right before me.

A little girl sat in the horse's saddle. She was perhaps six or seven years old. A red ribbon was tied in a bow on top of her head, and her dark brown hair spilled over her shoulders in carefully styled sausage curls. Her unblinking eyes were frosted blanks, windows to a world reflecting endless rolling grey mists. Her pale skin possessed a bluish tinge and was covered in patches of the same mould as the rocking horse, as though they both suffered the same affliction. She grinned at me, exposing teeth that were blackened stumps. It was a grin rimed in spite, and it sliced through me like a filleting knife.

She can't be real. She isn't real. The thought brought no comfort, because here in my son's bedroom, she had weight and texture. I could *smell* her, a foul smudge on the air.

She turned back to Benjie. My vision dimmed when I saw that the back of her head was missing, the curve of her skull pulverised like a dropped melon, revealing splinters of bone, pulped brain, ribbons of flesh. A meaty viscera slid down her shoulders.

I would not later remember grabbing Benjie from his cot, but suddenly my son was squirming in my arms and I was racing down the hall, yelling for Amanda. I burst into our bedroom, found her already pulling on her dressing gown. She pushed sleep-mussed hair from her eyes and looked at me, her face bright with alarm.

'What is it?' She swept forwards to take Benjie in her arms.

Down the hall, the crashing melodies were slowing as the wind-up toys grew still and then fell silent.

'What's wrong with him?' Amanda looked her son over, searching for some sign of injury or sickness. Distressed by his mother's fussing, Benjie arched his back and began to cry.

'He's fine,' I said, my voice clipped. 'Take him downstairs.'

'Shhh, baby, it's okay,' Amanda cooed, cradling Benjie to her chest. 'No, Mitch, look at him, he isn't fine. He's burning up. And what the hell was that racket?'

'Mandy, please. Just take him downstairs.'

Amanda stared at me, her expression morphing from concern to confusion.

'Mitch, what's going–'

The phone in the hallway rang, a shrill blare that was so unexpected, so sudden, we both jumped. The temperature dipped, an icy snap against my skin. I stared at the phone. It was almost three in the morning, a time to which a drilling ringtone did not belong.

I started towards it.

'No!' Amanda backed away, staring at the phone. A look of profound terror contorted her face, and she held Benjie closer to her body, cupping the back of his head in one hand. 'Don't answer it.'

'It's probably just a wrong number.'

'Mitch–'

'Dammit, Mandy! Please, would you just take him downstairs.'

The shrill scream of the phone tightened my scalp. I snatched it from the cradle mid-ring. The severed sound echoed through the house, a ghostly tone in the sudden lake of silence. I lifted the phone to my ear.

I heard a faint wash of crackling static. Then, ragged breathing and a voice, almost inaudible behind the curtain of silver hissing.

'Hello?' I said.

The breathing on the other end of the phone grew louder, as though the mysterious caller had moved the receiver closer to their mouth. My gaze shifted to Benjie's bedroom door. I knew if I saw the handle as much as twitch, I would scream.

On the line, a quavering inhalation, then one word, wetly gargled:

'Burn...'

The voice sounded choked, gasping, but I recognised it instantly.

'Father Heskin?'

On the other end of the phone, a sob. A liquid, burbling sound.

'Buuuurrrn...'

I stared at Benjie's bedroom door. Couldn't take my eyes off it.

'Father, I can't hear you. Where are—'

'Burrrrrrn... it... down...'

The line went dead. The instant it did, the cold dissipated, the tension on the air faded. I lowered the phone back into its cradle.

I saw the flash of the speed camera, but I didn't slow the car.

Burn it down.

Father Heskin's voice had sounded strange on the phone, pale as smoke, each wetly burbled word bitten with pain. I tried to ring him back, but his call went straight to voicemail. Now, the priest's words turned over and over in my mind as I tore through the night-dark streets.

Amanda recoiled when she saw me drag the rocking horse from Benjie's bedroom, shocked and disgusted that I had brought such a hideous thing home for our son. Her revulsion quickly morphed into anger, and I snapped at her, telling her that I would get rid of it, but when I grabbed my car keys and started to heave the rocking horse out of the front door, Amanda had tried to stop me, confused by the extremity of my distress, upset that I was going out so late without explaining myself.

You said you wanted it out of the house!

I do! But, Mitch, it's the middle of the night! Surely it can wait until morning.

But what I couldn't tell her, what she wouldn't understand even if I tried to explain, was that it *couldn't* wait.

Now, as I drove, the skin along the nape of my neck crawled. When I had returned to Benjie's bedroom for the rocking horse, there was no sign of the little girl, but I felt her presence now. It made my legs shake and my hands grip the steering wheel so hard my knuckles were sharp white caps. I avoided looking into the rear-view mirror, terrified that if I did, I would see that evil little face watching me from the back seat.

Temple Fall came into view, jagged and insane against the wildness of the moors. Every window was illuminated, rectangles of light blazing against the darkness. As though the house had awoken to welcome home a long-lost daughter. I turned down the long, rutted driveway. Petrol sloshed in the boot, and I drew comfort from the sound.

Burn it down.

I cut the engine, flung the car door open. Without bothering to close it, I moved to the boot, inserted the key into the lock. I hesitated, overwhelmed by the sudden certainty that the rocking horse wasn't inside. That somehow, in the seconds it had taken to close the boot and climb into the driver's seat, the little girl had opened it again and removed it. That as I drove away from my house, she was dragging the wooden horse back up the stairs into Benjie's bedroom.

I twisted the key, yanked the boot open.

The rocking horse was there.

I wrapped one hand around the horse's mane, curled the other around its flanks and heaved it out. Sweat beaded the nape of my neck, my muscles strained. I was a fit man, played football on weekends, lifted weights in the gym three times a week, but my calves, shoulders, back and arms all burned from the exertion of carrying the rocking horse earlier. And yet I was supposed to believe a little girl dragged it up the stairs to Benjie's bedroom, all on her own?

But she wasn't an ordinary little girl, was she?

No, she was a dead *little girl.*

I turned and looked up at Temple Fall. Wet veils of fog slid across its walls, like floating threads of silvery hair. I thought of Mum, her rapid mental decline in the aftermath of purchasing the house, her increasing desperation to raze it to the ground; I thought of Father Heskin, composed and articulate at the start of the house's blessing, a jabbering wreck by the time he fled.

I dragged the rocking horse up the porch steps. In my haste to flee Temple Fall earlier, I left the door wide open, which was just as well, as I had forgotten to bring the front door key with me now. I slid the horse across the wooden floorboards of the lobby, placed it back where I had found it, then returned to the car for the petrol.

I emptied the first can as I moved up the lobby stairs, drenching the carpet in petrol, sloshing it over the paintings. The second, I poured out in the sitting area, soaking the sofas and rugs, the side table, the curtains. I used the last can to douse the lobby. The astringent stench of petrol filled my nostrils, and I drew it deep into my lungs, as though it was fresh, green air. I thought of Mum, imagined her watching in silent approval.

I retreated to the porch, removed the matches from my pocket. Took one out and struck it.

Flame spurted from the head.

I was smiling when I held the flame in front of me. I hoped

the house could see what I was doing; I wanted it to know what was coming.

I tossed the lit match through the open door.

A gust of hot air washed over me, exhaled breath ripe with the scent of death and spoiled meat. It snuffed out the flame before it landed on the petrol-soaked floorboards.

A chill wrenched up my spine. I took another match from the packet, moved closer to the open door. I lit it, leaned forwards and threw it inside. But again, that foul breeze soughed over me and extinguished the flame.

The smile on my face had wilted. I tried to fumble a third match from the packet, but my hands shook so violently I dropped the box. Matches scattered across the porch decking. Sobbing, I sank to my knees, began to pick them up and stuff them back into the box. I set one match aside, then soaked the matchbox in the dregs of petrol from one of the cans. I struck the one remaining match against the ground, then dropped it onto the petrol-soaked box. It burst into flames as all the matches inside ignited, and I kicked the blazing conflagration into the house.

The box slid across the floorboards...

A small foot stamped on top of it.

The little girl from Benjie's bedroom grinned at me from inside the house. Flames flickered over her legs, the bottom of her dress caught fire.

I started forwards – I couldn't help it – the horror of seeing a child engulfed in flames overriding even my own terror, making me forget briefly why I was there. But then I saw something else that made my skin flare, a scald of horror hotter than any fire.

The space around the girl's small frame did not belong to the dark-panelled walls of Temple Fall.

It belonged to Benjie's bedroom.

It was impossible, because she was stood only a few paces

away from me, and yet beneath her soiled feet, I saw the grey-and-white tartan carpet of Benjie's room, part of his cot, the edges of his blue sailboat curtains. I saw Fozzie Bear, Bungle and Sootie propped against the wall in the background, their shiny glass eyes flickering with reflected fire: yellow, orange, red.

A burning rag of cloth dropped from the girl's dress onto the floor. Fire pulsed across the carpet. And I heard Benjie's sleep-soaked whimper.

I was falling, falling into a howling darkness.

The girl's grin spread like flame.

Watching me, with her blackened toe she pushed the burning matchbox beneath Benjie's cot.

I lurched forwards as a lash of fire spread beyond my vision but left Temple Fall untouched. It blazed across Benjie's bedroom, flared over his teddy bears. The fire was primal, alive, devouring everything, as though the accelerant I poured over the rooms in Temple Fall had slipped through space to soak into the walls of my own home.

Benjie's whimpers escalated to a searing scream. Heat rushed over my skin as I careened forwards. The power of the fire was a brute force, pushing me back, but I forged through it, Benjie's name on my lips. My skin tightened, my lungs burned. Fire singed the hairs on my forearms. I opened my mouth to call out for my son, but scalding heat dried my throat and stole my breath. Smoke in my nostrils, tears stung my eyes. I dropped to my knees, choking, covered my nose and mouth with my shirt. But I was disoriented now, smoke-blind, my consciousness slip-sliding.

Even over the roar of the fire, I heard Benjie's screams, high and desperate and agonised, and it felt like a fist squeezing my heart. But then the sound of his cries broadened, split into a hundred voices, men, women, children, and all of them screaming... screaming...

Another dry wave of heat pulsed over me. I lifted my head, groped with my hand.

My knuckles knocked against something – the edge of Benjie's cot? – and it was as though the contact doused the fire. The smoke cleared, silence dropped, not gradually, but in a stroke.

I sucked in a cold, damp breath of air and blinked my stinging eyes. My clothes were scorched, my lungs ached, and my mouth felt as though I'd wrapped my lips round a flame thrower. But Temple Fall betrayed not so much as a scorch mark, not a smouldering patch of carpet, not a rising wisp of steam.

The girl had gone, the rocking horse was where I left it. The opening to Benjie's bedroom had disappeared.

I staggered down the steps of Temple Fall, my son's dying screams echoing in my ears as I fumbled the car key into the ignition and tore home.

FLYNN

NOW

Mitchell falls silent. He looks exhausted, his eyes haunted, the retelling of what happened to him that day leaving him spent.

'I still hear his dying screams.' Mitchell's voice is crushed by emotion. 'Even after all these years... My boy. And there was nothing I could do.'

'The house tricked you,' Flynn says gently. 'You can't blame yourself for what happened to your family.'

Pain trembles in every line and wrinkle of Mitchell's face. He turns away from Flynn, stares out of the window. 'I was supposed to protect them.'

'But how could you have known—'

'Stop.' Mitchell lifts his gnarled hand to shield his eyes. 'Please. I've told you what happened, and I'm sorry, really, I am, but there isn't anything else I can do for you. I'd like you to leave now.'

'There must be something else you can tell me,' Flynn pleads. 'What about Father Heskin? Maybe I could reach out to him and ask—'

'Father Heskin died minutes after he drove away from Temple Fall. He was doing over seventy miles an hour on that country road when he wrapped his car around a tree. Apparently, the tyre tracks made it look like he'd swerved and skidded to avoid hitting something.'

'But you said you spoke to him that night, you said after–'

'He'd been dead for hours when he called.' A hardness creeps into Mitchell's voice, an unswerving rigidity that almost dares Flynn to challenge him. 'Sometimes I wonder whether it was even him, or whether it was the house… mimicking him.'

Flynn stares at Mitchell, and briefly considers the possibility that he really is insane, that his mind broke after the death of his family, that he fabricated a wild story to try to explain the tragedy that claimed their lives. But every word of Mitchell's account resounds with truth, and the shattered way he speaks of what happened echoes the haunted clarity of lived experience.

'Maybe an exorcism,' Flynn says. 'Another priest?'

'Call a priest,' Mitchell says, 'and you'll only have another death on your conscience.'

'But there must be something you can tell me that will help. *You* went inside that house and you survived.'

'Oh, I survived,' Mitchell says, his mouth twisting in a bitter smile, 'but I didn't *want* to.' He turns his hands over to show Flynn the deep twists of scar tissue down the insides of his wrists. 'Believe me, I've tried to end things more times than I care to recount. But the house won't let me go.'

Flynn feels a clutch of horrified pity. The injustice, the cruelty of what the house has done to Mitchell, what it is doing to him still, what it is doing to *all* of them, curls her hands into tight bulbs of rage.

'I'm trapped,' Mitchell says, 'trapped by this body and by the *thing* that lives inside it.' A look of fear flares in his eyes, a stricken, fathomless terror. 'That house – it knows what I'm doing, at the first drop of blood or the first skipped heartbeat or the first failed breath.' His hands move to his throat and his gaze acquires a haunted, faraway look. 'I haven't attempted to end things for a long time – not since I tried with the bleach. What's the point? It's always watching, waiting. It always *knows*.'

'The bleach...' Flynn whispers, appalled understanding stealing the strength from her voice. 'Oh my god, what did you do?' But even as she frames the question, she can picture Mitchell drinking bleach, his rheumy eyes streaming as he fights the urge to vomit the poison, his oesophagus burning, his central nervous system shutting down.

'I just want it to end.' Tears film his eyes. 'But the house always finds a way to save me.' That word, *save*, is imbued with such bitterness, it seems to seep into the air around them, briefly tainting everything a sour yellow. Mitchell offers Flynn a humourless smile. 'I think it likes the taste of my suffering.'

'How can it know?' Flynn says. 'How can it know what you're doing? How does it stop you?'

'You know how.' Mitchell taps his temple. 'It's inside me, just like it's inside you.'

His face buckles with despair, and he curtains his face with his hands. Flynn's throat tightens as she watches his narrow shoulders hitch with choked sobs. She sits forwards, her hand itching to reach out and comfort him.

'You're already dead.'

It isn't the words that make Flynn's blood run cold, as much as the voice Mitchell uses to speak them. It is a *woman's* voice, possessing none of Mitchell's guttural coarseness. It creaks with menace, and though it betrays no evidence of vocal damage, somehow it sounds even more abrasive than his natural voice. The smell of tobacco swirls on the air, mingling with the scent of sour meat.

Slowly, Mitchell lowers his hands. Flynn cries out, jerks to her feet, knocking her chair over.

His face looks the same, and yet it is utterly transformed.

As though some hidden shadow version of his personality has risen from beneath his skin. The anguish of moments ago has been replaced by an expression of spite and cruelty, and as Flynn stares at him, the milky cataracts that occlude his blue eyes fade, his irises darkening to a brown so deep they are almost black. The lines and creases in his face shift and flicker, as though freshly scarred. His mouth thins and flattens into a miserly line, his thin, white hair thickens and darkens as his hairline slopes lower, a sleek shadow sliding down in a widow's peak.

The face of the woman who had materialised behind Jackson swims beneath Mitchell's features, a flickering undulation beneath the skin.

Nausea washes through Flynn as she feels something rise inside her, a strange *recognition* that spills towards Mitchell, as powerful as metal shavings drawn to a magnet.

The woman grins, and it is a terrible, creeping thing. Flynn's hands cover her mouth, and horror screams through her when she feels an answering smile beneath her fingers, a fixed, rigid grimace that does not belong to her.

Mitchell's face contorts, his body stiffens. Cords stand up down his long, frail neck, and he grinds his teeth, like a prisoner strapped to an electric chair. A dark stain spreads across his crotch, and as it does, the rictus grin withers from his lips and the shadow woman dims and recedes.

Flynn reels round, looking for someone to help, but catching her own reflection in the window, her vision sways. Her face is blank, as though her features have been smudged, like soft clay pressed smooth. She tries to scream and the oval face in the mirror contorts, the space where her mouth should be flexing, a writhing blankness.

Flynn sits in a booth at Mrs Rafferty's Cafe, cradling a cup of tea and tensing every time the jangling bell above the door announces another customer. She is wearing a baseball cap in an attempt to conceal her face from people who might recognise her from the news, but still, she notices the double takes her appearance elicits, the way people's eyes keep slipping back to her, the girl who takes her phone from her pocket and snaps off a quick shot when she thinks Flynn isn't looking.

She wouldn't normally linger in a public place like this, open to scrutiny and curious whispers, but leaving Greenfields yesterday, she hadn't been thinking clearly when she'd texted Jonesy, Chloe and Tyrus, asking them to meet her here.

She has barely spoken to any of them since Jackson's death, and now that they are to be reunited her belly is knotted with nerves. It doesn't help that she has barely slept. All night, she replayed the moment Mitchell Lister's face changed, the way his bones slid beneath his skin, his hairline slithering forwards as shadows reshaped themselves around his features. And his voice, that *woman's* voice – *You're already dead* – had played over and over in Flynn's mind, as maddening as the music she had heard echoing through Temple Fall.

Happy birthday to you!

(you're already dead)

Happy birthday to you!

(you're already dead you're already dead already dead dead deaddeaddeaddead)

The doorbell jangles and Flynn looks up as Tyrus and Jonesy walk in. At the sight of them, something hisses inside her, as though scalded by their presence. *They think you pushed Jackson.* She can almost taste the anger that stiffens her spine, the bitterness of resentment coating her tongue. She itches to stand up, to push past Jonesy and Tyrus and hurry out of the cafe. Her hand even reaches reflexively for her coat, but then she freezes, closes her eyes. *These aren't my thoughts. It's the house. It wants to single us out.*

She clasps her hands together, watches Tyrus and Jonesy weave through the chairs and tables towards her.

Jonesy smiles as he approaches, but it falls far short of his usual megawatt grin. He opens his arms, and before she even realises what she is doing, Flynn has risen from the booth and is folded against his broad chest. The resinous stench of weed clings to his clothes, comforting for its familiarity.

'Hey,' Jonesy says, into her hair. 'It's good to see you.'

Flynn's heart clutches and for a moment she doesn't trust herself to speak. She glances at Tyrus as he slides into the booth, and he drops her a brief nod. Flynn can hardly blame him for the cold reception; out of all her friends, he has been the most persistent trying to reach her, sending her texts and leaving voicemails, all of which she had deleted without reading or listening to.

Flynn and Jonesy sit across from Tyrus, and for a few moments, silence pools around them, as though they have forgotten how to speak to each other. Flynn tries not to stare at her friends, but they almost look like strangers to her. Dark smudges squat beneath Jonesy's eyes and his blonde curls are grimy and matted. The twinkle of mischief has faded from his blue eyes, replaced by a haunted guardedness. Tyrus has lost weight, and he has the worn, crumpled look of an insomniac. His brown eyes are veined with burst capillaries, and his umber skin is dry, patched with ecthyma. The smell of stale booze seeps from his pores.

'You look like shit,' Jonesy says, breaking the silence.

'Self-care hasn't really been a priority over the last few months,' Flynn says with a shrug. 'And hey, if we're going there, you're not looking too hot yourself.'

'We thought we'd see you yesterday,' Tyrus says. His knee jitterbugs beneath the table.

'Yeah, I know. I couldn't... There was something I had to do.'

'Bullshit.' Tyrus glares at her. 'I'm sorry, but what could've been more important than Mei's funeral?'

Anger stabs behind Flynn's eyes, a flare of heat beneath the skin. She stares at the table, revulsion curling through her as she recognises the house's flex of alien rage. 'I don't want to fall out,' she mumbles.

'Oh, she doesn't want to fall out,' Tyrus says, flashing Jonesy a hard look. 'Hear that, TJ? She doesn't want to fall out.'

'Look, I didn't ask you to come here so we could argue,' Flynn says. 'I know I've been distant, and I'm sorry I've been a shit friend, but ever since that night...' She drops her eyes as the ache of tears presses against her throat. 'I haven't been myself, and I can't–'

The bell above the cafe door jangles, and silence seems to close around the sound as Chloe steps inside. A few months ago, every head would have turned in admiration towards the beautiful blonde with the exquisite face, colt legs and silky skin, but now, her appearance elicits shocked gasps and grimacing winces.

Flynn watches her approach the table with a plummeting in her gut. She has never known Chloe to leave the house without ensuring she is meticulously put together, but today she looks as though she has ripped an IV from her arm and absconded from her hospital bed. She is shockingly thin. Wearing scuffed ballet flats, a vest and skinny jeans, her clinging clothes only draw attention to her gaunt frame, her jutting clavicle, the xylophone of bones on her chest. Huge tortoiseshell shades cover half her face, but fail to conceal the sunken hollows of her cheeks. Her cornflower hair has thinned and hangs in greasy ropes.

''Sup, bitches.' Chloe slings her bag onto the table and slides into the booth beside Tyrus. She removes her sunglasses and picks up the menu, studiously avoiding looking at Flynn.

Chloe's face is make-up free, and her fingernails, usually so immaculately manicured and painted, are bitten down to stumps. Her eyes are flat, her skin is dull and dry. She looks worse than she had right before she received her diabetes diagnosis.

'You guys ordered yet?' Chloe says.

As though summoned by the question, a waitress sidles up to their table to take their order. Flynn and Tyrus ask for coffee, Jonesy gets a milkshake with fries, and Chloe a hot chocolate and a glass of water.

'So, to what do we owe the pleasure?' Chloe says, continuing to study the menu, even though they have ordered.

'Clo,' Jonesy says mildly. 'Don't start, okay?'

'Start what?' Chloe lowers the menu and glares at him. 'I'm not starting anything, I just want to hear what she has to say.' Her gaze swings to Flynn, her eyes bright and hard. 'Well? Where the fuck were you yesterday?'

'Fuck you, Chloe.' The words slip out, forked and spitting. 'I don't have to explain myself to you.'

'Yes, you do,' Chloe snaps. 'You don't get to give us all the cold shoulder after everything we've been through, then snap your fingers and expect us all to come running. You can't just treat people like shit and expect–'

'You think *I* treated you like shit? After what you and Jax did in that house, you think *I'm* the one in the wrong?'

Chloe drops her eyes. 'We didn't do anything.'

'You were making out with my boyfriend right in front of me.'

Chloe shakes her head, a shuttered look clattering down her face. She pinches a few strands of hair between her fingers, and with a quick tug, rips them out. Flynn flinches at the sound of the bulbs tearing from Chloe's scalp. She stares at her friend, chilled by the sudden violence of the gesture.

Jonesy reaches out, places a hand over Chloe's and shoots Flynn a warning look.

'Flynn, you wanted to see us, we're here,' he says. 'What's this about?'

Flynn sags, the anger rushing out of her. 'I didn't go to Mei's funeral yesterday because I went to visit Mitchell Lister at Greenfields Psychiatric Hospital.'

Jonesy frowns, his face blank. 'Who?'

'The guy who owns Temple Fall,' Tyrus says, watching Flynn.

Chloe flinches. 'I don't want to talk about that.'

'I had to see someone who knew the house, someone who'd been inside it,' Flynn says, ignoring Chloe. 'I needed answers.'

Tyrus leans across the table. 'Go on.'

'I know none of you believed me when I told you what I saw when Jax...' Flynn lowers her eyes. 'After a while, I almost managed to convince myself that I'd imagined it, imagined *her*. Standing behind Jackson right before he fell.'

The sounds of the cafe seem to grow muted, as though a curtain has been drawn around their table, deadening the noise. 'But I didn't imagine it. I saw a woman, she *was there* when Jackson died, and I think...' She swallows, lifts her gaze to her friends' expectant faces, reminds herself that they need to know the truth. 'I think she was there when Mei died, too.'

Flynn tells them everything, starting with her visit to Greenfields. She explains what happened to Mitchell's family, his mother's overdose shortly after purchasing Temple Fall, the death of his own wife and baby son; she tells them about the absences she has been experiencing since leaving the house and the dark thoughts that weave so seamlessly with her own; and finally, she tells them what she had seen and tried so hard to dismiss the night they visited Temple Fall: the number '18' carved into the surface of the table after the seance.

When she has finished, the others stare at her in silence. She shifts in her seat, cradling her coffee. The sounds of the room, which seemed to have quietened as Flynn spoke, suddenly swell: the clink and chatter of teacups against saucers, the cafe's jazz music, the background babble of customers, the squall of a baby. She takes a sip of her coffee but it has grown cold. She sets the cup back on the table with the sudden desire for something much stronger.

'What are you saying?' Jonesy breaks the silence. 'That Jax and Mei were *what*? Cursed?'

'This is bullshit,' Chloe sneers. 'She's just saying this because she blames herself for what happened to Mei.'

'Why the hell would I blame my–'

'Because maybe if you hadn't given us all the cold shoulder, she would've reached out to you,' Chloe snaps. 'Maybe then she wouldn't have been on her own doing stupid stunts on her birthday, she would've been with *us* and none of this would've happened.'

'This isn't all on me.' Flynn glares at Chloe. 'I didn't see you reaching out to her any more than I did. You were too busy hanging out with Nola and Macy, spreading rumours around college about me and–'

'Stop it, just *stop!*' Jonesy says, a pained look creasing his face. 'It was an accident, a terrible accident, and that's all there is to it, okay?'

'No.' Tyrus sets his mug of coffee on the table. A fissure of distress behind his dark eyes betrays the crack in his usual imperturbable manner. 'I don't buy it. This is fucking Spider-Mei we're talking about.' His eyes shift to Flynn. 'That building had railings and ledges all the way down. She could've scaled it with her eyes closed.'

'Ty, come on,' Chloe says, turning to him with a pleading look.

'I spoke to her mum after the funeral.' Tyrus speaks through the catch in his voice, his eyes distant. 'She said some bloke saw her fall, that he called the ambulance straight away, even though...' He shakes his head, digs his thumbnail into a groove in the table. 'She died on impact, it wouldn't have mattered if the ambulance was there on site, but he called 999 right after she fell.

'The call went through at 15:02. Mei's mum was so cut up about that, because she said that was the same time Mei was born.' He looks up, the lash of panic behind his dark eyes. 'Mei fell to her death the very moment she should have turned eighteen.'

Fear skims Chloe's face. 'Ty, what are you saying?'

'Ever since we left Temple Fall, I've felt strange,' Tyrus says. 'Like there's something moving beneath my skin, something...' A shudder passes through him, the edges of his mouth twist down. 'I have the most fucked-up thoughts, and it makes me sick coz I know they're not mine. It's like... like there's suddenly this other frequency inside me and my thoughts keep tuning in to it.'

'After what's happened over the past few months, it's no wonder you're a mess,' Chloe says. 'We all are.'

'No. This is something else. Look, before we went into that house, I'd never touched a drop of booze, and I would've sworn I never would, but now...' He shakes his head and laughs softly, but there is an expression of such profound terror in his eyes, Flynn has to look away.

'I had my first drink in that house and I don't even remember it. I told myself to forget it, that it was a one-off, but I was kidding myself. Since we left, I have these blackouts, and I guess I must start drinking, coz when I come round I'm so pissed I can barely stand. Sometimes, there'll be an empty bottle of vodka or whisky in my room. A couple of days ago, I woke up on the floor with my face in my own puke, this bottle of Jack

Daniel's knocked over beside me.' He looks up at them, horror welling in his dark eyes. 'I don't even remember opening it.'

'You were probably just caned.' Chloe's eyes are shielded. 'That's why you don't remember—'

'Clo, you're not listening,' Tyrus snaps. 'I'm not saying I was so pissed I don't remember opening it. I'm saying I don't remember taking a drink at all. Shit, I don't remember where I even got that bottle of Jack. It's like... like...'

'Like black ice in your mind,' Jonesy says tonelessly.

Flynn's scalp prickles. 'It's happening to you, too?'

'It started almost straight after that night.' There is no need for Jonesy to specify which night he is talking about; their time in Temple Fall – which had turned out to be so much more than one night – is like a line drawn in blood, dividing their lives into two parts: Before and After.

'I started smoking more, and at first, I figured it was just a reaction to everything that had happened, you know? But then I started sparking up without even realising what I was doing.'

'On autopilot,' Chloe says.

'No, it isn't that. I'm in a fucking trance or something, Clo, and when I snap back to reality, the ashtray's overflowing with stubbed-out joints and I'm stoned off my tits. Jesus.' He pushes his hands into his hair. 'Sometimes, I'm so baked I can't even stand up. It got so bad, I lost my job in The Dive and my mum kicked me out. I'm back at my dad's now, but he's always working away so he doesn't know what a mess I am.'

'Maybe if you lay off the dope you'll stop hallucinating,' Chloe mutters.

'Why aren't you listening to me?' Jonesy glares at her. 'I'm telling you I'm fucking scared, Clo. The other day, I flushed all my weed down the loo and I deleted Dizzy's name from my phone. I was *done* with it, man, I'm telling you. *Done*. The next day, I fog out again and when I come to, I'm wearing my coat and trainers like I've been out, and there are baggies on the bed. But not just weed – there was coke, too.'

'Fuck's sake, TJ.' Tyrus stares at him, his face pained. 'You said you'd never—'

'I don't touch that shit, man,' Jonesy says. 'You know I don't. But it was there on the bed. I bought it, I *must* have, even though I've got no memory of even leaving the house. Shit, I don't have any fucking money to pay for it, how did I even get hold of it?'

'There has to be a reasonable explanation.' Chloe's face is set. 'Some sort of post-traumatic stress—'

'Nah, man.' Jonesy shakes his head. 'This shit is real.'

'When it happens, I feel like I'm back in the house,' Tyrus says.

'Trapped and lost,' Jonesy says. 'And it's so dark, but I feel like something's watching—'

'Stop, just *stop*.' Chloe jerks to her feet, the ugly scratch of her chair drawing eyes to their table. 'Mei *fell*, and it's horrible and unbelievable, but that's the truth. There is no fucking curse.'

'Clo, who do you think you're kidding?' Tyrus speaks softly. 'You think if you pretend it's not happening, this will all just go away? It's happening to you, too. Anyone with eyes can see you're not well.'

Chloe blanches, and it is only then, in that small wince, that Flynn understands what is happening to her friend.

'You've stopped injecting, haven't you?' Flynn says.

Chloe bites her lip, shakes her head. But the truth is suddenly unavoidably clear, the symptoms of hyperglycaemia almost impossible to miss once you know to look out for them: weight loss, lethargy, excessive thirst, the near constant urge to pee. Flynn thinks of the way Chloe continued sipping from her water bottle in her handbag, even after she drained the glass of water the waitress brought her; the two quick bathroom trips she made since she arrived. Her dramatic weight loss, her dull, dry skin, the dark smudges beneath her eyes...

'Sit down, Clo,' Tyrus says gently. 'Please. Talk to us.'

'And don't fob us off with any of that high metabolism bullshit,' Jonesy says.

Chloe casts a furtive glance towards the door. Flynn can almost see the battle taking place inside her: dismiss all she has heard and pretend that everything will work out alright, or accept that Temple Fall has somehow infected her mind.

Her eyes flutter closed, she takes a deep breath.

'What you're saying,' she whispers. 'It's impossible. It's *crazy*.'

She opens her eyes, her gaze moving over each of them, as though daring them to argue, to give her a reason to walk out. But no one speaks because she is right: it *is* crazy. Her shoulders slump and she sinks back into the chair.

'It isn't that I want to stop injecting, but every time I try...'

'You lose time,' Flynn says.

Chloe nods, shoots Flynn a look that is both baffled and terrified.

'But that's not all,' she says. 'Sometimes, when I come round, I find empty packets of sweets in the bin and I can taste sugar. My glucose levels are so high my vision's starting to blur, but every time I get my insulin out–' She presses trembling fingers to her lips. 'Oh god...'

Chloe's fear stirs Flynn's, a sudden upswelling inside her, the realisation that the house is not only going to kill them, but it is going to squeeze every ounce of suffering from them it can before doing so.

'Do you think we should go back there?' Jonesy speaks the words reluctantly, as though the proposal is one that has to be tabled, if only to be rejected. He is twitchy with nerves, more antsy than Flynn has ever seen him.

It is his birthday in five days.

They are back in Nostromo, huddled beneath throws and blankets. Tyrus's old gas heater clicks with warmth that too quickly flees the poorly insulated room. They have returned here a few times since meeting in Mrs Rafferty's, drawn back by the comfort of their old haunt when, only a few months ago, they had been so close to outgrowing it.

Now, Flynn's gaze skims the shadowy room, stops on the Tipp-Ex marking on the bare brick wall. Jackson had drawn it there last year, not long after they started dating.

Jax ♡ FLYNN

Flynn had never thought a bit of graffiti could bring her such happiness, nor that it could cause her such pain now.

'No,' Chloe says. 'I can't go back to that house.'

'I don't see what it would accomplish, anyway,' Tyrus says, holding his hands to the heater to warm them.

'To try and communicate with whatever it was that we woke up?' Jonesy says. 'To try and... put it back.'

'No more seances,' Flynn says. 'Not after what happened last time.'

'Whatever we're dealing with, it's not a Jack-in-the-box,' Tyrus says. 'I don't think it will be that easy to put a lid on this.'

'There wouldn't be anything *easy* about walking back into that house,' Flynn mutters. 'I don't think I could do it.'

In truth, she knows she can't go back to Temple Fall. Just the memory of the house makes her chest tighten with dread.

'*Shit*, I need a smoke.' Jonesy removes his baseball cap and shoves his hands into his hair. Sections of his blonde curls, left unwashed and unbrushed, have knotted into thin ropes that look like dreads.

Straight after their meeting at Mrs Rafferty's, they had all gone to Chloe's house, where Flynn, Jonesy and Tyrus had convinced Chloe to check her blood glucose levels. She had been reluctant, nervous to see how severely hyperglycaemic she was, but even more scared that the house would sense what she was doing and steal her consciousness away, that she would come round surrounded by sweet wrappers, the taste of sugar coating her tongue and teeth.

Her blood sugar levels had been dangerously high, but she had been too scared to administer her insulin shot, and so Flynn had done it for her. The moment before the needle punctured Chloe's thigh, she had almost baulked, afraid that Temple Fall would smother her thoughts, cause her to stand up, drop the insulin pen, and walk away, but Flynn had managed to inject Chloe without incident.

In fact, none of them have suffered further lapses since meeting at Mrs Rafferty's three days ago, and the more time Flynn spends with her friends, the more she believes that the house's presence in her thoughts is fading, her anger and bitterness dissolving, like clouds burned away by the warmth of the sun. The toxic inner voice that had plagued her speaks up less frequently, flaring only now and again in a sudden pulse of hate that is becoming increasingly easy to ignore, and as it dissipates, she realises the positive effects her friendships have on her mental health were probably exactly why the house had tried to infect her against them.

To protect each other from further lapses, they had decided to spend as much time together as they could, at least until after Jonesy's birthday, with Chloe staying at Flynn's house, and Tyrus at Jonesy's.

'You make it sound like it's the house that's cursed us.' Jonesy looks at Flynn. 'But you saw a woman when Jackson fell. And Mitchell – he saw a little girl on a rocking horse, right?'

'The woman I saw in Mitchell's face,' Flynn says. 'I swear that was the same woman that appeared behind Jackson.

I think she's the one who placed this curse on us.'

'But we're all suffering very distinctive symptoms,' Tyrus says. 'It's like this curse is using our weaknesses against us, our own personal demons.'

'When we ran out of there, the way everything had changed...' Chloe's voice trails off with the memory. 'I don't know but it felt to me like the house itself was the ghost, that Temple Fall is the thing that's been haunting me.'

'Perhaps the house is what's holding the spirits here,' Flynn says. 'Preventing them from moving on, powering them.'

'Like an electrical grid,' Tyrus says.

'So we cut the source of its power,' Jonesy says. 'We destroy the house.'

'Eliza and Mitchell Lister tried that, remember?' Tyrus says. 'Didn't turn out so well for them.'

'Or Father Heskin,' Flynn says.

'I guess that rules out an exorcism,' Jonesy mutters.

'We can't drag anyone else into this,' Flynn says. 'Besides, finding a genuine exorcist could take months.'

A brief hush follows her words, and a chill rolls down Flynn's spine. She knows, in that moment, they are all thinking the same thing: Jonesy doesn't have months.

Chloe's phone pings, and she takes it from her pocket. 'Fuck's sake, Andy,' she mutters.

'What's wrong?' Flynn asks.

'He's taking this big brother thing way too seriously.' Chloe's fingertips fly across the screen as she taps out a reply. 'I can't go anywhere without him checking where I am and who I'm with. He's driving me mad.'

'He's just worried about you,' Flynn says, looking at her friend's sunken cheeks, her pale, drawn skin. *We're all worried about you.*

'Yeah, well,' Chloe says, tossing her phone onto the sofa. 'I can look after myself.'

Silence flows like pale smoke around her words, which sit jagged above it, craggy and harsh, a mirage they all stare at, wishing they could believe in while knowing it is a lie.

'I hate to say it,' Tyrus says. 'But I think we should go back. Not to the house,' he quickly adds, noting the flinch his words elicit from the others. 'But maybe we could go to the village, see if anyone can tell us anything about Temple Fall.'

Jonesy pops his knuckles, nodding. 'We could go to that pub from the article you found.'

'The Old Crown Tavern,' Flynn says.

'Yeah, see if anyone remembers the guy who wrote it.'

'It's a stretch,' Flynn mutters. 'We don't even know his name.'

'Or her name,' Jonesy says.

Chloe taps the name of the pub into her phone. 'Hey, I remember this place.' She turns the screen round so they can all see the photograph of the pub. 'We drove past it on our way to the house.'

'Okay, let's start there,' Flynn says. 'Get a few rounds in, we might loosen some tongues.'

'This old guy you visited – Mitchell.' Jonesy frowns. 'You said the house can get to him whenever it wants to, right? Like, it can tap into his mind and stop him from ending his own life.'

'Right.'

'Well, that's what I don't understand. I mean, how come the house is keeping him alive while it's taking us out one by one?'

'And why's it waiting until our eighteenth birthdays?' Tyrus says.

Flynn meets his gaze. 'Do you remember what you asked, right before the shot glass carved those numbers?'

Tyrus looks blank, but Chloe answers in a flat, toneless voice. 'He asked how old we'd be when we died.'

'Jesus, I said that?' Tyrus pales.

'It wasn't your fault, Ty,' Flynn says. 'We'd already opened the door by then. But that was when the woman stopped using the tiles and carved the infinity symbol into the table. By doing that, she freed herself and cursed us, all in one move.'

'That house is fucking evil,' Chloe says darkly. 'I mean, 666, the number of the beast.' At their bemused expressions, she shrugs, shakes her head. 'Maybe it's just a coincidence that it adds up to eighteen.'

Flynn and Chloe part ways with Jonesy and Tyrus, and arm-in-arm head back to Flynn's house. It is only early evening, but the winter sun fled the sky hours ago. Beneath silvery moonlight, tree branch shadows tangle on the pavement like swaying wreaths of fine black lace.

They walk through the estate, past houses lit from within, families gathering for dinner or reclining on sofas in front of TV screens. Chloe seems quieter than usual, but Flynn doesn't push her into conversation. Silence lingers between them often now, the spaces Jackson and Mei used to fill like potholes in a dark path that they must take care to manoeuvre around.

And yet, Chloe's silence feels different to those sad, haunted lulls. Taut as a strung bow, quivering with some unspoken sentiment. Flynn senses she has something to say, but that she is trying to work her way towards it, feeling for the right words.

Finally, when Flynn can no longer bear the tension and is about to ask Chloe what is bothering her, her friend abruptly unhooks her arm from Flynn's.

'Okay, I can't keep doing this, I can't keep it to myself anymore.' Chloe pushes her hands through her hair, takes a deep breath. 'I have to talk to you about that night.'

Flynn tenses, words knotting in her throat. Chloe is suddenly unable to meet her gaze, her eyes moving everywhere but to

Flynn's face. She pulls a packet of cigarettes from her pocket, slides one out and wedges it between her lips. Huddled in her puffer jacket, she looks small and frail, closer to fourteen years old than the eighteen she will turn in a few weeks' time.

She holds a lighter to the cigarette, and a gasp slips from Flynn's lips before she can stop it. The flame is like a blade, slicing all remaining softness from Chloe's face, cutting shadows into her cheeks and the grooves beneath her eyes. Her head looks disproportionately large, held up by the tender stem of her neck, her skin stretched taut across her skull. *She's lost weight since we left Nostromo ten minutes ago.* Flynn tries to dismiss the thought, but it lingers, certainty lending it a cold weight in her consciousness.

Chloe pulls on the cigarette, her hollow cheeks sinking as she inhales.

'I lied.' Her words chase the curl of smoke she blows into the night. 'I lied about what happened. With Jax.'

'It's over,' Flynn says, her voice clipped, cold. 'Let's not talk about that.'

'Please, Flynn. I have to tell you,' Chloe says, wrapping her arms round her waist. 'I can't carry it around inside me anymore. I can't. I just can't...' She shakes her head, a sob in her voice.

'Okay,' Flynn says, alarmed by the tears that fill Chloe's eyes. 'Okay, fine. Tell me.'

Chloe drops her weight against the wall at her back, her gaze drilling into the ground. She takes another deep drag on the cigarette, as though the heat from the fumes can burn away the pain inside her. 'You were right,' she says, eyes still downturned. 'What you said... about me and Jax.'

Flynn had known what Chloe was going to say but even so, anger burns beneath her skin. She feels the almost irrepressible urge to clamp her hands around Chloe's skinny neck and squeeze, to watch her beautiful almond-shaped eyes bulge and explode with starburst capillaries, to feel her leaping pulse slow beneath her tightening grip. Nausea crashes through her and she sways, catches herself against the brick wall. The violence of her reaction chills her to the bone, because in that moment, she knows that Temple Fall is still inside her, its consciousness garrotting her own.

'I know, Clo,' Flynn says, trying to make her voice gentle, as even as a priest listening to a penitent from the other side of a latticed confessional box. She knows she fails to pull it off.

'No, you don't,' Chloe says sadly.

'Okay.' Flynn swallows. 'Go on.'

Chloe watches her for a moment, gives a quick nod, pulls on her cigarette.

'I realise this is gonna sound like some bullshit excuse, but none of it felt real. It was like a dream, all of it, from the moment we stepped inside that house.'

That House. As though to speak its name might awake something within its walls, even all these miles away. *That House*.

Flynn remembers Chloe's glazed expression as she danced, her back arched, her pink mouth like a vulva, nipples puckered beneath her thin top, as though plucked by the notes of the music. Flynn had thought she had felt Jackson's eyes on her as she danced, that she had been seducing him, but that wasn't right. No. Temple Fall – *That House* – had seduced Chloe.

Flynn recalls the Titian pulse of light that had flashed behind Jackson's eyes as he watched Chloe, how his pupils had swollen to a cavernous black. And Flynn knows he too had been seduced by Temple Fall.

'It was like I was seeing him for the first time, like I'd never really opened my eyes before and *seen* him.' Chloe hesitates, her eyes flashing to Flynn before dropping back to the ground. 'I know it sounds awful but the truth is, I didn't even think about you. I couldn't think about anything but Jax, even though – and

I swear to god, Flynn, it's true, I *swear* it – there was nothing – *nothing* – between us.'

Jealousy punches Flynn, deep and low in her gut. She nods for Chloe to carry on.

'We left the room together and found a bedroom down the hall. I can't tell you exactly how it happened, like I say, it didn't feel real. It was like I was dreaming.' She shakes her head again, sucks hungrily on the dregs of her cigarette, pitches the roach. Her starved face is anguished, tortured, and Flynn wants to tell her to stop, that she doesn't need to hear it, doesn't *want* to hear it, while the skulking imposter in her consciousness basks in Chloe's torment.

'We were kissing...' Her throat bobs as she swallows. 'And he was gentle at first, but it got out of hand so fast. He started to get rough and... he bit me...' Her hand floats to the spot on her neck where Flynn recalls the hickey had been.

'I guess it was the shock of it, but I started to come round a little, and I pulled away, but he grabbed the back of my head and kept kissing me. Then he said your name, and it was like a hard slap waking me all the way up. I told him to stop, tried to push him off me because I couldn't believe it, Flynn, I couldn't believe what we were doing... But it was like he just couldn't *hear* me.'

Chloe's eyes acquire a faraway look, and her arms tighten round her waist.

'He pushed me onto the bed and climbed on top of me. He ripped my top trying to pull it off, but it was like he didn't notice. His eyes were huge and black, not his anymore, he wasn't Jackson. It was like... like he wasn't inside the house anymore. Like the house was inside *him*.

'He kneeled over me and he grinned, and I know it sounds stupid, but something about his face then scared me more than anything, because I realised I was looking into the soul of the *house*.

'He started to pull my shorts down, and I was punching and kicking him, trying to push him away. But he was so *heavy* and I... I screamed but he still wouldn't budge, he just pressed his hand over my mouth to shut me up and kept trying to pull my shorts down and I couldn't breathe. I thought... I really thought he was going to kill me.'

Chloe blinks, looks up at Flynn, a look of hurt bewilderment on her face. 'Can you believe that? Jackson, killing me?' She laughs, a small, humourless sound.

'I brought my knee up hard and caught him in the balls and he howled and fell off me, cupping himself and looking at me – looking at me like he had no idea why I'd hurt him. Like *I* was the monster. But I could see it happen, the way he came back to his senses because he looked so confused when he saw me on the bed, all messed up and crying. Like he had no idea what'd just happened. And I don't think he did know, Flynn – I don't think he realised what he'd been doing at all.'

Tears prism Chloe's eyes and she presses trembling fingers to her lips, as though these words are the worst she has yet spoken.

'He was the gentlest person I ever...' Her voice catches, tears drip from her eyes. 'What he did that night, it wasn't him, and I'm not saying it was out of character because it was, of course, it was. I'm saying that Jackson just didn't have that in him. And I would never... I want you to know – what I did, that wasn't me, either.'

Flynn's chest tightens and she pulls Chloe close.

'I'm so sorry, Clo. I had no idea.'

The words taste sour in her mouth because they are not entirely true; she had known all along that something was wrong. She has felt the house slide through her, a canker in her thoughts, a mental darkness clouding her mind. She has felt it graze her baser instincts and amplify them, awakening her to emotions and rages she had not known she was capable of feeling. Why had she refused to accept the same might have been true for her friends?

'I'd never do anything to hurt you, Flynn,' Chloe says. 'And Jax... he would have wanted you to know that. He was crazy about you.'

Flynn's heart twists at the memory of Jackson, the stumble in his eyes when she had accused him, the flash of pain in his face. She wishes there was some way she could take back her hate-filled words, undo that hurt she caused. But it is too late.

Andy pulls up outside Flynn's house, his expression scandalised as he watches Riley scramble into his van.

'Hey, what the fuck? This isn't Daddy Day Care. Can someone tell me why there's a tiny person in my van?'

Riley sits in front of Jonesy and Tyrus, who are in the back seat, flashes them a grin. Her swimming goggles are strapped to her forehead, as though at any moment she expects to take a high dive into a swimming pool.

'My mum had to work,' Flynn says, climbing in after Chloe. 'Last-minute thing.'

Flynn had tried to tell her mum that she couldn't watch Riley because she already had plans, but unable to tell her the truth – that those plans involved a trip to the Old Crown Tavern in Brinley Cliffe to ask questions about Temple Fall – her excuses fell flat.

'Buckle up, Ry,' Flynn says, as Andy, muttering under his breath, pulls away from Flynn's house.

'Can you tell him to step on it?' Riley says, jerking her head at Andy and clipping her seatbelt on. 'My swimming lesson starts at eleven.'

'About that,' Flynn says. 'I'm sorry, Ry, I can't take you swimming today.'

'What?! But you promised Jenna!'

'Nothing I can do about it,' Flynn says, pressing down the annoyance that flares at her little sister's continued use of their mum's Christian name. 'There's something important I have to do, okay?'

'*Swimming's* important.'

'I agree with the midget,' Andy mumbles. 'Swimming's important, we should take the midget swimming.'

'Andy,' Chloe groans. 'Don't start again, please.'

'I just don't know what you think you'll accomplish going back to that place.'

'I'm not a midget,' Riley says, glaring at the back of Andy's head. 'And you shouldn't use that sort of language. It's offensive.'

Andy glances at her in the rear-view mirror, but his eyes are hollow, devoid of his usual capering smirk.

Riley twists to Flynn. 'You heard him, he says you have to take me swimming.'

'Can't do it, I'm sorry.'

'This is *kidnapping*. Wait until Jenna hears, she'll be so mad.'

'Come on, Ry. I'll make it up to you, I promise.'

Riley folds her arms tightly across her chest, narrows her eyes. 'So where are we going that's so *important*?'

'It's... we're going to a pub.'

'A pub isn't important! Ugh, I hate pubs.'

'Hey, Batgirl, I brought you something.' Jonesy shuffles forwards in his seat, passes Riley a pack of Batman candy sticks. She brightens, takes them with a chirpy 'Thanks!' before remembering she's supposed to be sulking, and folding her smile away.

'Here, you can have your Switch, okay?' Flynn says, passing it to her. 'You don't have to come into the pub, you can stay in the van with Andy. We won't be long.'

'Hmm.' Riley flicks Andy a dubious glance, then twists her body away from Flynn, her little shoulders pinched tight. She pops a candy stick in her mouth, then starts to finger-sketch across the fogged window: a house, a stick figure of a little girl, a crooked tree, some kind of four-legged animal...

'What you drawing?' Flynn asks.

Riley freezes, her finger on the window. 'I'm not talking to you right now.'

Flynn sighs, turns to watch the scenery pass. She joins in half-heartedly when Riley and Chloe play a game of I Spy. The route Andy takes turns the hands of time back to the afternoon before Jackson's birthday when he had driven them down these very same roads on the way to Temple Fall. The moors had been a blaze of purple heather then, the trees thick with leaves, but now the sloped hills wear skeins of white frost and the trees are stripped bare. Still, the sense of abandonment the landscape evokes is the same, the sense of isolation just as acute.

When they get to the pub, Andy pulls into the car park and cuts the engine.

Chloe opens her door. 'We shouldn't be long. Why don't you head down to the village and I'll call you when we're done?'

'I'll wait here,' Andy says, his face set, grim. Dark memories turn in his troubled eyes, a nightmare image, a screaming scene. While Flynn's recollection of seeing Jackson's body is rendered in black and white, muted by shock and distance, she knows it is probably very different for Andy.

She imagines what it might have been like for him, discovering Jackson the way he had. Driving towards the house, seeing something on the ground, something that looked like a person but couldn't be, couldn't be. Driving faster, dread crushing his foot down on the accelerator. Cutting the engine and leaping out of the van, running towards the motionless body. Perhaps he skidded to a halt at the bloody sight, turned away too late, his hands grasping his hair, a scream splattering the back of his throat. Or perhaps he dropped beside Jackson, touched his cold white skin, then backed away, blood and brain matter on his hands, viscous body fluids congealing on his jeans, his trainers.

Riley unclips her belt, starts to climb out of the van with the others, but Flynn turns to her. 'Stay here, we won't be long.'

'I'm not staying with him!' Riley turns begging eyes on Flynn, lowers her voice. 'Even Clo hates him and they're *related*.'

'I can hear you,' Andy mumbles.

'Clo doesn't hate him, brothers and sisters just fight, that's all. Look, Andy's okay. And you've got your Switch. Why don't you show him how to play *Super Hero Girls*?'

Andy groans and closes his eyes, drops his head against the back of the seat. But the prospect of educating another person in the wonders of Batgirl, Livewire and Giganta instantly perks Riley up. She scrambles into the passenger seat beside him, turning on her Switch as she does, already explaining the characters, their skills and combat options. Flynn grins as her little sister swings the car door closed behind her.

'How are we going to play this?' Jonesy asks, as they walk towards the pub's entrance. 'We can't just rock up and start asking questions about Temple Fall.'

'That's exactly what we're going to do,' Flynn says. 'We don't have time to piss about.'

A muscle works in Jonesy's jaw. 'Copy that,' he says.

Flynn flashes him an apologetic look, inwardly cursing herself for her insensitivity. Only four days now stand between Jonesy and his eighteenth birthday. She wraps an arm round his waist, leans her head against his shoulder.

'You're gonna be okay,' she says.

'I know.' He smiles down at her, but his eyes are dark and his words ring hollow. He squeezes her arm gently, his gaze sliding past her face and into the uncertain future. 'I know.'

~

The pub is small, rustic, with an open fire burning in the corner and exposed beams running the length of the low ceiling. The bar is dimly lit, the walls dark panelled mahogany, hung with prints of the surrounding moors. It possesses the gravity of intimacy, the authenticity of age, and Flynn can easily imagine punters gathering here hundreds of years ago, woodchips on the floor to soak up spilled beer, candles on every table, the room thick with shadows and tallow smoke.

Now, the only drinkers are a group of old men gathered in the corner, playing dominoes and supping from dimpled pint glasses. A woman with cropped red hair and a She-Ra T-shirt stands behind the beer taps, scrolling on her mobile. She glances in their direction, her gaze ricocheting back to their faces as they sit at the bar.

'Oh my god, you're those kids what went missing from the house. I read all about it in the papers, you were even on the six o'clock news. Awful what happened to your friend—'

'I'll have a Baileys, please,' Chloe says, a cold snap in her voice.

She-Ra's eyes contract, a flush of colour to rival the red of her hair climbs her face. Flynn senses the table of old men grow still behind them, is sure she feels their eyes burning a hole in the back of her neck.

'Of course.' She-Ra slips her phone into her back pocket, turns away from them. 'Baileys coming right up. Do you want to make it a double for an extra quid?'

Chloe shrugs. 'Sure, why not.'

Flynn and Tyrus order Cokes, Jonesy asks for a J2O. She-Ra grabs four glasses from beneath the bar.

'So, what brings you kids out here?' She-Ra tries to sound nonchalant, but Flynn detects a forced quality to her voice.

'A research trip,' she says. 'We were hoping someone around

here might be willing to talk to us about Temple Fall.'

Flynn watches She-Ra shoot Coke from the soda gun into two glasses, and wonders whether she imagines the barmaid's flinch at the mention of the house. She-Ra sets the two drinks on the bar and takes a J2O from the fridge. Uncaps it, places it in front of Jonesy.

'I don't suppose you can tell us anything?' Flynn asks.

She-Ra turns round to take down a bottle of Baileys from the shelf behind her.

'Do you want ice, love?'

'No, thanks,' Chloe says.

She-Ra pours the drink without measuring it, almost filling the glass, which she pushes towards Chloe.

'Anything at all,' Flynn presses. 'The house isn't that far from here, maybe you've even visited—'

'No.' The sharp edge to her tone seems to take her by surprise, and she continues more gently. 'No, I've never been near that place, and you wouldn't either if you'd grown up round here. Anytime people go sniffing round that house, the only thing they find for themselves is a pile of trouble.'

'Tell me about it,' Chloe mutters, lifting her drink to her lips.

'I'm sorry I can't help you.'

'You said you'd read about our disappearance in the papers.' Flynn sits forwards, crosses her arms on the bar. 'You've probably heard the rumours that we've made a pact to commit suicide when we turn eighteen. It's not true.'

'Honey, I pay no mind to the shite they print in the papers. But that house...' She shakes her head, and a shadow passes across her brow. 'I know it sounds daft, but people round here are superstitious about it. They know it's there, but they'd sooner pretend like it isn't.'

'If only it were that easy,' Jonesy says, staring gloomily into his drink.

She-Ra watches them for a moment, taking in the dark half-moons beneath Flynn's eyes, Chloe's pale and shrunken face, the way Tyrus's leg bounces up and down on the bar stool and Jonesy watches her, his eyes tense and watchful.

She sighs, something in her face softening, then pulls her mobile from her pocket. 'Why don't you leave me your number and I'll ask around. I can't guarantee I can get anyone to call you, but I'll see what I can do.'

Flynn thanks her and recites her number, which She-Ra taps into her contacts. Tyrus asks what they owe for the drinks, but She-Ra waves them off. Flynn knows the gesture is well-meaning, but part of her wonders whether it is born from superstition rather than kindness, their money unwelcome, tainted as it is by Temple Fall.

They drain their drinks, and stand up to leave, but as they pass the domino table, one of the old men catches Flynn's eye. His gaze is a hard blue, chips of Arctic ice set in walnut skin. Stories swirl in the deep lodged lines of his face, and Flynn suspects more than a few of them involve Temple Fall.

He wordlessly passes her a scrap of paper, on which he has written a name and an address.

Mad Dog – 12 Moorfield lane, Thirsk.

Flynn looks from the paper in her hands to the old man. 'Mad Dog?'

'Maddon Dogharty.' The old man's voice is gruff, his words grudgingly measured. His gaze slides away from Flynn's face, already telling her to move along. 'If you want someone who knows about that house, he's your man.'

'He'll talk to us?' Chloe asks.

'Aye, just make sure you show up with a four pack.'

'A four pack,' Flynn repeats. 'Sure, okay. What does he drink?'

'Doesn't matter.' The old man frowns at his dominoes. 'So long as it comes in tins.'

Flynn shoots the others a baffled glance. 'Well, thank you,' she says, pocketing the slip of paper.

The old man nods once without looking up. He reaches for one of his dominoes and sets it on the table, and as he does, Flynn notices the tattoo on the back of his hand: the unfurled head of a single black rose.

Andy drives them to Mad Dog's house, which is only a few streets across from the pub. On the way, they pick up a four pack of Stella, a four pack of Carling and two four packs of Coke, hoping the extra drinks will bolster Mad Dog's willingness to talk, and that the beers will make him more garrulous.

Andy pulls up, and peers at the building with a buckled brow. 'I hope you've had all your shots.'

Mad Dog's house is a small detached bungalow, set in a garden overgrown with brambles. Foliage attacks the facade, slides across one of the ground-floor windows, as though seeking a gap in the pane through which to gain entry. The rendered walls are the colour of porridge and it flakes from the brickwork like leprotic flesh. A huge oak tree shades half the garden and a blue bin painted with the words *CANS ONLY!* stands beside a rusted gate.

'Mad Dog. Interesting name.' Andy looks pointedly at the house. 'I wonder how he came by it.'

'I'm sure he's harmless.' Chloe pops the door open. 'But if we're not out in an hour, come knock on the door, yeah?'

Riley climbs out of the van, catches Chloe's hand and grins up at her.

'Ry, you're staying here,' Flynn says.

'Oh no, she's not.' Andy twists in his seat. 'I'm not a fucking babysitter, and besides, she won't shut up about the bloody *Super Hero Girls*. Doing my head in.'

Riley drops Andy a curtsey and flips him the finger.

'Oh, that's nice,' Andy says. 'A lady like my sister. Really nice.'

'Fine,' Flynn snaps, shooting Riley a querulous look and ignoring Chloe's laughter. 'Come on, Ry.'

They walk down the path towards the house. All the curtains inside are drawn. Sunlight spills between the gaps in the clouds, a faint brush of warmth on the breeze. Jonesy presses the doorbell. The ringer drills through the house, muffled but audible from the doorstep.

'Who do we say sent us?' Chloe whispers, as though her voice might carry inside the house.

Riley looks from Chloe to Flynn, her eyes wide. 'Yeah, who sent us?' she echoes.

'I don't think it matters,' Jonesy says. 'Look at the place. There's probably no one even living here. That old guy was probably taking the piss.'

Riley ducks, lifts the flap of the letterbox and peers inside. 'There's a ton of post on the floor.'

Flynn pulls her back, the letterbox slaps down. 'Ry, you can't just shove your face into someone's house!'

'Who's Mad Dog?' Riley asks. 'Is he a bad person? Are you going to kill him?'

'What? *No!*'

Riley pushes forwards, holds the buzzer down. The bell rings, loud and insistent, through the quiet house.

'That's enough.' Flynn grabs Riley's hand, but Riley just uses her other hand, compresses the bell again. 'Ry, stop it! We'll come back later—'

The door opens a crack, admitting the sliver of a face. Riley steps back and grins up at the man in the doorway.

'Are you Mr Dog?' she says.

Flynn places her hands on Riley shoulders, eases her backwards.

'We were just in the Old Crown Tavern,' Tyrus says, 'and someone gave us your address.'

The eye framed in the narrow gap of the door slides from Tyrus's face to the beers in his hands.

'This guy, he said you might be willing to talk to us about Temple Fall, and so we–'

The door slams shut.

'Well, shit,' Jonesy mutters. 'Maybe we should've brought Peroni.'

From the other side of the door, they hear the scratch and scrape of chains, and then the door swings open, revealing a tall, bearded, scraggle-haired man, wearing a beanie hat and a dark blue dressing gown over stripy pyjamas. He motions them inside and shuts the door behind them.

'I've been expecting you,' Mad Dog says, shooting the bolts and chains back into their tracks. He tucks his long hair behind his ears and turns to them.

Any alarm Flynn might have felt by being barricaded inside the house is stifled by amazement as she stares around the small living room in which she is standing. A portable electric fire, a vintage leather armchair pocked with holes, and a TV that looks as though it dates from the eighties are mild eccentricities that barely register. Because the walls and ceiling of Mad Dog's living room are covered in empty Stella Artois cans. The electrical outlets, door casing, cornices, skirting boards, all are covered in reshaped tins. The furniture, too, is just as unconventional: a sofa made entirely of vertically stacked Heinz tomato soup tins, a table constructed from tins of Bud Light, a tower of pale blue aluminium alloy topped with a round sheet of glass.

But stacking and gluing empty cans is not the extent of

Mad Dog's talents. In one corner of the room stands a life-size statue of Darth Maul made from cans of Pepsi Max, and a half-finished model Ferrari, shaped from Coke cans, occupies the table. A wall of bookshelves are cluttered with ornaments crafted from empty drink cans: a Guinness racing car; a Red Bull Medusa head; a 7Up military jet; a San Miguel ballerina; a Carlsberg Nefertiti; a Pepsi Eiffel Tower; a Fosters Superman. A filing cabinet occupies the opposite corner, and beside it, books and folders climb the wall, relegated from their rightful position by sculptured aluminium. The house smells of old beer and glue and solitude.

Riley's mouth drops open as her gaze moves over the room.

'This place is really... *wow!*' Jonesy's face is awed. 'You did all this yourself?'

'I like sculpting things from cans,' Mad Dog says, turning to them. Flynn notices what looks like tomato ketchup stains marking the lapels of his dressing gown.

'No shit,' Riley mutters.

'Ry!' Flynn hisses.

'It's weird, isn't it? People say it's weird.' Mad Dog starts to clear the sofa, on which he has left a hammer and a pair of safety goggles. 'My dad, he was a big drinker, so there were always empties lying around the house.' He straightens, the hammer dangling from his hand. Flynn stares at it, her muscles tightening. 'He wasn't very nice when he was drinking, and he was always drinking. My mum hated him, hated his cans lying around everywhere. So I'd make things with 'em, see.' He shrugs his massive shoulders. 'It made her smile.'

Realising they are all staring at the hammer in his hands, he quickly sets it on the floor beside the goggles.

Jonesy moves towards Darth Maul. 'You made this, too?'

Mad Dog gives a small nod. Despite his enormous frame and the fact he has a hammer within easy reach, he seems to hold himself back, regarding them with a wariness incongruous to his size.

'It's incredible!' Jonesy bends down to inspect the piece.

'Oh, thanks.' Mad Dog tucks his hair back again, looking uncomfortable. 'Here, please, sit, sit.'

Tyrus eyes the Heinz tin sofa sceptically. 'Won't we break it?'

'Oh, no,' Mad Dog says. 'It's strong enough. Not right comfy, but I don't get many visitors, otherwise I'd have put out some cushions.'

'It's fine, thanks,' Jonesy says, sitting down. Flynn, Chloe and Tyrus squash up beside him on the small sofa, which is about as cosy as sitting on a cold brick wall. Riley perches on the floor. Mad Dog watches them, as though they are as exotic and strange to him as he is to them.

'Can I get you a drink?' His thumb rubs at his palm, as though, even now, his hands itch to bend and fold aluminium. 'Anything you want, I probably have it.'

'Urm, I'll take a lemon Fanta?' Tyrus says.

Mad Dog nods, looks at Jonesy.

'Do you have Dr Pepper?'

Mad Dog beams at them. 'Yes! I've just stocked up on those for my next piece!' His gaze moves to Chloe.

'Gin?'

'Gin in a tin, absolutely. Gordon's Pink Gin and Lemonade or Edinburgh Raspberry Gin Fizz?'

'Either one, thanks.'

Sensing Mad Dog's eagerness to impress them with his vast array of canned beverages, Flynn asks for a Sprite. He looks at Riley.

'I'll have what she's having.' Riley shoots her eyes at Chloe.

'A... gin?' Mad Dog frowns.

'She'll have a Coke,' Flynn says quickly.

Mad Dog nods and slips from the room to get the drinks.

'This guy's amazing,' Jonesy whispers, his smile the first genuine one he has given all day.

'He's certifiable,' Chloe mutters. 'Seriously, this is where we've come for advice?'

'I think he's a fucking genius,' Jonesy says.

Tyrus's eyes move over the tins of beer that cover the walls. 'I feel like I'm trapped in the weirdest room of Ripley's Believe It or Not.'

'He's just a little... eccentric,' Flynn says.

'Eccentric?' Tyrus says. 'The guy has pull-tabs looped through his shoelaces.'

'He does?' Flynn says.

Riley stands up, moves across the room, plucks a sculpture from the windowsill.

'It's a bum.' Riley giggles and turns it round so they can see the front. 'Look, it's a penis! It has hair on it and everything!'

Jonesy snorts on laughter, jabs Tyrus with his elbow. 'I bet that's what you say when you're with a girl you want to—'

'Here we go!' Mad Dog enters, carrying the drinks. He passes them round. Riley quickly sets the sculpture back on the windowsill and accepts her Coke with a smiling thank you.

'You said you'd been expecting us, so I guess...' Flynn's gaze drops to Mad Dog's shoes, the numerous pull-tabs snapped from cans looped through his laces. 'So, I guess the guy who gave us your address must've called you to let you know we'd talked—'

'No, nothing like that.' Mad Dog pops the tab on a can of Stella as he sinks into the armchair across from them. 'I recognised you from the news. I had a feeling that someone would point you my way eventually.'

'So, you can help us?'

'Well, I don't know. I can try. I mean, listen, I'll tell you everything I know about Temple Fall, I can do that much. But first,' he says, leaning forwards, all previous hesitance falling away as a hungry sort of curiosity lights his face. 'I was hoping you'd tell me what happened to you inside that house.'

'Mr Dog, can I pick these up?' Riley is standing by the shelf of aluminium statues, longingly staring at the San Miguel ballerina.

'Ry, don't touch them, they're not toys,' Flynn says.

'Yes, yes.' Mad Dog waves his hand. 'Do what you want with them. Play with them, play.'

'And put your headphones on,' Flynn says. Riley opens her mouth to protest, but Flynn shakes her head. 'No arguments, or else you're back in the van with Andy.'

Riley scowls, but pulls her headphones from her pocket, connects them to her Switch. Flynn waits until she hears music echoing from the tiny speakers, then turns to Mad Dog.

'If you've followed the news, then you already know what happened to us.'

'You're telling me half the stuff they printed is true?' Mad Dog's gaze drills into Flynn, his previous bumbling awkwardness replaced by a flash of intelligence. 'Yeah, I thought as much. I'll tell you what I know, of course I will. But first of all, I've got a question for you.' He leans forwards, his eyes moving over each of them. 'What made you go to Temple Fall in the first place?'

'It was my boyfriend's idea,' Flynn says, her chest tightening with the memory of Jackson. 'He loved photographing old houses, and when we came across photos of Temple Fall, he thought it would be fun to visit the place.'

'Photos of it are rare – very hard to come by,' Mad Dog says, his eyes narrowing.

'I'd been researching my family history,' Flynn says. 'I found out a woman, some distant relative, used to live in the house. I looked it up online, but it was like the place didn't exist. Jax suggested we–'

'What was her name?' A pulse of something, some subtle contraction, behind Mad Dog's eyes, a tightening in his focus.

'I'm sorry?'

'Your distant relative – the one who lived in Temple Fall. What was her name?'

'Lyda Gray,' Flynn says. 'She was my great-great-great grand–'

'You're related to Lyda Gray.' Mad Dog's voice is sharp as sliced aluminium, and something in the way he looks at Flynn has changed.

'Well... yeah, apparently.' Flynn shifts in her seat, glances at the others. 'Why? Who was she?'

'Lyda Gray was a baby farmer.'

'A baby farmer?' Flynn mutters, uncomprehending.

Instead of answering, Mad Dog stands up, moves to the filing cabinet. He opens it, rifles through the drawers, returns to his armchair with a folder.

'In the nineteenth century, women who fell pregnant and either didn't want their babies or couldn't care for them, often gave them to baby farmers, who they then paid to look after them.'

'So Temple Fall was an orphanage where Lyda Gray cared for babies?' Flynn asks, thinking of those small cots, their cold metal bars like little prisons.

'Lyda Gray didn't care for those babies,' Mad Dog says, opening the folder, rifling through the pages. 'She murdered them.'

His words land like a punch to Flynn's gut. Beside her, she hears Chloe's shocked gasp, Tyrus's softly muttered curse. *Those weren't beds I saw in that room – they weren't even prisons*, Flynn realises with a sinking horror. *They were coffins.*

'Lyda was pregnant when she stood trial for the murders, so her sentence was postponed until she delivered her baby. Her son, Budd Gray, was born in prison and adopted by one of the nurses attending the birth.'

'What was her sentence?' Jonesy asks.

'Death by hanging.'

Mad Dog unclips a sheet of paper in a plastic wallet and passes it to Flynn. Tyrus, Chloe and Jonesy lean towards her to read the small print.

It is a copy of an article, taken from an old newspaper called the *Leeds Mercury*. A grainy mugshot of a middle-aged, dour-faced woman accompanies the piece. She is holding a blackboard, chalked with her name – LYDA GRAY – and the year of her arrest – 1884. She glares into the camera, her marble black eyes seething with a ferocity that scatters chills down Flynn's neck. Her face is all hard lines and sharp angles. Deep parentheses bracket lips that are pressed into a flat line, folded over some terrible knowing that crackles in her gaze. Her dark hair is scraped into a high bun and her hairline slides forwards in a widow's peak.

'Flynn?' Chloe says, watching her worriedly. 'Are you okay?'

'It's her,' Flynn whispers. 'The woman who pushed Jax.' Her hands tremble, fear thick in her throat. She thinks of Mitchell Lister, his flexing features, the face that had shimmered beneath his own. *Lyda Gray's* face.

THE MURDER MANSION TRIAL CONCLUDES. VICTIMS RANGING FROM NEWBORN BABIES TO A FOUR-YEAR-OLD GIRL

At Leeds assizes yester-day, before Mr Justice Simmons and a jury, Lyda Gray (51) was indicted for the murder of fifteen infants. The Temple Fall murder trial, which will long hold the field for horror against all similar stories in ancient or modern times, has reached its conclusion.

Mrs Gray's crimes may not have been discovered at all, had it not been for the disappearance of Evelina Hill (18), who was reported missing by her brother, Hugo Hill (21), seven days after she visited Mrs Gray at Temple Fall to reclaim custody of her daughter. Miss Hill had spoken to the police in the days preceding her disappearance, accusing Mrs Gray, the recent dowager of Mr Nelson Thomas, of trying to pass off a stranger's child as her own.

Subsequent to Mr Hill contacting police about his sister's disappearance, Constable Levy visited Mrs Gray at Temple Fall to make enquiries. After speaking to her, his suspicions were suitably aroused to return that afternoon with a team of investigators, whereupon the full extent of Mrs Gray's crimes were revealed. Detectives discovered remains of more than a dozen bodies, bundled in gunnysacks and buried in clay in the basement. The victims were all infants. Five surviving babies were discovered in the nursery in an insensible state. They showed evidence of strychnine poisoning, and regular doses of laudanum, or 'The Quietness', had so withered their respiration that their rattled breaths were as laboured as those of the dying elderly. They were conveyed to the Holy Trinity Hospital for immediate medical attention.

After evidence for the prosecution had been heard (a report of which appeared in our later editions yester-day) Mr Smith, addressing the jury for the defence, said the case was launched before them in such a way calculated to lead one to believe the defendant was a deviant, where in fact she was a widow, doing her best to get by after the sudden death of her husband. If babies had died in Mrs Gray's care, that was because the good lady, in her infinite compassion, had advertised that 'a delicate child would have the greatest attention', and it was this frailty, not any negligence on her part, that had caused their expiration.

THE VERDICT

The jury retired, and after an absence of eight minutes, they returned and answered to their names. The Clerk of Assize upon asking the Foreman for the jury's verdict, was told the defendant was found GUILTY. Mr Justice Simmons put on his black cap and passed sentence of death. At his words, the baby farmer nodded and laughed. Mr Simmons advised her to devote her final weeks to prayer and repentance.

Flynn sets the article on the table, her stomach twisting queasily. She feels grimy just looking at Lyda Gray's face, sullied by association. This killer of children – of *infants*. She sees an echo of her own face in the baby farmer's, a kinship subtly betrayed by their shared angular brows, their dark, curly hair and sharp V-shaped hairline. Flynn wonders how deeply Lyda's crimes are encoded in her own DNA, to what extent they form part of her genetic memory.

'I researched the house myself,' Flynn says. 'How come I never read about this?'

'I found that article years ago on microfiche at the library,' Mad Dog says. 'But you won't find much about the house on the internet these days. Sometimes, unexplainable things have a way of conveniently slipping through the cracks.

'Listen,' Mad Dog says, 'I know people round here say I'm a bit weird, and they're right, they are. Weird, yes, okay fine. But I'm not an idiot. I knew as soon as you went missing after visiting the house that you hadn't run away. That's why I want to hear what happened from *you*.'

'You'll think we're insane,' Tyrus says.

Mad Dog barks a laugh. 'If *I* think you're insane,' he says, leaning forwards with a smile that contains a grim sort of twinkle, 'then you really are in trouble.'

Flynn explains everything that happened in Temple Fall, the others interjecting to fill the gaps in her narrative, as Mad Dog listens with rapt attention. As crazy as their story sounds, he does not scoff or express any disbelief, even when Flynn tells him how they had walked into the house on 7 September and walked out, a matter of hours later, on 16 January.

For months, Flynn has longed for someone to believe her account of what really happened to them within the walls of

Temple Fall, but now, she can't help but wonder whether she is seeking validation in the wrong place. Perhaps it is simply because she has become accustomed to other people's scepticism, but there is something unnerving about Mad Dog's singular focus. Her gaze keeps drifting to the stains on his dressing gown, to the unconventional furnishings and the pull-tabs looped through his shoelaces.

When they have finished, Mad Dog sits back in his armchair, his expression contemplative. For a few moments, he watches Riley, who has abandoned the ballerina sculpture and is now gaming on her Switch, then he stands up, moves to the filing cabinet again, and returns with two scrapbooks.

'The land on which Temple Fall stands used to be the location of a small church, Temple Fall Chapel,' he says, sitting back down, 'until the Black Death of 1348 swept through the local village. Apparently, many of the locals gathered in the chapel during the outbreak – women, children, the elderly. They all congregated to pray and take shelter together, probably believing it would offer them protection. But the sheriff, alongside the archbishop at the time, became convinced they could contain the spread of disease by boarding everyone up inside and setting fire to the building. Almost two hundred souls died in the flames.'

'Jesus,' Tyrus whispers.

A chill wrenches Flynn's spine as she recalls what Mitchell had said about hearing Benjie in the fire: *But then the sound of his cries broadens, splits into a hundred voices, men, women, children, and all of them screaming... screaming...*

'After that, the site was deconsecrated,' Mad Dog says. 'The chapel's ruins stood for centuries, though strange rumours persisted about the place, whispers that the land was cursed, that it was used for practising witchcraft and for secret satanic gatherings.

'Whatever the truth, I suppose we'll never know. What we do know is that, officially, the land where the chapel stood belonged to the church until Edmund Lonsdale bought it in 1860.'

Mad Dog passes one of the scrapbooks to Flynn. The first pages are comprised of newspaper clippings, deeds of sale, and an external black-and-white photograph of Temple Fall. Beneath the image, in a small, barely legible scrawl, is written: *Temple Fall, 1862.*

Flynn turns the page of the scrapbook. Edmund Lonsdale stares at her from a newspaper clipping, titled: *DEATH OF MR E. LONSDALE, MP FOR THE WEST RIDING OF YORKSHIRE.*

A photograph accompanies the piece, a stern-faced man wearing a waistcoat over a high-collared shirt with decorative cuffs. His furrowed brow, white hair and plunging sideburns lend him an imperious, aloof demeanour, but his chiaroscuro eyes are piercing and direct, bright flashes of light against the darkness of the photograph.

Beside the article about Edmund Lonsdale, there is another clipping, a photograph of a little girl, about seven or eight years old. Her dark hair, swept from her face by a bow, falls over her narrow shoulders in thick sausage curls. Though the photograph is black and white, her skin conveys a sickly pallor, which is heightened by the spreading bruises beneath her eyes. A fey quality lingers at the edges of her curved rosebud mouth and her gaze is distant, half-dreaming, as though skewering some inner dancing thought.

'Lonsdale was a prominent figure, practised law in the early 1840s, became a QC a decade later, but his main passion was clock-making. He was a renowned horologist and a member of both the Royal Astronomical Society and the British Horological Institute.'

'The British *what?*' Jonesy asks.

'British Horological Institute, an institute of timekeepers.' Mad Dog waves a hand, flippant. 'Basically geeks with a hard-on for clocks. Anyway, that other picture, the little girl, that's his daughter, Florence. Lonsdale lived alone with her after his wife died of tuberculosis when she was just twenty-eight. Florence was a poorly kid, suffered from a wasting sickness – a catch-all term the Victorians used when they didn't know what was wrong with someone. Fevers, persistent fatigue, recurrent nosebleeds. Looking back, it sounds like the kid might've had leukaemia, but the disease wasn't understood at the time. In any case, her illness took its toll on Lonsdale, who by all accounts doted on his daughter.

'It must have seemed strange to people back then, a single man building such a huge house for just himself and his daughter, and in such an isolated position, especially when you consider that he didn't just buy the land on which the property was built, but also the eleven acres that surround it, too. But what was *really* weird was the fact he employed a medium to help him find a suitable piece of land on which to build his house.'

'Do you think he was looking for ley lines?' Tyrus says.

'Dowsing for ley lines as we know it today didn't exist back then, and the term "ley lines" wasn't even coined until the 1960s.'

'I'm sorry, you've lost me.' Chloe shakes her head. 'Ley lines?'

'They're like... energy currents that run underneath the earth,' Tyrus says. 'Magnetic lines in nature that mammals and birds use when they migrate long distances.'

'Ley lines are believed to hold great energy,' Mad Dog says. 'Supposedly, the ancients knew they existed and deliberately built their monuments on top of them, places like Stonehenge, Machu Picchu, the Egyptian pyramids – even Glastonbury. They're all said to be built on top of these energy lines.'

'Sounds like pseudoscience bullshit,' Chloe mutters.

'Yes, okay, some people think so,' Mad Dog says. 'But I don't think Lonsdale was dowsing for ley lines. I think he was dowsing for *time*lines.'

'You mean...' Chloe frowns, as though trying to pick up the lost thread of her thoughts. 'I'm sorry, I haven't the foggiest what you mean.'

'Like a time-machine? In the *land?*' Tyrus asks.

'If you've heard of ley lines you probably know a little about geopathic stress?' Mad Dog asks, looking at Tyrus.

'Geological faults caused by underground water courses, drainage pipes or electromagnetic radiation,' Tyrus says. 'It's where the term "Sick Building Syndrome" comes from.'

Chloe side-eyes him. 'Jesus, you're such a geek.'

'But he's right,' Mad Dog says, warming to his subject. 'It's well documented that geostress can have harmful effects on both animals and humans. Body aches, palpitations, asthma, headaches, fatigue, depression, anxiety – they've all been linked to geostress, with strong evidence that prolonged exposure can lead to even more severe symptoms. Of course, the ancients were far more attuned to nature and their surroundings than we are today, and these areas of stress are hard for us to detect, but when the energy is strong enough...' His eyes swing to Flynn. 'You said yourself that you felt something was wrong as soon as you walked into the house.'

'I felt... something,' Flynn says.

'I did, too,' Tyrus says. 'Pins and needles, tinnitus. I guess I shrugged it off.'

'Man, I didn't feel anything like that,' Jonesy says.

'You were probably just stoned,' Chloe mutters.

'It didn't last long,' Flynn says, then frowns, recalling the flood of rage that overwhelmed her as she watched Chloe and Jackson together, anger moving through her like a sickness.

'Ley lines can cause geostress, just the way you described,' Mad Dog says. 'But the points where these lines intersect are even more powerful. They can create vortexes, charged spirals of energy. It probably won't surprise you to hear that Temple Fall is built on an intersection just like that. It's basically a powerhouse of energy that pools and condenses until it's so strong, it distorts time. Kind of like a black hole.

'I think Lonsdale knew it, or at least suspected it, and I think that's the reason why he bought that land and built his house where the church once stood. A place like that would have been a fascinating draw for a scholar who had not only an obsession with time, but also a sickly daughter who had very little of it left.'

'You think he was trying to manipulate time to save his daughter?' Flynn asks.

Mad Dog shrugs. 'I think it's possible. Like I said, he really did love her.' He cracks open another Stella, shoots them a cryptic smile. 'Which makes what he did to her all the more shocking.'

He works his beer in the silence.

'What did he do?' Jonesy asks.

Mad Dog lowers his drink, belches softly behind his clenched fist. 'Shot her in the back of the skull with his Baker rifle when she was playing on her rocking horse. Then he swallowed a bullet.'

Flynn stiffens, her thoughts again swinging back to Mitchell. She glances at Riley, wishing she'd insisted on making her stay in the van, but she is lost in her game, oblivious to Mad Dog's dark story.

'Fucking hell.' Chloe's gaze drops to the photograph of Florence, smiling dreamily from another era. 'But you said he *doted* on her.'

'Oh, he did. But by all accounts, as soon as he moved into

Temple Fall he started to change. He fired the girl's nanny and withdrew from society, pretty much disappeared from public life. I suppose you could say he became something of a recluse.' Mad Dog's voice drops away on these last words, awkwardness creeping back into his demeanour as his eyes flash round the canned walls of his living room.

Flynn turns the page of the scrapbook on her lap, stares at the articles pasted there, tightly cramped newsprint outlining details of Florence Lonsdale's murder, her father's suicide.

'This doesn't make sense,' she says. 'I found no mention of any murders when I researched the house.'

'Well, I doubt you found much of anything at all about Temple Fall,' Mad Dog says. 'Like I say, I printed all this from a microfiche years ago. Nowadays, the only people that know how dangerous that place is have the good sense to stay away.'

'What happened to the house after Lonsdale died?' Jonesy asks.

'He left the property to his sister, Louisa, but she died six months later when a section of masonry fell away from the stone window surround, crushing her.'

'Jesus,' Tyrus mutters.

'After that, the house sat empty until 1882, when Mr and Mrs Thomas bought it.'

Mad Dog passes Flynn the second scrapbook. Pasted to the first page is the mugshot of Lyda, beside another of a man Flynn does not recognise.

'The man is Nelson Thomas,' Mad Dog says. 'I couldn't find much on either Nelson or Agnes before they moved into the house. Nelson was a banker in London, Agnes was his second wife. They were both in their fifties when they married, and only a few months after they tied the knot, they bought Temple Fall.'

'Who is Agnes?' Chloe asks.

'Agnes Devlin was an alias Lyda used before she was married, probably an attempt to shake off the criminal charges in her past. Presumably she wouldn't have wanted her new husband to know about any of that. It would have also made it harder for mothers to track her down, should they try and reclaim the babies they'd placed under her care.'

Nelson is a young man in his daguerreotype portrait, with wavy dark hair and a thick handle-bar moustache. Faint crinkles around his eyes lend him a kind, affable countenance.

Beneath these two shots, a wedding photograph of them both together: Lyda, in a white dress with puffed sleeves and a white lace veil, sits in a chair clutching a bouquet of flowers. Nelson stands behind her, dressed in a dark frockcoat, white waistcoat and striped trousers. A flower on his lapel, a black top hat in one hand.

The newly married couple stare into the camera, neither of them smiling. Their poses are rigid, stilted, and while Lyda leans slightly towards Nelson, he does not respond in kind. His free hand is clenched by his side, and a vaguely baffled look creases his brow. They look like strangers beside each other.

'Lyda had served six months in prison for an incident of child neglect, before she moved into Temple Fall.'

'And Nelson?' Chloe asks.

'Had a great reputation,' Mad Dog says. 'A bit of a philanthropist, subscribed to a few charities, helped fund a local night shelter for the homeless, made contributions to the parish church where volunteers raised money for the poor. Who knows, maybe Lyda was part of that community, helping on a Sunday to crochet blankets and socks for the needy.'

Flynn's eyes creep back to the image of Lyda Gray. She knows, deep down, that on this point, Mad Dog is mistaken: the only way Flynn imagines the woman in the photograph involving herself in charity would have been under the guise of ensnaring Nelson Thomas.

'Nelson dropped a clanger when he married her, that's for sure. Anyway, not long after they moved into Temple Fall, Nelson was dead.'

'How did he die?' Flynn asks.

'Coroners entered a verdict of accidental death after he took a stumble down the stairs, and no one seemed to question it at the time. Apparently he'd started to drink heavily after he re-married and he was drunk when he fell. But if Lyda thought marrying him was her passport to riches, she was sorely mistaken. Nelson was a rich man, but he only left his pregnant wife one shilling in his will. The rest of his fortune? Gave it all away to charity.'

'A shilling doesn't sound like much,' Chloe says.

'In today's money, that'd be about five or ten pence,' Mad Dog says.

'Wow, that's a stone-cold bitch slap from the grave,' Chloe mutters.

'She got the house though,' Jonesy says.

'Yeah,' Mad Dog concedes, shooting Jonesy a loaded look. 'She got the house. But a big place like that would've taken a lot of looking after, a lot of money that she didn't have. She'd have had to find a way of making some, or she'd have ended up queuing for handouts outside the same charities her husband used to support.'

'So that's when she started the baby farming stuff,' Chloe says.

'Well, she'd already been involved in that business before she met Nelson, but after his death, she took it up again in earnest. What she did to those babies...' Mad Dog breaks off, shaking his head.

'Who owned the house after that?' Flynn asks.

'Well, it stood empty until around 1983, then it was sold to a private developer.'

'Eliza Lister,' Tyrus says. 'The woman who killed herself before she could bulldoze the house.'

'"Killed herself",' Mad Dog scoffs, takes another tug on his beer. 'Yeah, right.'

Frustrated, Flynn stands up and moves to the window. Andy is still sitting in his van, eyes closed to the sun that hits the windscreen. Clusters of snowdrops shiver in the quiet breeze, the branches of the oak tree shake like old bones.

'There must be something we can do to stop it,' she mutters.

'Listen, hey,' Mad Dog says. 'I said I'd tell you what I knew about the house, and I did. But if you're asking how you can stop what's coming – I'm sorry, but I just don't know. In all honesty, I don't know if there *is* anything you can do.'

Chloe says something, but Flynn doesn't hear her. She is staring at the dappled shadows swaying beneath the oak tree. Clouds spill across the sun, the day darkens. Cold air brushes Flynn's neck. The branch shadows shiver, thicken, twisting together to take the shape of a figure. A woman in black, stood beneath the tree's canopy.

Fear sears Flynn, the sudden presentiment that this woman has come for her. That it is her time. Her *turn*.

She blinks, and the woman has gone. The branches swing, scattering shadows that dance to the beat of the breeze.

Tyrus's voice pulls her from her thoughts. '... something more than just sitting round and waiting until it's our turn to die!'

'Look, I don't know what to say. You could drop a bomb on Temple Fall and I don't think it would make any difference. That house – it's built on foundations that straddle both the living world and the dead. It's a place we can't reach, a place that isn't meant for the living.'

'But people *do* survive that house,' Jonesy says. 'Mitchell Lister – he's still alive.'

'The difference is that Mitchell *wants* to die,' Mad Dog says. 'He never recovered from what happened to his family. That house is like a parasite inside him, feeding on his pain, just like it's feeding on your terror of dying.

'It's like... like a tree that has its roots deep beneath the ground. You look at it and all you can see is what's above the surface, right? But somehow, you know it's diseased, you feel it. Because those roots, they burrow into some other liminal place, like they've punctured reality the way a tree's roots can puncture stone. And it's from that place that it draws its strength, feeding on that darkness in just the same way a tree draws nutrients from deep in the soil. But that other place – it's a place we can't reach, a place on the margins. A place that isn't meant for the living.'

'Yeah, well,' Flynn says, staring at the swaying oak, 'trees can be chopped down.'

'I'm sorry, really I am,' Mad Dog says. 'Maybe you can chop this tree down, but I don't think you'll ever be able to destroy its roots.'

I'm sat on the floor, staring at the seven Scrabble tiles stacked on the rack:

E P T P A R D

Heather watches me from the other side of the table. Her eyes look strange, the whites tinged pink, splodged with tiny red dots. Her skin is swollen, bloated, and her feet poking from the bottom of her nightgown are a reddish-purple colour. The smell of bleach that always clings to her is undetectable beneath the thicker, heavier stench of decay. Her bathrobe's belt is knotted around her neck, a garrot squeezing her skin which bulges over the tight band, stopping her breath.

It doesn't bother her though, the not breathing, because Heather is dead. She died years ago, hung herself from the belt of the bathrobe that knots her throat now. She called 999 before she did it, not for herself – she was determined to be quite dead by the time the ambulance showed up – but for me.

The front door stands open, sunshine splashes the carpet in a spill of gold. I close my eyes, slant my ear to the rustle of the wind outside, imagine it is Heather's breath, moving in and out of her rotting lips, filling her lungs with air; imagine her heart jerking to life beneath her decomposing chest, blasting blood through her dried-out veins.

I open my eyes again. Heather is still watching me, her red eyes unblinking, her chest still as the grave. Sand drains through the timer.

I consider my tiles again, but I can't see a word. I'm not fast like Heather, who doesn't even flip the sand timer when it is her go, just places her letters on the Scrabble board, as though each word presents itself the instant I take my turn. The words she plays are ugly, each one scraping a chill down the back of my neck: DANGER; DEADLY; MURDER; MASSACRE; OUTSIDE; KILLERS; TORTURE.

A word suddenly shouts out at me, and it's one that fills my lungs with fresh air.

DEPART

I spell the word on the Scrabble board, using the D from Heather's DANGER. I look up at her, grinning. Something shifts in the red bolts of her eyes, a flick of anger behind her brow. She shakes her head, leans over the board. The smell of death stirs on the air as she slides my letters around on the board, rearranging them. She takes the P that is still on my rack, adds that to the word, the word she wants me to play.

TRAPPED

I stare at that word and suddenly I can't breathe. Anger swells inside me, and my hand shoots out before I can stop myself, knocking the board over. I surge to my feet with a cry as tiles topple across the floor, but Heather rises too, reaching black-tipped fingers towards me, ready to wrap round my throat and squeeze, to drag me into death with her. I throw up my hands to protect myself, but already she is choking me, squeezing the breath from my lungs, pushing me down into a swooping darkness...

Flynn lurches up in bed, her hands laced round her neck, feet tangled in the churned sheets. Her heart thwacks her sternum, her breath is ragged. She pulls herself up, presses the heels of her hands into her eyes as the jerk of her pulse steadily slows.

She knows instantly she has slept late; light glows around the edges of the curtains, and the sofa bed Chloe has been sleeping on is folded up, the blankets heaped on top.

Flynn's nightmare clings to her thoughts, the details so visceral, they almost feel like a real memory: the starbursts of blood in her mother's eyes, the bloated corruption of her flesh, the belt of her bathrobe, buried so deep in her throat it was barely visible.

She pushes her hands through her hair, reminds herself she has other things to worry about.

Today is Jonesy's birthday.

Wary of causing alarm or suspicion, and conscious of the rumours swirling about birthday suicide pacts, Jonesy had been reluctant to ask his parents about the time of his birth. Instead, he had contacted the maternity ward at St James's Hospital, where he had been born. They had emailed him back only yesterday to inform him of the time they had recorded: 17:45.

Flynn checks her phone, hoping to have a message from either She-Ra or Mad Dog, but there is nothing. Even though she knows deep down that she will never hear from them again, a sinking weight settles in the pit of her stomach. The day's sand timer has been turned, the hours and minutes draining until their final conclusion, and they will have to see it through on their own.

She showers, brushes her teeth and gets changed. Then she throws everything she will need for an overnight stay at Jonesy's house in her rucksack and goes downstairs.

As she moves down the hallway, she hears her mum talking in the kitchen. Quietly, Flynn moves to the door. Jenna is sat at the breakfast table, her back to Flynn, speaking into her phone. She finishes the call, her tone polite but formal, then slouches at the breakfast bar, staring at the mobile in her hands. The bowed shape of her body, the tilt of her head and the curve of her shoulders emanate a bone-deep weariness, a helplessness that borders on despair.

'Hey,' Flynn says, walking in.

Her mum instantly straightens, pushes her hair from her face. Flynn notices the way she swipes the back of her hand over her cheeks before turning round to flash her a smile.

'Hey, I didn't expect to see you up this early.'

'Sarcasm doesn't suit you, Mum.'

'There's coffee in the pot if you want some.'

'Thanks.' Flynn moves to the counter and pours herself a mug. 'Where's Chloe?' She slides onto the stool beside her mum, who nods towards the living room.

'You two are spending a lot of time together.'

Flynn blows across her coffee. 'I thought you'd be pleased. You kept telling me to mend bridges with the others.'

'I only want what's best for you, for all of you.' Exhaustion drags in her voice, and her gaze flicks towards the door. 'What's going on with Clo? Has something happened at home? It's just she's over here all the time now, and you know I don't mind, but I just... I'm worried about her. She looks seriously unwell, Flynn.'

'She's okay.' Flynn avoids her mum's gaze. 'I mean, she *will* be okay.'

Her mum lowers her eyes to the blank screen in her hands.

'Who was that?' Flynn says.

'Hmm?'

Flynn takes a sip of her coffee, nods to the mobile. 'On the phone.'

'Oh – Riley's teacher.' She slides the phone onto the counter. 'There's been another incident at school. Riley pushed some other kid off the climbing wall, tried to blame it on her imaginary friend. This kid, he wasn't badly hurt, thank god, but Riley had a tantrum when her teacher told her she had to stay in at break.' She shakes her head. 'Her behaviour's getting out of control. Honestly, I don't know what to do with her anymore.'

The defeat in her mum's voice surprises Flynn. If Jenna has ever felt self-doubt as a mother, she has never before revealed it. Flynn knows it can't have been easy for her, opening her heart and home to two troubled and traumatised kids, but she always made it seem effortless, natural. With the deftest touch and a few well-chosen words, she could take the sting out of a hurt, dissolve the anger from a rage, lift spirits when they slumped.

'She's been through a lot,' Flynn says, scrabbling for the words of encouragement that usually come from her mother. 'She'll snap out of this imaginary friend stuff soon.'

'Will she?' A hardness creeps into Jenna's tone and her eyes pin Flynn, a silent glinting challenge. 'You still don't understand, do you? She thinks she's going to lose you again.'

'She isn't going to lose me.'

'Flynn, you didn't see what your disappearance did to her. Now, every time you leave the house, she's in a panic you won't come back. When I pick her up from school, the first thing she asks is where you are, and when you're out with your friends, she's a nervous wreck. Is it any wonder she's so angry? *I'm* angry.

You disappeared on us, Flynn. What's to stop you from doing it again?' She drops her face into her hands. 'I lost you, and now all this "Jenna" bullshit. I feel like I'm losing her, too.'

'I'm here,' Flynn says, her insides wrenching. 'You haven't lost me, and as for Riley – it's just a phase.'

'She looks up to you, Flynn. I don't think you realise how much she needs you.'

Riley isn't the one I'm worried about right now, Flynn thinks. But she can't say that, can't expect her mum to believe the truth. So she pushes back the heaviness in her chest and stands up, shoulders her backpack. Her mum stands too, alarm flickering behind her eyes.

'You're going already? You've not eaten breakfast.'

The worry in her voice makes Flynn's heart clench. Her mum, who has always before seemed larger than life, capable, strong, is looking at her with a look of such frailty and fear that Flynn can suddenly imagine how she will look as an old woman. An unwelcome thought chases the image: *Will I still be around when she's old?*

Flynn hugs her mum, places her hands on her shoulders and steadies her with her eyes, wondering as she does it, when she became the taller of the two, when she became the one seeking to reassure.

'It's going to be alright, Mum. And as for Riley, you know I'll always look out for her. Try not to worry, okay?'

Jonesy's house is less than a ten-minute walk away, but Flynn quickly finds herself wishing she had booked a taxi. Chloe walks painfully slowly, and has to frequently stop to catch her breath, which rasps in and out as though she is physically pushing her body beyond endurance. A few months ago, she would have skipped out of the house in a crop top and skirt, regardless of the cold, but today, despite the mild weather and the fact she has wrapped herself up in multiple layers, she shivers convulsively.

Flynn's eyes keep flitting nervously to her friend, to her dry, chapped lips, the sores at the edges of her mouth, to the thinning hair that spills beneath her bobble hat. Trying to catch a glimpse of the old Chloe in place of this gaunt and hollow-eyed imposter.

'I dreamed I was back in the house last night,' Chloe says, stuffing her hands deep into her pockets. Her sugared breath hangs on the air, powdered pear drops, yet another symptom of her high blood sugar levels. 'I couldn't find my way out.' She shudders, passes a frightened glance to Flynn. 'Do you think that's what happens when we die? That we somehow end up back inside that house?'

'No,' Flynn says. 'I don't think we go anywhere. When we die, we're just... gone.'

'How can you say that after everything we've seen?'

'I haven't seen anything,' Flynn says, but her voice catches like a rag nail on the memory of Lyda Gray, sliding behind Jackson in a sweep of tar-black shadows, the basalt glitter of eyes in sunken sockets. 'Only... *her*.'

'And that's not enough?'

Flynn doesn't answer, locked in the memory of Lyda's cold grin.

'It's strange though,' Chloe says, 'how Lyda lived in that house for so many years without it turning on her.'

'Why *would* it hurt her?' Flynn says. 'She was doing its work. Those poor babies... It's like that saying, don't bite the hand that feeds you.'

'It really bothers you, doesn't it?' Chloe says, watching her.

'What?'

'That you're related to the baby farmer.'

'She isn't exactly the family history I was hoping for.'

'Let it go. It was almost a hundred and fifty years ago. She has nothing to do with you.'

'I know.'

Yet even as she speaks, an image of Lyda Gray coalesces in her mind. Standing in front of the gallows, her belly slack from the baby she had just delivered, her breasts leaking milk for the child she could not feed. Had she been allowed to hold him after he was born, or was he whisked away as soon as the cord that bound them was cut? What went through her mind as she stood on the trapdoor, a sack over her head and a noose around her neck? Had she spoken any last words? Were her thoughts consumed by her son, or was he as insignificant to her as all those other babies she had brutally murdered?

Flynn tries to push these thoughts from her mind, but she feels tarnished, as though the baby farmer has reached out from her unmarked grave and placed a hand against her cheek.

'You're obsessing,' Chloe says, nudging her shoulder. 'Seriously, who doesn't have a black sheep in the family?'

'Clo, *Jonesy's* a black sheep, but he wouldn't turn round tomorrow and start killing babies.'

'It's hard to imagine, isn't it?' Chloe says. 'Knowing you were going to be hanged as soon as you delivered your baby? Talk about barbaric.'

'What she did to those babies was barbaric,' Flynn mutters.

'What I can't understand is how the fuck she managed to get pregnant in the first place. I mean, *woof*.'

'I imagine the same way all other women get pregnant.'

'Poor bastard.' Chloe shoots her a sly look. 'You know, you and Lyda... There *is* a family resemblance.'

'Fuck off!' Flynn grins, goes to shove her friend, but when she grabs Chloe's arm and feels the slide of bone beneath her paper-thin skin, she thinks better of it.

They reach Jonesy's house and let themselves in without

knocking, something they only do when Jonesy's dad is working away. Both Tyrus and Jonesy are in the living room, sprawled on the sofas. Tyrus is channel surfing, Jonesy stares at the screen, working his way through a family-sized pack of Maltesers.

Chloe grimaces. 'It smells like armpits in here.'

Flynn parts the curtains and throws open a window.

'Have you two been up all night?' she says, her eyes moving over the empty pizza boxes on the floor, crumpled cans scattered around the room.

'We were playing *Crash Bandicoot*,' Tyrus says.

'Yeah, it was wild,' Jonesy mutters sardonically. 'I mean, my eighteenth birthday and I'm sat at home drinking alcohol-free beer and gaming.'

'He's been like this all night,' Tyrus mutters.

'Yeah well, I don't need babysitting,' Jonesy says.

Flynn drops onto the sofa beside him. 'We're not babysitting you. We always see you on your birthday.'

Jonesy rolls his eyes. 'Not like this though, not sat round like a fucking *knitting* party.'

'He's just grumpy coz he wants a smoke,' Tyrus says, picking up a pizza box, rifling through the leftovers for a crust.

Flynn's eyes flash to Jonesy. 'You told me you flushed everything away.'

'I did! Jesus, don't you start on me and all.'

Chloe comes back in carrying four cups of tea. She passes them round, keeping one for herself, then slumps onto the sofa beside Tyrus.

'Oh, a cup of tea,' Jonesy quips. 'Exactly what I need.'

'Stop being such a whiny bitch.' Chloe turns the PlayStation on, scrolls to *Fortnite* and drops onto the floor in front of the television.

Jonesy tosses Chloe a controller and she uses it to scroll to her skin, Jinx, a Disney princess version of her with flowing yellow hair, creamy skin and wide blue eyes. She is last on the leaderboard. Jonesy, aka Snoop, is in top spot, his fluffy blonde hair half-covered by a baseball cap, a box of chips sticking out of his pocket. Tyrus, or DeLorean, is fourth, umber-skinned and dimpled, an ammo belt strapped to his chest, his black hair buzzed with faded sides. He is closely tailed by Flynn, renamed Ripley, in fifth place. Jonesy had created her skin, giving her a bouncy ponytail, huge headphones and, inexplicably, an eye-patch.

Flynn's heart clutches at the sight of Mei's and Jackson's skins, Aerial and Dallas, holding second and third places. Aerial's hair is scraped into a topknot that exposes her shaved back and sides, her left ear is riddled with piercings, and her bare arms are covered in the tattoos she talked about getting when she turned eighteen. Dallas wears a cardboard box on his head, a smiley face painted on the front. A camera hangs round his neck and he carries an axe in each hand.

Flynn realises this is the first time they have played *Fortnite* since Jackson and Mei died. The knowledge that Dallas's and Aerial's scores will never change, that they will drop lower down the leaderboard until the day Jonesy deletes the game or their accounts, presses a pain against her throat.

Flynn realises it is an insignificant detail beside everything else that is going on, but every breath she takes feels suddenly too small, too heavy. The heat of tears presses behind her eyes. She stands up, turning so the others can't see her face, and walks into the kitchen. She leans against the sink, takes a long, deep breath.

Chloe and Jonesy shout over the stutter of gunfire. It is so easy for Flynn to imagine Jackson and Mei in there with them, she can almost trick herself into thinking it is an ordinary Saturday afternoon.

Almost.

She needs something to busy her hands, a task to distract her from the ticking clock. She opens the fridge, peers at the measly contents inside, and starts to grab ingredients at random: onions, garlic, chicken breasts, some drooping celery. She sets everything on the worktop, opens the cupboards, takes out a jar of passata.

Tyrus pokes his head round the doorframe.

'You okay?' His look of concern shifts to one of dismay as he takes in the assembled ingredients on the counter. 'You're not cooking, are you?'

'Wow, your confidence in me is overwhelming.'

Tyrus moves towards her. 'Yeah, well, I still remember the Snoopy cake you made Chloe for her birthday.'

'Oh, come on,' Flynn says. 'I was, like, ten.'

'Snoopy looked like he'd died in a pool of blood.'

'He was sleeping on his red roof. It's an iconic image.'

'Yeah, I mean. That's not how it looked. It looked like a beagle bloodbath. Amelie cried when she saw it.'

Flynn chuckles at the memory of Chloe's little sister, only four years old then, running out of the room in tears after seeing Snoopy lying in a bath of dripping red icing.

Tyrus washes his hands and pulls the chopping board from the cupboard. 'Then there was your scrambled egg with Frosties?'

'That was an experiment.'

'Was your jackfruit risotto an experiment, too?'

'Granted, I was overreaching there.' Flynn grimaces at the memory of the meal, which she had brought home from food tech in a Tupperware box. It had looked like something scooped from the pavement outside a pub on a Saturday night, and when her mum had gamely tasted a forkful, she had promptly gipped and fled the room.

Tyrus claps his hands together, assesses the ingredients. 'So, what are we making?'

Flynn shrugs. 'I was just gonna chop it all up and sling it in a pan—'

'Stop, you're killing me! Let's see...' He tosses the wilted celery in the bin, then opens the fridge, pulls out some fresh coriander, tomatoes, a pack of red bell peppers, a chunk of ginger. 'Looks like tomato and chicken spiced curry to me.'

'I'll be your sous-chef,' Flynn says.

'Right, you chop the chicken and the peppers.'

'Yes, Chef.'

'And stick the kettle on.'

Tyrus pulls a skillet from the cupboard, drops a glug of oil into it, sets it on the stove and turns on the heat. He starts dicing the onions, the blade falling so close to his fingertips it makes Flynn wince.

For a few minutes, they work in silence, the complex soundboard of Chloe and Jonesy's game punctuated by their frustrated shouts.

'I'm worried about Clo,' Tyrus says, scooping onions and chicken into the pan. 'I don't think she's injecting properly.'

Flynn pauses with the blade. 'She's just distracted by everything that's going on.'

'She looks ill.' Tyrus crushes a bulb of garlic with the flat side of a bread knife then begins to finely chop it. His hand rocks back and forth with practised precision. 'She needs to see a doctor.'

'She promised me she'd make an appointment with the GP as soon as Jonesy's birthday's out of the way.'

Tyrus adds the garlic and peppers to the pan, then starts to chop a chunk of ginger. His face is drawn, set. Watching him, Flynn feels a cold knot tighten the base of her spine.

She folds her arms and leans against the counter. 'What's eating you, Ty?'

A muscle in his jaw flickers, and Flynn senses some kind of struggle taking place behind his eyes.

'Whatever it is, spill it,' Flynn says. 'I don't think we should be keeping secrets from each other right now.'

Tyrus adds the chopped ingredients to the skillet, sets the lid on top and lowers the heat. He flips the dish-towel over his shoulder and turns to Flynn.

'Mei's mum called me yesterday.'

The words drop a silence behind them, and Flynn feels herself grow still inside.

'She found my combat jacket, the one I lent Mei that she refused to give back.'

An image of Mei, wearing Tyrus's green coat, fills Flynn's mind. The way her hands disappeared in the too-long sleeves, her habit of chewing on the zip beneath her chin. Grief closes its walls around Flynn again, that terrible black weight, so hard to breathe around. She remembers Tyrus shivering in the cold outside Temple Fall, annoyed with Mei for failing to return his coat, Mei's flippant remark, the teasing smile in her voice: *You can have it back when I'm dead.*

'I went over to get it this morning,' Tyrus says. 'I don't know why, it's not like I'll ever wear it again, not now.' His eyes drill into the floor, a muscle in his jaw twitches. 'Anyway, when I got there, her mum told me to go and get it from her wardrobe. Standing in her room, all our old photos tacked to her wall, her things everywhere...' He shakes his head, brushes a hand over his tightly shaved hair. For a moment, Flynn is sure he is about to break down, but then he looks at her, and she sees more than grief in his eyes.

'I found something.'

'Go on,' Flynn says.

'Her GoPro.' Tyrus slides his mobile from his pocket, scrolls through it and passes it to Flynn. 'She was wearing it when she fell.'

Flynn's heart quickens as she takes his phone. Over the years,

Mei had sent her countless GoPro videos of her parkour runs, and so the triangular PLAY button centred over a grey expanse of concrete is so heartbreakingly familiar, it almost undoes her.

'It was just sitting there on her desk,' Tyrus says. 'I watched it, then I sent it to my phone.'

Flynn's finger hovers over the PLAY button. Her pulse thrashes her eardrums.

'Have you shown the others?'

Tyrus shakes his head.

Mei used to wear the camera in a head strap across her forehead, saying it gave the viewer the most immersive POV footage. In the paused frame on the screen, Mei is looking at the ground. Flynn can see her scuffed sweatpants, the tops of her trainers.

She knows this video will not be edited like all the others Mei sent her. No soundtrack layering each daredevil stunt, no time-warp transitions, frame splits or location switches. Only Mei, running the clock on the last moments of her life.

Flynn swallows, breath shaking in and out. She doesn't want to watch, but she knows there might be something in this raw footage that can help them understand what happened to her friend, some clue to help them figure out what is stalking them. But more than that, she feels an obligation to Mei, to watch and bear witness to her final minutes alive, almost as though by doing so, she will somehow be reaching out, holding her friend's hand as she took her last breath.

She presses PLAY.

The image jerks into motion, wind blasts through the built-in microphone. It muffles and distorts Mei's ragged breath as she races across the concrete. The camera shakes to the beat of her footfalls, her bandaged hands whip up and down. A stretch of blue sky above, so clear it looks smug, bragging.

One hand flashes out, plants on a wall to help propel her

over it. Her feet flick briefly into shot, then hit the ground running again. Another low wall veers into shot, and this time she flips her body 360 over it. The camera glides smoothly as her body spins in flight, nothing but sky and the tips of Mei's tucked knees. She lands, and again she is running, her body always in motion, graceful and fluid, as though she has to cover every inch of space.

She scrambles over a chain-link fence, drops into a pile of leaves. Shifts direction, a jag to the side, and now Flynn can see the blade of her shadow racing alongside her. She jumps onto a wall and the sunlight hits her from a different angle, shrinking her shadow to a distant shape at the bottom of a flight of steps.

The video slices up and down as she pivots, leaps, flips over obstacles and railings, and Flynn starts to feel dizzy watching. Mei launches herself at a wall, scales its metal pipes, using ledges and grooves in the brickwork to heave herself towards the top of the building. The camera follows the movement of her head, records everything she sees. And as it slashes up and down, there is nothing and no one with her, only a stomach-wrenching drop beneath her that steadily grows as Mei climbs higher and higher.

Her head flashes up, revealing a taunting glimpse of the railing at the edge of the roofline, so close, only a few metres away now. And Flynn knows how it all plays out, knows there is nothing she can do to change the outcome, yet she wills Mei to reach up, to snap her bandaged hand around that cold rail and haul herself onto the safety of the roof. Her own fingers twitch, every fibre of her being straining towards the metal bar, towards safety.

A ribbon of distortion rolls slowly up and down the screen, and then the image scrambles, the pixels sticking and stretching, as though the film is bring pulled in opposite directions. Flynn can't see anyone, but she is struck by the sudden impression that

Mei is no longer alone, that another presence is right there on the wall with her, even though it is quite obviously impossible.

Goosebumps break across Flynn's skin.

Mei's breath seizes, a shocked inhalation.

The sound of static wipes out all other noise.

She falls.

If she screams, the sound is scratched out by the strange static roar, the deadly plummet erased by the corrupted video.

Mei lands with a thud that punches a hole in Flynn's gut. The image on screen suddenly clarifies, the sound of the wind replaces the scream of static. As though the impact of her fall worked on the GoPro the way a percussive slap might fix an old-fashioned TV when it scrambled. The faces of the grey walls slide up to the bragging blue sky, showing just how far she has fallen.

Flynn covers her mouth with her hand, pressing back a sob. She passes the phone back to Tyrus.

'There was something up there with her,' Tyrus says.

'I don't know,' Flynn whispers.

But she does. She knows it in her bones. Knew it the moment she heard Mei's sharp intake of breath. It was only for a second, a blink of an eye, but for that beat of time, she was not alone on the wall. Someone – some*thing* pushed her.

'What are we going to do?' Tyrus asks.

Flynn shakes her head, meets his gaze. 'I don't know.'

They pass the next few hours watching TV and gaming. Jonesy, Tyrus and Flynn go into the back garden to shoot hoops, while Chloe sits on the old tyre swing, wrapped up in layers, watching them. At three o'clock, they go back inside, and Tyrus dishes up the curry, which they eat in front of the television. The scrape of spoons against bowls abrades Flynn's nerves like the scratch of nails down a blackboard. Her eyes keep shifting to the clock above the mantelpiece, wishing the time would run down faster while also dreading its inevitable passage.

Just after four o'clock, Tyrus gets up to check all the windows and doors are locked. Flynn resists the compulsion to tell him that his efforts are futile; all the locks in the world can't protect them from the coming danger. Chloe sits cross-legged on the carpet, playing a game on her mobile, Jonesy's leg bounces as he stares vacuously at the TV, Flynn chews her bitten down nails, channel surfing until she settles for an episode of *The Simpsons*, which she knows Jonesy loves.

She glances again at the clock. 16:52. Time has grown sticky, the third hand on the clock stubbornly refusing to sweep forwards at an ordinary pace. Chloe scans her blood sugar levels and Flynn tries not to watch as she administers her insulin shot. *The Simpsons* finishes, credits roll.

17:01. Someone knocks on the front door. Tyrus goes to see who it is. He leaves the chain on the lock, opens it a crack. On the television, the opening jingle of a quiz-show plays. Flynn moves to the hallway, straining to hear what Tyrus is saying. He closes the door, shakes his head. Collecting for charity, he tells her. His dark skin looks ashen.

The strain in the living room has a physical quality. It presses against the back of Flynn's skull, thrums beneath her skin. Where ordinarily, they would all be shouting the answers to the quizmaster's questions, now they sit quietly, barely registering what they are watching.

Unable to abide the tension any longer, Flynn gets up and gathers all the curry bowls. She takes them into the kitchen, scoops the leftovers into the bin then dumps the dirty pots into the sink. She adds a squirt of washing up liquid and fills it with hot, sudsy water. Resting her hands on the porcelain, she stares out of the window at the back garden. Daylight has fled and darkness squats in stagnant pools beneath the trees.

She glances at the clock on the oven. 17:12. The air feels heavy, soupy with tension. Flynn stirs her hand through the hot water in the sink, watches the bubbles break apart and reshape, like wind-stirred clouds. The quizmaster's voice drifts into the kitchen, parting the silence: *The term 'fractal expressionism' was coined to describe the painting style of which famous artist?* A buzzer sounds, but the answer comes to Flynn before the contestant answers: *Jackson Pollock*.

Her gaze shifts to her face in the glass. She looks exhausted, haggard. Wisps of hair have escaped her ponytail, and the way they frizz up makes her think of the baby farmer. As she stares at her reflection, her eyes fill with a darkness that quickly spreads, sinking her sockets into black pools. The shadows shuffle down her face, her widow's peak slides lower, her eyebrows thin, her mouth flattens.

Lyda Gray smiles at her from the glass.

The air whooshes from Flynn's lungs as though she has been kicked. Her eyes widen, but now all she can see is her own pale, scared reflection.

The air feels tight with cold, so she lowers her hands into the hot water. Warmth trickles through her fingers, up her wrists and arms. It spreads through her chest, soothes her drumming heart. A delicious lassitude seeps into her muscles and her eyelids droop.

The quizmaster's voice from the other room: *Who was the founder and original lead guitarist of The Rolling Stones?* His voice sounds different. Snide. Mocking. But Flynn is so tired, the seascape of her mind darkening, growing silted, clouded. Blood pulses softly at her temples. She closes her eyes and a ribbon of calm slides through her. She is flotsam, floating on a drifting tide. The answer – *Brian Jones* – rises from the murk of her subconscious, turns upon the surface of her thoughts, like a dead and bloated fish.

Bruce Lee fought in only one official boxing match, the Hong Kong High School Boxing Tournament in 1958. The quizmaster's voice carries a sly twist of cruelty. *How old was he when he won it?* He sounds far away, and the silence that folds around his words is vast as an ocean.

Jackson Pollock... Brian Jones... Bruce Lee...

Jackson Darrow... Teddy Jones... Mei Lee...

With a rising howl, a gust of wind cracks against the window. Flynn's eyes snap open, as the answer – *18* – screams through her mind.

A woman, dressed head to toe in black, is stood on the other side of the glass. She is young, a girl, really, on the cusp of womanhood. Her eyes, set within impossibly dark sockets, are a striking grey-blue and her face possesses a fine-boned delicacy, though she has a worn look about her, a scrappiness that hints at hard-living and lean days. Her skin is so pale, she might have been woven from the fog that cloaks the garden, but there is nothing pale about the emotion in her expression, a rage so powerful, Flynn is sure it will crack the glass between them.

She glares at Flynn like a malevolent reflection, her eyes blazing pits, her mouth a chasm framing a mute scream. Still, Flynn feels the edges of that soundless cry, and senses an anguished rage pouring from those split lips. Flecks of darkness float from the woman's mouth, black petals that twist on the air and flutter slowly to the ground.

Her silent scream builds, widening like a broadening deluge of rain, a haze of static that fills every part of Flynn's consciousness. The smell of crushed roses, metallic and earthy, scents the air. Her shape blurs, turns translucent and begins to fade, like a polaroid in reverse.

Flynn staggers away from the window, breathing hard. Shock briefly pins her to the spot, but then she turns, hurries towards the living room, her movements clumsy, stilted, her limbs numb with shock. The gameshow has finished and Jonesy is scrolling through the channels again.

The bulb hanging from the ceiling flickers with a low buzz.

Flynn glances at the clock on the mantelpiece, dread spilling a leaden cold through her guts. The seven LED segments of each digital number flash, as though time is streaming forwards too fast to track.

A cold snap in the room, Flynn's pulse spasms in her throat, her heart is a crashing cymbal. The bulb's rapid flickering slows, the light dying like a fading pulse.

Jonesy stands up, frowning at the light bulb. He mutters something about faulty electrics, moves to the switch.

The image on the TV screen stretches, the pixels stick. The sound cuts out, the screen goes black.

And it is then that Flynn glimpses a figure, stood in the corner of the room. A shape revealed only in the darkness, vanishing in each faltering blink of light.

Lyda Gray.

Flynn starts towards Jonesy, but her movements feel slow, drugged. Even the motion of inflating her lungs feels protracted, the air thick as tar.

The light flickers back on, and the baby farmer isn't there. It dies again and her dim outline appears. Inching towards Jonesy in each spasm of darkness.

'Jonesy, *no!*' Flynn tries to shout the warning, but her lungs are drenched in cold, and the air in the room feels solid, unbreathable. Tyrus is bent over the back of the TV, fiddling with the cables, Chloe frowns, jabs at the remote as she aims it at the screen.

Jonesy reaches for the light switch.

The lights gasp out.

The dim outline of Lyda Gray is beside Jonesy. Time has

slowed, the seconds sticking to the frosted air. The room feels unnaturally still. Flynn watches the fog of Jonesy's breath swirl from his lips, an impossibly long exhalation.

He flicks the switch at the same time as Lyda's fingers touch his chest. It is the lightest contact, but it lifts Jonesy off his feet, flings him backwards. He crashes against the mirror, cracking the glass, and his body crumples to the floor.

Heat floods back into the room, the light bulb stops buzzing and stays on, the foul smell dissipates. Flynn pulls in a convulsive gulp of air and falls forwards as the world comes unstuck and time regains momentum.

'Jonesy!' She drops beside him, shakes his shoulder. '*Jonesy!*'

'Oh my god.' Chloe crouches beside her. 'Is he okay? Oh Jesus, his fingers...'

The tips of Jonesy's fingers are black where they touched the light switch. Flynn grabs his wrist. No pulse.

'He's not breathing,' she says.

Tyrus is already speaking into his phone, asking the 999 call handler for emergency services. Reeling off Jonesy's address. Begging them to hurry.

Flynn's thoughts flash back to the rudimentary CPR lesson she'd had at school, but panic lights a fire to the memory. She turns Jonesy onto his back, places the heel of her hand over his chest. *Thirty chest compressions, press down about 5 centimetres, two rescue breaths, repeat...*

She starts the compressions, dropping her weight onto Jonesy's chest.

1... 2... 3...

Tyrus: 'I don't know the postcode. He isn't breathing. Please hurry up.'

8... 9... 10...

Tyrus: 'No, no he isn't bleeding. Yes, my friend. She's just started chest compressions.'

'Please, please, please.' Chloe sobs, standing behind Flynn, her hands covering her mouth.

Despair stalks through Flynn's fingertips, down her wrists and arms. She feels as though she is dying alongside Jonesy.

Tyrus: 'His fingers are badly burned. He must've been electrocuted. Oh god. No, he doesn't have any medical conditions. Yes, he's on his back. Please hurry. What? How old?'

Tyrus's voice catches, trips on the answer.

16... 17... 18...

'Eighteen. He's eighteen.'

A sway of dizziness, Flynn's thoughts stutter. Darkness laps at the edges of her vision.

18...

The number is a net cast over her, dragging her down. A wash of grey buffets her vision, and for a moment she is sure she will black out. She focuses on Jonesy, pushes away the drowning darkness.

19... 20... 21...

She pins these numbers to the front of her mind, pictures them as Jonesy's future birthdays, Jonesy growing older, moving forwards with his life.

Tyrus: 'Yes, she's still doing chest compressions. How far away is the ambulance?'

28... 29... 30.

Flynn tips Jonesy's chin back, pinches his nose and blows two rescue breaths into his mouth. The touch of his cooling lips against hers presses a sharp jag against her throat. She resumes the compressions, trying to ignore the pounding of tears behind her eyes.

Tyrus: 'His lips are blue. Oh fuck, his lips are blue. Oh god.'

Chloe is crying.

Tyrus: 'Yes, one other person. Yes. Okay. Okay, I'll tell her.'

He turns to Chloe. 'Clo. *Clo!* Go outside, wait for the

ambulance on the street.'

Chloe stands there, staring at Jonesy, sobbing.

Tyrus: '*Go!*'

Flynn counts each compression, but Jonesy's eyes are open and fixed and his heart is a stone beneath her hands and she feels his departure, a sudden lacking beneath his skin, an absence that speaks of infinity. And she knows in her gut it doesn't matter how quickly the ambulance arrives.

Jonesy has already gone.

She doesn't stop, refuses to give up on him, but as she works his chest, her eyes slip to the clock on the mantlepiece. The digital display has stopped its erratic dance, the numbers standing clear and still as the letters on a freshly chiselled gravestone.

17:45.

PART 3

One need not be a Chamber – to be Haunted –
One need not be a House –
The Brain has Corridors – surpassing
Material Place –

EMILY DICKINSON, *POEM 407* (1862),
THE POEMS OF EMILY DICKINSON

EVELINA

JULY 2ND, 1882

Evelina had made every attempt to avoid coming here. She had taken the feminine ailments the midwife gave her, chased with gin the monthly pills the apothecary had recommended for 'relieving obstructions', and when these measures failed, had flushed her insides with alum and sulphite of zinc. Yet still, here she is, a chloroform handkerchief pressed to her nose, stirrups around her ankles bracing her legs apart. The tea that Doctor Katz gave her has turned her thoughts soupy and slow, but at least it has dulled the terror.

Still, she isn't so souped that she doesn't realise she is in a serious fix. Her gaze keeps sliding to the tray of instruments on the small table. They gleam dully in the shadowy room: long scissors, metallic hooks, a pair of pincers. What looks like an iron skewer.

The windows are cracked open but the air feels stagnant, soured by the smell of fear and butchery. The fading daylight provides little by the way of illumination, and she wonders, *Will he be able to see what he's doing?* Panic paints the thought so loud, Evelina is sure Doctor Katz must hear it. His back is turned to her as he washes his hands in the basin. Hands that will soon take up those cruel instruments and turn them on her to cut and scrape her baby away.

She takes a deep, trembling breath, pulling in a blast of chloroform that makes the room swirl. *Don't flinch or fight, it will be safer that way.*

She thinks of Julian and grits her teeth around her anger. While they had not yet declared their suitability to the world, and he had not placed a ring on her finger, in secret, they had been promised to each other. Yet when she told him about her condition, he had turned her away, ignored her desperate appeals, and on the one occasion she had managed to catch him alone to beseech his help with the abortionist's fees, he had refused to acknowledge any obligation to her. What proof, he asked, did he have that the child was even his, when he had seen her more than once making eyes at other men.

His false accusation had pierced her heart, but his final words delivered the blow that sent her scuttling away, bewildered and betrayed. Even now, they echo in her mind, so vivid he could be standing beside her, whispering them in her ear. *There are cheaper ways to rid yourself of the problem. A tumble down the stairs should do it, and if not there's always the river.*

Evelina's parents had arranged – *insisted* – upon this visit to Doctor Katz, after making it quite clear they would turn her out onto the streets if she kept the child. Evelina had not argued. She recognised the narrowness of her options; respectable society would sooner turn its back on a single woman with a baby than hold out its hand.

A small sob swells in her throat. She feels like a carcass strung up in a butcher's shop. Already dead. So many girls have been killed this way, their insides ravaged by nurses with rudimentary training or doctors struck off for malpractice. Their last hours spent in an agony of pain and blood.

Tears burn her eyes and she turns her face towards the grimy window. Wild, red roses grow across the panes, a spray of colour that, set against the dour surroundings, are almost violent in their beauty. Something in her chest loosens at the sight of them. Those roses are a lifeline to which she must cling, a raft in a storm-tossed ocean. A scream of life in this room of death.

She bites her lip when she hears Doctor Katz pick something up from the tray, but she does not turn away from the roses. The window is cracked open and the musky scent of the flowers wafts into the room. As it does, she feels a quickening inside her, a flutter beneath the hardening drum of her belly. As soft as wind-blown petals, so gentle it could almost be imagined, so powerful it changes everything.

Evelina's hands move to her stomach, red roses kiss the glass, the world is reframed.

NOVEMBER 12TH, 1884

Evelina stands on the porch of Temple Fall. She is wearing a new yellow dress and has attached a nosegay of red roses to her bodice, daubed her wrists in lavender and orange blossom. She wants her daughter to love her as soon as she sees her, and first impressions are so important.

She glances over her shoulder at the black mare yoked to the wagon. The cab driver, dressed in coat-tails and top hat, watches her, his expression one of guarded curiosity. Evelina wonders what he makes of her, a young woman travelling alone. She is dressed as a lady, but she knows she doesn't look like one: thin to the point of emaciation, shoulders curved from hours of oakum picking in the workhouse, fingertips scarred by the fibres in the old ropes, she looks like a dipper, her finery a costume, a deception. At least she can hide her hands in gloves, a luxury she could not indulge in the ringer-house, where her bared hands and hitched skirts were subtle as a costermonger hawking his wares.

She takes a deep breath, reaches for the knocker. It is shaped like a snake eating its own tail, its body curved in a perfect circle. As soon as she touches it, she snatches her hand back with a gasp. Despite the cold day and her gloved skin, the cast iron felt warm, and she would swear the snake's scales had shifted beneath her palm.

She closes her eyes. *You're just tired. Keep it together now, for Rose.*

She holds this thought in her mind as she opens her eyes, grabs the knocker, raps it sharply against the strike plate. The metal is grave-cold, no murmur of life beneath the snake's ebony scales.

She smooths her hands over her skirt and wonders how Rose will react when she sees her. Almost two years old now, she will have no memory of Evelina, but perhaps she will intuit the bond between them and greet her mother with a shy smile. Evelina expects no such warmth from Mrs Thomas. She knows it is cruel, showing up so unexpectedly, but in all fairness, she *had* tried to get in touch with the woman, repeatedly, at the address Mrs Thomas had given her, only for all her letters to go unanswered.

In the workhouse, Evelina had been powerless to discover the reason for this loss of contact, but a few weeks ago, her brother, Hugo, had written to her with news that changed everything. Their parents had died of consumption, both expiring within days of each other. Still shamed by their daughter's indiscretion with the baker's son, they had left the entirety of their fortune to Hugo, but Evelina and her brother had always been close, and there was no way he would continue to see her languish in the workhouse. He split the inheritance equally with her, and though it was not a vast amount, it was enough to liberate her from her grey prison and ensure her relative comfort for years to come.

Upon leaving the workhouse, Evelina had hired a private investigator to track down the woman who had adopted Rose. It had taken him weeks to find her, his search complicated by the fact that Mrs Thomas's husband, Nelson Thomas, had recently died, and Mrs Thomas had not only reverted to her maiden name, Gray, but had also changed her first name. The woman who had adopted her daughter, Mrs Agnes Thomas, now went by Mrs Lyda Gray.

Evelina shivers on the doorstep. She knocks again.

She feels she has lived many lives since the day she walked out of Doctor Katz's house. Upon hearing that she had changed her mind about the abortion, he had refused to return any of the money she had given him for the procedure, and her parents, true to their word, had cast her out onto the streets. She'd had nowhere to go but the dosshouse, where she was forced to share a narrow bed of filthy straw with another woman, and her room with thirteen more.

She can still recall the stink of the place: sweat-soured air mingling with the toxic miasma of the streets below, the stench of sickness and despair. The noise was relentless: the early organ-grinders, the clatter of wheels over cobblestones, the squabbles of the other women, paperboys yelling the news, drunks singing or brawling on the streets, match-sellers, streetwalkers, drunks. An endless din that precluded rest but at least drowned out the sound of rats scuttling across the floorboards.

Evelina's money had dwindled as swiftly as her hope, and in her darkest moments, she began to regret her decision to keep her baby. But then she had seen the advertisement in the local newspaper:

RESPECTABLE couple looking to entirely ADOPT a young child. Nice country home and a mother's love and care. Premium required £10. Apply by letter only to Mrs Agnes Thomas. Post Office. Church Road, Leeds.

—

Evelina had replied, the adoption was arranged. To raise the required funds, she had moved from the dosshouse to a ringer-house, where meagre food rations, stress, and a crippling corset helped conceal her condition for almost four months.

Even now, her thoughts shrink from those rouged and powdered nights. Greeting men with a smile, their rough hands pawing at her aching, swollen breasts. Pushing her down to her flea-bitten knees, as though she had not already sunk far enough. Her belly growing hot and hard so that she imagined the baby inside burning with shame for her. But the rattle of coins in her pocket was all that mattered to Evelina, the knowledge that even as each illicit encounter stole a little more of her, it brought her one step closer to securing her child's safety.

Once her pregnancy could no longer be concealed, the madam kicked her out and it was in the workhouse that she delivered Rose. Her labour had been long and complicated, leaving her delirious with fever, almost too weak to nurse. And yet, despite her illness, in the days that followed, Evelina had fallen in love with Rose, and would have done anything to keep her. It was a selfish desire; she knew she would never find work as an unmarried mother, and Rose would starve.

The day Mrs Thomas collected Rose, Evelina had dressed

her in a faun-coloured pelisse and a white bonnet, and packed a small box with tiny garments she had sewn and embroidered during her pregnancy. How hard it had been to place her squalling baby in Mrs Thomas's arms, how agonising the rending inside her then.

Later, shivering on her filthy bunk, she would imagine Rose swaddled in fresh linen. As she forced down the watery broth she and the other women were served at mealtimes, she pictured her child sitting down to a meal of faggots in gravy, sugar cookies and fresh milk. When her fingertips were raw and bleeding from picking oakum and the desperate sobs of other women in her dormitory were too much to bear, she pictured Rose snug in Mrs Thomas's arms, safe, content, loved. And she told herself that someday, she would hold her baby again.

Footsteps from inside the house tug her back to the present.

A hopeful smile touches Evelina's lips, and as she stands at the door of Temple Fall, she no longer looks like a hard-eyed young woman who has known the pain of hunger, the savagery of lustful strangers, the bone-weary days of the workhouse – she looks like the child she is, swept away by a moment of unbridled joy.

A key rattles in the lock.

And the door swings open.

Evelina takes a step back, her smile dimming as she stares at the dishevelled woman framed in the doorway of Temple Fall.

Evelina had been gravely ill the day she gave Rose away, but the aches wracking her body were nothing to the pain she felt in those last moments holding her baby. The world had ceased to exist as she committed every detail of her face to memory: the delicate scoop of her nose, the bow of her lips, the curve of her soft cheek, her dark, pellucid eyes.

But she had been so focused on Rose, now she can barely recall the woman who took her away. She has a vague recollection of a dignified lady dressed in black crinoline skirts, dark hair swept up in a neat chignon, but the image is blurred, as though viewed through obfuscating opium clouds.

And yet, despite the treachery of memory, she is sure she has never before seen the woman leering down at her from the doorway of Temple Fall.

Her long dress is black, but the edges of her sleeves are smeared with muck, the material, grime-stiffened. Her hair is dark, but threaded with grey, and while she has attempted to pin it back, it has come loose of its grips in short, wild sprigs that tuft at her temples. Her eyes are sinkholes, set in bruised sockets and rimed in smudged black kohl. They slide over Evelina, dull and phlegmatic.

'What do ye want?' The woman's voice possesses the coarse, gravelled texture of an inveterate smoker.

Even without the sour stink of booze that seeps from the woman's pores, Evelina would have known from her ruddy complexion, the broken capillaries scrawled across her nose and cheeks and the way her eyelids droop loosely over those beetle-black eyes, that she is a lush.

Evelina glances past her into the house, sees a lobby wreathed in shadows, an imperial staircase, a crystal and bronze chandelier hanging from the ceiling. Despite the fact it is a clear, bright day, the curtains are drawn, the gloomy space illuminated by oil lamps and candles. The house looks large enough to accommodate an orphanage, but Evelina sees no evidence of children within. No tiny shoes by the door, no small coats hanging on the coat stand, no toys scattered across the floor.

'Mrs Thomas?' Evelina hears the doubt in her own voice, but a sudden flare of recognition sharpens the woman's stony eyes, and in that moment, Evelina knows there is no mistake.

She could almost have sunk to the ground and wept tears of relief, were it not for the realisation that the draggle-tailed drunk standing before her has been looking after Rose for almost two years.

Mrs Thomas's eyes click to the hansom cab, a shifty, caught-out look.

'My name is Evelina Hill. A little under two years ago, you took my daughter, Rose. I've come to collect her, Miss. I'm so sorry, I know this must be awful hard for you to—'

'It is my only condition of taking on their care that the mothers of unwanted babies don't contact 'em again.'

'Oh, Rose weren't never unwanted, Miss! If you could only see the babies what are born into the workhouse, you'd understand why—'

'I understand better than ye think.' Bitterness laces the voice, a swerve in the words betraying the alcohol Evelina can already smell. 'I ain't exactly had an easy time of it meself, but we don't all have the luxury of choice.'

'Please, Miss. If there were any other way, I'd have taken it.'

'She were adopted entirely, correct?'

'I'm sorry, I—'

'Your girl. She weren't a lodger here, is what I'm asking. You 'ent been sending me money every week, like what some others do. She were adopted entirely.'

'Well, yes... but—'

'Ye should've said if ye wanted her back.'

Mrs Thomas speaks with a cold finality that opens the ground beneath Evelina's feet.

'I'd have given any sum to keep Rose safe, if I'd only had it. But the money...' She falters, presses back images of crude tousles in the dark, hard mouths and calloused hands and semen-scented sheets. *The luxury of choice.* Those words gnaw at her fraying composure, but she pushes her emotions down, folds away her anger, resentment, shame, so her voice is smooth, crease-free. 'The money were no small sum for me, Miss, it took a while.'

'My conditions were clear and they 'ent for negotiatin'. If ye want a child, then I suggest ye go make another.' Mrs Thomas glides a palm over her distended belly. 'They 'ent hardly difficult to come by.'

It takes a moment for Evelina to interpret the gesture, and when she does, a pulse of shock ricochets through her. Despite her inestimable years, the unhealthful pallor of her skin, the reek of alcohol that seeps from her pores, Mrs Thomas is heavy with child.

How could I have given Rose to this woman? Evelina thinks, appalled. But then she had not been herself after the delivery. Feverish and sick, half-drugged on opiates and so exhausted she had barely possessed the capacity to hold her baby. And besides, she is quite sure Mrs Thomas had not presented herself back then in the same disordered and slovenly manner as she does now.

Mrs Thomas starts to close the door, but Evelina stops it with her hand.

'My circumstances have changed, Miss. I can look after her now.'

The older woman's eyes narrow, a sneer twists her features. 'Hoors, yer all the same. Give yer quim for a sov, then offload yer brats onto others to do the mothering for ye. Now if ye'll excuse me—'

Evelina shoots her foot between the door and the frame before Mrs Thomas can close it. Her back tightens, her shoulders lift.

'I will not leave without my child.'

Mrs Thomas's gaze flicks again to the hansom cab and something slithers behind her face. Perhaps realising that the young woman before her will not be easily dismissed, she dips her head. Her smile is broad, lipless. Reptilian.

She opens the door wide, and gestures Evelina inside.

The moment she crosses the threshold of the house, nausea rocks Evelina back on her heels. Sweat springs up on her brow, her head aches and her thoughts feel febrile, scattered. Outside, the cabman shivers in his heavy greatcoat, icy wind bends the grass, but Evelina feels no shelter within the walls of the house. Rather, the cold seems to contract, snatching her breath like a tightened corset.

Mrs Thomas closes the door. As Evelina steps past her, she catches the scent of something foul. Offal... or greasy meat on the turn.

Pillar candles burn in tiered stands, oil lamps cast a yellow, flickering light. Paintings of hunting scenes decorate the dark-panelled walls: a pack of dogs rip into a felled wildebeest, a wild boar frames a soundless scream as men sink spears into its flanks, three hyenas tear shreds of glistening red meat from a lion cub. The malice and pleasure in the predators' eyes betray a cunning beyond the remit of beasts, a viciousness that belongs only to humans.

Movement within the shadowy recess beneath the split staircase makes Evelina turn. The darkness wavers, shapes itself into a figure. A girl. No – not a girl. A young woman. Crouched and trembling on the floor.

Evelina starts towards her, but the woman shrinks back, shakes her head. *No!* Evelina can't make out her features in the darkness, but the way she bends into the shadows and angles her face to the wall, begs concealment.

Mrs Thomas, noticing Evelina's expression, starts to turn to see what she is looking at. Evelina senses a spike in the figure's terror, a spark on the air between them. She quickly sweeps her hand out, knocks over a vase standing on a side table by the door. It crashes against the floor and shatters.

'I'm sorry,' she mutters, stooping to collect the jagged pieces. 'Please, let me—'

'Leave it!' Mrs Thomas glares down at her. 'Come with me.'

Evelina stands up, brushes at her skirts. She follows Mrs Thomas through an archway that opens onto a dimly lit sitting room. Even in the gloom, Evelina can tell the furnishings are expensive. The thick, textured curtains are richly coloured, the red and mustard carpet feels quilted and lush underfoot.

Mrs Thomas opens a door and leads Evelina down a long, dark corridor. Her lantern-light slides over the walls, candles waver as they pass. Something about this woman, this house, makes Evelina's heart tick faster. The air feels warm, oddly mushy. Fungal. As though every breath is laced with spores that fill her lungs with a dank fetor. She strains to hear children's voices, a distant giggle, the padding of small feet. The answering silence spreads cold through her chest.

Though it must once have been a grand manor, the house now possesses an air of neglect and abandonment. Dust swirls in what little watery light penetrates the grimy windows of the rooms through which they pass, and grey cobwebs wreathe the wall-mounted sconces.

'I was sorry to hear of your husband's death,' Evelina says. 'It must have been terrible for you... to discover him the way you did.'

'Oh, aye,' Mrs Thomas says, a smile in her voice. 'Terrible.'

'And Rose—' Evelina stumbles on her daughter's name.

'Hmm?' Mrs Thomas swings round, her brow corrugated, a smudge of confusion in her gutter-dark eyes. As though baffled by the emotion in Evelina's voice. 'Oh, the child. She's fine, didn't see it happen, if that's what yer asking. No, it were late at night, the babies were sleepin'. Nelson had been out drinking, soused out of his skull when he came home, sot that he wah. Probably din't feel a thing when he fell.' An odd, grudging tone creeps into Mrs Thomas's voice as she says this. 'It might even have taught him a lesson, if he'd survived, but there weren't much chance of that.' The smile that had greased her voice now slips over her lips, the shadows slide over her face as she leans close to Evelina. 'He'd split his skull, you see, cracked it wide open, like a smashed ceramic pot.'

Evelina's scalp tightens. Her face feels frozen, but she must betray her revulsed shock because Mrs Thomas's smile creeps higher.

'Aye, a terrible thing,' she says, though the dry glitter in her eyes tells a different story. 'Just terrible. He were still breathing, you know, when I found him lying there, but beyond all possible help, poor dear.'

She stops at a door, reaches for the handle. 'I held him in my arms and his brain leaked out like meat juice running from a beef joint.' Her lips seem to grip her teeth, and her eyes are as cold as a dead fish. She gives her head a small shake, more bemusement than distress. 'Impossible to wash out, those stains.'

She twists the handle, opens the door.

'Here we are,' she says, gesturing Evelina inside.

The odorous smell is the first thing Evelina notices. The sourness of unwashed bodies and dirty linen, the faint apple tang of laudanum.

The room is cavernous and sparsely furnished, with dusty wooden floorboards and dark-panelled walls. Drawn curtains thicken the shadows. A heavy, walnut rocking chair is set beside a low-burning fire and a scuttle of coal. On the other side of the room, far from the warmth of the fire is a row of four metal cribs.

Evelina starts forwards, her daughter's name on her lips as her eyes move over the little occupants in each cot.

Since her parents turned her out in disgrace, she has lived through horrors she had never before imagined. She has watched a woman rummage through the pockets of a corpse lying on the street, seen children fighting over fly-blown scraps stolen from the cart of the cat's meat man. She has endured the depraved demands of the men in her chamber, has lain in stirrups and stared at the abortionist's hooks on their tray. But nothing she has seen or endured has prepared her for the sight before her now.

Two or three infants occupy each small bed. Sallow-skinned, faces filthy, they lie in eerie quietness, barely moving. There are no mattresses to soften their hard cribs, just bare metallic mesh and soiled blankets. Evelina doubts the eldest can be older than two years of age, yet they are so emaciated, so hauntingly watchful, they put Evelina in mind of the ravaged elderly in the workhouse.

Evelina notices one of the babies has been shackled by the ankles to the bars of his cot. He flinches as she leans towards him, then watches her with bleak exhaustion as she hurriedly unties his bonds. A pool of vomit crusts the corner of the cot.

Evelina feels a kick of anger so intense it dizzies her. She grabs the bars to steady herself, and turns to Mrs Thomas, speechless with horror as she watches the woman pluck a gunge-nosed child from one of the cots.

'Here, take yer baby.' She thrusts the infant into Evelina's arms. 'I've too many mouths to feed anyway, and this one's more trouble than she's worth.'

The girl is so thin, Evelina feels as though she is cradling a bundle of toothpicks. Her breath is laboured, and each laudanum-tinged sip makes her narrow shoulders hitch spasmodically. Her filthy gown is tattered, pocked with holes, and a dark collar of vomit spills down her chest. Evelina recoils from the faecal stench of her unchanged nappy.

'This is not my child.'

Mrs Thomas shrugs, her spit-black eyes flat, emotionless. 'Ye'd hardly recognise her after all this time.'

With trembling hands, Evelina lifts the child's dress, seeking the sickle-shaped birthmark just below Rose's hip bone. The girl's skin is an angry storm of bruises, fading lavender down the back of one leg, swirling shades of blue and black across her thighs. But there is no birthmark.

'Where is Rose?' Evelina's voice trembles, frail as autumn's last leaf, clinging to its branch. Barely holding on.

'Stupid girl,' Mrs Thomas smirks. 'She's right there in yer arms.'

'No.' Evelina's chin wobbles like a child's. 'No.'

Mrs Thomas waves a dismissive hand. 'If ye don't want her, leave her. Ye 'bandoned her once, it will mean nowt to her if ye 'bandon her again.'

The girl is so light, it is as though she is made of skin and feathers. Sores mark her ankles and heels, muck cakes the creases of her skin. Three of her fingernails are missing. Each cruelty is a blow that drives a nail into the lid of Rose's coffin, because holding this small body in her arms, Evelina knows that no child can survive in Mrs Thomas's care for long.

If she leaves the child here, she will undoubtedly die.

The girl's eyes brighten at the sight of Evelina's nosegay. She gently brushes the roses with her fingertips, as if she is skimming a butterfly's wings. Light fills her face, and the awe in her expression tells Evelina she has never seen flowers, or if she has, they are nothing but a distant memory, a half-remembered dream.

Evelina's vision swims, her heart beats thickly. She realises she is going to black out, but she understands intuitively, that if she does, she will not walk out of this house alive. Her daughter is gone, yet in the cruellest of twists, she will have to pretend they have just been reunited.

'It has been a long time.' Tears spill down her cheeks, a mother's tears at being reunited with her child. The room solidifies around her, but her pain persists, a spreading wound in her chest. 'She is much changed.'

Mrs Thomas leads Evelina back outside, and she stumbles into the sunlight. Clutching the child, she climbs into the hansom, and with a whip-crack, they roll away. Temple Fall recedes, but the pain in her chest grows. Hate spills through her, burrowing deep. A seed buried in a bleak and sunless place, growing thorns sharper than those of any rose, and sprouting buds darker than any sin.

NOVEMBER 14TH, 1884

Evelina watches Temple Fall from the concealment of the trees. Dressed in widow's weeds, a weeping veil drawn over her face, the only slash of colour she wears comes from the blood-red roses pinned to her bodice. She stands, still and silent, a half-dreaming shadow pressed beneath the trees. Her thoughts swirl, dark and dangerous.

Almost five hours have passed since she arrived, her driver leaving her by the bridge where she had instructed him to collect her at dusk. Her feet ache from standing still for so long, the cold air gnaws at her skin.

Only two days have passed since she arrived at Temple Fall in her yellow sundress, yet it feels like much longer. Upon leaving the house, she had taken the sickened child directly to Richmond Hospital, but she had not lingered to speak to the doctors and nurses. Leaving the girl in reception, she had returned to her hansom and instructed her driver to take her directly to the police station.

Even now, she burns with humiliation and rage at the way the officers had dismissed the accusations she levelled against Mrs Gray.

Mrs Gray. That is who she is to Evelina now, as though the woman has emerged from the chrysalis of Mrs Thomas, something foul and unholy, sloughing away the veneer of dignity and cleanliness which had concealed her true nature.

The door to Temple Fall suddenly opens and Mrs Gray steps outside. Evelina tenses, blinking into the midday light as though she is waking. The mistress of Temple Fall looks more presentable today in a dress of silk twill and cut velvet with mother-of-pearl fastenings. Polished black boots, hair swept back and tucked into a bonnet. To all outward appearances, she appears the respectable widow the constable had described. A pillar of the community. A kind-hearted, charitable woman, caring for the unwanted infants abandoned by their feckless mothers.

She locks the door, pockets the key within the folds of her dress and descends the porch steps. Evelina had always considered the waddling gait of heavily pregnant mothers to possess an endearing charm, but watching Mrs Gray shuffle gracelessly towards the stable induces in her sharp contractions of black hate.

The baby farmer yokes her horse to the dogcart. Evelina's hands clench into fists by her sides. Why should that woman get to bear and keep a child after so cruelly stealing Evelina's? The injustice of it is more than she can bear.

Mrs Gray cracks her whip and the wheels on the dogcart turn. Evelina waits until it slips round the bend in the road and she can no longer hear the clop of the horse's hooves or the wheels rattling over the ground. Then she starts towards the house.

As she approaches, she feels the pressure of observation tingle her skin. She falters, struck by the fancy that Temple Fall is watching her, its black windows like hollowed eye sockets.

She tries to shake off the thought, but her heart kicks harder as she draws close to those towering grey walls. She picks up a large stone, eyes the windows, wondering which one she should smash to gain entry. The sense of being watched sharpens to conviction. Her hand tightens on the stone. A glance over her shoulder reveals no one behind her. The only movement is the soft sway of the tree branches, the long grass rippling in the breeze.

She turns back to the house.

A figure is standing in the upper turret window.

A small, pale face framed by a storm of dark curls. A pair of large brown eyes, a delicately pointed chin, a snub nose, spattered with freckles. That face... She knows that face, has seen it over and over in her dreams for the past two years. Her heart seizes, then starts to clap wildly.

Rose.

But she is not alone. Behind her, there stands a tall man, dressed in a dark jacket and waistcoat with a white collared shirt and necktie. Steep sideburns lend him an aristocratic look, but his hair is white and wild around his haggard face. The darkness of his scowling brow serves as a startling counterpoint to his clear, almost opaque eyes. A savage kind of malevolence radiates from his burning gaze.

And his hand is resting on Rose's shoulder.

At first, Evelina is too scared to take another step, fearful that any movement will cause her daughter's face to fade, and so she stands there, staring at Rose, as though she is the sun, thawing the frost inside her heart.

The man's grip tightens on Rose's shoulder, the shadows of his face spill and pool as he leans closer to her. As though oblivious to his presence, Rose places her palm against the window. She smiles at Evelina, and that is all it takes to break the spell. Evelina starts towards the house with a sob, tears streaming down her cheeks unchecked.

She has taken only a few steps when she stutters to a stop.

Her daughter's smile is a creeping thing, slow and cruel. As Evelina watches, the warm blush in Rose's cheeks fades and her skin turns mottled and grey. Her plump face narrows, flesh shrivelling as though she is rapidly decomposing. The shine in her eyes fades but the grin grows sharper, lips skinning back, exposing shrinking gums, teeth gummed with soil and grime. Shadows spread like darkening bruises around her sockets and her curls turn brittle, fall in clumps from her scalp. Rot staggers through the hand on the glass.

'No!' Evelina runs towards the house, up the porch steps.

She pumps the handle, forgetting, in her panic, that Mrs Gray had locked it. With a cry of rage, she launches the stone at the window. Glass smashes in huge jagged slices. Evelina pulls at a serrated tooth lodged in the pane, widening the hole so she can climb through.

As she steps inside, her skin tightens with cold, as though she has just pushed through an invisible snowdrift.

The lobby is dark, empty, but Evelina races up the stairs, screaming her daughter's name. Refusing to think of the way Rose's face had changed, withering and wilting like a plucked flower, or how her eyes had shrivelled into their sinking sockets as her hair fell from her scalp. That was nothing but a misfiring thought, a trick of the light, a shadow passing over the glass. *Rose is alive!*

A foul stink clings to the air, the cloying sweetness of infection that Evelina remembers from the last time she was here, the opium tang of bitter flowers. She slows in the darkness. The upper corridor is dimly lit by wall-mounted black candles, and she takes one down, holds it in front of her as she moves down the hallway.

'Rose!'

Silence swirls around her voice, yet she senses she is not alone, the feeling of being watched like static against her skin.

She opens a door and steps hesitantly into a darkened room. The stench in here is so thick, she presses a hand over her mouth and nose. Moonlight slants through the tall windows, the shadows waver. Four crowded cots stand on one side of the room, on the other, a fireplace and a rocking chair. She falters. *The nursery was downstairs. I* know *the nursery was downstairs.*

She opens her mouth to call again for Rose, but her eyes shift to the windows and her voice is suddenly dust in her dry throat.

Even though she stepped into the house a matter of minutes ago, the sky is pitch-black, thick with stars. The candlelight quivers as her hands begin to shake. Hot wax slides over her fingers, but she barely flinches from the scalding heat. She moves towards her own dark reflection, her gaze fixed upon the night sky.

'No...'

The moon is full and bright against the black lake of the night. Its soft light kisses the gently sloping fields and the contours of the trees.

It's not possible, not possible...

It isn't only that the night has so swiftly dropped its black curtain on the day that sways shocked horror through her, but the moon tonight – it should be a waning crescent, not the swollen silver ball that now spotlights the sky. If the moon has cycled through five of its phases, then almost three weeks have passed since she entered the house.

Or time has... slipped.

She tries to tell herself she's wrong about the moon cycle, but she knows she isn't. Since leaving the workhouse, she has become a veteran of sleepless nights, and often spends the dark and solitary hours walking, or lying beneath the cold sky, staring into the black expanse of space. Only last night, her heart heavy, her thoughts racing, she had trekked across the moors beneath a sky pierced by stars, and the silver scythe of a waning moon.

Her tremors turn to violent convulsions as she backs away. *The house has tricked me!* It is a lunatic thought, yet the truth of it is as unavoidable as the sudden and certain knowledge that Rose is dead.

Ye should've said if ye wanted her back.

Only now do Mrs Gray's words take on their true meaning. Confident Evelina would never return for Rose, convinced she would receive no more money for her ongoing care, Mrs Gray had killed her.

A smell steps into the room, overpowering the meaty stench of the tallow candle and the infective stink. It is the smell of the workhouse: the foul miasma of the water-closet, the deadhouse that it abuts, the sourness of unclean flesh and unwashed hair, of night-sweats and despair.

Evelina's vision shimmers, dims. She squeezes her eyes closed and takes a deep breath. But when she opens them again, her surroundings have changed. The room has narrowed, the ceiling lifted. Instead of cots, two long rows of wooden beds line bare brick walls. The windows are smaller and set too high to reach. Wooden posters adorn the walls, an assortment of biblical quotes and dire warnings. One reads: *GOD IS GOOD.* Another: *Go to the ant, thou sluggard; consider her ways and be wise.*

She is in the dormitory of the workhouse.

Threads of pain sear her fingertips and she cries out, drops the candle. The flame snuffs out but Evelina lifts her hands to her face. Moonlight touches the scars on her fingertips. They are red and sore, stained black with tar from the oakum. The wounds throb in synch with her pulse. A dull ache corkscrews up her spine, as though she has been hunched over piles of oakum for hours.

This isn't right! Sweat greases her palms, her heartbeat staggers. *This isn't right!* Her eyes travel down her body. Her black mourning clothes have been replaced by the blue and white cotton shift and smock of the workhouse. Long stockings cover her legs, knee-length drawers. On her feet, hob-nailed boots.

Her shaking hands move to her head. The black veil that had been fastened there is gone, in its place, the standard issue poke bonnet of the workhouse. She feels her sanity unravel, like the twists of rope over which she used to labour, shredding to fibres.

Lightning flares at the windows. She looks around and everything is as it was, her mourning clothes, the room, the cots.

She stumbles back towards the door, turns and flees the way she came, her body twisting down corridor after corridor, through empty dining rooms and abandoned parlours. Her skirts snap at her ankles, her midnight veil flows behind her like black smoke. Rose petals drop from her nosegay as she runs. They darken as they fall, crimson as they twist one way, the maroon of old blood as they twist another, and by the time they touch the dusty floor, they have acquired a blackness deeper than the darkest night.

The shadows ripple, slide apart.

A figure steps forwards, and Evelina skids to a stop.

Mrs Gray's eyes are like hardened berries, flat and black. A quick glean of light slips over the blade in her hand.

Before Evelina has time to react, pain flourishes in her side, a slick silvery heat, and petals of blood open like sun-warmed flowers in her gown. She slides to the floor, pressing her hands to the wound. A wet warmth soaks through her bodice.

By the flickering candlelight, she watches her blood slide between the gaps in the floorboards. It crawls up the walls, as though the house is absorbing her, pulling the sanguine flood into its own veins.

Fear sinks through her like fangs, a bite of sharp terror. It is not death she fears, but the prospect of dying without knowing what happened to Rose is more than she can bear.

'Where is she?' Her voice is a fading whisper, pale as tallow smoke. 'What did you do to my baby?'

Mrs Gray stands over her, watching her the way a cruel child might watch a fly struggle and twitch across the ground after plucking its wings.

'She's with the other babies now,' she says. 'The ones what don't cry no more.'

Evelina had known that Rose was dead, but even so, the confirmation sinks a pain in her deeper than any blade can reach. She closes her eyes, tears spilling over her cheeks.

'Tell me...' A choked cough brings a fine spray of blood, crimson against her paling skin. 'Tell me... what you did.'

Mrs Gray shrugs. 'Like I said before, she'd have had a chance if ye'd been paying me on the weekly to care for her.'

Care for her. Evelina thinks of the men she had received in the ringer-house, the abuses she endured, the debasing acts she had been made to perform, all of it after seeing the advertisement in the penny paper. The bindings she had worn to stop her milk after giving Rose away, the tears she had shed every night over what she had done, the fervent, desperate prayers she had offered, begging God to protect her baby. The ache of missing her, a pain that she had only been able to abide because she had thought Rose was in a better place, that her PREMIUM OF £10 had secured for her A MOTHER'S LOVE AND CARE.

But all that time, Rose was dead, murdered by MRS AGNES THOMAS, that RESPECTABLE woman in her NICE COUNTRY HOME.

Evelina's anguish must reveal itself on her face because Mrs Gray's dull eyes acquire a dark sort of rapture, the avaricious creases of her face contract. She crouches beside Evelina, as though drawn, titillated, by the younger woman's torment. A smile slithers across her lips.

'I remember now.' Her grimy face inches from Evelina's, a putrid smell wafts on her breath. 'You gave her to me in't mornin' but she were dead by nightfall. I choked her 'til the house said I could stop, and then I buried her in the basement wi' the rest of 'em.'

A fit of trembling passes through Evelina, waves of cold breaking across her skin. The dim hallway grows darker still, and she knows she doesn't have long.

'Please, promise me...' Pain contracts in her side, a spear of hot agony, but it anchors her, stops her spinning into the dark. 'Promise you'll bury me beside her.'

The words barely carry, and Evelina knows they are her last. Her final wish. And she longs for it with a desperate wanting, with a craving that overrides everything else. For her bones to lie beside her daughter's. They had not been reunited in life, but at least in death, they can rest together.

Her thoughts stutter, darkness crowds her vision. The searing pain in her side is unravelling and she is fading, sinking into a feather-soft darkness. Her eyes drift closed.

The pain in her side widens in a sudden bright pulse, and she gasps back to consciousness. Mrs Gray leans over her. She has pulled the knife from her side, and she holds it between them, turning the blood-soaked blade.

'No,' Mrs Gray says. 'The house don't want you.'

She drives the knife into Evelina's chest. Heat and pain swirl beneath the blade. She feels herself sinking, tries to thrash back to the surface, grasping at life if only to once more plead for this one thing. But death has snapped cold chains around her ankles and it is dragging her down.

She opens her mouth to beg, but blood clogs her words, choking her; it spills down her chest, soaking what remains of the red roses she wears every day for her daughter. Their colour deepens as her skin turns pale. The light in her eyes dims and her twitching body stills.

NOW

Flynn gasps awake, snatching back a scream before it bursts from her lips. Snowflakes blur her vision, her thoughts feel scrambled, full of static. She shivers, standing in the middle of a street. *Where am I? Oh god, where am I?*

With a pulse of alarm, she realises that she is wearing a dressing gown over her pyjamas, slippers on her feet. She tries to ground herself as panic whirls. It is dark, the snow beginning to settle on the ground. The few people out on the street do a double take when they glance her way, gazes lingering on her drenched and dripping figure.

She lowers her eyes, fearful she will be recognised, and retreats into the nearest bus shelter, thankful to find it empty. The smell of Temple Fall clings to her nose, the taste of ash and dust, decay and disease. As though, in her dark dream, she really had been walking the halls of the house. As though it hadn't been a dream at all.

The frequency of these fugues has increased since Jonesy's death, but are no less frightening for their regularity. She casts her mind back to the last thing she remembers. *I was home with Riley, and Mum called to say she was running late*. Flynn's breath catches. *Shit, I've left Riley home alone!*

She rifles through the pockets of her dressing gown, hoping to find her mobile to call a taxi, but they are empty. She doesn't even have her house keys. Her eyes move over the dark street, at the slow-moving cars, the pedestrians walking past, chins tucked into their collars. *It isn't far. If I hurry, I can be back in less than ten minutes.*

Cursing under her breath, she strides out into the snow. *These blackouts are going to get me killed.* The thought possesses the clarity of truth, and all too clearly, she pictures how it will happen: lost inside a dream, her body a mindless puppet, her consciousness stalking the rooms of Temple Fall, she imagines herself stepping out into the road, oblivious to the car (*bus? lorry?*) tearing towards her. Perhaps she turns at the last moment, snaps from her dream in time to see the vehicle speeding down the street. Perhaps she is still dreaming the moment before she is ploughed down, the ghost lights of Temple Fall swirling in her blind eyes.

The cars on the road seem to sharpen in clarity, their shapes hulking behind the veils of snow, metallic beasts, sleek as shotguns and just as deadly. Their headlights gouge bright paths through the darkness, engines purring, roaring, rending the night with their growls.

Flynn keeps her head down, quickens her pace. The snow melts into her fluffy dressing gown and her slippers are soaked through. She tells herself Riley will be fine, that she will be happily gaming or ensconced in the living room watching TV.

She tries to cling to an image of Riley, but instead Jonesy's face swims to the front of her mind. His glazed eyes, his pallid skin, his blackened fingertips. Five weeks have passed since his death, a stretch of time that is punctuated by little more than eating, sleeping and looking after Riley when their mum is working. Submerged in grief, Flynn feels half-dead herself, like something that subsists beneath the surface of a stagnant river, rising only to absorb the minimal oxygen required to survive before sinking to the murky streambed again.

On Jonesy's death certificate, the coroner had written: *Cardiac arrest. Contributing factor: electrocution.* An accident. A terrible accident. That's what people said, but still rumours about the Hocking Estate Kids continue to swirl. *Third Suicide in Death Cult Gang*; *Another Hocking Teen Dies on 18th Birthday*; *Peter Pan Kids Refuse to Grow Old.* A dark glamour permeates every article Flynn reads, an invisible stitch that dances between the printed words. As though the prematurity of their deaths imbues them with some unspeakable allure.

Conscious of the way people stare at her, the reporters who chase her with their questions, the photographers following her with their cameras, Flynn finds it increasingly difficult to leave the house. Last week, someone had taken her picture when she had been buying sleeping tablets at the supermarket pharmacy. The paper that ran the article – *Hocking Girl Plans Sleeping Pill Overdose?* – had enlarged the image of her hand and circled the medication in red.

Flynn can see how strange it all must seem to other people: five teenagers go missing, leaving no trace of where they could have gone, only to reappear over four months later dressed in the same clothes they wore the night of their disappearance and claiming to only have been gone for one night. It had to be an elaborate prank, one which was fuelled by some sort of juvenile derangement, some sick, shared malady born from delinquency: a suicide pact to be enacted the day each of them turned eighteen.

A car skids on the icy road and briefly mounts the pavement, so close to Flynn the wing mirror almost clips her. The driver blares his horn, a shadow rolls inside the car. Cruel black eyes flash in the rear-view mirror, a glance that Flynn feels like the slash of a blade. She staggers back, blood roaring in her ears. A woman in the passenger seat winds the window down, leans out. Her features waver, and all Flynn sees is dark hair pulled back from a pale face, lips pulled into a hard, tight line, and cold black eyes, sunk deep as tombs in her skull.

Her breath stops, the certainty that she is about to die solidifies time. All she feels in that moment is her heart, mashing itself to pulp as it throws itself against her sternum. But the woman is yelling curses at her through the open window, and the car is turning the corner, and sweet, cold air fills Flynn's lungs in a rush as she realises it isn't Lyda Gray.

She is still breathing, her heart still beating.

She is still alive.

For now.

She ducks her head and keeps walking.

The moment Flynn steps inside, she sees Riley, sat on the bottom of the stairs. Her little face flashes up, a heart-snatch of a glance. Tear-streaked cheeks, eyes red-rimmed. In that darted look, relief spars with fear before anger sweeps both away. Riley scrambles to her feet, hands fisted by her sides, and when Flynn starts towards her, she turns and runs up the stairs. Flynn flinches when she hears the door bang.

She goes to her own bedroom, peels off her wet clothes and changes into dry pyjamas, then, still shivering, wraps herself in a thick cardigan. She grabs her mobile from her desk to check the time. 19:03. The last thing she can remember is making Riley tomato soup, and that was at about 17:00. Which means she has left her seven-year-old sister home alone for almost two hours.

She has fifteen missed calls, thirteen of them from her home landline. Guilt spears Flynn at the thought of Riley desperately trying to get hold of her, panic-stricken by the possibility that her big sister had disappeared on her again. The other two calls are from Tyrus. Flynn hasn't seen him since Jonesy's funeral and on the few occasions she has spoken to him on the phone, his speech had been slurred with drink. Chloe has been almost as elusive, hardly ever answering when Flynn calls her, and when she does, sounding as though she can't get off the phone fast enough. Concerned, Flynn had gone to her house, but Andy had answered the door and told her Chloe was too ill for visitors, and that she would probably need a few weeks to recover.

The implication was clear: Flynn should not try to get in touch with Chloe until after she had turned eighteen. While Andy might not believe his sister's account of what had happened to them all in Temple Fall, it was an indisputable fact that three of her closest friends had died on the day of their eighteenth birthdays, and though he knew deep down that the 'Peter Pan Kids' were not responsible, separating his sister from them was the only way he thought he might be able to protect her.

Flynn tucks her phone into her cardigan pocket, then goes to Riley's bedroom and knocks on the door.

'Go away!'

'I can't do that, Ry.' Flynn cracks the door open.

Riley is sat on her bed. Crumple-haired, pale-faced, her legs crossed and knees wedged beneath her chin. Lavender bruises squat beneath her eyes.

'You left me.' The words are tightly wadded syllables that she spits at Flynn.

'I'm so sorry.' Flynn sits on the edge of the bed. 'I didn't mean to.'

'You just walked out, even after I hit my head!'

'You hit your head?' Flynn says, only now noticing the tender lump lifting on her sister's temple.

Riley's eyes flash. 'You know I did! You pushed me over!'

'I... *what?*'

'You were making me soup and soldiers and then you were just... gone.' Riley shivers. 'I tried to stop you but when I grabbed your sleeve, you *pushed* me.'

'Oh, Ry. I'm so sorry.' Flynn reaches to hug her, but Riley shrugs her off.

'You're sick, aren't you?' She picks at her fingernail and Flynn's stomach clenches as she peels a strip of skin from her nailbed. A nervous tic she had shaken off years ago, but picked up again in recent months.

'I'm not sick. I just... I guess I was distracted.'

'Yes, you are, you're sick. You're sick like me.'

Flynn's phone vibrates in her pocket. She ignores it.

'What do you mean?' She places her palm over Riley's cool brow. 'You're feeling sick?'

'Not that kind of sick.' Riley pulls another skintag from her nailbed, drawing a bead of blood. 'You're going to go back to that house. I know you will. Florence told me.'

Dread licks down Flynn's spine. 'What did you say?'

'Florence.' Riley's eyes grow distant, her voice drops to a whisper. 'She gets so angry when I won't play.'

I had to go and collect Riley from school, she's been fighting. Jenna's words turn over in Flynn's mind, but now they sink a weight through her that makes it hard to breathe.

'Is she the girl who hits your friends?'

Riley's small shoulders lift and drop. 'The teachers don't believe me when I tell them what she does.' She taps her bruised temple with her ravaged fingertips, confusion flickering behind her eyes. 'It's like she climbs inside me and bad things happen, but she just wants someone to play with. She gets so lonely in that house. She says I'll live with her soon, but I don't want to go back there ever again.'

'Ry, what do you mean? What house?' But even as she asks the question, Flynn realises she already knows.

'Jenna told me to wait in the car.' Riley's voice is hushed, barely there. 'But she was taking so long. I thought maybe she was in trouble.'

Flynn has a sudden flashback of Riley sitting beside her in Andy's minivan. The faint smell of chlorine lifting from her swimming bag, her goggles strapped to her forehead. Her small shoulders twisted angrily away from Flynn as her finger slid across the fogged window. Drawing a house, a girl, and what Flynn had assumed was a dog or a cow. But she'd been wrong. Because the house was Temple Fall, the girl was a ghost, and the animal was her rocking horse.

'You went inside.' Flynn's voice is flat, heavy.

Flynn feels as though she is sinking. She knew her mum had driven to the house looking for clues, praying to find a lead the police had missed. But she had never considered that she might have taken Riley with her.

Fear tightens Flynn's ribs. 'What did you see, Ry?'

'I saw *her*. Florence.' Riley frowns, her eyes sliding to the corner of the room again. 'And I saw someone else, too.'

You're not the only one who disappeared, Flynn. Riley was devastated when you left and she hasn't been the same since.

Her behaviour's getting out of control.

You didn't see what your disappearance did to her.

Flynn takes Riley's hands in hers. Her heart aches to think of Temple Fall crawling through her little sister's thoughts, manipulating her darkest instincts, corrupting her. She tries to dismiss the idea as paranoia, but suspicion swiftly hardens to a conviction that shapes itself like poured concrete to the contours of her mind.

Temple Fall has infected Riley, too.

RILEY

25 SEPTEMBER 2024

Riley huddles in the car, staring at the house. It feels mean. Watchful. Strange to think of a house like that, but there it is. Her skin scritches with the sensation of eyes on her, a feeling so intense, there could be a person stood at every one of its many black and empty windows, staring down at her.

She has tried turning round in her seat to face the frost-stiffened moors, but that had felt too risky, like showing her back to someone who was about to come at her with a knife. She doesn't make the mistake of telling herself she is being silly, or trying to dismiss her intuitions. Her early years have instilled in her an instinct for danger, a particular sensitivity to the pervading atmosphere in which she finds herself, and right now that inner needle is dialled to the max. So she sits and watches the house and is not fooled by its stillness.

She tucks her knees up to her chin, wraps her arms round her legs. Pulls at a hangnail on her thumb, drawing blood. She doesn't notice. Her eyes flick from Temple Fall to the clock on the dashboard. Her mum went inside the house at 15:38, and the clock now reads *15:39*, but it must be broken, because it feels like hours have passed since she left. She had told Riley to stay put, that she would be in and out, that if she was good and patient, they would grab a takeout pizza on the way home. The thought had cheered Riley up a little, but now her patience is all run out and the hollowness in the pit of her belly has filled with a dread that banishes hunger.

The sun is sinking into the sloped hills, darkness edges across the sky. The cruel house watches her from the thickening shadows. Predatory.

She doesn't want to go inside, but she is beginning to feel as though something is very wrong. What if her mum has fallen down the stairs and needs help? What if she is in danger? What if the house has eaten her, the way it ate Flynn? She has been missing for eighteen days now. Riley knows, because she marks each day of her absence in her diary. She has started sleeping in Flynn's bed, falls asleep every night hoping that when she wakes, her big sister will be there. But the mornings bring only renewed disappointment, and the hard knock of cold, empty space beside her.

Her mum's words turn in her mind. *Stay put. I won't be long.* But she *has* been long. She's been *ages*, no matter what the stupid clock says. And Riley can't sit out here forever. She'll end up like Jack Torrance at the end of *The Shining*, frozen solid with icicles dripping from her chin and frost sheeting her eyes. Riley feels a pang, remembering how she had snuck downstairs and hidden behind the curtains when Flynn and Jackson had watched it.

Jackson. She misses him. He had almost been like a brother to Riley, always made time to talk to her, to play games. He died here, fell from one of the high windows. Riley thinks the house probably ate him, too. Ate him and spat him out, like a chunk of regurgitated meat.

Riley pops the car door open, climbs out. The wind curls round her hair, slides cold fingers down her neck. She stares at the open door of the house, willing her mum to appear there, to hurry down the porch steps, scolding Riley for her impatience and telling her to get back in the car. But the open door stands empty, the space within hollow, dark.

Riley takes a deep breath, puffs out her chest. 'It's not who I am underneath,' she says, lowering her voice as she affects her best Batman impression, 'but what I do that defines me.' Being Batman always makes her feel braver, even though she knows it's just pretend.

She moves to the boot, opens it, rummages beneath all the empty shopping bags for the torch Jenna keeps there.

'You wanna get nuts?' She is Michael Keaton's Batman now, psyching herself up to face the Joker. She flicks the torch on, as though she is cocking the trigger of a gun, and drops the boot closed. '*Come on!* Let's get nuts!'

She starts to walk towards Temple Fall, even though every instinct in her body screams at her to turn and run. The house seems to grow taller as she nears it, the weight of its consideration lowering like a dark sky. The hairs along her arms bristle. She tries to imagine a bullet-proof suit wrapped round her torso, a scalloped cape floating on the breeze behind her, a cowl with peaked bat-ears covering her head. But as she moves up the porch steps, the last dregs of her bravado falter, vanishing faster than her beloved superhero on Commissioner Gordon.

She hesitates in the open doorway, aims her light at the couched darkness.

'Mum?' Her voice is a hushed croak, a frightened wisp of sound.

She places her hand against the doorframe. At the contact, her mind swirls dizzily, the sensation of being suddenly knocked off balance, a plummeting in the pit of her stomach. She blinks, and behind her eyes, worms curl through rotten soil, blood clogs bubbling screams, diseased skin bulges, splits, spilling a flood of beetles, their hard shells shining as they flow outwards in a slick black tide.

Riley takes a deep, shuddering breath. *Come on, get it together! It's just the house playing tricks on me. It isn't real.*

She steps inside.

The beam of her torch crawls over crumbling walls and mouldering curtains, over faded paintings and dust-thickened cobwebs. As she breathes in the stagnant air, a feeling of bleak desolation fills her, spreading through her chest, dragging at her bones. Tears pool in her eyes, spill down her cold cheeks. Her skin sings with old pains, the ghost hand of every hard slap her first mummy ever dealt her, the burning scald of a razor strap folded double.

'Mum?' The torchlight quivers, and darkness peels from the light like rot from an infected wound. Shadows stand solid as sculptures. 'Mum! Mum, please. I want to go home.'

The door slams shut, coughing clouds of dust. Riley shrieks, lunges towards it, jogs the handle. It doesn't open.

'No! No no *no! Let me out! Please, let me out!*'

The cold bites harder, and the scent of the grave floods the room. The patter of footsteps, light and quick, fast approaching. She turns, swings her torch up with a cry.

A little girl stands at the foot of the stairs, motionless in the beam of light. She is wearing a filthy, tattered dress, and her skin possesses an eerie cast, like mould on an old stone wall. Her shoulders are coated in a gunge of filth that gleams wetly in the darkness.

Follow me!

The girl doesn't open her mouth to speak, but her words hang on the air, cold and silvery as a frosted cobweb. Riley's torchlight dims, flickers.

The girl moves up the stairs, the darkness slipping over her head and shoulders as she turns. Riley doesn't move, and the girl pauses, one pale hand on the banister.

Come on! She's up here!

Riley swallows. She doesn't want to follow the girl, but she also doesn't want to leave her mum in here, alone.

She takes a deep breath and moves up the stairs, one hand on the banister, the other gripping the torch. The steps are buckled, covered in debris. Riley doesn't like the way they creak and sigh beneath her feet. The wood feels spongy, as though it might give out beneath her at any moment. Darkness lies thick above her.

At the top of the stairs, Riley moves her torch over the branching corridors, looking for the girl.

This way!

Again, her torchlight fizzes, dims. She turns towards the voice, sees the faint outline of the girl, before she folds herself into the shadows. Riley quickens her step to catch up. The girl stops in front of a window, staring at the moors, her expression hungry, yearning.

You can live with me now. This will be your home, too.

She turns away from Riley, and moonlight slides over the back of her head. Her skull is a shattered ruin, a mush of imploded meat and bone that spills in glistening ropes over her shoulders.

Riley's pulse spikes. She staggers away, a mute scream welded to her throat. Tearing her eyes from the grisly vision, she flees back down the corridor, sobs catching in her throat, her chest convulsing. Her torchlight slashes the walls, her heart crashes like a timpani drum.

'*Mummy!*'

She screams the word, and it echoes round the house, blistering with raw need. And suddenly, as though summoned by the desperate force of her daughter's cry, Jenna appears, her tall, slender figure draped in shadows at the end of the corridor.

She opens her arms, and, sobbing, Riley runs towards her mother's embrace.

Her torchlight slips over parch-white skin, a face hidden by a gauzy black veil, two cavernous eyes, hollow pools that burn within sunken sockets.

Riley skids to a stop, frozen in terror, her breath wheezing like a broken scream.

Black petals float on the air around the woman, as though swept up by the ghost of a non-existent breeze.

Riley's mouth opens, horror stacked up in her throat, choking her. But the woman moves towards her on a swirl of lavender and roses. She reaches forwards, places a cold palm over Riley's eyes, and sinks her into the cradle of sleep.

NOW

'Mum never told me you went into the house,' Flynn says.

'I didn't tell her,' Riley says. 'When I woke up, I was back in the car and Jenna was driving. I don't think she knew I'd got out at all. I bet she just found me asleep coz we went and got takeaway like she promised, and no way she'd have done that if she thought I'd gone inside the house. And when I asked her why she'd left me for so long, she said she hadn't and that she'd only been gone a minute. She said the door to the house had been locked and all the windows were barred so she couldn't get in. And that's just a lie, because I got in easy-peasy.'

'Is it possible that you just fell asleep?'

'I didn't dream it.' Riley's voice is hard, uncompromising. The memory of Temple Fall darkles behind her haunted gaze.

'Okay, but how did you get back in the car?'

'I can't remember! Maybe the lady put me there. Don't look at me like that, Flynnie, I'm not making it up, I went inside that house. I *know* I did because when we got out of the car at Pizza Palazzo, Jenna said I had something caught in my hair.'

Her chin trembles, the fear that she has folded inside herself for so long shimmering in the bloated darkness of her pupils. Flynn catches her hand, gently squeezes.

'What, Ry?'

Her sister's eyes swivel to her face, glossy with tears. 'A black petal.'

Flynn's heart grates her ribs. She drops a soft kiss on Riley's bruised temple, tugs the covers up to her chin. 'It's okay now, you'll be okay,' she says, with a ferocity that shapes truth into the words, like hammer blows shaping hot steel. 'I won't let anything happen to you.'

Riley's eyelids slip closed, but the little V between her brows doesn't fade, as though even the reprieve of sleep can't soothe her fear.

Flynn quietly closes the door behind her and goes to her own bedroom. She checks her phone. The call she ignored had been Tyrus again, but this time he has left her a voicemail. She listens to his slurred message, dismay over his evident intoxication sliding into horror as his words sink in.

'Hey, it's me. I don't know if you've heard. It's Clo. She's... fuck, I can't believe this is happening. Her mum couldn't wake her up this morning. She's in a coma, Flynn. Her sugars are off the charts, they've had to intubate her. She's at St James's now, but they don't think... They don't think she's going to wake up.'

Flynn deletes the voicemail, sinks onto her bed. Shock blurs the edges of her distress, the realisation that she has almost been expecting this. A cold, flat thought slides like a palette knife over the jagged edges of her fear: *Maybe she will wake up, maybe she won't, but either way, three weeks and two days from now, Chloe's going to die. They'll say her wasted body gave up, that she died as a result of her poorly controlled diabetes. No one will suspect the truth: that Lyda Gray killed her on her eighteenth birthday.*

She takes the printout Mad Dog gave her from her pocket. Lyda Gray's black eyes blast into her, her pupils like bullets, burying themselves deep in Flynn's subconscious. The intensity of her gaze is so powerful, Flynn feels as though she is in silent communion with the past somehow, as though Lyda Gray can really *see* her.

She shoves the clipping back into her pocket and tries calling Tyrus back, but he doesn't answer. She doesn't leave a voicemail to tell him what she is planning, fearful he will try and talk her out of it. She doesn't have room for self-doubt.

It's always watching, waiting. It always knows.

Mitchell Lister's words spin on the turnstile of her mind, and for the first time, they do not sound like an ominous declaration, but a warning. A warning to someone who might be thinking about returning to Temple Fall. Because there *is* a way she can go back to that house, a way to move unseen through those terrible rooms, and to do so without physically taking a single step inside.

She recalls what Mad Dog said about the house. *It's a place we can't reach, a place that isn't meant for the living.*

But Flynn *can* reach it.

The Split.

She has not travelled in the Split since the night she damaged the elastic energy that binds spirit to host, knowing that to do so would likely snap it completely, leave her lost forever. But she doesn't see what other option she has. She doesn't know how long she has left, and she can't just sit around and wait for those closest to her to die. She has to do something while she still can.

Doubt crowds her mind. *I haven't Split for years. What if I can't do it anymore?* She shoves the thought aside. *It will work – it* has *to work.*

Her heart quickens with fear. She thinks of the leeches, those dark shimmers on the air, entities she has only ever detected in the Split and that radiate sadness, rage, bitterness, confusion. She has always known, instinctively, to keep her distance from such spirits, has felt their *wrongness*, the obscenity in the way they cling to and drain the living. Temple Fall, more than any other place she has ever visited in the Split, will harbour many such entities. Wary of accidentally bringing them back with her and passing them on to Riley or her mum, she decides to use Nostromo as the base for the Split.

Flynn quickly packs her rucksack: sleeping bag, jumper, torches, mobile, charger. She realises, as she shoves everything into her bag, that the last time she packed these things was the day she and her friends went to Temple Fall together. That night had been the beginning of the nightmare, but now, she is going to end it.

She goes into the kitchen, grabs some snacks from the fridge, then rifles through the drawers for a lighter. She debates taking sleeping tablets with her, worried her nerves will preclude sleep, but decides against it, unsure how the medication will affect the Split. She needs to be clear-headed when she reaches Temple Fall.

She hears the scrape of a key in the front door, and hurries upstairs. She climbs into bed and flips her light switch off. A few minutes later, her mum knocks gently on her bedroom door, opens it a crack. Flynn lies still, feigning sleep, and her mum retreats to check on Riley. Flynn listens to her move round the house, then to the quiet that follows, letting the minutes curl around her, silent and slumberous.

It is a little after midnight by the time she creeps down the stairs, opens the front door and slips outside. The black sky is encrusted with stars, the moon so bright and clear, Flynn can make out the dark pits in its surface. Thick petals of snow float from the night, twirling lazily in the glow of the street-lights. As Flynn walks down the muted street, she feels as though she could be the only person in the world. The snow-skinned trees are still, the houses dark. Her boots *crump-crump* through the thick cold powder that quilts the pavement, denting the silence.

As she walks, she is struck by the sudden conviction that she won't be coming back. So jarring and sudden is this thought, so absolute, that her footsteps falter and her scalp tingles. She glances over her shoulder, at the disturbances in the snow, footprints that she is sure, in that moment, will only ever lead in one direction.

Keep going, don't look back.

She turns, keeps walking, finding her resolution in every fresh footstep. The house has already taken too much from her. She won't let it take any more.

Against the night's shadowy canvas, The Pitfalls looks stark, inhospitable. Flynn hesitates, staring up at its scaffolded walls. A thousand memories collide, pressing a piercing pain against her throat. Blood beads beneath the steel point of her grief.

She switches her head torch on and the beam of light parts the darkness. She pushes open the flimsy mesh gate, picks her way across the construction site. She reaches the opening to the building, steps inside. The fecund smell of soil tangles on the air with the scent of stagnant rainwater, the musty tang of mould. The light from her head torch traces the contours of the vast steel pipes stacked in the corner, rolls of insulation material, scattered planks of wood and broken bricks.

She passes beneath the archway, her footsteps echoing through the cavernous space as she starts up the stairs. There is no handrail to prevent a drop to the hard cement floor below, and she presses close to the brick wall, taking care on the uneven surface.

When she reaches the second floor, she moves down the corridor towards Nostromo. A few of the empty bedroom doors are ajar, and the cold moon shines against the windows, slides fingers of light across the walls.

Flynn opens the door to Nostromo, and her breath catches in her chest.

The beam of her head torch glances over the ghost of Jonesy, sat on the beanbag smoking a joint while he plays on his Switch; Mei hangs from the bar Andy fastened above the doorframe, doing pull-ups; Chloe lies on the tatty old sofa, filing her nails beside Tyrus who is doing his homework. And Jackson... Jackson sits on the window ledge, his camera aimed at the grey expanse of concrete below, making poetry of the rubble-filled skips, the piles of shattered bricks, the snarled bracken that pushes through the mesh gate.

Overlaying the pervasive scent of brick dust and mildew, the smell of Jonesy's weed clings to the fabric of the room, Chloe's oil-infused candles, the almost imperceptible tang of sweat that permeates Mei's pull-up bar and hand weights, the eucalyptus of her joint spray.

Memories slice through Flynn, glass-sharp, and she bends over, tears suddenly streaming from her eyes. Only now, standing alone in Nostromo, does she truly understand her friends are gone. Shock and denial peel away, twin curtains sliding apart to reveal a stage upon which actors depict a scene of unparalleled horror. Unable until now to comprehend the enormity of all she has lost, understanding barrels through her, and it drops her to her knees.

A faint breeze soughs through the open doorway behind her.

Flynn swallows the lump in her throat, brushes the tears from her cheeks. *It isn't too late. Not for Riley. Not even for Chloe or Tyrus. I can still save them.*

She flicks the switch on the fairy lights, and plastic stars bathe the walls in a soft glow. She turns on the gas heater and pulls the sleeping bag from her rucksack, taps her pocket to make sure the lighter is still there.

Her heart claps hard, her palms are greased with sweat, but she wriggles into the sleeping bag, zips it up to her chest. Then, she lies down on the ratty sofa, one hand squeezing the lighter through the fabric of her pocket.

Fire. It began with fire, a terrible fire that claimed hundreds of lives, an atrocity that left a scar in the land, some unseen malignancy that corrupted the powerful magnetic forces that converged in a vortex deep beneath the earth. And perhaps, fire is the only way it can end. Mitchell tried it, but he had been standing in the physical world when he struck his match, his feet planted in the realm of the living, a world that could never hurt Temple Fall. But Flynn can slip between the cracks and walk through those rooms in a way no one else can. She can straddle the world of the living and the dead and enter the house when its guard is down, its naked leer exposed, mask-less.

Flynn is wide awake. Muscles twitching, adrenaline thunders through her veins. Her eyes throb behind lids she holds forcibly shut, scrunched and squeezed, as though cringing from a coming blast. It isn't surprising, the way her body staves off sleep – and yet it is. She has slept little over the past few weeks, and last night she had tossed and turned until birdsong ushered in dawn's grey light. All day, her thoughts have felt blurred and woolly, sodden with exhaustion.

She sighs, turns over on the sofa, trying to adjust herself so that she isn't lying on any of the jutting springs. Her eyes move over the fairy lights strung across the wall, the Tippex'd Jax ♡ FLYNN bright as a fresh promise beneath one glowing white star. She swallows, closes her eyes, wishing she could shut off her thoughts.

She knows for the Split to work, she has to will it, to keep her intention forefront in her mind, to focus on the way it will feel: the rending in her core, that tug behind her navel, the rushing sensation of her physical body falling away. She has to *want* it, the way she had wanted it the first time it happened, six years old and convinced the Outsiders were going to kill her. Her mind then had been like a wild bird thrashing in a too-small cage, blind to everything but the desperate urge to escape. Even after, when she was passed from the hospital to the children's home to foster care and back to the home, that essence of fear had remained, and it was this that had driven her spirit from its shell.

The difference now is that the danger she longs to escape is the very thing she must face. And she knows, this time, she might not wake up.

She rolls over, checks her phone. 02:44. Over an hour has passed since she climbed into her sleeping bag. Annoyed, she sits up, reaches for the sleeping pills in her rucksack before remembering she left them behind. She flops back onto the sofa, one arm thrown over her forehead. She tries to console herself with the knowledge that, if she fails to Split tonight, she can return tomorrow, but the thought of creeping out of the house again, making that solitary journey through the darkness, and spending another night here, alone, only sinks her into a deeper despair.

She feels grimy with tiredness, her eyes gritty with exhaustion, yet still, she can't sleep. Her head and shoulders, peeking out of the top of the sleeping bag, feel cold. She snuggles deeper. The wind sighs through the old building, darkness wavers and pulses behind her eyelids. The busted springs in the old sofa feel like knuckles pressing into her hip bone.

Her thoughts spin back to the day Andy and his mate dragged the sofa from the skip and brought it to Nostromo. A smile touches Flynn's lips at the memory of Chloe jumping onto the sofa as they carried it from the back of the minivan, how Andy had yelled at her to get off so they could wrestle it up the staircase.

Flynn sighs, shifts position. Pinpricks of light glow through the thin blanket that hangs across the window as dawn creeps closer. She realises she will have to pack up and head home before her absence is noticed.

She takes a deep breath, closes her eyes again. She feels herself sinking, comforted now by the knowledge that she will have to delay her return to Temple Fall. *I'll come back later, when Mum and Riley are asleep. I'll try again. But now, I can go home...*

Warmth seeps through her temples, and a blissful lassitude infuses her body. Her breath steadies, slows as she sinks. Sleep lowers, a feather-soft pillow smothering consciousness.

Now I can go home...

Flynn jettisons from her body, as though her spirit is a projectile fired from a slingshot. She lands on her hands and knees. She does not feel the cold floor beneath her skin, does not graze her knees against the abrasive concrete. She can no longer feel the chill in the air or smell brick dust, or oil-infused candles, or the old cigarette smoke of Nostromo. She is severed from the physical realm, as deadened to sensation as an amputated limb.

She stands up, looks round with the sense she is observing everything at a remove. The edges of her vision shimmer, as though bordered by falling skeins of water. Distantly, she hears her heartbeat, sleep-slow, hypnotic, the almost imperceptible whisper of her breath.

She tentatively feels for the cord that tethers her to her sleeping body. It is intact, but she thinks she can feel the buckle in the connection, an ache somewhere deep in her core.

She turns to look at herself. If anyone were to walk in and see her lying on the sofa, they would probably think they had stumbled upon a corpse before they noticed the faint rise and fall of her chest. She feels a faint pang of nostalgia for her own physical body, as though she is saying goodbye to a close friend she might not see again. She thinks of the scar on her knuckle from where she had sliced it on a nail at The Pitfalls, the stick-and-poke Leo symbol Jackson tattooed on her wrist, the burn scars on her feet from her tumble into the scalding water when she lived with Heather. Her body tells the story of her life, of *living*, and she hopes she gets to return to it, to add to the complex tapestry written into her skin.

Flynn's hand moves to her pocket, feels the weight and shape of the lighter there. Her fear is dulled by the Split, but not eradicated, and it thrums faintly within her at the thought of what she is about to do. But she knows she can't back down.

She closes her eyes and pictures the lobby of Temple Fall.

The first thing Flynn feels is the hard wrench in her core, the pull of her body, screaming at her to come back, to wake up. Her cord is fraying, that damaged connection thinning by the second, snapping like the stretched fibres of a thick rope.

She will have to move quickly.

When she opens her eyes, she is standing in the vast shadow of Temple Fall. A clammy chill rushes over her at the sight of the house. The shock of seeing it again is so overwhelming, at first, Flynn doesn't even process the fact she is not in the lobby, where she had expected to apport to.

The snow has stopped falling, and it clings to the trees like ermine furs. The rising sun shatters light across the sky, the powdered landscape dazzles, but Temple Fall crawls with shadows. Without the dark glamour that had enticed her inside last time, the house's ugliness is bared, like gnashing teeth: the rotting fascias, the corroding woodwork, the collapsing roof and shattered roof tiles.

Because it doesn't know I'm here.

Her eyes track to the upper-floor turret window. With savage clarity, Flynn recalls the heartbreak in Jackson's face when she told him they were finished, the terrified rigidity of his posture as Lyda Gray materialised behind him, the flare of horror in his eyes the moment she pulled him backwards through the window. The sound of his body smacking against the porch decking.

Tears slide down her cheeks. She lifts her fingers to her face, feels the wetness there. The *wrongness* of it hits her with a force that makes white spots flash at the edges of her vision. Because, except for the tug that binds her to her physical body, she shouldn't be able to feel *anything*. And yet she feels it all: the bitter cold, the tears on her face, the snow seeping through her trainers. Her teeth chatter, her breath steams. She can taste the house on the air, a metallic sharpness that mingles with the bosky smell of the snow-smothered woodland.

She starts towards the house, the conviction that something is wrong growing with every step. The cord pulls tight, and Flynn can almost hear its silent creak, a thin, anguished sound. But while this is alarming, something else is troubling her. This Split is *different*.

She looks down at her feet, at the footsteps she has sunk deep in snow. Her heartbeat staggers, her pulse thrums. *This is wrong!*

She briefly considers following the insistent drag at her core and snapping awake. But she can't. She won't. Temple Fall has taken so much from her, and it hasn't finished yet. Besides, standing here now, staring up at the house, Flynn feels there is something *inevitable* about her returning.

She walks towards the front door. The physical world asserts its presence where it has no right: her heartbeat, usually no more than a faint echo in the Split, pounds her sternum hard enough to bruise; snow that should remain untrammelled by her passage sinks beneath her weight, leaving tracks that scream her presence; her breath plumes on the cold air and beads of sweat stand on her brow.

It's always watching, waiting. It always knows.

She closes her eyes, tries again to imagine herself inside the lobby of Temple Fall, focusing on the memory of its wood-panelled walls, the deep claret carpet and imperial staircase. But it is no good. She feels shackled to reality, grounded by the brute physicality of her surroundings.

Because in Temple Fall, the physical world isn't the reality – the spirit world is.

She reaches the porch steps. Her terror rises and the pull beneath her navel quivers with tension. The remaining threads pulled taut as steel cords. But she can't go back. She won't go back.

Jackson.

His face pulses in her mind: the painted bruises beneath his eyes, the sculpted curve of his lips, the lopsided kink in his smile. Flynn imagines him standing beside her now, his warm hand sliding into her cold one. Grief squeezes her throat but with it anger flares, a flickering heat over her skin. She takes another step.

Jackson. Mei. Jonesy. Her hand tightens around the lighter as she reaches the top step. *I won't let you take anyone else.*

Flynn reaches for the door. Rather than pass through it, her fingers connect with solid wood. She twists the handle and it swings open with a sly creak.

And she steps inside.

The moment Flynn crosses the threshold of the house, the band that tethers her to her body snaps like a jerked leash. She takes a steadying breath, slowly closes the door, as though sudden movement might fray and rupture the failing connection.

Her eyes move over the lobby. The light slanting through the dirty windows seems to curdle when it strikes the glass, tracing a bilious glow over the room. Debris covers the floorboards. Veins of ivy have grown through the window frames, nature clamouring to reclaim the space. An animal musk hangs on the air, mingling with the scent of death and rot.

Flynn walks deeper into the lobby, slides the lighter from her pocket. Her shadow spills across the floor, reminding her again that she has weight and texture in this Split. Crusts of snow drop from the bottom of her tracksuit bottoms, the floorboards pop beneath her feet.

She moves towards the thick curtains, her heart ticking faster. She tries not to think of what happened to Mitchell Lister when he returned to the house to burn it down, but his face sharpens in her mind when she flicks the lighter on.

Flame spurts from the wick.

Flynn's ears pop, as though the barometric pressure has altered. The floor tips and the taste of copper pennies floods her mouth. She feels a tearing deep inside her, a savage rending. The tether that connects her to her sleeping form drops away, as though it has been cut. She reaches for it, fear surging now like hot acid, but it has gone. In its place there is only an emptiness, a hollow cave inside her. A terrible absence. *I'm dead! Oh god, I'm dead!*

She stares round the lobby, too shaken at first to take in what she is seeing.

The debris that had covered the floorboards has disappeared, as have the vines that had been growing through the crumbling masonry. The broken window is intact, and the age-faded paintings are now untarnished. Candles flicker against the walls, releasing the heavy reek of tallow smoke. An oil lamp burns on the table by the door. The curtains, which had been stood open, are now all drawn, and their edges glow, as though they block bright, midday light.

The clatter of the knocker against the door startles Flynn and she drops the lighter. It skitters across the wooden floorboards, disappears beneath the side table. She drops to her knees, swipes her hand back and forth as she grasps for the lighter, her shoulder winched at an angle that makes tears spring to her eyes.

A door bangs upstairs. Flynn's heart seizes and she scrambles to her feet, the lighter forgotten. *There's someone in the house!* She backs into the oval of darkness between the two staircases, squeezes her eyes shut, reaching for the severed connection, willing herself to wake up. It's no good. She feels rooted to the spot, as surely as if her feet were cemented to the floor.

Again, the rap of the knocker against the strike plate echoes through the lobby. Approaching footsteps from deeper in the house turn Flynn's guts to liquid and she presses deeper into the shadows. With a drop in her stomach, she thinks of the clumps of snow that had fallen from the bottom of her trousers, tell-tale signs of her presence, but just like the debris and the ivy, they have disappeared.

The creak of floorboards above her, the sigh of aged timbers beneath a heavy tread. She clamps her hands over her mouth to smother her panicked breathing.

A figure descends the stairs: a pair of leather lace-up boots with wooden heels, the swish of a black hem, a waist, thickened by pregnancy.

The woman reaches the bottom step, and the lantern-light glances across her profile. A square jaw, a stern, thin-lipped mouth framed by deep parentheses, kohl-blackened eyes that are as hard as glass. Wiry strands of hair have escaped her bun, a frizzy wisp that does nothing to soften her face. Flynn catches her scent, a miasma of stale booze, sweat and sour meat.

This isn't real, this can't be real!

Lyda Gray moves to the door. There is a key in the lock that had not been there moments ago. She twists it, opens the door. Flynn winces from the glare of bright sunlight. Lyda's broad back blocks Flynn's view of whoever is stood on the porch, but she can see the sky above Temple Fall is clear blue, the gravel drive covered not in snow, but fall leaves, burnished yellows, golds, browns that glitter beneath a glaze of frost.

'What do ye want?' Lyda's voice is a hoarse scratch, cold and sunless as an ancient cavern. It is the voice Flynn heard on the lips of Mitchell Lister. *You're already dead.*

'My name is Evelina Hill. A little under two years ago, you took my daughter, Rose. I've come to collect her, Miss. I'm so sorry, I know this must be awful hard for you to—'

'It is my only condition of taking on their care that the mothers of unwanted babies don't contact 'em again.'

'Oh, Rose weren't never unwanted, Miss! If you could only see the babies what are born into the workhouse, you'd understand why—'

'I understand better than ye think. I ain't exactly had an easy time of it meself, but we don't all have the luxury of choice.'

'Please, Miss. If there were any other way, I'd have taken it.'

'She were adopted entirely, correct?'

'I'm sorry, I—'

'Your girl. She weren't a lodger here, is what I'm asking. You 'ent been sending me money every week, like what some others do. She were adopted entirely.'

'Well, yes... but—'

'Ye should've said if ye wanted her back.'

'I'd have given any sum to keep Rose safe, if I'd only had it. But the money... the money were no small sum for me, Miss, it took a while.'

'My conditions were clear and they 'ent for negotiatin'. If ye want a child, then I suggest ye go make another. They 'ent hardly difficult to come by.'

She starts to close the door, but Evelina stops it with her hand.

'My circumstances have changed, Miss. I can look after her now.'

'Hoors, yer all the same. Give yer quim for a sov, then offload yer brats onto others to do the mothering for ye. Now if ye'll excuse me—'

Evelina shoots her foot between the door and the frame.

'I will not leave without my child.'

A sudden steel in the voice that had not been there before, a strength Flynn wishes she possesses herself, because fear has stolen the strength from her legs, and she huddles on the floor, tremors shaking her body. She presses her eyes shut. *I'm not here, I'm not here. I'm miles away, fast asleep in Nostromo. I'm not here...*

And yet, she *is* here. The physical world abrupt and crude, rooting her to Temple Fall. The chill of the lobby, the glare of sunlight, the sour tang of the house, the faint swirl of lavender and moss that whisk through the open door, all of it real. Flynn is certain that if Lyda turns and looks into the dark recess beneath the stairs, she will see her there.

No no no, it isn't real, it can't be. I'm stuck in a memory, a memory that belongs to Temple Fall. But it isn't real, it can't be real. I just have to wake up!

But without the connection tethering her to her body, she is grounded. And it strikes her then, truth sparking like flame. *Perhaps it isn't because I've died that I can't wake up – perhaps it's because I haven't been born yet.*

Lyda opens the door wider, and Evelina steps inside. Flynn feels a bolt of recognition. This is the same young woman she saw standing outside Jonesy's kitchen window moments before he died, the dark cavern of her soundless scream swirling with black petals.

Now, she is wearing a yellow sundress with a posy of red roses pinned to her bodice. Her strawberry blonde hair is parted down the centre and braided into buns that curl over her ears. She looks painfully thin, and the blush to her cheeks fails to conceal her unhealthy pallor, and yet there is a robustness about her, a wiry competence. Her grey eyes glitter as they move over the lobby.

Something in Evelina's demeanour seems to dim as she takes in her surroundings. Her narrow shoulders slump. Flynn sees realisation dawn behind her eyes, the understanding that this is not a place for children, that whatever discovery she is about to make is not the one she had hoped for.

Evelina's gaze suddenly snaps to Flynn, crouched in the recess beneath the stairs. Flynn's terror sharpens, a spike at the base of her skull. *Please don't tell her I'm here! Please don't tell her I'm here, please don't–*

Lyda starts to turn, but Evelina swoops forwards, swipes at the vase standing on the side table. It crashes against the floor, scattering slices of porcelain.

'I'm sorry. Please, let me–'

'Leave it!' Lyda glares at Evelina. *'Come with me.'*

The two women move off together through the lobby, but Flynn hangs back, watching them slide into the darkness. Her eyes move to the door, her feet itching to flee. But where can she go? If she steps outside into 1884, can the world hold its shape around her? No, she is sure if she leaves Temple Fall, her consciousness will shatter and she will cease to exist. If anything is holding her together now, it is the walls of the house.

Flynn hears the low grate of Lyda's voice, the gentle lilt of Evelina's reply. She recalls how Evelina had gone missing shortly after filing a report against the baby farmer. Her body was never discovered.

I have to warn her.

Flynn's throat is dry, her heart beats so hard she feels its pulse in her fingertips.

She stands up and follows the two women deeper into the house.

~

The candles flicker in their fixings, light jerks across the walls. Lyda and Evelina glide ahead, seem to gather speed as Flynn staggers to catch up with them.

An icy hand closes on her shoulder, and she gasps, spins round. An old man is standing beside her. Tall, gaunt, white-haired, with thick sideburns covering his jawline. His eyes are clear lakes, his face a crawl of shadows. Hate and rage seethe from his skin, branding the air like a silent scream.

Flynn takes a staggering step away from Edmund Lonsdale, away from the terrible heat that burns in his glacial eyes, but already he is fading, darkness billowing across his skin, erasing him.

Flynn pivots, looking for Evelina, but she too is fading, the bright yellow of her dress dimming to a sooty grey. Beside her, Lyda's figure blurs into the darkness. Flynn quickens her pace, fearful of losing them, but they are mere shadows now, dark husks curling into the air like candle smoke.

Flynn breaks into a run as the two women disappear. She stares at the spot where they had been a moment ago with disbelieving eyes, feels the house move through her, a twinge in her consciousness.

She takes a step back, and her foot strikes something solid. She spins round, sees that the hallway has disappeared, a wall closing like a door behind her. Biting back a sob, she stumbles forwards, forced to follow the path the two women took.

She opens the first door she comes to, steps into a shadowy room.

The dry rasp of wool carpet beneath her feet is replaced by bare floorboards that slide into darkness. Pale moonlight falls through a row of seven Palladian windows. A faecal stench tangles with a sharp, medicinal tang on the air.

'No,' she whispers. 'No-no-no-no-no...'

Her throat shrinks to the width of a pin, the roots of her hair stiffen.

She is in the nursery.

She spins back round with a cry and stumbles down the

corridor until she reaches a narrow staircase that corkscrews up into darkness.

A door creaks in the distance, the sound dragging like nails down Flynn's spine.

Then... footsteps.

Swelling as they approach.

Flynn tears up the stairs as those terrible footsteps grow into a cacophony in her ears. The landing leads onto three dark corridors and Flynn sprints down one of them. The threadbare carpet seems to shift beneath her feet, lifting and rolling like a huge tongue to pull her back. The footsteps pound in her skull. She senses something reaching out to grab her, a tightening cold across her shoulders.

She cries out, pulls open another door, swings it closed behind her.

Breathing raggedly, she sags against the door. Her eyes move over the room.

Cold wooden floorboards, seven high, curved windows, a row of cots beside an unlit fireplace.

She is back in the nursery.

A scream pushes against her throat, a swollen, choking horror. Her cheeks are wet with tears, fear swells her eyes in their sockets. She flings the door open again, staggers back the way she came, opens the next door she comes to—

Backs away, her eyes fixed on those same arched windows. An unholy stink bakes from the room. A snatch of music on the air makes her spin round.

Happy birthday to you!

Panic-blind, she runs through the house. Corridors and rooms appear where they have no right to be, the house rearranging itself like a shuffled deck of cards, and the music keeps pace with her, an unwelcome companion, lifting from the walls like bubbling plaster, singing up from the floor like clouds of thick dust.

Happy birthday to you!

The shadows spill forwards, and Flynn realises the walls are narrowing, pressing closer to her. She looks round for a door, but the walls of the corridor stretch on and on, unbroken.

A soft, hissing static fills Flynn's head, grows in volume to a blizzard that blurs her thoughts and hazes her memory. She sobs, clamps her hands over her ears, trying to think past the noise that fills every corner of her mind. Her thoughts collide like cymbals, a nonsense band. She knows she came here with a purpose, but she can't think... can't think... cognition pulverised by the wall of sound.

Flynn's throat is suddenly dry, her tongue thick and heavy. The walls closing in, the space diminishing in size. The scent of stale popcorn and bleach tangle on the air, the smell like a hard shove knocking her back in time. She turns on the spot, convinced that if she reaches her hand into the darkness, she will feel the solid walls of The Cupboard closing in on her.

The candles mounted in their sconces wink out, darkness plunges into Flynn's eyes. She gropes at the wall, arms swiping blindly, telling herself there has to be a door, there has to be... She grasps the ridge of a doorframe. Tears shake down from her eyes as she fumbles for the handle, swings it open and throws herself inside.

The hail of static drops to a background murmur and she blinks into the light of a familiar room. Pebbledash plaster walls, a dark green carpet, windows covered in old newspaper. There is a table in one corner with a Scrabble box on top, a TV on a stand in front of an olive-green sofa. The smell of greasy meat and sickness fades, replaced by the astringent smell of bleach.

Flynn realises she is wearing her old Care Bears pyjamas, the ones with the nibbled and frayed cuffs. On the side table sits a cloth doll. The room's dim light glints in its one button eye, storm-cloud grey. The other eye is missing, snapped black thread dangling from where it should be. Its mouth is a small, pinched rosebud, its hair a dark velvet cap.

It can't be, it can't be Mama?!

But that stitched mole on its cheek is as telling as a birthmark.

Flynn doesn't realise she is edging away until her shoulder knocks into the wall.

Fear whitewashes her thoughts, so she doesn't at first notice the tang of crushed pills at the back of her throat. Not until darkness surges behind her lids, and sleep presses its leaden hand against her brow.

The trembling of her body turns to palsied convulsions, but the terror is swiftly smothered. Her head swims, her vision blurs. Nausea sways through her, and with it, a slumberous apathy. She is tired. So tired… Her thoughts still, then sink to the seabed of her mind as her eyes drift closed.

Without thinking, she starts to walk, softly counting each footstep, her fingertips trailing the wall. Temple Hall watches and smiles as Flynn's features ripple and blur and are smoothed to a blank oval.

She walks from one room to the next, counting softly under her breath as, at first by degrees and then all at once, she forgets herself.

Time slips and slides, but it no longer means anything to the girl. She is part of Temple Fall now, just as it is part of her. She floats in the specks of dust that hang on the air, she skulks in the shadows that slide across the floor as the sun arcs across the sky, she exhales on the breeze that sweeps through the gaps in the windowpanes.

Decades slide by in seconds, seconds snag on the hooks of time and drag on for years. Past, present, future, all exist at once, tripartite threads on a loom that twine under and over each other. Temple Fall is an ouroboros, consuming itself, both the beginning and the end of time. Cyclical. Eternal.

The girl knows she is not alone, that there are others like her, lost souls, held hostage by the house, but she avoids them, just as she avoids the Outsiders who come and go. They scare her almost as much as the mistress of Temple Fall, that woman with the black stare and empty smile.

Time passes, and the girl's mind exists in a state of dreamless hibernation as she walks the rooms and halls of the house. The only time she stops is in brief pauses at the turret window, where she is drawn over and over for reasons she can't understand, and doesn't try to.

Is there anyone there?

The girl's footsteps falter. The dust motes slow in their aerial ballet, the wind drops, the bats roosting in the loft space grow still. An unnatural hush falls over Temple Fall, as though it strains to hear the direction of the girl's thoughts.

'Izzanybodythere?'

The girl normally ignores Outsiders, just as she ignores the restless denizens of Temple Fall, but something about this voice makes her want to answer. She tries to hear through the rain of static trapped inside her. The muted sound of excited chatter sharpens, the brazen buzz of life to which she no longer belongs. She can't bring her surroundings into focus, her vision blurred by the silver skeins that sheathe her eyes.

'Come out and play, we don't bite!'

'This is a bad idea.'

'It's Jackson's eighteenth! Say happy birthday!'

That name – *Jackson* – flares in the girl's mind. The static trapped in her head fades, and the obfuscating veil that sheathes her eyes lifts so that she sees she is standing in the turret room.

The wind rattles the windows in their frames, a fire burns in the grate. A group of people, no more than shimmers on the air, sit around the low wooden table. *Outsiders.* Threads of fear pulse through the girl and she starts to turn away, but something about the whispering voices makes her hesitate.

What is your name?

She moves towards the table. Her vision is blurred, but she can make out the lettered tiles, set in a wide circle. A glass is placed upside down in the centre, and the Outsiders rest their fingertips upon it.

Again, the static swells in the girl's ears, a rising tide of sound that dims the voices she is trying to hear. *My name... What is my name?* She reaches for the shot glass, and it quivers beneath her touch. The Outsiders gasp and the girl feels their fear, a cold snap on the air.

What is your name?

A strange quickening inside her, a cryogenically preserved soul, awakening. She tries to wipe a hand over her eyes to clear her vision, but the house blots her senses. She feels its agitation, her flare of autonomy like a mosquito bite on the hide of a huge predator. Something tears inside her mind, her consciousness ripping free from the walls of the house. Temple Fall pulses with anger and the wick of every candle in every room and hallway suddenly bursts into flame.

Did you die here?

The girl's breath snatches, cold rushes through her. She senses the Outsiders recoil, as though her gasp stirs the small hairs down their necks. She tries to open her mouth to answer – *No!* – but her face is a blank tile, a desperate and featureless flexing.

As though sensing her distress, the house whispers through her, calls to her. It wants to fold her back into its embrace, and the girl longs to do just that, to walk through dreams of forgetting and blunt the terrible ache in her chest. But those voices... They draw her in, pulling questions like corpses from the cemetery of her mind. *What is my name? Am I dead? Did I die here?*

Enraged, the house tightens its grip on her, and its gravity tugs her, but there is an opposing gravity at work now, in this table of Outsiders.

Keep your hands on the glass!

Thinking the command is aimed at her, the girl places her other hand on the glass. Her eyes flicker blindly. She can almost feel her subconscious straining to free itself from the bricks and mortar that bind it.

She turns the last question over in her mind: *Did I die here?*

She does not move the glass consciously, and yet she feels it slide beneath her touch, the truth appearing from some hidden, repressed part of her.

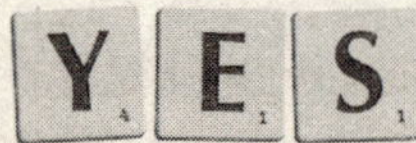

The girl senses the Outsiders recoil, their fear as palpable as a scream rending the air.

Why haven't you moved on?

A quaver in the voice now, a tremble of uncertainty. The glass feels more solid beneath the girl's fingers, the figures in the room and the lettered tiles a little clearer, as though every communication frays the barriers between them. A roar of static tries to wipe her thoughts, but she tunes it out.

Her mouth frames the word as she guides the glass to the lettered tiles. She hears it echoed on the Outsider's lips, and only then does she feel the truth of it. The desperate agony of being imprisoned in this house, her free will smothered, her consciousness bound. Trapped, like a fly on a spiderweb.

She reaches over, ready to say more, but her hand passes through one of the Outsiders, a blonde shimmer on the air. The girl feels as though she has placed her cold hand into a warm patch of sunlight, but the Outsider tenses.

Something touched me! Oh my god, something touched *me!*

The Outsiders are arguing, voices fear-strained, the excitement of a few moments ago curdling with fear, but the girl holds the question in her mind, turns it over. Her name holds a weight and texture in her mind, but she can't reach deep enough to feel its shape.

How old will we be when we die?

The question slices through the girl's consciousness, and the instant it does, the glass beneath her hand splinters, a jagged crack slicing from the upturned base to the lip. A sense of danger cleaves her as she realises that she is not alone in the room with these Outsiders. Temple Fall has been riding quiet on her thoughts, and it has summoned someone to stop her.

The girl looks up as the mistress of Temple Fall slides towards her. Where the Outsiders are amorphous wisps on the air, the woman is solid flesh, an aberration of sour meat and malignancy. Her vermillion grin is stretched tight, the black scribbles of her eyes darkle in their shrouded sockets.

Before the girl can pull away, the woman lunges, slaps her hand over the glass. Her touch is clammy, repellent. The girl tries to pull away, but the woman's broad hand pins her. The smell of her is a violence, the sour-sweat that radiates from her armpits, the infective tang on her breath, the stale scent of booze that seeps from her pores.

She glares at the girl, eyes ablaze with febrile hatred, lips stretched in a knowing grin as she drags the glass down the table in a long, straight line. The Outsiders are screaming, their panic tightening the air.

Spirit, leave in peace!

But the woman doesn't leave, only scars her message deeper, her hand sweeping faster and faster round the table, a swift, jerking motion, almost impossible to track. The girl tries again to pull free from her grip, but the woman's grasp is a manacle, possessing a tensile strength as powerful as the house's will.

We thank you, spirit, leave in peace!

With a strangled cry, the girl dashes the shot glass against the wall. It shatters in an explosive hail of jade, falls to the floor glittering like spite. But the girl isn't looking at the glass; she is staring at the tabletop, at the message scarred deep as a vow into the wood.

18.

The girl sways, blinking into the shadow-cluttered turret room. The fire is unlit, she is alone. The house feels empty. The storm-darkened window now admits the rose-blushed light of dawn. The Outsiders disappeared from the turret room only moments ago, but deep down, the girl knows they have been gone a long time.

The quiet is broken by the soft crackle of static, and more distantly, the intermittent squall of babies crying, a sound that makes the girl want to cover her ears and curl into a ball. She feels an inexplicable sense of abandonment, and an overwhelming loneliness fills her. *They left me here*. It makes no sense, this crippling pain, this intense sadness.

The Outside isn't safe for you.

The voice is not her own, yet she feels as though she has been hearing it all her life.

You belong in here.

Her gaze slides to the window. The sun peeks over the horizon in a spill of gold that sweeps brushstrokes of reds, pinks, oranges, through the clouds. The purpled heather-clad ridges of the open moorland, the cobalt spray of bluebells, the hills, rising and falling in countless shades of green. So much colour, and all of it outside the grey and crumbling walls of Temple Fall, as though all that beauty, all that *life* belongs to another world altogether.

Come away from the window.

The voice speaks from deep in her subconscious, but she resists its pull, held captive by the view. She longs to walk outside, to breathe in the fresh green air, to brush her fingertips over the lemon-scented ferns, to lie in the heather and watch the clouds glide against the high blue sky.

Come away from the window.

Despair thickens, a soupy quicksand that weighs her down. Because she knows the house won't let her leave. That she is destined to walk these halls forever. The dark realisation spills through her and she feels herself sinking, the house weaving its webs over her eyes and mouth again. She lets it happen, her resolve slackening. Why should she leave? The world is frightening and cold and cruel, but in Temple Fall, she is safe, sheltered from the Outside.

She turns from the window and the ache in her chest slackens, as though the house has delivered a dose of novocaine to her pain-filled thoughts. She closes her eyes, wills Temple Fall to hurry up and take her, eager for it to be over.

A wash of grey in her mind, her senses dull. She passes a hand over her face. Her features have flattened into a featureless waxen plane. Her consciousness unravels, floods into distant rooms and melts into the walls. It flickers in the oil lamps, curls in twists of candle smoke and groans in the rafters.

The heady scent of roses fills the turret room.

The girl opens her eyes. Her vision is clouded, her thoughts scattered, but she pulls the scent of roses deeper into her lungs, an aroma that works like smelling salts, sharpening her senses.

She lowers her gaze to the carpet. It is covered in black rose petals.

A dark crush of velvet beneath her feet, fecund and earthy. A ripple passes through them, as though a breeze stirs the dead air, then they swirl to life, a blizzard of black snow that flutters over the girl. Beating across her eyes, fluttering over her ears, kissing her numbed skin. Their quiet music silences the static wash in her head and the fog that sheathes her vision clears.

The girl steps back, transfixed by the rising storm of petals. They swirl and spin higher, a massed, rotating darkness that slows on the air to take the shape of a figure.

A young woman, beautiful and terrible. Dressed head to toe in black, her sepaled feet hover above the floor, petals drift across her face. A veil covers her eyes, a fine gauzed undulating darkness that shadows her features.

The figure slides closer, shedding petals like dead skin. Her eyes blaze behind the floating skeins of black. She lifts her hand to her chest, as though pressing a palm to her heart. Something in her shaded features conveys a grief so deep, the girl feels grateful for the shroud that covers it.

From the dark dance of the petals, the woman plucks a single black rose and holds it out.

The girl takes it.

The stem is long and thin, spiked with thorns. She twirls it between thumb and forefinger, and as she stares at the blurred petals, she feels suddenly unsteady. As though she is the rose, spinning violently in the grip of some unknowable power.

A thorn cuts her thumb, a bite of pain that moors her.

Blood wells.

And memory spills.

A life flickers through her consciousness, *her* life, reclaimed from the sucking walls of the house. *Flynn... My name is Flynn.* The floorboards shiver beneath her feet, a fresh crack splinters the wall, but she doesn't notice. Each memory sparks another, and she drops to her knees, her bulbed fists pressed to her temples. *Jackson... Mei... Jonesy...* Her lungs seize, can't breathe around the grief that barbs each breath. *Chloe... Tyrus... Riley.*

The house is going to take them all.

Perhaps it already has.

Rage fills Flynn. She screams and a draught of icy air blows through the house.

She turns to where the veiled figure had been, but she has gone. Flynn's eyes track to the window, to the black roses that scramble the low stone wall. *Evelina.* And she knows then that she is buried there, beneath the dark snarl of flowers.

She feels the house grapple to regain control of her consciousness, a sly, almost imperceptible uncurling at the back of her mind. And it is then, in that oily shift within her, that she realises what she has to do.

She had thought that she was helpless, powerless, because the house was inside her, fused to her consciousness. But if the house is part of her, then she in turn is part of the house.

And if the house can shuffle time, then perhaps she can, too.

She moves to the window. Her heart beats jaggedly, her pulse flails, her body awakening to the memory of itself... to *her*self. Excitement quickens inside her, daring her to hope even though hope feels dangerous. *This might work. This* has *to work.*

She stares at the vast expanse of the moors and spins the reel of time in her mind back to the day she first visited Temple Fall.

Jackson taking her photo in the minivan, his knuckles grazing her cheek as he tucked her hair behind her ear, sending an electric jolt through her; his sculpted lips, his crooked smile; Andy shouting at Chloe when she turned the music up too loud; the pop of Chloe's prosecco bottle; Jonesy's giggle when the cork struck Andy on the back of his head; everyone singing 'Happy Birthday' to Jackson; Mei snapping her gum; the menthol, eucalyptus smell of her magnesium joint spray; Tyrus popping the tab on a can of Coke; the squirm of unease Flynn had felt when she saw the house, the conviction, so much stronger than déjà vu, that she had been there before...

Because you had been here before. This is where you belong. Come away from the window.

She grinds her teeth together, closes her ears to the voice of the house, focuses on the memory of that day. The rising sense of dread she had felt watching the tail-lights of Andy's minivan disappear as he drove away, the grim chill that wrenched up her spine when she turned back to the house. The feel of rain against her skin, the distant rumble of thunder.

The house digs its heels in, a sudden searing at the back of her mind. Static fills her ears and greyness feathers her vision, seeking to obliterate her, but she clings stubbornly to memory – Jackson's hand sliding down the curve of her back, the warm solidity of his arms, the smell of his skin, the shy smile on his lips when he passed her the black rose.

The house screams, a desperate howling that shivers through the masonry and lengthens the shadows, but Flynn is lost in Jackson, lost in his dark eyes, the sooty fringe of his lashes, the dusting of stubble on his chin.

Temple Fall sinks grappling hooks in her mind, tries to reel her thoughts back, but it is Jackson's fingers Flynn feels, hooking into the waistband of her jeans and pulling her close, Jackson's breath against her ear, Jackson's lips she tastes, filling her cold body with heat.

A blinding flash sears her eyes.

She blinks, confused. The dawn sky outside has been replaced by a storm-dark evening. Thunder prowls the rolling hills, veins of lightning pulse within metal-grey clouds.

But the snap of brightness behind Flynn's eyes wasn't the lightning.

Standing at the foot of Temple Fall, Jackson lowers his camera and stares up at Flynn, framed in the turret window. A frown caught between his brows. Chloe skips down the porch steps, her cornsilk hair rippling down her spine. Mei and Tyrus are laying tent poles on the ground while Jonesy watches them, smoking a joint. Flynn sees herself, wearing Jackson's beanie hat, her arms twined around his waist.

She backs away from the window. I did it... *I did it!*

For a moment, shock overwhelms her, and she can't think beyond the enormity of what she has done, can only watch as a fine patter of rain starts to fall outside. It quickly thickens, spreading into a merciless downpour. Thunder cracks the sky.

Don't let them in!

The thought snaps her from her shock and she starts towards the door, but hot needle points of pain pierce her feet. She gasps, stumbles, as unbearable heat flows over her skin. The soles of her feet blister and bubble, and heat rushes up her legs as though they have been doused in hot oil.

Or boiling water.

Inside her mind, Temple Fall smiles.

It's just the house, it isn't real, just a bad memory. It isn't real.

The pain peels back like scalded skin. Flynn grits her teeth, staggers to the door and throws it open. She hurries down the hallway. The house screams at her in the voice of her childhood home, a blaze of static that roars through her consciousness, threatening to eradicate her, but she holds her purpose firmly in her mind, lurches towards the stairs.

Down the steps, her face sweat-lathered, feet blazing. *Are we on the porch yet? Are we already inside?*

At the bottom of the stairs, down the next corridor, the house tries to buckle and shift around her, but she knows the shape of these walls now, the natural pattern of rooms and corridors, and she holds them firmly in her mind, refuses to let them change. She senses the house's frustration, a grating vibration at the back of her skull. The skin on her feet feels as though it is peeling away in layers, her toenails loosening from their scalded beds.

Nausea rocks her back on her heels. Her throat swells, the heat that blazes in her feet spreads through her entire body. Her breath shrinks to snatched gasps as the illness that had hospitalised her as a child, again stalks through her.

But she can't stop, stumbles onwards, pushing through the roar of static that seeks to blind her, the agony of her scalded feet, the ache in her oxygen-starved lungs. Holds determinedly to that first visit to Temple Fall as she staggers through the dining room, into the morning room, down another hallway.

But every step is becoming slower than the last. Her breath wheezes, her friends' faces dim in her mind. She grabs onto the furniture, sure at any moment her legs will fold beneath her. She is in the lobby... almost there... sees the front door...

Her vision blurs, her hearing dims. A blankness rolls across her thoughts as her lips begin to seal, her eyes occlude. Her heart lurches, and she throws her mind towards her friends, painting the scene from memory: dripping rainwater onto the porch, Jackson's hand squeezes hers, Tyrus turns troubled eyes on the storm, Jonesy screams as lightning strikes the tree, Chloe is *so f-fucking c-cold* and Mei pushes forwards, raps the knocker against the strike plate and all the time, Flynn can't shake the feeling that she has been here before.

Dimly, she can hear them out there, gathered on the porch. But her movements are agonisingly slow, too slow... She won't make it... the house is pulling her back, enveloping her, turning her into dust and masonry and bricks and shadow. She can feel it happening, a slow *unbecoming*.

No! You can't have them!

She can barely see, but she feels for the key, twists it. The click of the lock resonates deep inside her, the knowledge that she is locking herself in as much as she is locking everyone else out. She sinks to the floor, her back pressed against the door. But then she remembers Jonesy. The hammer. Shattered glass...

Mei raps the knocker against the door.

I can't stop them! They're going to come in and I can't stop them!

Something glints beneath the side table, catching her eye. The lighter – she dropped it when Evelina knocked on the front door.

Flynn thinks of Mitchell Lister, standing in the doorway to Temple Fall, trying to light a match to set the house on fire. She thinks of a chapel standing where she is now, full of innocent people, burning alive. At the thought, the acrid scent of smoke floods the lobby, the stench of burning meat. Dying cries scorch the air, hoarse and agonised, as though the victims of that terrible crime have not stopped screaming since it happened.

Flynn crawls towards the lighter. The house fastens its grip, a fierce contraction that floods her body with pain. Her vision blanches, the static in her head builds. Not enough air... There is not enough air... But in the darkening cave of her mind, the faces of those she loves gains a clarity they have not yet possessed.

She gropes for the lighter.

You can't have them!

Her hand wraps round it and she pulls herself to her feet. Flicks the flint wheel. She can't see the fire, can't see anything, but she knows it is there from the way the house roars through her. She staggers towards the curtains, reaches blindly for the feel of the cloth, then guides the small tongue of flame to it.

Fire catches, a sudden blaze. Heat flares over her, tightening her skin, scalding her lungs. And this time she knows it will work, because unlike Mitchell, she is outside of time and space, her feet firmly planted in Temple Fall in a way no other living person's have ever been. The chorus of dying screams sharpen on the air, willing her on, begging her to end their pain.

I won't let you take them!

She lurches across to the next pair of curtains and holds the flame to them. The house's roar becomes a scream of agony that splinters her skull.

Leave them alone! You can't have them! Take me instead!

The fire spreads, bubbles the plaster on the walls and blisters the air. It blazes beneath her skin, because she is part of the house, too. She holds her hands in front of her and stumbles towards the direction of the door. Faces swim in her mind, and though they seem familiar, she doesn't know who they are. Her consciousness is flooding back into the house, her memories unravelling.

Take me instead.

The words turn in her mind, but she does not understand what they mean, just as she does not understand this dogged compulsion to keep the door shut. Only that it exists. That it is everything. Her hands knock against the door and she sinks to her knees, her back pressed against the solid wood. Her scream blends with the scream of Temple Fall as the flames steal over her, as her clothes catch, her hair flares, and her features melt like tallow.

Take me instead...

NOW

Flynn scrolls through the recruitment website on her phone, searching for a part-time job. It is lunchtime, and the bar of The Dive downstairs is quiet. Chloe is sitting beside her on the sofa, reading a magazine, Tyrus is playing *Street Fighter* on the club's ancient Super Nintendo, Mei and Jonesy are playing cards. Eighties rock plays through the speakers of the bar's ancient music system.

It is the middle of August, but outside the window, rain lashes down from the sky. The background wash of sound that others find so soothing, makes Flynn feel antsy. She has never liked listening to the rain, the sound too easily bringing back memories of the static Heather used to play through the house night and day.

She slips her pumps off, tucks her bare feet up on the sofa. She sees a waitressing job advertised, fifteen hours a week, close to her university accommodation. She clicks on the little heart beside it, then scrolls to the next page of jobs.

She still can't quite believe that in just over a month's time, she is going to university. Moving out, moving on. She knows the transition will be easier for her than her best friends, with Jackson going to Manchester Metropolitan to study for his degree in photography, just a stone's throw from Flynn at the University of Manchester, where she has secured a place on the English course.

She struggled with indecision over where to go and what to study for so long, she almost missed the application deadline. It was Mei who had pointed out that she was putting way too much pressure on herself. After all, she was only seventeen, and she had years to decide what she wanted to do with her life. One way or another, she would figure it out.

Jonesy groans as Mei turns her cards face up on the carpet. He tosses his own hand down in disgust.

'You're cheating,' he says. 'No one wins this many times on the trot.'

'You always were a sore loser.' Mei smiles and spins one of the cards on the tip of her middle finger.

Jonesy flicks the card, his expression sulky. Mei laughs. Shuffles the cards one-handed.

Flynn lowers the phone, her concentration knocked askew by a sweeping déjà vu. Unease skims her mind. Her eyes grow unfocused, and she is aware of her attention folding inwards, seeking, searching, as though there is something she is missing, some vital kernel of knowledge lurking just beyond the edge of memory.

'Shall I deal you in again?'

'I'm out.' Jonesy heaves himself to his feet. 'I need to go for a slash.'

Lost in thought, Flynn doesn't notice Jackson enter the room until his hands slide over her shoulders. She whirls round, knocking her pint glass onto the floor. Jackson steps back too late, beer splashing his trousers.

'Shit, I'm sorry!' Flynn says.

Jackson picks the glass up, sets it back on the table, absently brushes a hand over his beer-soaked jeans. Flynn notices a small crack running through the glass, a tiny chip in the rim. She stares at the hairline fracture, that brush of unease sharpening into an inexplicable anxiety.

'Jacko, where've you been?' Jonesy comes out of the bathroom. 'I was just gonna get a pint downstairs, you want one? I still owe you for—'

'Not now,' Jackson says, flicking Jonesy a glance then turning his attention back to Flynn. 'I have to show you something.'

His words are freighted with excitement, yet dread drops like a stone in Flynn's stomach.

'What's going on?' Jonesy picks up the remote and turns the TV off, ignoring Tyrus's outraged cry.

Jackson takes an envelope from his inside pocket, hands it to Flynn. The music playing through the room slows, a brief lull of tempo, an orchestral interlude. Something about the sound makes Flynn frown and look over her shoulder, the feeling someone has whispered her name in a distant room.

'I developed them this morning.' A beat of silence chases Jackson's words, a catch in his dark eyes as they land on Flynn. 'They're from Temple Fall.'

At the mention of the house, tension cracks the room like a whip, everyone falls silent. Tyrus, who had been reaching for the remote to turn his game back on, freezes, Mei looks a question at Jackson, Chloe lowers her magazine, Jonesy freezes, the pint he had just picked up from the table halfway to his lips. The muted chatter from the bar downstairs brushes against the silence, the oppressive sound of rain outside swells.

Almost eleven months have passed since their doomed camping trip, but still a tremor ricochets through Flynn at the memory of what had happened at Temple Fall.

She slides the photographs from the envelope onto the table as the others gather round.

'I almost didn't bother developing them,' Jackson says. 'After what we saw... well, I was so spooked, I buried the camera and tried to forget all about it.' He shrugs, his dark eyes darting to Flynn's face. 'I guess curiosity got the better of me in the end.'

Flynn's thoughts flood back to that stormy afternoon, their trip for Jackson's eighteenth birthday. Standing on the rain-dashed porch of Temple Fall, looking through the glass pane in the door she had glimpsed a figure darting forwards, a slice of movement that had chilled her to the marrow. She couldn't have said what it was about that distorted shape that had terrified her, only that she had been so unnerved, she had insisted they wait out the storm on the porch.

Perhaps, if that was all she had seen, she would have since been able to convince herself that she had imagined it. But it wasn't. Because as they huddled together, hunched against the rain and wind, Jonesy twitching to break in, Chloe complaining about the cold, every single hair on Flynn's body had suddenly stood on end. Static crackled over her skin, the taste of batteries flooded her mouth, and a faint crackling filled her head.

Convinced that she had just felt the electrical charge of lightning striking the house, she had looked up at the building, and seen fire blaze behind every glass pane. The windows had exploded, and she had cried out, staggered back, thrown her arms over her head to protect herself from the falling shards. But the glass never hit the ground, and when she cast her gaze flinchingly upwards, she was stunned to see the windows were intact, the rooms within cold, dark.

It was as though she had hallucinated the whole thing, but when she had turned to the others, she had seen her own shock reflected in their eyes.

Clutching at each other, they had backed away from Temple Fall and as they did, the house had *withered*, as though centuries were passing in the blink of an eye, leaving behind a rotting carcass of crumbling masonry.

They had huddled beside the low stone wall, over which the

tumbling vines of black roses grew, watching the house with wary eyes, but after its sudden degeneration, the storm had quickly passed, and they had managed to pitch their tent on the grass.

Now, Flynn studies the black-and-white photographs Jackson had taken on the old Brownie camera. Their grainy resolution lends them a mysterious, vintage effect: Flynn in the back of Andy's minivan, staring out of the window; Chloe draped over the porch railing, her long hair tangling on the breeze; numerous images of the house before the storm; lightning streaking down from the dark sky, sparking white wisps against the darkness; their tent, pitched in the sodden grass; the sprawling expanse of the moors, jewelled by rainfall, Temple Fall glimmering darkly beneath scrubbed skies; Flynn and Chloe crashing plastic cups inside the tent; the photograph that Flynn had taken of Jackson blowing out eighteen candles on the camera cake Jonesy had made for him.

'What are we looking at exactly?' Tyrus asks, peering over Chloe's shoulder.

Jackson taps the image of Chloe posing on the porch railing. Flynn has a sudden memory of Chloe demanding he take her photo. Jackson peering through the viewfinder, focusing the shot. The bemused expression on his face as he looked up from the camera towards the upper turret window.

'Do you see it?' Jackson asks, watching her.

Like the others, the photograph's resolution is poor, shapes blurring together in a static wash of blacks and silvers and greys. At first, all Flynn sees is Chloe, her head flung back, her legs tangled round the metal railing, wild hair framing her perfect profile. But then Flynn's gaze travels over the house.

A clammy chill grips her. She leans closer, squints at the gritty image. A granular figure is standing at the turret window. A girl. Dark-haired. Gaunt and pale, her eyes a socketed black. Something about her posture, the angles of her face...

'Oh my god...' Mei whispers.

Flynn feels as though the ground beneath her feet has shifted, a tectonic crack opening deep within the earth. Cold splinters down her spine. The music playing through the bar's sound system scratches, notes bending to shape a different tune.

Happy birthday to you!

'It's crazy, isn't it?' Jackson's voice carries a tremor of excitement. 'The resemblance? I mean, it looks just like you!'

The music cranks louder, the lyrics catching like barbs in Flynn's mind. The air in the room smells suddenly ferric and foul. She opens her mouth to speak, to say it must be a trick of the light, double exposure, some malfunction of the antique camera, but the words don't come. She is transfixed by the pale and haunted face. Those dark eyes on the other side of the glass that seem to swirl with terror.

Jackson is right. But the shape in the window doesn't just look like her.

It *is* her.

Happy birthday to you!

Flynn feels as though she is going to throw up. Her head aches, her mouth is dry. Her gaze shifts to her friends' faces. She tries to ground herself, but she is spinning away.

The floor tips beneath her, the bar's music grows to a cacophony in her skull.

'Flynn?' Jackson grabs her hand, and the contact pulls her back into the room. She tries to focus on the warmth of his skin, the sound of his voice. In that moment, his face looks unearthly beautiful, his gravid, searching eyes and dishevelled hair. She aches to wrap her arms around him, to hold fast to this moment. But it is slipping already, and he is swimming out of focus. A cold spills through her, and as Jackson fades, she sees only the crumbling walls of a house.

Happy biiirthday, dear Flyyyyynnnnnnnn!

'Flynn, where are you going?' He sounds so far away.

She tries to tell him she loves him, but her lips are fusing. Memory blurs. She hopes he knows. She hopes they all know, that she would do anything to keep them safe.

Somewhere, in a distant room, babies are crying.

The house solidifies around her, a dark grey ruinous mass.

The music stops, dead air fills Flynn's ears. A beat of awareness, brief as a camera's shutter-click.

She is standing, barefoot, on the side of the road. Rain dashes from the sky, seethes against the concrete. She is soaked and Jackson is screaming, screaming her name, screaming in a voice squeezed by terror. She turns towards him, rain dripping from her lashes, streaking down her face like tears. She wonders why he is running towards her. Jackson, Mei, Tyrus, Chloe and Jonesy, they are all there. All rushing towards her.

Someone else is there, too. A woman. She stands on the other side of the road. Still. Quiet. Cars flash past her from both directions, briefly concealing her from view. But she doesn't move, just stands there, staring at Flynn with unblinking eyes. Malice crackles on the air around her, a malevolence so intense, it draws a gasp from Flynn's lips.

'Lyda Gray.' Flynn whispers the name, even though she has never heard it before, even though she knows that if she had ever seen that terrible face, she would remember.

She blinks and the woman has gone. But a bone-shattering cold pierces her, a cold that floods her lungs and turns each breath into a puff of ice. Her breath snatches as she senses the woman standing behind her, but she can't move, can't cry out, can't even close her eyes against the frost stealing across her vision.

The cold sinks deeper as the woman leans closer, the smell of her foul as an exhumed grave. She breathes two words into Flynn's ear before the hard shove that sends her stumbling into the path of oncoming headlights:

Happy birthday.

ACKNOWLEDGEMENTS

My deepest thanks to my incredible agent, Clare Wallace, and everyone at Darley Anderson, for their efforts and support with this book. To George Sandison, for picking it up when I was tearing my hair out with it, for fixing the wrong bits and making it so much better. Thanks to Julia Lloyd for another gorgeous cover, Louise Pearce for her thorough copy edit, Rich for the beautiful typesetting, Charlotte and Katharine in publicity, Rachel in editorial, and the whole team at Titan Books.

Thank you, Beth, for being there through thick and thin and ka-kow. Sarah, for the gongs and deer. Alison, for the support, book chats and prosecco. Marion, for making those mad drives just to check in. Becky, Nicole, Tina, Paul, Juan, Vicki, Miller, who all know what for.

Thank you, Father McGillicuddy for entertaining my morbid questions about exorcisms, and Jonny, for your patience fielding all my questions about teen disappearances and police procedures. Katie, for helping with the 'Unknown Female Child.'

A huge thank you to everyone who has been there for our family over the past five years, and who are still there for us now. Special thanks to Nalini, Sharon, Juliet, Gill. A huge thank you to every single member of staff at Park Lodge Nursing Home, and to the staff and volunteers at St Gemma's Hospice, with an extra big hug for Jen and Sita.

Thank you, Mum. I miss you. Te voglio bene assaje. Thank you, Owen, for literally everything. Your courage over the past few years has been superhuman, but then I've been in awe of you ever since I begged ten pence for the chocolate bar vending machine at college. Thank you, Dad, for always being in my corner. Thanks to Aldo, Richard, Daniel, Vicky, Ruth, Madge, Big Frankie, Little Frankie, Dec and Gemma.

And thank you Barney, Milo and Eric, who have been braver than I could ever have asked or imagined. You guys are the reason I keep going with it all, even when it feels impossible.

ABOUT THE AUTHOR

R. L. Boyle studied Classical Civilisation at the University of Leeds, after which she worked in a variety of jobs – none of which had anything to do with her degree. Her debut, *The Book of the Baku*, was published in 2021. It was shortlisted for a Bram Stoker Award® in the YA category, 2021.

Rosanna lives in Leeds with her husband and three sons.

You can follow R. L. Boyle on Instagram *rosannaboyle79*